A TEXT BOOK OF

ENVIRONMENTAL ENGINEERING – II

FOR
SEMESTER – I

FINAL YEAR (B.E.) DEGREE COURSE IN CIVIL ENGINEERING

As Per the New Revised Syllabus of Savitribai Phule Pune University
(2012 Pattern)

Dr. RK LAD

B.E. (Civil), M.E. (Env. Engg.), Ph.D. (Engg.)
Dean,
Dr. D. Y. Patil Institute of Engg. & Tech.
Pimpari, Pune 18

Dr. MR GIDDE

B.E. (Env. Engg.), M.E. (Env. Engg.) Ph. D
Professor, Dept. of Civil Engineering,
BVDU's College of Engineering,
Dhankawadi, Pune

NIRALI
PRAKASHAN
ADVANCEMENT OF KNOWLEDGE

N3686

Environmental Engg. II (B.E. Civil SEM. I PU)   **ISBN 978-93-5164-688-4**

First Edition	:	July 2015
©	:	Authors

Published By :   POLYPLATE
NIRALI PRAKASHAN
Abhyudaya Pragati, 1312, Shivaji Nagar,
Off J.M. Road, PUNE – 411005
Tel - (020) 25512336/37/39, Fax - (020) 25511379
Email : niralipune@pragationline.com

☞ **DISTRIBUTION BRANCHES**

PUNE

Nirali Prakashan : 119, Budhwar Peth, Jogeshwari Mandir Lane, Pune 411002, Maharashtra
Tel : (020) 2445 2044, 66022708, Fax : (020) 2445 1538
Email : bookorder@pragationline.com, niralilocal@pragationline.com

Nirali Prakashan : S. No. 28/27, Dhyari, Near Pari Company, Pune 411041
Tel : (020) 24690204 Fax : (020) 24690316
Email : dhyari@pragationline.com, bookorder@pragationline.com

MUMBAI

Nirali Prakashan : 385, S.V.P. Road, Rasdhara Co-op. Hsg. Society Ltd.,
Girgaum, Mumbai 400004, Maharashtra
Tel : (022) 2385 6339 / 2386 9976, Fax : (022) 2386 9976
Email : niralimumbai@pragationline.com

☞ **DISTRIBUTION BRANCHES**

JALGAON

Nirali Prakashan : 34, V. V. Golani Market, Navi Peth, Jalgaon 425001,
Maharashtra, Tel : (0257) 222 0395, Mob : 94234 91860

KOLHAPUR

Nirali Prakashan : New Mahadvar Road, Kedar Plaza, 1st Floor Opp. IDBI Bank
Kolhapur 416 012, Maharashtra. Mob : 9850046155

NAGPUR

Pratibha Book Distributors : Above Maratha Mandir, Shop No. 3, First Floor,
Rani Jhanshi Square, Sitabuldi, Nagpur 440012, Maharashtra
Tel : (0712) 254 7129

DELHI

Nirali Prakashan : 4593/21, Basement, Aggarwal Lane 15, Ansari Road, Daryaganj
Near Times of India Building, New Delhi 110002
Mob : 08505972553

BENGALURU

Pragati Book House : House No. 1, Sanjeevappa Lane, Avenue Road Cross,
Opp. Rice Church, Bengaluru – 560002.
Tel : (080) 64513344, 64513355, Mob : 9880582331, 9845021552
Email:bharatsavla@yahoo.com

CHENNAI

Pragati Books : 9/1, Montieth Road, Behind Taas Mahal, Egmore,
Chennai 600008 Tamil Nadu, Tel : (044) 6518 3535,
Mob : 94440 01782 / 98450 21552 / 98805 82331,
Email : bharatsavla@yahoo.com

niralipune@pragationline.com | www.pragationline.com

Also find us on 🇫 www.facebook.com/niralibooks

PREFACE

It gives us great pleasure in presenting the book on **"Environmental Engineering-II"**, which is written as per Savitribai Phule Pune University's revised syllabus (2012 course) and in most concised form. The book will also be very useful for the students preparing for Engineering Service Examination and AMIE Examination.

The subject matter is presented in simple and easy form so as to enable the students to understand the subject easily. Sufficient care is taken to present the subject matter in the point wise form in most of the chapters.

It consists of eleven chapters, which cover all the syllabus. At the end, objective questions are given, which will be useful for GATE, Engg. Services, AMIE examinations.

Special features of this book are lucid theory, solved examples including examples from University of Pune, Engineering Services and AMIE papers.

We are sincerely thankful to **Shri Dineshbhai K. Furia, Shri. Jignesh C. Furia, Mrs. Nirali Verma, Shri. M. P. Munde** and the entire team of Nirali Prakashan who really have taken keen interest and untiring efforts in publishing this text. We are also thankful to Mrs. Deepali Lachake (Co-ordinator) Mrs. Ulka Chavan, Miss. Rani zinjade for their kind co-operation throughout the work.

Also, it is important to mention invaluable moral support of our beloved family members, who consistently encouraged us for better work.

Despite the best efforts taken by authors, it is possible that some unintentional errors might have taken place. Authors would gratefully acknowledge if any of these is pointed out.

Suggestions and comments for further improvement of this book will be gratefully received and acknowledged from the students, teachers and others.

Pune   **Authors**

July 2015

SYLLABUS

CONTENTS

Trickling Filter

Unit IV

Unit V

Unit VI

✠ ✠ ✠

Chapter 1

INTRODUCTION

Wastewater engineering is that branch of environmental engineering in which the basic principles of science and engineering are applied to the problems of water pollution control.

Related to sources of generation, wastewater may be defined as a combination of the liquid or water carried wastes removed from residences, institutions and commercial and industrial establishments, together with such ground water, surface water and storm water as may be present.

1.1 IMPORTANT TERMS AND DEFINITIONS

1. **Sullage :** Sullage is a term used to indicate the wastewater from bathrooms, kitchens, wash basins etc.

   As organic matter in it is either absent or is of negligible amount, so it does not create bad smell.

2. **Sewage :** It includes sullage, discharge from latrines, urinals, stables, industrial waste and also the ground surface and storm water that may be admitted into the sewer.

3. **Domestic Sewage :** It consists of liquid wastes originating from urinals, latrines, bathrooms, kitchen sinks, wash basins etc. of the residential, commercial or institutional buildings. Since, it contains human excreta and urine, it is extremely foul in nature.

4. **Industrial Sewage :** It consists of liquid wastes originating from the industrial processes of various industries, such as distillery, dairy, paper mill, textile, brewing etc.

   The quality of the industrial sewage depends upon the type of industry. It may contain objectionable organic compounds and thus may require extensive treatment before being disposed of in public sewers.

5. **Sanitary Sewage :** It is the sum total of domestic and industrial sewage.

6. **Storm Sewage :** The run-off resulting from the rain storms is called storm sewage or storm drainage or simply drainage.

7. **Night Soil :** It is a term used to indicate the human and animal excreta.

8. **Sewer :** It is an underground conduit through which sewage is carried to a point of disposal.

Sewers can be classified as follows :

- **Separate Sewers :** These type of sewers are carrying the household and industrial wastes only.
- **Storm Water Sewers :** These type of sewers are carrying rain water.
- **Combined Sewers :** These type of sewers are carrying both sewage and storm water.
- **House Sewer :** It is a pipe to carry sewage from a building to street sewer.
- **Lateral Sewer :** This type of sewer collects sewage from the houses.
- **Branch Sewer (Submain Sewer) :** This is a sewer which receives sewage from laterals and discharge into a main sewer.
- **Main Sewer (Trunk Sewer) :** This is a sewer which receives sewage from tributary branches and sewers.
- **Depressed Sewer :** This type of sewer is at lower level than adjacent sewers. This sewer runs full under the force of gravity and at more than atmospheric pressure.
- **Intercepting Sewer :** This type of sewer flowing parallel to a natural drainage channel, into which a number of main sewers discharge.
- **Outfall Sewer :** This type of sewer receives the sewage from the collecting system. It's location is at final discharge.

9. **Sewarage :** This term is applied to the art of collecting, treating and finally disposing of the sewage.

10. **Oxygen Deficit :**

   Oxygen deficit = [Saturation dissolved oxygen – Actual dissolved oxygen]

11. **Bio-Chemical Oxygen Demand (BOD) :** The amount of oxygen consumed by aerobic bacteria for the decomposition of wastewater (ofcourse upto oxidation is completed) is called BOD.

12. **Chemical Oxygen Demand (COD) :** A known quantity of wastewater is mixed with a known quantity of standard solution of potassium dichromate and the mixture is heated. The organic matter is oxidised in presence of H_2SO_4 by potassium dichromate. The resulting solution of potassium dichromate is titrated. The oxygen used in oxidising the wastewater is known as COD.

13. **Total Organic Carbon (TOC) :** TOC test is the method for measuring the small concentrations of organic matter.

14. **ThOD :** Theoretical oxygen demand.

15. Treatability Index (T.I.) :

$$\text{T.I.} = \frac{\text{BOD}}{\text{COD} - \text{BOD}}$$

16. Dilution Factor :

$$\text{Dilution factor} = \frac{\text{Volume of the diluted sample}}{\text{Volume of the undiluted sewage sample}}$$

17. Population Equivalent :

$$\text{Population equivalent} = \frac{\text{Standard } BOD_5 \text{ of the industrial wastewater in kg/day}}{\text{Standard } BOD_5 \text{ of domestic sewage per kg per person per day}}$$

Generally, the BOD_5 of domestic sewage is 0.08 kg/day/person.

18. Relative Stability :

$$\text{Relative stability} = \frac{\text{Oxygen available in the effluent}}{\text{Total oxygen required to satisfy its first stage BOD demand}}$$

19. Detention Period :

$$\text{Detention period} = \frac{\text{Volume of the tank}}{\text{Rate of flow in the tank}}$$

20. Volumetric BOD loading / Organic Loading :

$$\text{Volumetric BOD loading/Organic loading} = \frac{\text{Mass of BOD applied per day in gm}}{\text{Volume of the aeration tank in m}^3}$$

21. Food to Micro-Organisms Ratio (F/M) :

$$\text{F/M ratio} = \frac{\text{BOD load applied per day to the aerator system in gm}}{\text{Total microbial mass in the system in gm}}$$

22. MLSS : Mixed liquor suspended solids.

23. MLVSS : Mixed liquor volatile suspended solids.

24. Sludge Age :

$$\text{Sludge age} = \frac{\text{Mass of suspended solids in the system}}{\text{Mass of solids leaving the system per day}}$$

1.2 SYSTEMS OF SANITATION

Depending on the type of waste, the following two systems may be employed for its collection, conveyance and disposal :

1.   Conservancy system.
2.   Water carriage system.

Table 1.1. shows advantages of the modern water-carriage sewage system over the old conservancy system.

Table 1.1 : Advantages of the Modern Water-Carriage Sewage System Over the Old Conservancy System

Sr. No.	Factors	Water-Carriage Sewage System	Conservancy System
1.	**Hygienes and Sanitary Aspects**	The system is very hygienic. The wastewater is conveyed through closed conduits which are not directly exposed to the atmosphere.	The system is very unhygienic, since in this system, the society's wastes have to be collected and carried in buckets or carts.
2.	**Foul Smell**	No foul smell as no chances of putrefication.	There is lot of foul smell due to putrefication.
3.	**Epidemic Aspect**	As flies and other insects do not have direct access to the sewage, there are no chances of outbreak of epidemic.	There are more chances of outbreak of epidemic due to improper disposal of night soil.
4.	**Pollution Aspect**	Pollution problems are rare as the liquid wastes etc. are directly conveyed through the sewers.	Pollution problems are more since the liquid wastes from lavatories etc., may soak in the ground, thus contaminating the soil.
5.	**Compactness in House Design**	Compact design is possible since the latrines can be kept clean after every use, excreta does not remain and therefore no foul smells. So the latrines can be attached to the living and bedrooms.	Compact house design is not possible.
6.	**Labour Aspect**	Labour required is negligibly small for the operation and maintenance.	The working of this system wholly depends on labour (sweepers).
7.	**Final Disposal**	Final disposal easier because of treatment works.	Possibility of risk may be at final disposal.
8.	**Land Disposal Requirements**	Land required for the disposal of treated sludge is less.	Land required for the disposal of untreated sewage is large.

Contd...

9.	Cost Consideration	Initial cost is high, but running cost is very less as labour requirement is less.	Initial cost is small, but the running cost is high as labour requirement is more as compared to water-carriage sewage system.

1.3 TYPES OF WATER CARRIAGE SYSTEM

The following are the types of water carriage system :

    (a)   Separate system.

    (b)   Combined system.

    (c)   Partially separate system.

    (a) **Separate System :** When the drainage (storm drainage) and sewage are taken independently of each other through two different sets of conduits, it is called a separate system.

    (b) **Combined System :** When the drainage is taken along with sewage, it is called a combined system.

    (c) **Partially Separate System :** Sometimes a part of drainage water (rain water from roofs of buildings), is allowed to be admitted into the sewers and similarly, sometimes the domestic sewage is allowed to be admitted into the drains, the system is called a partially separate system.

Table 1.2 gives comparison between separate system and combined system.

Table 1.2 : Comparison between Separate and Combined System (Dec. 2010)

Sr. No.	Factors	Separate System	Combined System
1.	Cost Consideration	**(a)** **Maintenance Cost :** Two sets of sewers prove to be costly. **(b)** **Construction Cost :** Less	**(a)** **Maintenance Cost :** As this system requires only one set of sewers, maintenance cost is less. **(b)** **Construction Cost :** Very high because of large dimensions of the sewers to be constructed at sufficient depth to receive the sewage from the basement.

Contd...

2.	Load of Influent On Treatment Units	As only the foul sewage carried by the separate sewers need be treated, the load on the treatment units will be lowered.	Due to the addition of storm water, the load on the treatment plant increases.
3.	Chocking Problem	Due to smaller size of sewers, they are likely to get chocked.	Due to larger size of sewers, the chances of their chocking are rare.
4.	Lifting of Sewage	In this system, sewage can be lifted mechanically, so the system is economical.	When pumping is required for lifting of sewage, the system is uneconomical.
5.	Ventilation	As size of sewers is small, they can be ventilated easily.	As size of sewers is large, they are more difficult to be ventilated.
6.	Foul Smell	Foul smell may be there because of lesser air contact in small size sewers.	Due to more air in the larger sewers, the sewer gas, that may be formed, gets diluted.
7.	Storm Water Polluted	In this system, no question of pollution of storm water as it is flowing from separate open channels or sewers.	Storm water is unnecessarily polluted as it is mixed with sewage.
8.	Pollution due to Overflow Problems	Due to heavy rains, sewers may overflow but unhygienic condition will not be there as rain water is not mixed with sewage.	Due to heavy rains, the sewers may overflow and may thus create unhygienic conditions as it is mixed with sewage.
9.	Provision of Automatic Flushing Tanks	As flow in a sewer of smaller section is more efficient, there is no necessity of providing automatic flushing tanks for use in dry weather.	When rain water is not available, they may become foul in dry weather, so there is necessity of providing automatic flushing tanks.

In the modern days, "separate system" is generally preferred to a "combined system", although the selection of system depends on individual merits, keeping the above points into consideration.

Table 1.3 : Factors Governing Choice of Separate and Combined System   (May 2010)

Sr. No.	Factors	Separate System	Combined System
1.	Financial Aspect	If sufficient funds are not available at the beginning, then this system is preferred.	If sufficient funds are available, then this system is preferred.

Contd...

2.	**Rainfall Pattern**	If rainfall is for shorter duration, then this system is preferred.	If rainfall is evenly distributed for the year, then this system is preferred.
3.	**Development Pattern**	This system is preferred, when the sewers are laid before the area is developed.	This system is preferred, when the sewers are laid in already developed area.
4.	**Subsoil Condition**	Where subsoil is hard, this system is economical compared to larger size of combined system.	Where subsoil is hard, this system is not economical.
5.	**Pumping Requirements**	This system is economical, where only sewage is required to pump.	Where both sewage and storm water is required to pump, this system is preferred.
6.	**Flat Topography**	If the country is flat, required more depth to achieve reasonable gradient, in such a case this system is more economical.	For such cases, for laying bigger size sewers at a great depth will not be economical.
7.	**Space Considerations**	When space available for laying the sewers is restricted, this system will not be preferred.	This system is preferred where the space available for laying the sewers is restricted.

IMPORTANT POINTS

- Definitions and terms.
- Systems of sanitations.
- Comparison between separate system and combined system.

EXERCISE

1. Define :

   (a) Sewage, (b) Sullage.

2. Explain :

   (a) Conservancy system.   (b) Water carriage system.

3. What are the advantages and disadvantages of conservancy and water carriage system ?

4. Discuss the advantages of the separate and combined system of sewage and give the conditions favourable for the adoption of each of them.

5. Write short notes on :

    (i)   Sewage and drainage.

    (ii) Combined and separate systems of sewage.

    (iii) Domestic and industrial sewage.

UNIVERSITY QUESTIONS

1. Differentiate between separate and combined sewerage system.   **[4 M] (Dec. 2010)**

2. Explain giving reasons, when to adopt separate and combined systems.

                                                             [4 M] (May 2010, 2011)

✠ ✠ ✠

Chapter 2

SEWAGE OR WASTEWATER QUANTITY

Estimation of the rates of wastewater flows is an important step in the design of wastewater collection, treatment and disposal facilities. Reliable data on existing and projected flows must be available, otherwise the sewers may either prove to be inadequate, resulting in their overflow or may prove to be of too much of size, resulting in unnecessary wasteful investments. Proper design sewer is also helpful to minimize the cost.

2.1 SOURCES OF SEWAGE OR WASTEWATER FLOWS

The following are the sources of wastewater flows, which are dependent on the type of collection system:

1. Domestic or sanitary wastewater.
2. Industrial wastewater.
3. Infiltration / Inflow.
4. Storm water.

1. Domestic Wastewater :

The principal sources of domestic wastewater are residential and commercial buildings, other important sources include institutional and recreational facilities.

(a) Residential : For small residential areas, wastewater flows are commonly determined on the basis of the average per capita contribution of wastewater and population density.

For large residential areas, wastewater flows are determined by considering 75 to 80% of the accounted water supplied from the water works. Residential sources of wastewaters are apartments, hotels, individual dwellings, etc.

(b) Commercial : Commercial wastewater flows are generally based on existing or anticipated future development or comparative data.

Commercial sources of wastewater are airports, automobile service stations, hotels, industrial buildings (excluding industry and cafeteria), laundries (self-service), motels, motels with kitchen, offices, restaurants, shopping centers, etc.

(c) Institutional Facilities : Institutional sources of wastewaters are hospitals (medical), hospitals (mental), prisons, schools, etc.

(d) Recreational Facilities : Recreational sources of wastewaters are apartments (resorts), cafeteria, coffee shops, country clubs, day camps (no meals), dining halls, hotels (resort), swimming pools, theaters, stores (resort), etc.

2. **Industrial Wastewater :**

Industrial wastewater flow rates vary with the type and size of the industry, the supervision of the industry, the degree of water reuse, etc.

3. **Infiltration / Inflow :**

• **Infiltration :**

Ground water or subsoil water may enter into the sewers through leaky joints.

• **Inflow :** The water discharged into a sewer system, including service connections.

Infiltration / Inflow : The total quantity from both infiltration and inflow.

4. **Storm Water :**

Storm is generated due to rain water flowing over the ground surface, pavements, roofs, etc.

2.2 ESTIMATING WASTEWATER DISCHARGE

Theoretically the quantity of wastewater (i.e. domestic and industrial) that is likely to enter the municipal sewers under design, should be equal to the quantity of water supplied to the contributing area, from the water works. But in actual practice, it is not possible. The quantity of wastewater depends upon the following additions and subtractions.

(a) **Additions due to Unaccounted Private Water Supplies :** The records of water supplied to the public through the public distribution system are easily available from the waterworks office, but only this water is not consumed by the public. The other sources of water for consumption are private wells and tubewells may sometimes used by the public for the domestic needs and similarly, certain industries may utilize their own sources of water. This quantity can, however, be calculated by actual field observations.

(b) **Additions due to Infiltration :** Infiltration is much more important from the point of sewer design. Also, infiltration unnecessarily increases the load on the treatment works.

Infiltration of water into the sewer depends upon the following factors :

1. Sewer material.
2. Size of sewer.
3. Depth of sewer below ground water level.
4. Nature and type of soil through which sewer is laid.
5. Type of joints.

Infiltration Design Allowances for Sewers :

Infiltration of water into sewer line may be calculated by the following methods :

- **Diameter-Length Basis :**

The rate of infiltration will increase with the increase in the diameter of the sewer.

Unit for Rate of Infiltration : Litres per cm diameter of sewer per km length per day.

- **Area-Basis :**

Unit for Rate of Infiltration : Litres per hectare of area per day.

Range of Infiltration : 0.2 to 28 m³/ hectare/day.

Example : If infiltration rate is 2000 litres per hectare per day and the area of the sewer line is 10 hectares, then the total infiltration volume per day will be

$$2000 \times 15 = 30,000 \text{ litres/day.}$$

In the absence of relevant flow data, average infiltration allowances presented in Fig. 2.1 may be used for new sewers or recently constructed sewer systems having precast manholes and pipe joints made with gaskets of rubber or rubber like material.

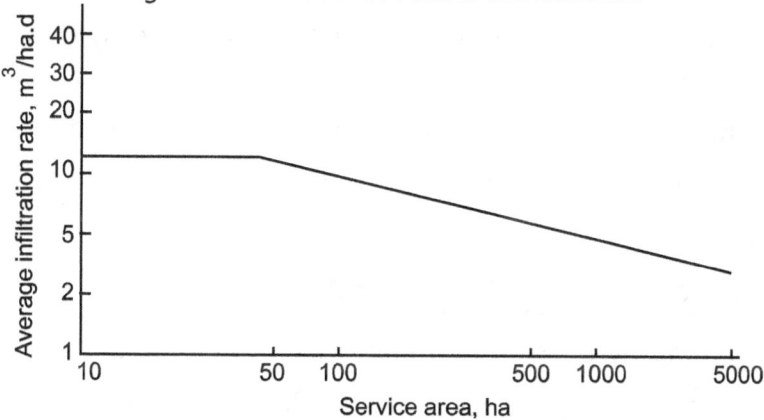

Fig. 2.1 : Average infiltration allowances

- **Length Basis :**

Unit for rate of infiltration : Litres per unit length per day.

Range of Infiltration :

- 10,000 to 50,000 litres per km per day.
- 11,000 to 2,25,000 litres per km per day (In U.S.A.).

Example : If infiltration rate is 15,000 litres per km length of sewer per day and the length of sewer through the ground water zone is 7 km, then the total infiltration volume will be 15,000 × 7 = 1,05,000 litres/day.

No allowance for infiltration should, however, be made when sewers are provided with under-drains which have free outlets.

(c) **Subtractions due to Losses of Water :** The water lost, because of leakage in the distribution system and connections of the water supply scheme, does not reach to consumers, and thus, never appears as wastewater.

(d) Subtractions due to Water not Entering the Sewerage System : The wastewater generally does not generate from the following uses :

- Water sprinkled over the roads, streets, gardens and lawns.
- The water used for automobile washings.
- The water consumed in industrial products, such as beverages, paper mill, etc.
- The water used in boilers for steam generation.

Net Quantity of Wastewater Produced : Net quantity of wastewater produced = The accounted quantity of water supplied from water works + additions due to above factors (a) and (b) – subtractions due to above factors (c) and (d).   ... (2.1)

= 75 to 80% of the accounted water supplied from the water works.

2.3 SEWAGE OR WASTEWATER QUANTITY

To design sewer, it is necessary to know the total quantity of sewage or wastewater which will flow through the sewer.

The total wastewater flow can be divided into the following two components :

1. Dry weather flow (D.W.F.) and

2. Storm water flow.

2.3.1 Dry Weather Flow (D.W.F.) / Sanitary Sewage

It is defined as the quantity of wastewater that flows through a sewer in dry weather when no storm water is in the sewer.

2.3.1.1 Factors Affecting D.W.F.

Following are the factors affecting D.W.F. :

(i) Population growth; (ii) Type of area served (residential, commercial or industrial); (iii) Infiltration of ground water; (iv) Rate of water supply.

2.3.1.2 Design Period

Design periods for different components of a sewerage scheme are different. For example, we can keep less design period for pumping plant, because the additional pumps can be installed in future very easily and also within a short time. For branches, mains and trunk sewers, design period is required more, because addition of sewer pipes at a future date cannot be accomplished without digging the roads or disrupting the traffic. So it is difficult and costly to enlarge.

Table 2.1 shows design periods for different components of a sewerage scheme.

Following are the guidelines for deciding design period of different components of sewerage scheme :

    (a) Rate of Interest : If rate of interest on borrowings is small, a higher value of design period can be fixed.

    (b) Useful Life of Components of a Sewerage System : The design period should not exceed these values.

    (c) Difficulties in Expansion : The design period should be of higher value for more difficult expansions.

    (d) Availability of Funds : If funds are not easily available, then keep a smaller design period.

Table 2.1 : Design Periods for Different Components of a Sewerage Scheme

Sr. No.	Types and Name of the Component Structure	Design Period in Years
1.	Lateral sewers, less than 150 mm in dia.	Full development
2.	Branches, mains and trunk sewers	30
3.	Treatment units	15 – 20
4.	Pumping plant	5 – 10

2.3.1.3 Population Forecast and Estimating Design Wastewater Discharge

The quantity of wastewater which is passed through the sewer (Q_1) at the end of design period = Per capita production of wastewater (q_1) × Expected population at the end of the design period.   ... (2.2)

Note : Per capita production of wastewater (q_1) = 75 to 80% of the per capita water supplied to the public (q).

Expected population at the end of the design period can be estimated by collecting the past census data generally available with the local bodies like panchayat, municipality or corporation and then by extrapolating the future population by using any one of the following different methods :

- Arithmetical increase method.
- Geometrical increase method.
- Incremental increase method.
- Decrease rate or Declining growth method.
- Simple graphical or Graphical extension method.
- Graphical comparison method.
- Zoning method or Master plan method.
- The logistic curve method.
- The ratio method or Apportionment method.

These above methods have been described in details in article 16.2 in "Environmental Engineering – I".

In above equation (2.2), we have mentioned about per capita production of wastewater. This per capita production of wastewater may be increasing in future as the future population may also increase the per capita demand, so this factor should be considered while estimating design wastewater discharge. For normal Indian conditions, some norms may be adopted which is tabulated in Table 2.2.

Table 2.2 : Effect of Growth of Population

Sr. No.	Population	Per Capita Water Demand (Litres/Day/Person) (q)	Per Capita Sewage or Wastewater Production (Litres/Day/Person) $q_1 = 80\%$ of Col. (3)
(1)	(2)	(3)	(4)
1.	Less than 20,000	110	90
2.	20,000 – 50,000	110 – 150	90 – 120
3.	50,000 – 2 lakhs	150 – 180	120 – 150
4.	2 lakhs – 5 lakhs	180 – 210	150 – 170
5.	5 lakhs – 10 lakhs	210 – 240	170 – 190
6.	Over 10 lakhs	240 – 270	190 – 200

In case the desired information on population is not available in the Master Plan of the town, the most suitable approach for estimation of population is density of population, which one is tabulated in Table 2.3 may be adopted as suggested by the Manual on Sewage and Sewage Treatment prepared by the Public Health and Environmental Engineering Organisation.

Table 2.3 : Population Densities

Sr. No.	Population	Population Density / Hectare
1.	Upto 5,000	75 – 150
2.	5,000 – 20,000	150 – 250
3.	20,000 – 50,000	250 – 300
4.	50,000 – 1,00,000	300 – 350
5.	More than 1,00,000	350 – 1000

2.3.1.4 Variations in Rate of Wastewater

The per capita wastewater production (q_1) is based upon *annual average daily flows per person*. This average value is not sufficient, although it is very useful for the design of various components of a sewerage scheme, because the rate of sewage flow is not constant. It varies with every hour of the day, every day of the season and with every season of the year. The designer should consider both maximum and minimum flow while designing sewer. So the designed sewer can take the maximum load and at the same time, they should be laid on such longitudinal gradient that there are no deposits in the sewers at the minimum flow. The variations in the sewage flow may be due to the following factors :

(a) Type of industries.   (b) Habits of the people.

(c) Climatic conditions.   (d) Timings of water supply, etc.

Fig. 2.2 shows hourly variation of sewage flow compared to that of water supply.

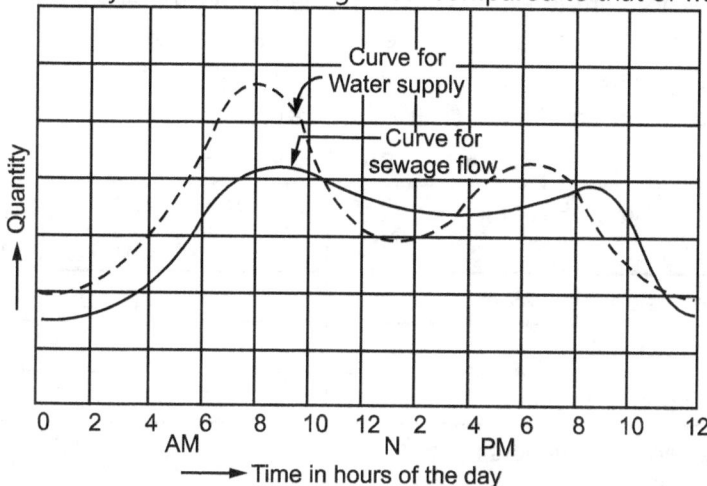

Fig. 2.2 : Hourly variation of sewage flow compared to that of water supply

- Sewage flow rises by about 6 A.M.
- Maximum between 8 and 10 A.M.
- Minimum flow between 1 to 4 P.M.

Fig. 2.3 shows daily variations of sewage flow.

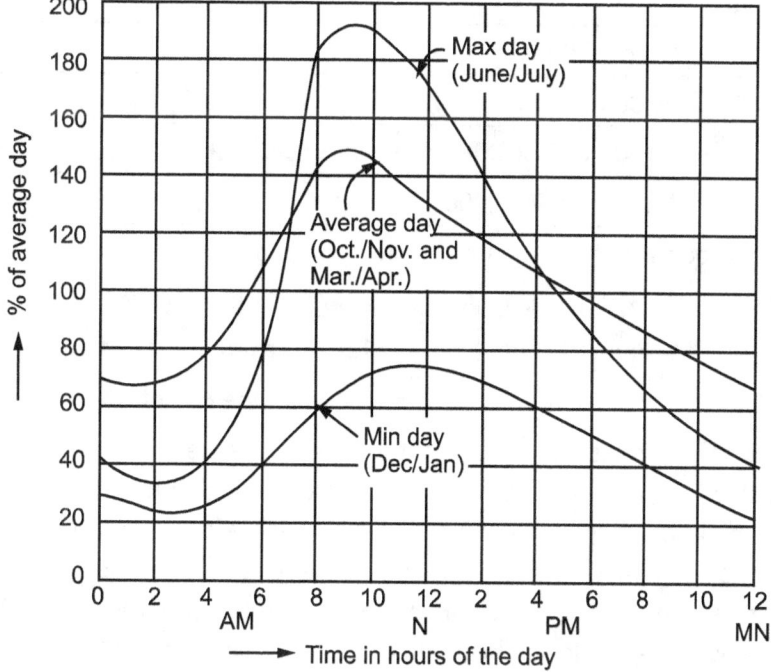

Fig. 2.3 : Daily variations of sewage flow

Peak Flows/Maximum Flows, Minimum Flows and Sustained Flows

Peak Flows/Maximum Flows : If the sewage is gauged near its origin, the peak flow will be quite pronounced. Therefore, the peak flows will be much greater for smaller lateral sewers as compared to those for larger trunk sewers. Various sewers in a sewer-network are designed not for the average annual flow rate, but for a flow rate which is higher than the average flow rate by a peaking factor. (See Table 2.4).

Table 2.4 : Peaking Factors

Sr. No.	Type of Sewer	Peaking Factor = Ratio of Maximum Flow to Average Flow
1.	Trunk mains above 1.25 m in dia.	1.5
2.	Mains upto 1 m in dia.	2.0
3.	Branches upto 0.5 m in dia.	3.0
4.	Laterals and small sewers upto 0.25 m in dia.	4.0

The peaking factors also depend upon population as tabulated in Table 2.5.

Table 2.5 : Peaking Factors

Sr. No.	Population	Peaking Factor
1.	Upto 20,000	3.5
2.	20,000 to 50,000	2.5
3.	50,000 to 7,50,000	2.25
4.	More than 7,50,000	2.0

For areas of moderate sizes, such as involved for branch sewers :

$$\text{Maximum daily flow} = 2 \times \text{Average daily flow} \qquad \qquad ... (2.3)$$

$$\text{Maximum hourly flow} = 1.5 \times \text{Maximum daily flow}$$

$$= 3 \times \text{Average daily flow} \qquad \qquad ... (2.4)$$

Minimum Flows : This is also an important factor in the design of the particular sewer. Because due to low flow rate, velocity of flow will reduce, which may cause silting. The flow in the sewers is minimum during night hours when people are at sleep. The use of flushes and bath rooms during these hours is minimum. The effect of these minimum flows is maximum on lateral sewers. Thus, the minimum flows through laterals may be even lesser than 25% of the average, while in the mains, they can be 50 to 70% of the average. For moderate areas (for branch sewers), the following minimum flows may be assumed.

$$\text{Minimum daily flow} = 0.67 \times \text{Average daily flow} \quad\quad \text{... (2.5)}$$

$$\text{Minimum hourly flow} = 0.5 \times \text{Minimum daily flow}$$

$$= 0.33 \times \text{Average daily flow} \quad\quad \text{... (2.6)}$$

Sustained Flows : Of equal importance to information on the expected peak flows is information on the expected sustained flows, especially in the design of sewage or wastewater treatment facilities. Sustained flows are flows that persist for various time durations (say 2 hours or larger). Sewage flows that are higher than the average flow or those lower than the average flow are of importance in design of sewer.

2.3.1.5 Measurement of Wastewater Flows

There are two methods for measurement of wastewater flows :

(a) Direct – Discharge methods and

(b) Velocity – Area methods.

(a) **Direct – Discharge Methods :** Direct-discharge methods are those in which the rate of discharge has been related to one or two easily measured variables. The following methods or apparatus are used for measurement of flow rate.

- Venturi meters
- Venturi flumes
- Orifice
- Weirs
- Tracers, chemical and radioactive
- Flow nozzles
- Magnetic flowmeters
- Computation
- Direct weighing.

(b) **Velocity – Area Methods :** In this method, the flow rate is determined by multiplying the velocity of flow by the cross-sectional area through which flow is occurring. The following are methods and devices for determining velocities :

- Electrical methods
- Current meters
- Float measurements.

2.3.2 Storm Water Flow

In a separate sewerage system, the sewers and drains should be designed for the maximum sewage discharge and the maximum rain run-off respectively.

In a combined system, the sewers should be designed for sewage discharge plus rain run-off.

When rainfall takes place, a part of it infiltrates or percolates into the ground surface and the remaining water flows over land towards the valleys, as storm run-off. This storm water is ultimately drained through the sewers, otherwise streets, roads etc. which would have been flooded. The amount of peak storm water flow or maximum rate of storm run-off is generally very high, say 20 to 25 times that of the sewage discharge, called Dry Weather Flow (D.W.F.). In a combined system, the sewers are normally not designed to passing this combined maximum flow only, but they should also be capable of passing the low sewage discharge (D.W.F.) during non-mansoon periods with minimum permissible velocities.

The peak rate of run-off depends upon the following factors :

- Intensity of rainfall
- Duration of rainfall
- Type of precipitation
- The rainfall distribution
- The soil moisture deficiency
- The climatic conditions
- Ground slope
- Permeability of the ground
- Size, shape and type of catchment basin
- Extent of vegetation growth
- The direction of the prevailing storm etc.

The following two methods are used for computing the peak drainage discharge :

- Rational method and
- Empirical formulae.

(a) Rational Method :

Firstly, we will discuss about time of concentration and critical rainfall duration.

When a rainfall is applied to an impervious surface at a constant rate, the rate of flow in the beginning is very small, but it gradually increases as more and more area contributes to the flow; it means that the water will start reaching the outlet from the entire area; and in this case, the runoff rate would become equal to the rate of rainfall. The period required from the beginning of rainfall to the entire area will start contributing to the runoff, is known as the *time of concentration*. The maximum runoff will be obtained, when the rainfall duration is equal to the time of concentration and this is called as *critical rainfall duration*. It means that even if the rainfall duration is more than the time of concentration, the runoff will not be maximum (see example 2.10) because in such a case, the intensity of rain reduces with the increase in its duration.

The following rational formula is based upon above principles, which was evolved by Kuichling (America), Fruhling (Germany) and Lloyd Davis (England).

$$Q_P = K \cdot C_R \cdot I_C \cdot A$$

where, Q_P = Peak rate of runoff or storm water flow

K = Constant related to conversion of I_C and A units in convenient units.

Now, consider

Q_P = Peak rate of runoff in **cumecs**

C_R = Coefficient of runoff

= The ratio of precipitation to runoff

I_C = Critical rainfall intensity of the design frequency in **mm/hr**

A = Catchment area in **hectares**

Now we will convert the units of I_C and A in m/sec and m² respectively, so corresponding value of K will be,

$$Q_P = C_R \cdot \left(\frac{I_C}{1000 \times 3600} \right) \cdot (10000 \cdot A)$$

$$\therefore \quad \boxed{Q_P = \frac{1}{360} \, C_R \cdot I_C \cdot A} \quad \text{cumecs} \qquad \qquad ... (2.7)$$

So value of K = $\frac{1}{360}$.

Catchment Area : In above equation (2.7), *the catchment area (C.A.)* served by a given storm water sewer can be found directly from the map of the town showing the positions of roads, houses, sewers, etc.

Coefficient of Runoff (C_R) : The storm water flow depends upon the imperviousness of the surface over which rainfall takes place. The percentage of rain water, that is available in the form of runoff, is called as coefficient of runoff or impermeability factor (C_R). The value of *coefficient of runoff* or *impermeability factor* increases as the imperviousness of the area increases, means greater is the imperviousness of an area, lesser will be the infiltration and hence more will be the runoff.

Table 2.6 shows values of runoff coefficient (C_R) for various surfaces (Kuichling's runoff coefficients or Kuichling's impermeability factors) and Table 2.7 shows values of runoff coefficients (C_R) for different types of localities (Fruhling's factors).

Table 2.6 : Kuichling's Runoff Coefficients (C_R) for Various Surfaces

Sr. No.	Type of surface	Value of C_R
1.	Water-tight roof surface	0.70 – 0.95
2.	Asphalt pavement in good order	0.85 – 0.90
3.	Stone, brick, wood-block pavement with cemented joints	0.75 – 0.85
4.	Same as above with uncemented joints	0.50 – 0.70
5.	Inferior block pavements with open joints	0.40 – 0.50
6.	Water bond macadam (W.B.M.) roads	0.25 – 0.60
7.	Gravel roads and walks	0.15 – 0.30
8.	Unpaved streets, rail road yards and vacant lands	0.10 – 0.30
9.	Parks, gardens, lawns, meadows etc., depends on characteristic of subsoil.	0.05 – 0.25
10.	Wooden lands or forest land	0.01 – 0.20

Table 2.7 : Fruhling's Runoff Coefficients (C_R) for Different Types of Localities

Sr. No.	Type of Locality	Average Approximate Population Density in Persons/Hectare	Value of C_R
1.	Business areas	Above 625	0.85
2.	Area closely built-up	500 to 625	0.75
3.	Areas with 50% attached houses and 50% detached houses	375 to 500	0.65
4.	Suburban areas with widely detached houses	125 to 150	0.45 – 0.55
5.	Extreme suburban areas with 20 to 40% parking and widely detached houses	75 to 125	0.35

Average Runoff Coefficient : A given catchment area may consist of various types of surfaces for which different runoff coefficients are applicable. The average runoff coefficient can be determined by the following relation :

$$C_{R\,(ave)} = \frac{C_{R_1} \cdot A_1 + C_{R_2} \cdot A_2 + \dots C_{R_n} \cdot A_n}{A_1 + A_2 + \dots A_n} = \frac{\Sigma\, C_R\, A}{\Sigma\, A} \qquad \dots (2.7\,a)$$

where,　　$A_1, A_2 \dots A_n$ = Areas of the different surfaces of the catchment area

　　　　$C_{R_1}, C_{R_2} \dots C_{R_n}$ = Corresponding runoff coefficients for the different surfaces

Intensity of Rainfall : The value of intensity of rainfall in mm/hr (or cm/hr) can be worked out from the rainfall records of the area. The intensity of rain is the rate at which it is falling. A rainfall at a place also depends upon duration and frequency of the storm. The duration is the time for which it falls with that given intensity and frequency is the number of times it falls.

Duration of Storm : It is the time after which the entire area will start contributing to the runoff. It means the duration of storm is taken equal to the time of concentration.

Intensity of rainfall can be determined from the following formulae :

1. For areas of heavy and frequent rainfall (frequency once in 5 years),

$$I_C = \frac{3430}{t + 18} \qquad \qquad \text{... (2.8)}$$

2. For storm occurring once in a year,

$$I_C = \frac{150}{t^{0.625}} \qquad \qquad \text{... (2.9)}$$

3. For storm occurring once in 10 years,

$$I_C = \frac{380}{t^{0.5}} \qquad \qquad \text{... (2.10)}$$

4. Kuichling's formulae :

    For storm occurring once in 10 years,

$$I_C = \frac{2667}{t + 20} \qquad \qquad \text{... (2.11)}$$

    For storm occurring once in 15 years,

$$I_C = \frac{3048}{t + 20} \qquad \qquad \text{... (2.12)}$$

5. General formula :

$$I_C = \frac{25.4\,a}{t + b} \qquad \qquad \text{... (2.13)}$$

where, I_C = Critical rainfall intensity, mm/hr

              t = Duration of storm in minutes

                = Time of concentration

The United States Ministry of Health recommend the following values of constants a and b.

Duration of Rainfall	Constant 'a'	Constant 'b'
5 to 20 min	30	10
20 to 100 min	40	20

Intensity of rainfall can also be determined for any given time of concentration from following intensity curves. Fig. 2.4 shows rainfall intensity curves for various frequencies of storm.

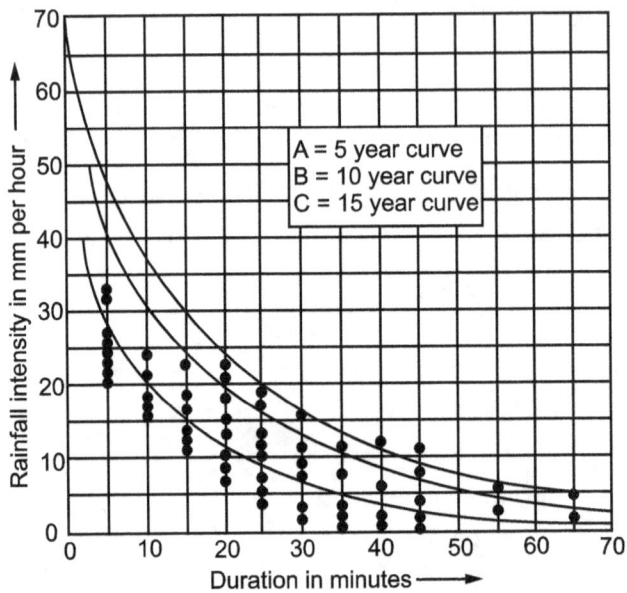

Fig. 2.4 : Rainfall intensity curves for various frequencies of storm

The Time of Concentration :

The time of concentration is equal to the longest combination of overland flow time (inlet time, t_i) and channel flow time or gutter flow time (t_f).

1. **Channel Flow Time (t_f) :** It is defined as the ratio of length of the drain to the average velocity in the drain.

$$\therefore \quad t_f = \frac{\text{Length of the drain or channel}}{\text{Average velocity in the drain or channel}} \qquad \text{... (2.14)}$$

2. **The Overland Flow Time or the Inlet Time (t_i) :** It is a time that the water to flow overland from the critical point upto the point where it enters the mouth of drain.

The following formula can be used for evaluating the inlet or overland flow time.

$$t_i = \left(0.885 \, \frac{L^3}{H_T}\right)^{0.385} \qquad \text{... (2.15)}$$

where,

t_i = Inlet or overland flow time in hours

L = The distance from the critical point to the mouth of the drain in kilometres.

H_T = Total fall of level from the critical point to the mouth of the drain in metres.

The total time of concentration (t_c) can be determined from the following equation :

$$t_c = t_i + t_f \qquad \text{... (2.16)}$$

In above equations value of t_i and t_f can be calculated from equations (2.15) and (2.14) respectively.

The intensity of rainfall during this much of time can be easily obtained from the standard intensity duration curves.

In the absence of the standard intensity-duration curves, the value of I_c can also be determined by equations (2.8) to (2.13) and the following equation (2.17) :

$$I_c = I_o \left(\frac{2}{1 + t_c}\right) \qquad \text{... (2.17)}$$

where, I_o = One hour rainfall value

(b)   Empirical Formulae :

In previous article, we have discussed about rational method, but this method is useful for smaller areas only, hence used only for the design of drains having catchments less than 400 hectares. For larger area (say more than 400 hectares), empirical formulae are more suitable.

Some of the following empirical formulae are based on local conditions only, and can be adopted only when certain specific conditions are fulfilled. Other formulae can be used for many localities, as they are based on experimental studies and results obtained over wide areas.

   (i)   Burkli–Ziegler Formula : This is the earliest empirical formula used for determining the peak runoff rate, originally given by a Swiss engineer for local conditions, but was soon adopted in U.S.A

$$Q_p = 296 \, C_R I A \left(\frac{S}{A}\right)^{1/4} \qquad \text{... (2.18)}$$

where, Q_p = The peak runoff in litres per second. (Same meaning for equations (2.18) to (2.25)

I = The maximum rainfall intensity over the entire catchment and is usually taken as 25 to 75 mm/hr

A = The drainage area in hectares

C_R = Runoff coefficient depending upon the permeability of the surface. It may vary between 0.5 to 0.9 (or adopting an average value of 0.7)

S = The slope of the ground surface in metres per thousand metres.

(ii) Metcalf and Eddy's Formula :

$$Q_p = 28.32 \left[\frac{25000}{2.47 A + 125} + 15 \right] \qquad \text{... (2.19)}$$

(iii) McMath's Formula :

$$Q_p = 292 \, C_R I \, A \left(\frac{S}{A} \right)^{1/5} \qquad \text{... (2.20)}$$

The value of C_R varies between 0.3 to 0.9, though an average value of 0.75 is recommended.

(iv) Dicken's Formula : This formula is generally useful for North India.

$$Q_p = 14 \, K \, A_M^{3/4} \qquad \text{... (2.21)}$$

where, A_M = Catchment area in sq.km.

          K = Constant depending upon factors which affect the runoff

          = 1600 for small areas

          = 850 for areas of average size with annual rainfall varying between 600 to 1200 mm

          = 250 for very large areas

(v) Fanning's Formula :

$$Q_p = 3125 \, A_M^{5/8} \qquad \text{... (2.22)}$$

where, A_M = Catchment area in sq.km.

(vi) Ryve's Formula :

$$Q_p = 15 \, K \, A_M^{2/3} \qquad \text{... (2.23)}$$

where, K and A_M have the same meaning as in Dicken's formula.

The value of K may vary between 450 to 625.

(vii) Inglis Formula : This formula was adopted to the fan shaped catchments in old Bombay.

$$Q_p = \frac{123100 \, A_M}{\sqrt{A_M + 10.4}} \qquad \text{... (2.24)}$$

where, A_M = Catchment area in sq.km.

(viii) Talbot's Formula :

$$Q_p = 87000 \, A_M^{1/4} \qquad \text{... (2.25)}$$

where, A_M = Catchment area in sq.km.

SOLVED EXAMPLES

Example 2.1 : Find out density of population/hectare, for city, the municipal authorities has the following reservations for different land uses fixed :

Roads	:	20%
Gardens	:	15%
Schools	:	5%
Markets	:	3%
Hospitals and dispensaries	:	2%
Floor space index (FSI)	:	1.

Solution :

Total reservation is 45%.

$\therefore$ Area available for residential development $= 100 - 45 = 55\%$

Let us consider an area of 1 hectare ($= 10^4 \, m^2$)

$\therefore$ Actual total floor area of residential development

$$= (0.55) \times 10^4 \times FSI$$

$$= 0.55 \times 10^4 \times 1$$

$$= 5500 \, m^2$$

Assuming a floor area requirement of 9 m^2 per person,

$\therefore$ Density of population/hectare $= \dfrac{5500}{9} \; = 611.11 \cong \mathbf{612}$ ... **Ans.**

Example 2.2 : Estimate the total quantity of a sewage of a town (whose design population is 50,000). The water supply is 150 litres/capita/day (average) and the estimated infiltration of ground water is 8000 litres/km line per day. The proposed sewerage system will have 65 km of sewer line; out of which nearly 50% will be below ground water table.   **(Civil Services)**

Solution :

   Given :

Population	=	50,000
Average water supply	=	150 l/capita/day
Rate of infiltration	=	8000 l/km/day
Length of sewerage system	=	65 km of sewer line
Length of the sewer under ground water table	=	0.50×65
	=	32.5 km

The water supply in l/day $= 50,000 \times 150$ l/day

$\qquad = 7.5 \times 10^6$ l/day

$\qquad = 7.5$ Ml/day

The quantity of sewage generated due to supplied water

$\qquad = 80\% \times 7.5$ Ml/day

$\qquad = 6$ Ml/day   ... (i)

The quantity of ground water filtration for 32.5 km length of sewer line

$\qquad = 8000$ l/km/day $\times$ 32.5 km

$\qquad = 0.26 \times 10^6$ l/day

$\qquad = 0.26$ Ml/day   ... (ii)

Total quantity of a sewage of a town

$\qquad =$ The quantity of sewage generated due to supplied water + The quantity of ground water filtration for 32.5 km length of sewer line

$\qquad =$ (i) + (ii)

$\qquad = 6 + 0.26$

$\qquad = \mathbf{6.26\ M}l\ \mathbf{/day}$ ... **Ans.**

Example 2.3 : Assuming that the surface on which the rain falls in a district is as follows :

20% of the area consists of roofs with runoff ratio is 0.90, 25% of the area consists of pavements for which the runoff ratio is 0.85, 50% of the area consists of lawns and gardens for which runoff ratio is 0.10 and the remaining 5% of the area is wooded for which the runoff ratio is 0.05, determine the runoff coefficient.

If the total area of the district is 1.5 hectares and the maximum intensity is taken as 60.5 mm/hr, what is the total runoff for the district ?   **(Civil Services)**

Solution :

Given :

$\qquad A$ $=$ Total area of the district $= 1.5$ hectares

$\qquad A_1$ $=$ 20% of the area (A) consists of roofs with runoff ratio (C_{R_1}) is 0.90

$\qquad A_2$ $=$ 25% of the area (A) consists of pavements for which the runoff ratio (C_{R_2}) is 0.85.

$\qquad A_3$ $=$ 50% of the area (A) consists of lawns and gardens for which runoff ratio (C_{R_3}) is 0.10

A_4 = 5% of the area (A) is wooded for which the runoff ratio is 0.05

Maximum intensity of rainfall,

$$I_C = 60.5 \text{ mm/hr}$$

Average runoff coefficient can be calculated by equation (2.7 a).

$$C_{R \text{ (ave)}} = \frac{C_{R_1} A_1 + C_{R_2} A_2 + C_{R_3} A_3 + C_{R_4} A_4}{A_1 + A_2 + A_3 + A_4}$$

Now,

$$C_{R_1} A_1 = \frac{20}{100} A \times 0.90 = 0.18 A$$

$$C_{R_2} A_2 = \frac{25}{100} A \times 0.85 = 0.213 A$$

$$C_{R_3} A_3 = \frac{50}{100} A \times 0.10 = 0.05 A$$

$$C_{R_4} A_4 = \frac{5}{100} A \times 0.05 = 0.0025 A$$

and

$$A = A_1 + A_2 + A_3 + A_4$$

∴

$$C_{R \text{ (ave)}} = \frac{0.18 A + 0.213 A + 0.05 A + 0.0025 A}{A}$$

$$C_{R \text{ (ave)}} = \textbf{0.4455} \qquad \textbf{... Ans.}$$

The total runoff or the peak rate of runoff may be determined by using equation (2.7).

∴

$$Q_p = \frac{1}{360} \cdot C_R \cdot I_C \cdot A$$

$$= \frac{1}{360} \times 0.4455 \times 60.5 \times 1.5$$

$$Q_p = \textbf{0.112 cumecs} \qquad \textbf{... Ans.}$$

Example 2.4 : Assuming that the surface on which the rain falls in a district is classified as follows :

15% of the area consists of roof for which the runoff ratio is 0.90, 25% of the area consists of pavements for which the runoff ratio is 0.90, 5% of the area consists of paved yards of houses for which runoff ratio is 0.85, 20% of area consists of macadam roads for which runoff ratio is 0.60, 30% of the area consists of lawns and gardens for which the runoff ratio is 0.15 and the remaining 5% of the area is wooded for which the runoff ratio is 0.1. Determine the coefficient of runoff for the area.

If the total area of the district is 40 hectares and the maximum rain intensity is taken as 70 mm/hr, what is total runoff for the district ?

Solution :

Given :

A = Total area of the district = 40 hectares

A_1 = 15% of the area (A) consists of roof for which the runoff ratio (C_{R_1}) is 0.90

A_2 = 25% of the area (A) consists of pavements for which the runoff ratio (C_{R_2}) is 0.90.

A_3 = 5% of the area (A) consists of paved yards of houses for which runoff ratio (C_{R_3}) is 0.85

A_4 = 20% of the area (A) consists of macadam roads for which runoff ratio (C_{R_4}) is 0.60

A_5 = 30% of the area (A) consists of lawns and gardens for which the runoff ratio (C_{R_5}) is 0.15

A_6 = 5% of the area (A) is wooded for which the runoff ratio (C_{R_6}) is 0.1

Maximum intensity of rainfall, I_C = 70 mm/hr.

Average coefficient of runoff can be calculated by equation (2.7 a).

$$C_{R\,(ave)} = \frac{C_{R_1} A_1 + C_{R_2} A_2 + C_{R_3} A_3 + C_{R_4} A_4 + C_{R_5} A_5 + C_{R_6} A_6}{A}$$

Now,

$$C_{R_1} A_1 = \frac{15}{100} A \times 0.9 = 0.135 A$$

$$C_{R_2} A_2 = \frac{25}{100} A \times 0.9 = 0.225 A$$

$$C_{R_3} A_3 = \frac{5}{100} A \times 0.85 = 0.0425 A$$

$$C_{R_4} A_4 = \frac{20}{100} A \times 0.6 = 0.12 A$$

$$C_{R_5} A_5 = \frac{30}{100} A \times 0.15 = 0.045 A$$

$$C_{R_6} A_6 = \frac{5}{100} A \times 0.1 = 0.005 A$$

$$\therefore \quad C_{R\,(ave)} = \frac{0.135\,A + 0.225\,A + 0.0425\,A + 0.12\,A + 0.045\,A + 0.005\,A}{A}$$

$$C_{R\,(ave)} = \textbf{0.5725} \qquad \text{... Ans.}$$

The total runoff may be determined by equation (2.7).

$$\therefore \quad Q_p = \frac{1}{360} \cdot C_R \cdot I_c \cdot A = \frac{1}{360} \times 0.5725 \times 70 \times 40$$

$$\therefore \qquad Q_p = \textbf{4.45 cumecs} \qquad \text{... Ans.}$$

Example 2.5 : The total area of the district is 15 hectares. The following data shows various types of area and the corresponding runoff coefficient of a town. Determine the coefficient of runoff for the area.

Type of Surface	% of Total Surface Area	Runoff Coefficient
Roof surface	20%	0.85
Unpaved shreets	15%	0.25
Wooded area	10%	0.15
Parks and lawns	40%	0.20
Hard pavements	5%	0.85
Macadam roads	10%	0.30

Find the maximum runoff for a rainfall intensity of 40 mm/hr having a frequency of once in five years.

Solution :

Given :   A = Total area of the district = 15 hectares

Type of Surface	% of Total Surface Area	Runoff Coefficient
Roof surface	$A_1 = \dfrac{20}{100} \times A = 0.2\,A$	$C_{R_1} = 0.85$
Unpaved streets	$A_2 = \dfrac{15}{100} \times A = 0.15\,A$	$C_{R_2} = 0.25$
Wooded area	$A_3 = \dfrac{10}{100} \times A = 0.1\,A$	$C_{R_3} = 0.15$
Parks and lawns	$A_4 = \dfrac{40}{100} \times A = 0.4\,A$	$C_{R_4} = 0.20$
Hard pavements	$A_5 = \dfrac{5}{100} \times A = 0.05\,A$	$C_{R_5} = 0.85$
Macadam roads	$A_6 = \dfrac{10}{100} \times A = 0.1\,A$	$C_{R_6} = 0.30$

Maximum intensity of rainfall, I_c = 40 mm/hr.

Average coefficient of runoff can be calculated by equation (2.7 a)

$$\therefore \qquad C_{R\,(ave)} = \frac{C_{R_1} A_1 + C_{R_2} A_2 + C_{R_3} A_3 + C_{R_4} A_4 + C_{R_5} A_5 + C_{R_6} A_6}{A}$$

Now, $C_{R_1} A_1$ = $0.85 \times 0.2\,A$ = $0.17\,A$

$\qquad C_{R_2} A_2$ = $0.25 \times 0.15\,A$ = $0.0375\,A$

$\qquad C_{R_3} A_3$ = $0.15 \times 0.1\,A$ = $0.015\,A$

$\qquad C_{R_4} A_4$ = $0.20 \times 0.4\,A$ = $0.08\,A$

$\qquad C_{R_5} A_5$ = $0.85 \times 0.05\,A$ = $0.0425\,A$

$\qquad C_{R_6} A_6$ = $0.30 \times 0.1\,A$ = $0.03\,A$

$$\therefore \qquad C_{R\,(ave)} = \frac{0.17\,A + 0.0375\,A + 0.015\,A + 0.08\,A + 0.0425\,A + 0.03\,A}{A}$$

$$C_{R\,(ave)} = \mathbf{0.375} \qquad\qquad \text{... Ans.}$$

The maximum runoff can be determined by using equation (2.7).

$$\therefore \qquad Q_p = \frac{1}{360} \cdot C_R \cdot I_c \cdot A$$

$$= \frac{1}{360} \times 0.375 \times 40 \times 15$$

$$Q_p = \mathbf{0.625\ cumecs} \qquad\qquad \text{... Ans.}$$

Example 2.6 : The total area of the district is 25 hectares. The following data shows various types of areas and the corresponding runoff coefficients of a town. Determine the coefficient of runoff for the area.

Type of Surface	% of Total Surface Area	Runoff Coefficient
Roof surface	20%	0.80
Unpaved shreets	20%	0.20
Wooded area	15%	0.20
Parks and lawns	30%	0.25
Hard pavements	5%	0.85
Macadam roads	10%	0.40

If the time of concentration for the area is 30 minutes, determine the maximum runoff.

Solution :

Given :   A = Total area of the district = 25 hectares

$t \approx t_c$ = Time of concentration = 30 min.

Type of Surface	% of Total Surface Area	Runoff Coefficient
Roof surface	$A_1 = \dfrac{20}{100} \times A = 0.20\ A$	$C_{R_1} = 0.80$
Unpaved streets	$A_2 = \dfrac{20}{100} \times A = 0.20\ A$	$C_{R_2} = 0.20$
Wooded area	$A_3 = \dfrac{15}{100} \times A = 0.15\ A$	$C_{R_3} = 0.20$
Parks and lawns	$A_4 = \dfrac{30}{100} \times A = 0.30\ A$	$C_{R_4} = 0.25$
Hard pavements	$A_5 = \dfrac{5}{100} \times A = 0.05\ A$	$C_{R_5} = 0.85$
Macadam roads	$A_6 = \dfrac{10}{100} \times A = 0.10\ A$	$C_{R_6} = 0.40$

Average coefficient of runoff can be calculated by equation (2.7 a).

$\therefore \quad C_{R\ (ave)} = \dfrac{C_{R_1} A_1 + C_{R_2} A_2 + C_{R_3} A_3 + C_{R_4} A_4 + C_{R_5} A_5 + C_{R_6} A_6}{A}$

Now,

$C_{R_1}\ A_1 = 0.80 \times 0.20\ A = 0.16\ A$

$C_{R_2}\ A_2 = 0.20 \times 0.20\ A = 0.04\ A$

$C_{R_3}\ A_3 = 0.20 \times 0.15\ A = 0.03\ A$

$C_{R_4}\ A_4 = 0.25 \times 0.30\ A = 0.075\ A$

$C_{R_5}\ A_5 = 0.85 \times 0.05\ A = 0.0425\ A$

$C_{R_6}\ A_6 = 0.40 \times 0.10\ A = 0.04\ A$

$\therefore \quad C_{R\ (ave)} = \dfrac{0.16\ A + 0.04\ A + 0.03\ A + 0.075\ A + 0.0425\ A + 0.04\ A}{A}$

$C_{R\ (ave)} = \mathbf{0.3875}$ ... **Ans.**

Maximum intensity of rainfall, I_c can be calculated by equation (2.13).

$\therefore \qquad I_c = \dfrac{25.4\ a}{t + b}$

As duration of storm is 30 minutes, a = 40 and b = 20

$$\therefore \quad I_c = \frac{25.4 \times 40}{30 + 20} = \frac{1016}{50}$$

$$I_c = 20.32 \ mm/hr$$

$$\cong 20 \ mm/hr$$

The maximum runoff can be determined by using equation (2.7 a).

$$\therefore \quad Q_p = \frac{1}{360} \cdot C_R \cdot I_c \cdot A$$

$$= \frac{1}{360} \times 0.3875 \times 20 \times 25$$

$$Q_p = \textbf{0.5382 cumecs} \qquad\qquad \text{... Ans.}$$

Example 2.7 : The drainage area of one sector of a town is 12 hectares. The classification of the surface of this area is as follows.

Type of Surface	% of Total Surface Area	Coefficient of Runoff
Hard pavement	20%	0.85
Roof surface	20%	0.80
Unpaved street	15%	0.20
Gardens and Lawns	30%	0.20
Wooded area	15%	0.15

If the time of concentration for the area is 30 minutes, find the maximum runoff.

Use the formula

$$R = \frac{900}{t + 60} \qquad\qquad \textbf{(A.M.I.E.)}$$

Solution :

Given :   A = Total drainage area of one sector of a town = 12 hectares

$$t \cong t_c = \text{Time of concentration} = 30 \ minutes$$

Type of Surface	% of Total Surface Area	Coefficient of Runoff
Hard pavement	$A_1 = \frac{20}{100} \times A = 0.2\,A$	$C_{R_1} = 0.85$
Roof surface	$A_2 = \frac{20}{100} \times A = 0.2\,A$	$C_{R_2} = 0.80$
Unpaved street	$A_3 = \frac{15}{100} \times A = 0.15\,A$	$C_{R_3} = 0.20$

Contd...

Gardens and lawns	$A_4 = \dfrac{30}{100} \times A = 0.30\,A$	$C_{R_4} = 0.20$
Wooded area	$A_5 = \dfrac{15}{100} \times A = 0.15\,A$	$C_{R_5} = 0.15$

Average coefficient of runoff can be calculated by equation (2.7 a).

$$\therefore \qquad C_{R\,(ave)} = \frac{C_{R_1}A_1 + C_{R_2}A_2 + C_{R_3}A_3 + C_{R_4}A_4 + C_{R_5}A_5}{A}$$

Now,

$$C_{R_1}A_1 = 0.85 \times 0.2\,A = 0.17\,A$$

$$C_{R_2}A_2 = 0.80 \times 0.2\,A = 0.16\,A$$

$$C_{R_3}A_3 = 0.20 \times 0.15\,A = 0.03\,A$$

$$C_{R_4}A_4 = 0.20 \times 0.30\,A = 0.06\,A$$

$$C_{R_5}A_5 = 0.15 \times 0.15\,A = 0.0225\,A$$

$$\therefore \qquad C_{R\,(ave)} = \frac{0.17\,A + 0.16\,A + 0.03\,A + 0.06\,A + 0.0225\,A}{A}$$

$$C_{R\,(ave)} = 0.4425$$

Now, in the given formula,

$$R = \frac{900}{t + 60}$$

R is the maximum rainfall intensity (I_c) and t is the time of concentration (t_c).

$$\therefore \qquad R = I_c = \frac{900}{t_c + 60} = \frac{900}{30 + 60}$$

$$= 10 \text{ mm/hr}$$

The maximum runoff can be determined by using equation (2.7).

$$Q_p = \frac{1}{360} \cdot C_R \cdot I_c \cdot A$$

$$= \frac{1}{360} \times 0.4425 \times 10 \times 12$$

$$Q_p = \textbf{0.1475 cumecs} \qquad\qquad \text{... Ans.}$$

Example 2.8 : The total area of the district is 25 hectares. Assuming that the 15% of the area consists of roof for which the runoff ratio is 0.90, 5% of the area consists of paved yards of houses for which runoff ratio is 0.85. The runoff from remaining area will not be allowed to enter the sewers. The maximum rain intensity is 40 mm/hr.

The density of population is 200 per hectare and the water demand is 160 litres per capita per day. Calculate the quantity of

1. Sewage for which the sewers of a separate system should be designed.

2. Storm water for which the sewers of a partially separate system should be designed.

3. Sewage and storm water for which the partially separate system should be designed.

Solution :

Given :   A = Total area of the district = 25 hectares

A_1 = 15% of the area (A) consists of roof for which runoff ratio (C_{R_1}) is 0.90

A_2 = 5% of the area (A) consists of paved yards of houses for which runoff ratio (C_{R_2}) is 0.85

Density of population = 200 per hectare

The demand of water = 160 litres/capita/day

Maximum rain intensity = 40 mm/hr.

(i)   The Quantity of Sewage :

Population = 200×25

= 5000

Average quantity of water supplied to the district per day

= 160×5000

= 8,00,000 litres

= 800 cu.m.

∴   Rate of water supplied in cumecs

$$= \frac{800}{24 \times 60 \times 60} = 0.009 \text{ cumecs}$$

Assuming the sewage generation is 80% of the water supplied,

∴   Average rate of sewage generation

$$= \frac{80}{100} \times 0.009$$

= 0.007 cumecs

Now, assuming the peak rate of sewage to be three times the average,

∴   The peak rate of sewage discharge

$$= 3 \times 0.007 \text{ cumecs}$$

$$= \textbf{0.022 cumecs} \qquad\qquad \text{... Ans. (i)}$$

The sewers of the separate system, should be designed for the quantity of sewage is 0.022 cumecs.

(ii) The Quantity of Storm Water : In case of partially separate system, the storm water from roofs and paved yards of houses will be allowed to enter the sewers.

Area of roofs $(A_1) = \dfrac{15}{100} \times 25 = 3.75$ hectares

Coefficient of runoff for roofs $(C_{R_1}) = 0.90$

Area of pavements $(A_2) = \dfrac{5}{100} \times 25 = 1.25$ hectares

Coefficient of runoff for roofs $(C_{R_2}) = 0.85$

∴   The discharge from roofs and pavements can be determined by rational formula

$$= \frac{1}{360} \times 0.90 \times 40 \times 3.75 + \frac{1}{360} \times 0.85 \times 40 \times 1.25$$

$$= 0.375 + 0.12$$

$$= 0.49 \text{ cumecs}$$

$$\cong \textbf{0.5 cumecs} \qquad\qquad \text{... Ans. (ii)}$$

The quantity of storm water for which the sewers of a partially separate system should be designed is 0.5 cumecs.

(iii) The Quantity of Sewage and Storm Water :

The quantity of sewage (i) and storm water (ii) for which the sewers of a partially separate system should be designed is (i) + (ii) i.e. 0.022 + 0.5 = **0.522 cumecs.**

Example 2.9 : A population of 40,000 is residing in a town having an area of 70 hectares. If the average coefficient of runoff for this area is 0.55 and the time of concentration of the rain is 40 minutes, calculate the designed discharge for the sewers of a proposed combined system. Use general formula for the maximum intensity of rainfall. Assume necessary data.

Solution :

Given :   Population = 40,000

Total area (A) = 70 hectares

Average runoff coefficient $(C_{R \text{ (ave)}}) = 0.55$

Time of concentration (t_c) = 40 minutes

$$= t$$

Assume the water demand is 130 litres/capita/person.

∴   Average quantity of water supplied to the town per day

$$= 130 \times 40{,}000$$

$$= 5.2 \times 10^6 \text{ litres}$$

$$= 5200 \text{ cu.m.}$$

∴   Rate of water supplied in cumecs

$$= \frac{5200}{24 \times 60 \times 60}$$

$$= 0.06 \text{ cumecs}$$

Assume the sewage generation is 80% of the water supplied.

∴   Average rate of sewage generation

$$= \frac{80}{100} \times 0.06$$

$$= 0.048 \text{ cumecs}$$

Now, assume the peak rate of sewage to be three times the average.

∴   The peak rate of sewage discharge

$$= 3 \times 0.048$$

$$= 0.144 \text{ cumecs} \qquad \text{... (i)}$$

The storm water discharge can be determined from equation (2.7).

∴ $$Q_p = \frac{1}{360} \cdot C_R \cdot I_c \cdot A$$

Using general formula (2.13) for maximum intensity of rainfall (I_c),

$$I_c = \frac{25.4\,a}{t + b}$$

For time of concentration of 40 minutes, value of a = 40 and b = 20.

∴ $$I_c = \frac{25.4 \times 40}{40 + 20} = \frac{1016}{60}$$

$$= 16.93 \text{ mm/hr}$$

$$\cong 17 \text{ mm/hr}$$

By substituting,

$$Q_p = \frac{1}{360} \times 0.55 \times 17 \times 70$$

$$Q_p = 1.82 \text{ cumecs} \qquad \text{... (ii)}$$

Total peak discharge = Maximum sewage discharge

+ Maximum storm water discharge

= (i) + (ii)

= 0.144 + 1.82

= **1.96 cumecs**   ... **Ans.**

The designed discharge for the sewers of a proposed combined system is 1.96 cumecs.

Example 2.10 : The area of 30 hectares which is an impervious, is to be served by a sewer line. This area is subject to four storms P_1, P_2, P_3 and P_4 with equal frequency of occurrence. The duration of the four storms is 25 minutes, 35 minutes, 45 minutes and 40 minutes respectively. Taking the time of concentration is 35 minutes, determine the peak rate of runoff from each storm. Use general formula for maximum intensity of rainfall.

Solution :

Given :   Total area (A) = 30 hectares

Duration of storm for P_1 storm = 25 min.

Duration of storm for P_2 storm = 35 min.

Duration of storm for P_3 storm = 45 min.

Duration of storm for P_4 storm = 40 min.

Time of concentration (t_c) = 35 min.

Impervious area   ($\therefore$ Runoff coefficient is 1)

(i) P_1 Storm of 25 Minutes $(t)_1$ Duration :

Intensity of rainfall can be calculated by using equation (2.13).

$$\therefore \qquad I = \frac{25.4\, a}{t + b}$$

For duration of storm of 20 to 100 minutes, value of a = 40 and b = 20.

$$\therefore \qquad I = \frac{25.4 \times 40}{25 + 20} = \frac{1016}{45}$$

$$= 22.58 \text{ mm/hr}$$

Rate of runoff can be calculated by using equation (2.7).

$$\therefore \qquad Q = \frac{1}{360} \cdot C_R \cdot I_C \cdot A$$

$$= \frac{1}{360} \times 1 \times 22.58 \times 30$$

$$= 1.88 \text{ cumecs}$$

However, the storm (P_1) for a duration of 25 minutes (t_1) while the time of concentration (t_c) is 35 minutes. The storm stops much before the whole area starts contributing.

$$\therefore \quad \text{Maximum flow from storm } P_1 = 1.88 \times \frac{25}{35} = 1.34 \text{ cumecs} \qquad \qquad \text{... (i)}$$

(ii) P_2 Storm of 35 Minutes $(t_2 = t_c)$ Duration : For duration of storm of 20 to 100 minutes, value of a = 40 and b = 20.

$$\therefore \qquad I = \frac{25.4 \times 40}{35 + 20} = \frac{1016}{55}$$

$$= 18.47 \text{ mm/hr}$$

$$\therefore \qquad Q = \frac{1}{360} \times 1 \times 18.47 \times 30$$

$$= 1.54 \text{ cumecs}$$

As, $t = t_c$, the whole area starts contributing.

(iii) P_3 Storm of 45 Minutes (t_3) :

$$I = \frac{25.4 \times 40}{45 + 20} = \frac{1016}{65}$$

$$= 15.63 \text{ mm/hr}$$

$$\therefore \qquad Q = \frac{1}{360} \times 1 \times 15.63 \times 30$$

$$= 1.3 \text{ cumecs}$$

(iv) P_4 Storm of 40 Minutes (t_4) :

$$I = \frac{25.4 \times 40}{40 + 20} = \frac{1016}{60}$$

$$= 16.93 \text{ mm/hr}$$

$$\therefore \qquad Q_p = \frac{1}{360} \times 1 \times 16.93 \times 30$$

$$= 1.411 \text{ cumecs}$$

From (i), (ii), (iii) and (iv), we find that **Q$_{max}$. i.e. Q$_p$ = 1.54 cumecs,** and this occurs when the duration of storm is equal to the time of concentration.

Remark : From above example, we have concluded that even if the rainfall duration is more than the time of concentration, the runoff will not be maximum, because in such a case, the intensity of rain reduces with the increase in its duration.

Example 2.11 : A population of 60,000 is residing in a town having an area of 50 hectares. Find the design discharge for the sewer line, if the rate of water supply is 150 litres per capita per day, average runoff coefficient of the entire area is 0.4 and time of concentration is 40 minutes.

The sewer line is to be designed for a flow equivalent to the wet weather flow (W.W.F.) plus twice the dry weather flow (D.W.F.).

Solution :

Given : A = Total area of town = 50 hectares

Population = 60000.

Water demand = 150 litres/capita/day

Average runoff coefficient = 0.4

Time of concentration, t_c = 40 minutes = t.

Average quantity of water supplied to town per day

$$= 150 \times 60000$$
$$= 9 \times 10^6 \text{ litres}$$
$$= 9000 \text{ cu.m.}$$

∴ Rate of water supplied in cumecs

$$= \frac{9000}{24 \times 60 \times 60}$$
$$= 0.104 \text{ cumecs}$$

Assuming the sewage generation is 80% of the water supplied,

∴ Average rate of sewage generation (D.W.F.)

$$= \frac{80}{100} \times 0.104$$
$$= 0.083 \text{ cumecs}$$

The rainfall intensity can be calculated by using equation (2.13).

∴ $$I_c = \frac{25.4\,a}{t + b}$$

For t = 40 minutes, the value of a = 40 and b = 20.

$$\therefore \quad I_c = \frac{25.4 \times 40}{40 + 20} = \frac{1016}{60}$$

$$= 16.93 \text{ mm/hr}$$

$$\cong 17 \text{ mm/hr}$$

The W.W.F. can be calculated by using equation (2.7).

$$\therefore \quad Q_p = \frac{1}{360} \, C_R \cdot I_c \cdot A$$

$$= \frac{1}{360} \times 0.4 \times 17 \times 50$$

$$= 0.94 \text{ cumecs}$$

Hence, the design discharge is given by

$$Q = 2 \,(D.W.F.) + W.W.F.$$

$$= 2 \times (0.104) + (0.94)$$

$$= \textbf{1.148 cumecs} \qquad \qquad \textbf{... Ans.}$$

Now, ratio of designed D.W.F. to W.W.F.

$$= \frac{2 \times 1.04}{0.94} = \frac{1}{4.52}$$

As this ratio is not very large, it is preferable to use a combined sewer system.

Example 2.12 : The surface water from airport road is drained to the longitudinal side drain from across one half of a bituminous pavement surface of total width 7.0 m, shoulder and adjoining land of width 8.0 m on one side of the drain. On the other side of the drain, water flows across from reserve land with average turf and 2% cross slope towards the side train, the width of this strip of land being 25 m. The inlet time may be assumed to be 10 min for these conditions. The runoff coefficients of the pavement, shoulder and reserve land with turf are 0.8, 0.25 and 0.35 respectively. The length of the stretch of land parallel to the road from where the water is expected to flow to the side drain is 400 m. Estimate the quantity of runoff flowing in the drain assuming 10 year frequency. The side drain will pass through clayey soil with allowable velocity of flow as 1.33 m/s. Intensity-duration chart for 10 year frequency is

Duration (min)	5	10	15	20	30
Intensity (mm/hour)	160	150	125	110	95

(Engineering Services)

Solution :

Given :

Surface	Area of Surface	Runoff Coefficient
Bituminous pavement	$A_1 = 7 \times 400 = 2800$ m^2	$C_{R_1} = 0.80$
Shoulder and adjoining land	$A_2 = 8 \times 400 = 3200$ m^2	$C_{R_2} = 0.25$
Reserve and turf land	$A_3 = 25 \times 400 = 10000$ m^2	$C_{R_3} = 0.35$

Inlet time, $t_i = 10$ minutes

Average coefficient of runoff can be calculated by equation (2.7 a).

$$\therefore \qquad C_{R\,(ave)} = \frac{C_{R_1} A_1 + C_{R_2} A_2 + C_{R_3} A_3}{A_1 + A_2 + A_3}$$

$$= \frac{0.80 \times 2800 + 0.25 \times 3200 + 0.35 \times 10000}{2800 + 3200 + 10000}$$

$$= 0.40875$$

Now, time of concentration can be calculated by using equation (2.16).

$$\therefore \qquad t_c = t_i + t_f$$

where, $\qquad t_i = 10$ minutes (given)

t_f = Channel flow time in drain in 400 m length

$$= \frac{\text{Length of the drain}}{\text{Average velocity in the drain}}$$

$$= \frac{400}{1.33} = 300 \text{ sec.}$$

$$= 5 \text{ minutes}$$

$\therefore$ Time of concentration, $t_c = 15$ minutes.

Corresponding rain intensity for 15 minutes duration rain = 125 mm/hr (from given table)

The quantity of runoff flowing in the drain can be calculated by using equation (2.7).

$$\therefore \qquad Q_p = \frac{1}{360} \; C_R \cdot I_c \cdot A$$

$$= \frac{1}{360} \times 0.40875 \times 125 \times 1.6$$

$$\left(\text{As area in ha.} = \frac{16000}{10^4} = 1.6 \text{ ha} \right)$$

$$= \textbf{0.227 cumecs} \qquad \qquad \textbf{... Ans.}$$

IMPORTANT POINTS

Sewage or waste water quantity.

- Sources of sewage.
- Estimating wastewater discharge.
- Variations in sewage flow.
- Methods for computing peak drainage discharge.

EXERCISE

1. Describe the three types of sewerage (drainage) systems indicating the conditions warranting the adoption of each system and the respective treatments. Also indicate the method of estimating flow in a combined system.

   [**Note :** For description of three types of sewerage systems, refer chapter 1. Three types of sewerage systems means separate, combined and partially separate system.]

2. What are the sources of sewage ? Explain the variations in sewage flow.

3. Enlist the different sources of sewage and explain the variations in the sewage flow.

4. What do you understand by dry weather flow ? Discuss in brief various factors affecting the dry weather flow.

5. Briefly discuss about guidelines which you will adopt for deciding the design period of various laterals, branch sewers and main sewers of a sewerage system.

6. In brief write about hourly variations of sewage flow.

7. Discuss the variations in the rate of sewage. What are its effects on the design of a sewer ?

8. State the factors on which the infiltration of water into sewer depends.

9. State the factors on which the runoff or storm water flow depends.

10. What is time of concentration and how is it used in design of sewer ?

11. Briefly explain about ground water filtration with regard to sewage flows.

12. How do you estimate the quantities of storm water runoff and sanitary wastewater in order to design storm sewer and sanitary sewer, separately ?

13. Explain intensity of rainfall. How do you determine intensity of rainfall ?

14. Differentiate between 'Sewage' and 'Drainage'. Discuss and explain the Rational formula and its limitations in calculating the quantities of storm sewage.

15. Discuss the use of Ryve's formula for the Indian catchments, and also discuss that upto which catchment area Rational formula can be used.

16. Give various empirical formulae for estimating drainage discharge of Indian catchments.

17. Write short notes on :
    (a) Storm duration and its effect on imperviousness.
    (b) Minimum and maximum D.W.F. in sewers.
    (c) Estimating the design sewage discharge.
    (d) Inglis formula.
    (e) Per-capita sewage.
    (f) Design periods for different components of a sewerage scheme.
    (g) Average runoff coefficient for business areas.
    (h) Time variations in sewage.
    (i) Rational formula for estimating run-off.
    (j) Different sources of sewage.
    (k) Sustained flow.
    (*l*) Time of concentration and its significance.

18. Define :
    (a) Critical rainfall duration.
    (b) Coefficient of runoff.
    (c) Peak rate of run-off.
    (d) Inlet time or overland flow time and channel flow time or gutter flow time.

19. The total area of the district is 20 hectares. The following data shows various types of area and the corresponding runoff coefficient of a town. Determine the coefficient of the runoff for the area.

Type of Surface	% of Total Surface Area	Runoff Coefficient
Roof surface	15%	0.80
Unpaved streets	20%	0.25
Wooded area	15%	0.20
Parks and lawns	35%	0.20
Hard pavements	5%	0.85
Macadam roads	10%	0.40

Find the maximum runoff for a rainfall intensity of 50 mm/hr.

(**Ans.** : $C_{R\,(ave)}$ = 0.3525; Q_p = 0.979 cumecs)

20. A population of 80,000 is residing in a town having an area of 80 hectares. If the average coefficient of runoff for this area is 0.65 and the time of concentration is 30 minutes, calculate the designed discharge for the sewers of a proposed combined system. The maximum rainfall intensity is 50 mm/hr. Assume water demand is 160 litres/capita/day.

21. An impervious area of 40 hectares is to be served by a sewer line. This area is subjected to four storms P_1, P_2, P_3 and P_4 with equal frequency of occurrence. The duration of the four storms is 35 minutes, 25 minutes, 15 minutes and 30 minutes respectively. The time of concentration is 25 minutes. Determine the maximum runoff from each storm.

✠ ✠ ✠

Chapter 3

SEWER DESIGN AND CONSTRUCTION OF SEWERS

DESIGN OF SEWERS

Generally the design of sewer pipes and water supply pipes is same excepting two major differences, which we will be seen in detail in next article.

In modern days, a separate sewerage system is mostly adopted, in which the circular sewer pipes are laid below the ground level, keeping steep gradient towards the outfall point and the storm water drains (S.W. drains) are separately constructed (open or covered, rectangular or trapezoidal surface drains) at suitable gradients.

The sewer pipes are designed to carry the maximum quantity of sanitary sewage.

The storm water drains are designed to carry the maximum drainage discharge i.e. storm run-off.

The combined sewers are designed to carry the sewage as well as the drainage.

3.1 COMPARISON OF DESIGN OF WATER SUPPLY PIPES AND SEWER PIPES

As we have seen that the design of water supply pipes and sewer pipes is the same related to finding out their sections and gradients. But there are two major differences which are tabulated in the following table related to the characteristics of flows in sewers and water supply pipes.

Following Table 3.1 shows comparison of design of water supply pipes and sewer pipes.

Table 3.1 : Comparison of the Design of Water Supply Pipes and Sewer Pipes

Sr. No.	Item	Water Supply Pipe	Sewer Pipe
1.	Presence of solid matter	No presence of solid matter.	• Contain particles of solid matter (both organic as well as inorganic). • Heavier of these particles may settle down at the bottom of the sewers and leads to clogging of the sewers at low velocity, so to avoid clogging of sewers, they must be laid at such a gradient that self cleansing velocity is achieved.

Contd...

2.	Pressure	Carry water under pressure, so they may be carried up and down the hills and the valleys.	• Carry sewage as gravity conduit or open channels, hence they must be laid at continuous downward gradient.
			• Sewers run under pressure only when they are designed as force mains and as inverted siphons.

3.2 HYDRAULIC FORMULAE

To determine velocities, the following empirical hydraulic formulae are used :

(1) Chezy's formula, (2) Kutter's formula, (3) Bazin's formula, (4) Manning's formula, (5) Crimp and Bruge's formula, (6) Hazen and Willian's formula.

1. Chezy's Formula : Chezy (1775) gave the following formula :

$$V = C\sqrt{R \cdot S} \qquad \qquad \text{... (3.1)}$$

where,

V = Velocity of flow, m/sec

S = Hydraulic gradient or slope of the sewer

R = Hydraulic mean radius, m = A/P

A = Area of cross-section, m^2

P = Wetted perimeter, m

C = Chezy's constant.

The Chezy's constant C depends upon several factors, such as roughness of inner surface of sewer, hydraulic mean radius, size and shape of sewer, slope etc. Generally, the value of Chezy's constant C is found either by Kutter's formula or by Bazin's formula.

The channel section is designed by the general formula :

$$Q = A \times V \qquad \qquad \text{... (V is obtained from equation 3.1)}$$

where,

Q = Discharge in m^3/sec.

(i) Kutter's Formula : As per this formula, the following value of C to be used in equation (3.1).

$$C = \frac{23 + \dfrac{0.00155}{S} + \dfrac{1}{N}}{1 + \left(23 + \dfrac{0.00155}{S}\right)\dfrac{N}{\sqrt{R}}} \qquad \qquad \text{... (3.2)}$$

where,

R = Hydraulic mean radius, m

S = Slope

N = Rugosity coefficient, the value of which depends upon the nature of inside surface of the sewer (Table 3.2).

Usually, the values corresponding to *fair condition* of the interior surface are taken in the design.

Table 3.2 : Values of Kutter's or Manning's Coefficient (N)

Sr. No.	Pipe Material	Condition of Interior Surface	
		Good	Fair
1.	Salt glazed stoneware	0.012	0.014
2.	Cement concrete	0.013	0.015
3.	Cast iron	0.012	0.013
4.	Brick unglazed	0.013	0.015
5.	Asbestos cement	0.011	0.012
6.	Plastic (smooth)	0.011	0.011

(ii) **Bazin's Formula :** As per this formula, the following value of C to be used in equation (3.1).

$$C = \frac{157.6}{1.81 + \frac{K}{\sqrt{R}}} \qquad \qquad ... (3.3)$$

where,   K = Bazin's constant, the value of which may be taken from Table 3.3.

Table 3.3 : Bazin's Constant (K)

Sr. No.	Type or Nature of Inside Surface of Sewer or Drain	K
1.	Very smooth surface	0.11
2.	Smooth brick and concrete surface	0.29
3.	Rough brick and concrete surface	0.50
4.	Smooth rubble masonry surface	0.83
5.	Good earthen channels	1.54
6.	Rough earthen channel	3.17

2. **Manning's Formula :** Manning (1890) gave the following expression for velocity of flow. The formula is widely used in U.S.A. as well as in India :

$$V = \frac{1}{N} R^{2/3} S^{1/2} \qquad \qquad ... (3.4)$$

where, V, N, R, S have the same meanings as above. The value of rugosity coefficient, N is the same as suggested by Kutter and is represented in Table 3.2.

3. Crimp and Bruge's Formula : This formula is commonly used in England and it is very simple.

$$V = 83.47 \, R^{2/3} S^{1/2} \qquad \qquad ... (3.5)$$

where, V, R and S have the same meanings, as given earlier. Comparing this with Manning's formula, we have

$$V = 83.47 \, R^{2/3} S^{1/2} = \frac{R^{2/3} S^{1/2}}{N}$$

which gives N = 1/83.47 = 0.012. Hence, Manning's formula becomes Crimp and Bruge's formula when N = 0.012.

4. Hazen and William's Formula : Allen Hazen and G.S. Williams (1902) gave the following formula, which is mostly used for flow under pressure for designing water supply pipes and rarely used for designing sewers.

$$V = 0.85 \, C_h \, R^{0.63} S^{0.54} \qquad \qquad ... (3.6)$$

The coefficient C_h may be taken from Table 3.4.

Table 3.4 : Hazen and William's Coefficient (C_h)

Sr. No.	Type of Material	C_h
1.	Steel pipe with rivetted joints	95
2.	Old C.I. pipes; brick sewers in good condition	100
3.	Steel pipes, with welded joints	100
4.	Stoneware pipes in good condition	110
5.	Cement lined pipes	110
6.	Asbestos cement pipe	120
7.	Plastic pipes	120
8.	New C.I. pipes	130
9.	Pipes with very smooth inside surface	140

3.3 FREEBOARD

Sewers :

- Dia. less than 0.4 m → designed as running half full at maximum discharge.

- Dia. greater than 0.4 m → designed as running $\frac{2^{rd}}{3}$ or $\frac{3^{th}}{4}$ full at maximum discharge.

Storm Water Drains : Keeping nominal freeboard for storm water drains, which is shown in Table 3.5.

Table 3.5 : Freeboard for Design of Storm Water Drains

Sr. No.	Peak Discharge, Cumecs	Freeboard, Meters
1.	Less than 0.3	0.3
2.	0.3 to 1.0	0.4
3.	1.0 to 5.0	0.5
4.	5.0 to 10.0	0.6
5.	10.0 to 30.0	0.75
6.	30.0 to 150.0	0.90
7.	Greater than 150	1.0

3.4 MINIMUM AND MAXIMUM VELOCITIES OF FLOW

3.4.1 Minimum Velocity of Flow

As we know that, sewage contains solid matter, the minimum velocity of flow is required to keep the solid matter in suspension, is called *self-cleansing velocity*.

Because of fluctuations in sewage flow, it is not possible to maintain the self-cleansing velocity throughout the day.

Self-cleansing velocity should be maintained at least once a day, because if certain deposition takes place and which is not removed, it will obstruct free flow or may lead to blocking of sewer.

Shild's Expression for Self-Cleansing Velocity :

Self-cleansing velocity can be determined as follows with reference to Fig. 3.1.

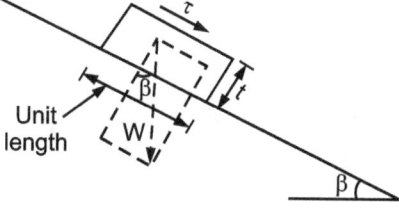

Fig. 3.1

Consider a layer of sediment of unit width and unit length and of thickness t deposited at the invert of a sewer of gradient β.

1. The submerged unit weight of the sediment is given by equation,

$$\gamma_{sub} = \gamma_w \left(\frac{S_s - 1}{1 + e} \right) \qquad \dots \text{(i)}$$

where, γ_{sub} = Submerged unit weight of the sediment.

$$\gamma_w \;=\; \text{Unit weight of the water.}$$

$$e \;=\; \text{Voids ratio.}$$

But the porosity (n) of sediment,

$$n \;=\; \left(\frac{e}{1+e}\right)$$

$$\therefore \qquad\qquad (1-n) \;=\; \frac{1}{(1+e)} \qquad\qquad\qquad \text{... (ii)}$$

Substituting this in equation (i),

$$\therefore \qquad\qquad \gamma_{sub} \;=\; \gamma_w\,(S_s-1)\,(1-n) \qquad\qquad \text{... (iii)}$$

2. The weight of the sediment of unit length and unit width is given by equation,

$$W \;=\; \gamma_{sub} \times \text{Volume}$$

$$=\; \gamma_{sub} \times (1) \times (1) \times (t)$$

Substituting value of γ_{sub} from equation (iii),

$$\therefore \qquad\qquad W \;=\; \gamma_w\,(S_s-1)\,(1-n)\,t \qquad\qquad \text{... (iv)}$$

3. When the sediment is just on the point of sliding, then,

$$\left[\begin{array}{c}\text{The drag force } (\tau) \text{ exerted by the flowing} \\ \text{water on the surface of the channel}\end{array}\right] = \text{The frictional resistance, R}$$

$$\tau \;=\; R$$

Now, first we calculate value of τ and R separately and then equating the same, the drage force,

$$\tau \;=\; \gamma_w \cdot R \cdot S \qquad\qquad\qquad \text{... (v)}$$

where,

$$\tau \;=\; \text{Drag force}$$

$$R \;=\; \text{Hydraulic mean depth of the channel}$$

$$S \;=\; \text{Bed slope of the channel}$$

$$R \;=\; W \tan \beta$$

But for smaller values of β, $\tan \beta = \sin \beta$

$$\therefore \qquad\qquad R \;=\; W \sin \beta$$

or

$$\tau \;=\; R \;=\; W \sin \beta$$

or

$$\tau \;=\; \gamma_w\,(S_s-1)\,(1-n)\,t \sin \beta \qquad\qquad \text{... (vi)}$$

Now, equating equations (v) and (vi),

$$\therefore \qquad\qquad \gamma_w \cdot R \cdot S \;=\; \gamma_w\,(S_s-1)\,(1-n)\,t \sin \beta$$

Considering $(1 - n) \sin \beta = a$, as an important characteristic of the sediment, we get

$$(S_s - 1) \, a \cdot t = R \cdot S$$

or

$$S = \frac{a}{R} (S_s - 1) \, t$$

For single grains the volume per unit area i.e. t becomes the function of the diameter of the grain d_g as an inverse measure of the surface area of the individual grains exposed to drag or friction.

$\therefore$

$$S = \frac{a}{R} (S_s - 1) \, d_g \qquad \ldots \text{(vii)}$$

Therefore, equation (vii) gives invert slope at which the sewer will be self-cleansing.

4. **Chezy's Equation :** From Chezy's formula, the velocity,

$$V = C\sqrt{RS} \qquad \ldots \text{(viii)}$$

5. **Self-Cleansing Velocity :** Self-cleansing velocity can be calculated using equation (viii), by substituting value of S.

$\therefore$

$$V_s = C\sqrt{R} \sqrt{\frac{a}{R} (S_s - 1) \, d_g}$$

or

$$V_s = C\sqrt{a \, d_g (S_s - 1)} \qquad \ldots \text{(ix)}$$

For calculating value of Chezy's constant, C, let us use Darcy-Weisbach formula for head loss, H_L.

$$H_L = \frac{f \, L \, V^2}{2 \, g \, D} \qquad \ldots \text{(D is the pipe diameter)}$$

as slope,

$$S = \frac{H_L}{L} = \frac{f \, V^2}{2 \, g \, D}$$

Now,

$$V = C\sqrt{RS}$$

$\therefore$

$$C\sqrt{R} = \frac{V}{\sqrt{S}} = \sqrt{\frac{2 \, g \, D}{f}}$$

For circular pipes running full, R = D/4.

$\therefore$

$$C\sqrt{\frac{D}{4}} = \sqrt{\frac{2 \, g \, D}{f}}$$

or

$$C = \sqrt{\frac{8 \, g}{f}} \qquad \ldots \text{(x)}$$

Substituting this value in equation (ix),

$\therefore$
$$V_s = \sqrt{\frac{8\,a}{f}\,(S_s - 1)\,g \cdot d_g} \qquad \text{... (3.7)}$$

where, V_s = Self-cleansing velocity.

f = Darcy-Weisbach friction factor, the common value of which may be taken as 0.03.

a = Characteristics of solids flowing in the sewage, in suspension. The actual values of 'a' for relatively clean inorganic and organic matters present in sewage are 0.04 and 0.6 respectively. i.e. value of 0.04 for initiating scour of clean grit and 0.6 for full removal of sticky grit.

S_s = Specific gravity of solids. 2.65 for inorganic sediments and 1.2 for organic sediments

g = Gravitational acceleration constant

d_g = Diameter of solid particles

Table 3.6 shows required self-cleansing velocity related to specific gravity and size of particle.

Table 3.6 : Self-Cleansing Velocity

Sr. No.	Diameter of Solid Particle	Specific Gravity	Self-Cleansing Velocity
1.	1 mm (inorganic sand particles)	2.65	0.45 m/sec.
2.	5 mm (organic particles)	1.2	0.45 m/sec.

From above table it is concluded that, for removing the impurities mostly present in the sewage i.e. sand upto 1 mm diameter and organic particles upto 5 mm diameter, it is necessary that a minimum velocity of about 0.45 m/sec and an average velocity of 0.9 m/sec is developed in sewers.

Generally, the sewers design for 0.8 m/sec or so (for full design depth). But sewers are generally designed for $\frac{1}{2}$ to $\frac{3^{th}}{4}$ full so the velocity at running full condition will even be more than 0.8 m/sec, say 1 m/sec or so.

Table 3.7 shows the value of self-cleansing velocities for various types of particles, as recommended by Beardmore.

Table 3.8 shows gradient and velocity, recommended by **N.B.O.**

Table 3.9 shows sewer gradient required to generate self-cleansing velocities in different sized pipes.

Table 3.7 : Self-Cleansing Velocities

Sr. No.	Sewer Material	Self-Cleansing Velocity (m/sec)
1.	Angular stones	1
2.	Round pebbles (12 mm to 25 mm dia.)	0.5 – 0.6
3.	Fine gravel	0.3
4.	Coarse sand	0.2
5.	Fine sand and clay	0.15
6.	Fine clay and silt	0.075

Table 3.8 : Gradients for Small Sized Sewers

Sr. No.	Dia. of the Sewer (m)	Gradient Required to Generate Self-Cleansing Velocity	Velocity Generated in the Sewer when Running Half Full (for Which Small Sewers are Designed)
1.	0.1	1 in 60	0.58 m/sec [*]
2.	0.15	1 in 100	0.61 m/sec [*]
3.	0.225	1 in 120	0.79 m/sec [*]

[*] These values have been calculated by considering the variations in value of n at lower depth.

Table 3.9 : Sewer Gradients
(to Generate Self-Cleansing Velocities in Different Sized Pipes (Running Full))

Sr. No.	Dia. of Sewer (m)	Gradient 1 in ... for Developing Velocity of		
		0.75 m/sec	0.90 m/sec	1.05 m/sec
1.	0.100	90	75	60
2.	0.150	150	105	78
3.	0.225	265	180	135
4.	0.300	385	270	195
5.	0.375	520	355	265
6.	0.450	660	460	340
7.	0.525	820	570	415
8.	0.600	970	680	500
9.	0.675	1100	790	580
10.	0.750	1300	910	670
11.	0.900	1700	1200	850
12.	1.050	2100	1450	1050
13.	1.200	2500	1700	1250

3.4.2 Maximum Velocity of Flow

Due to the presence of suspended solids in sewage, the continuous abrasion is caused and hence the smooth interior surface of sewer pipes gets scoured.

To avoid the scouring action or abrasion, the maximum velocity is also limited. The maximum velocity at which no any scouring action takes place is called as **non-scouring velocity**.

This limiting maximum velocity or non-scouring velocity will mainly depend upon the type of material used for the construction of sewers.

Table 3.10 shows non-scouring limiting velocities.

Table 3.10 : Non-Scouring Limiting Velocities

Sr. No.	Sewer Material	Non-Scouring Velocity (m/sec)
1.	Earthen channels	0.6 – 1.2
2.	Ordinary-brick lined sewers	1.5 – 2.5
3.	Cement concrete sewers	2.5 – 3.0
4.	Stone ware sewers	3.0 – 4.0
5.	Cast iron sewers	3.5 – 4.5
6.	Vitrified tiles and glazed bricks	4.5 – 5.5

3.4.3 Effects of Discharge Variation on Velocity in Sewers

The sewage flow varies from time to time. Due to the variation in flow, the depth of flow varies and therefore, hydraulic mean depth varies and as a velocity of flow is related to hydraulic mean depth, the velocity of flow also varies.

The following points should be considered related to minimum velocity (self-cleansing velocity) and maximum velocity (non-scouring velocity) at time of designing sewers.

- As the velocity of sewage developed in a sewer of a given section and grade will be less as and when the discharge reduces. At such situation, it is necessary to check the sewer for maintaining a self-cleansing velocity of about 0.45 m/sec at the time of minimum flow and also see that a velocity of about 0.9 m/sec is developed at least at the time of maximum flow, but it should not exceed scouring value.

- In flat countries, the sewers should be designed to develop minimum velocities of 0.9 m/sec at maximum discharge only, thus, it leads to avoiding deep excavations.

- In case of steep slopes, the sewers may be designed to develop velocity of 0.9 m/sec even at minimum discharge, but the velocity is exceeded during maximum discharge, and it may be exceeded than non-scouring velocity. So drop manholes should be provided to bring down the velocity within the non-scouring value.

3.5 NOMOGRAMS AND TABLES FOR HYDRAULIC COMPUTATIONS

The different formulae described in article 3.2 involve lot of mathematical calculations. The computational work becomes very much complex while designing a full fledged sewerage scheme. To avoid such complex computational work, readymade charts, tables and nomograms are available based on different flow formulae.

(a)   Nomogram :

A nomogram shown in Fig. 3.2 is based on Manning's formula for sewers running full, for N = 0.013.

This nomogram can be used by placing a straight edge across any two known variables such as velocity and discharge (e.g. velocity is 2.1 m/sec and discharge is 0.14 m³/sec) and so read out two remaining variables such as gradient i.e. 0.024 and diameter i.e. 280 mm.

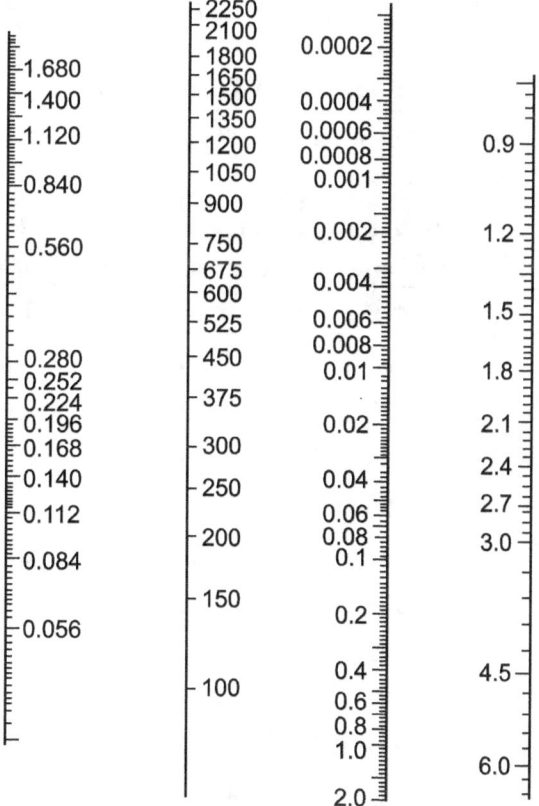

Fig. 3.2 : Nomogram based on manning's formula (n = 0.013) for circular sewers running full

For different values of N, say N = 0.012 (i.e. other than 0.013), the following multiplication is required.

- **Case I :** If velocity or discharge not known,

$$\left[\begin{array}{c}\text{The real velocity or discharge} \\ \text{produced at N = 0.012}\end{array}\right] = \left[\begin{array}{c}\text{The velocity or} \\ \text{discharge obtained} \\ \text{from the chart} \\ \text{for N = 0.013}\end{array}\right] \times \frac{0.013}{0.012}$$

- **Case II :** If velocity or discharge is given,

  - First correcting the velocity or discharge by multiplying them by $\left(\dfrac{0.012}{0.013}\right)$.

  - Placing the straight edge across the two known values.

  - Read out the remaining two variables.

(b)   Santo Crimp's Tables :

These readymade tables are based upon the Crimp and Burg's formula (equation 3.5) and mostly used in India. A sample page of Santo Crimp's tables is shown in Table 3.11 for circular sewers running full.

Table 3.11 : Santo-Crimp's Table

Sr. No.	Dia. of Sewer (mm)	Grade : 1 in 225		Grade : 1 in 100	
		Velocity (m/sec)	Discharge (litres/sec)	Velocity (m/sec)	Discharge (litres/sec)
1.	100	0.479	3.76	0.560	4.400
2.	150	0.628	11.12	0.942	16.67
3.	200	0.760	23.90	1.140	35.83
4.	250	0.833	43.34	1.324	65.01
5.	300	0.996	70.52	1.494	105.80
6.	375	1.156	127.70	1.735	191.70
7.	450	1.306	208.00	1.960	312.30
8.	525	1.447	313.30	2.170	470.10
9.	600	1.582	448.10	2.373	672.00
10.	675	1.711	611.20	2.566	918.50
11.	750	1.837	812.50	2.754	1219.00
12.	900	2.073	1320.00	3.200	2038.00

3.6 HYDRAULIC CHARACTERISTICS OF CIRCULAR SEWERS

(A)   Running Full Condition :

Area of cross-section,

$$A = \frac{\pi}{4} D^2$$

where, D is the diameter of the pipe

Wetted perimeter, $P = \pi D$

∴   Hydraulic mean depth,

$$R = \frac{A}{P} = \frac{\frac{\pi}{4} D^2}{\pi D} = \frac{D}{4}$$

(B)   Running Partially Full Condition :

(Say at a depth d, see Fig. 3.3)

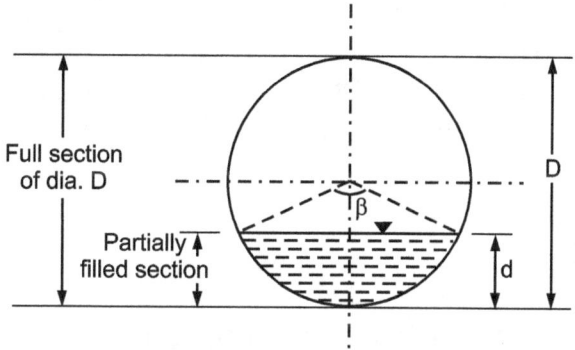

Fig. 3.3 : Partially filled circular sewer section

(a)   Depth :

$$d = \left[\frac{D}{2} - \frac{D}{2} \cos \frac{\beta}{2} \right]$$

where, β is the central angle in degrees.

∴   Proportionate depth,

$$\frac{d}{D} = \frac{1}{2} \left(1 - \cos \frac{\beta}{2} \right) \qquad \dots (3.8)$$

(b)   Area :

$$a = \frac{\pi D^2}{4} \cdot \frac{\beta}{360°} - \frac{D}{2} \cos \frac{\beta}{2} \cdot \frac{D}{2} \sin \frac{\beta}{2}$$

$$= \frac{\pi D^2}{4} \left[\frac{\beta}{360°} - \frac{\sin \beta}{2\pi} \right] \qquad \dots (3.9)$$

$$\left[\because \sin\beta = 2\sin\frac{\beta}{2} \cdot \cos\frac{\beta}{2} \right]$$

∴   Proportionate area,

$$\frac{a}{A} = \left[\frac{\beta}{360°} - \frac{\sin\beta}{2\pi} \right] \qquad \text{... (3.10)}$$

(c) Wetted Perimeter :

$$p = \pi D \cdot \frac{\beta}{360°} \qquad \text{... (3.11)}$$

∴   Proportionate wetted perimeter,

$$\frac{p}{P} = \frac{\beta}{360°} \qquad \text{... (3.12)}$$

(d) Hydraulic Mean Depth (H.M.D.) :

$$r = \frac{a}{p}$$

$$= \frac{D}{4}\left[1 - \frac{360° \sin\beta}{2\pi\beta} \right] \qquad \text{... (3.13)}$$

∴   Proportionate H.M.D.,

$$\frac{r}{R} = \left[1 - \frac{360° \sin\beta}{2\pi\beta} \right] \qquad \text{... (3.14)}$$

(e) Velocity of Flow :

$$v = \frac{1}{n} \, r^{2/3} \sqrt{S_0} \qquad \text{(v = velocity at partial flow)}$$

$$[\because \ S = S_0, \text{ i.e. bed slope}]$$

∴   V = Velocity, when running full

$$= \frac{1}{N} \cdot R^{2/3}\sqrt{S_0}$$

(Bed slope S = S₀ remaining constant whether pipe runs full or partially full)

∴   Proportionate velocity,

$$\frac{v}{V} = \frac{N}{n} \cdot \frac{r^{2/3}}{R^{2/3}} \qquad \text{... (3.15)}$$

Assuming that roughness coefficient n does not vary with depth, we have n = N.

i.e. $\dfrac{N}{n} = 1.0$

∴   Proportionate velocity,

$$\frac{v}{V} = \frac{r^{2/3}}{R^{2/3}} = \left[1 - \frac{360° \sin\beta}{2\pi\beta} \right]^{2/3} \qquad \text{... (3.16)}$$

(f) Discharge :

$$q = av \quad \text{(running partially full condition)} \qquad \text{... (3.17)}$$

$$Q = A \cdot V \ \text{(running full condition)} \qquad \text{... (3.18)}$$

∴   Proportionate discharge

$$\frac{q}{Q} = \frac{av}{A \cdot V} = \frac{a}{A} \cdot \frac{v}{V} = \left[\frac{\beta}{360°} - \frac{\sin \beta}{2\pi}\right] \left[1 - \frac{360° \sin \beta}{2\pi\beta}\right]^{2/3}$$

... (3.19)

By using proportionate depth (d/D) as reference, values of other elements can be calculated from Table 3.12.

Table 3.12 : Hydraulic Elements for Circular Sewers When Flowing Partially Full (Without being Corrected for Variations of Roughness with Depth)

Sr. No.	Proportionate Depth d/D	Proportionate Area a/A	Proportionate Wetted Perimeter p/P	Proportionate H.M.D. r/R	Proportionate Velocity v/V	Proportionate Discharge q/Q
(1)	(2)	(3)	(4)	(5)	(6)	(7)
1.	1.00	1.00	1.00	1.000	1.000	1.000
2.	0.90	0.949	0.857	1.192	1.124	1.066
3.	0.80	0.858	0.705	1.217	1.140	0.988
4.	0.70	0.748	0.631	1.185	1.120	0.838
5.	0.60	0.626	0.564	1.110	1.072	0.671
6.	0.50	0.500	0.500	1.000	1.000	0.500
7.	0.40	0.373	0.444	0.857	0.902	0.337
8.	0.30	0.252	0.369	0.684	0.776	0.196
9.	0.20	0.143	0.296	0.482	0.615	0.088
10.	0.10	0.052	0.205	0.254	0.401	0.021
11.	0.00	0.000	0.000	0.000	0.000	0.000

● **About Maximum Velocity :**

We concluded from Table 3.12 that the velocity in partially filled circular sewer sections are equal or more than those in full sections. The maximum velocity is obtained when the depth of flow is 0.81 D and it is about 12.5% greater than that at time of running full. It means that velocity is not maximum for running full.

● **About Maximum Discharge :**

The discharge is maximum at 0.95 D and is about 7% greater than that at time of running full. It means that discharge is also not maximum at running full.

The above two statements are correct only when the rugosity coefficient (n) is assumed to be independent of depth. But as Sudin has demonstrated that the rugosity coefficient (n) is not constant theoretically as well as experimentally, but it varies 20% or more with depth. [See table 3.13, Col. (3)]. Due to the effect of variation of n the proportionate velocities and discharges at lower depths of flow also reduces, so, if these variations of n are also considered, more accurate values of proportionate velocities and discharges can be computed out. (See Table 3.13, Col. (4) and (5)].

Table 3.13 : Hydraulic Particulars of Circular Sewers, Accounting Variations of n with Depth

Sr. No. (1)	$\dfrac{d}{D}$ (2)	$\dfrac{n}{N}$ (3)	$\dfrac{v}{V}$ (4)	$\dfrac{q}{Q}$ (5)
1.	1.0	1.00	1.000	1.000
2.	0.9	1.07	1.056	1.020
3.	0.8	1.14	1.003	0.890
4.	0.7	1.18	0.952	0.712
5.	0.6	1.21	0.890	0.557
6.	0.5	1.24	0.810	0.405
7.	0.4	1.27	0.713	0.266
8.	0.3	1.28	0.605	0.153
9.	0.2	1.27	0.486	0.070
10.	0.1	1.22	0.329	0.017

Fig. 3.4 shows standard chart for proportionate hydraulic elements for circular sewers. The curves are drawn related to Table 3.13 and Table 3.12 shows as firm lines and dotted lines respectively. These curves are very useful for determining different elements by knowing any one of them.

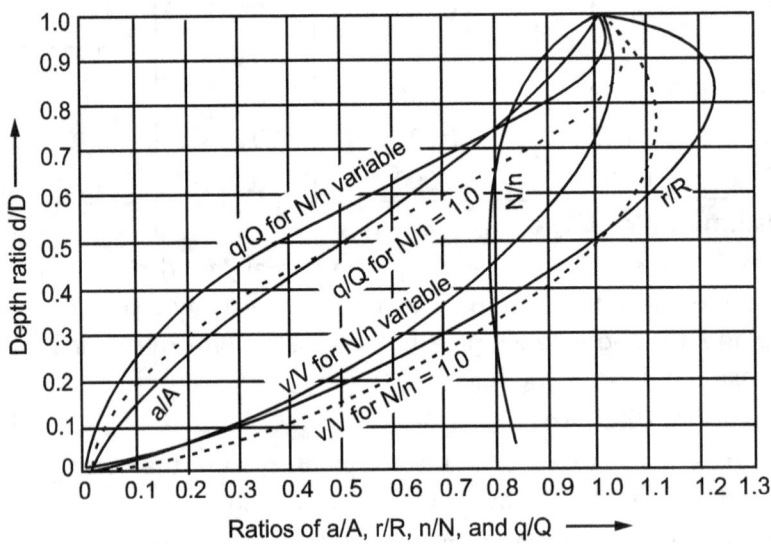

Fig. 3.4 : Standard chart for proportionate hydraulic elements for circular sewers

Self-Cleansing Flow at Partial Depth : When the sewers flowing with depths between 0.5 D and 0.8 D, need not be placed on steeper gradients and they should be taken as self-cleansing sewers running full. Because the velocity and the discharge are functions of tractive force intensity, which is based upon the friction coefficient as well as velocity. Required ratios of v_s/V, q_s/Q and s_s/S, (where the subscript s denotes self-cleansing equal to that obtained in full section) can be determined by using equation (v) of article 3.4.1 on the assumption that equality of tractive force intensity implies equality of cleansing, or

$$\tau = t$$

or
$$\gamma_w \cdot r \cdot s_s = \gamma_w RS$$

or
$$S_s = \left(\frac{R}{r}\right) S \quad \dots \text{(where } S = s_s) \qquad \dots \text{(3.20)}$$

and
$$\frac{V_s}{V} = \frac{N}{n}\left(\frac{r}{R}\right)^{2/3}\sqrt{\frac{S_s}{S}}$$

or
$$\frac{V_s}{V} = \frac{N}{n}\left(\frac{r}{R}\right)^{1/6} \qquad \dots \text{(3.21)}$$

and
$$\boxed{\frac{q_s}{Q} = \frac{N}{n}\left(\frac{a}{A}\right)\left(\frac{r}{R}\right)^{1/6}} \qquad \dots \text{(3.22)}$$

Fig. 3.5 shows various curves for values of $\dfrac{q_s}{Q}$, $\dfrac{V_s}{V}$ and $\dfrac{S_s}{S}$ for different values of $\dfrac{d}{D}$.

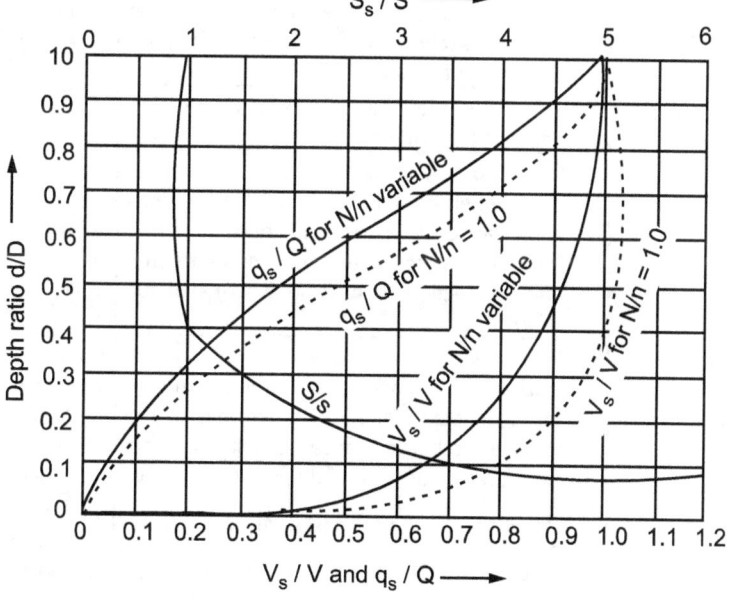

Fig. 3.5 : Standard chart for proportionate elements, to ensure self-cleansing equivalent to all depths, in circular sewers

From Fig. 3.5, we conclude that the minimum gradients are enough, so long as circular sewers flow more than half full. However, the curve for s_s/S indicates that when the depth of flow d reduces to less than 0.3 D, the grades must be increased. At a depth of 0.2 D, the grade must be doubled for equal self-cleansing and at a depth of 0.1 D the grade must be tripled i.e. $s_s = 3\,S$.

3.7 LIMITATIONS ON DEPTH OF FLOW DUE TO VENTILATION CONSIDERATIONS

Due to ventilation considerations, sewers should not be designed to run full even at ultimate peak flows.

- Upto 400 mm dia. sewers : Designed for $\frac{1}{2}$ depth.

- Between 400 mm to 900 mm dia. sewers : Designed for $\frac{2}{3}$ depth.

- Larger sewers at ultimate peak designed discharge : Designed for $\frac{3}{4}$ depth.

3.8 EGG SHAPED SEWERS

Table 3.14 shows advantages and disadvantages of circular shaped and egg shaped sewers.

Table 3.14 : Advantages and disadvantages of circular shaped and egg shaped sewers

Sr. No.	Type of Sewer	Advantages	Disadvantages
1.	Circular shaped sewer	• Manufactured very easily. • Cheapest and most economical because circular section utilizes the minimum quantities of materials. • Possibility of less deposits as circular section being of uniform curvature all round. • Providing the maximum hydraulic mean depth when running full or half full, because a circular sewer provides the maximum area for a given perimeter and therefore, the efficient section at running full or half full condition.	• The poorer the performance for lesser discharge.
2.	Egg shaped sewer	• In combined sewer system the variations in discharge are more, because the storm run-off is generally 20 to 25 times that of the sewage discharge. Hence, combined sewers will have to run at low discharges of about $\frac{1}{20}$ to $\frac{1}{25}$ times the maximum during non-monsoon periods. In such a case, egg shaped sewers are useful i.e. for low discharges and it maintains hydraulic depth nearly uniform and give 2 to 15% higher velocities than provided by **hydraulically equivalent** (hydraulically equivalent means two sewers of different shapes are discharging at the same rate, while flowing full, on the same grade) circular sections carrying the same low discharges.	• More difficult to construct. • More costly because they require more material. • They are less stable, because the smaller base has to support the weight of the upper broader section.

Egg shaped sewers were quite often used in olden days, more than at present. Due to the above mentioned disadvantages, these are becoming obsolete these days.

The following are the two common forms of egg shaped ovoid sewers :

   (i)   Standard or Metropolitan sections [Fig. 3.6 (a)].

   (ii) New shaped section [Fig. 3.6 (b)].

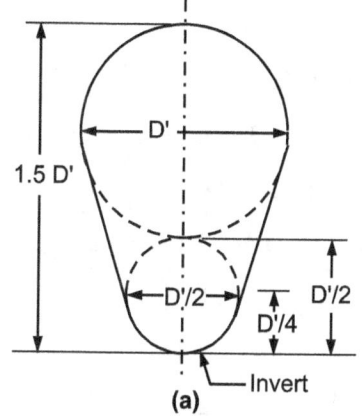 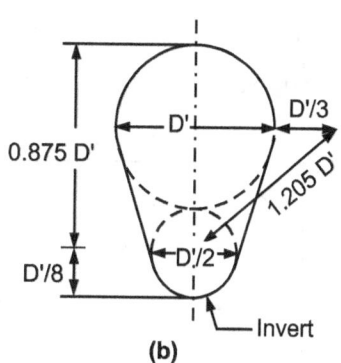

(a) "Standard" or "Metropolitan" egg shaped section   **(b) "New" egg shaped section**

Fig. 3.6 : Egg shaped sewer sections

3.9 DESIGN OF STORM WATER DRAINS

We have seen that, instead of combined sewers, to carry the storm water through storm water drains are preferred. These are generally accomplished by providing surface drains. (Surface drains are used to carry both sullage as well as storm water from houses and roads).

3.9.1 Depth Fixation Criteria

The following certain empirical formulae and curves are given which are based on experimental results for depth fixation.

   (i)   For Drains having Discharge upto 15 Cumecs :

$$y = 0.5 \sqrt{B}$$

where,   y = Depth of flow, m

                               B = Width of drain, m

For example, for trapezoidal section (depth of flow, y and width of drain, B as shown in Fig. 3.7).

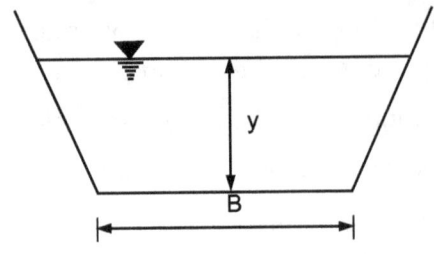

Fig. 3.7

(ii) For Drains having Discharge More than 15 Cumecs :

Table 3.15 shows value of depth for discharge above 15 cumecs.

Table 3.15 : Depth Related to Discharge

Sr. No.	Discharge (Cumecs)	Depth (y) (Metres)
1.	15	1.7
2.	30	1.8
3.	75	2.3
4.	150	2.6
5.	300	3.0

(iii) Central Water Commission's (C.W.C.) Recommendation :

C.W.C. has given graphical relationship for unlined drains representing B/y ratio for different discharges, as shown in Fig. 3.8.

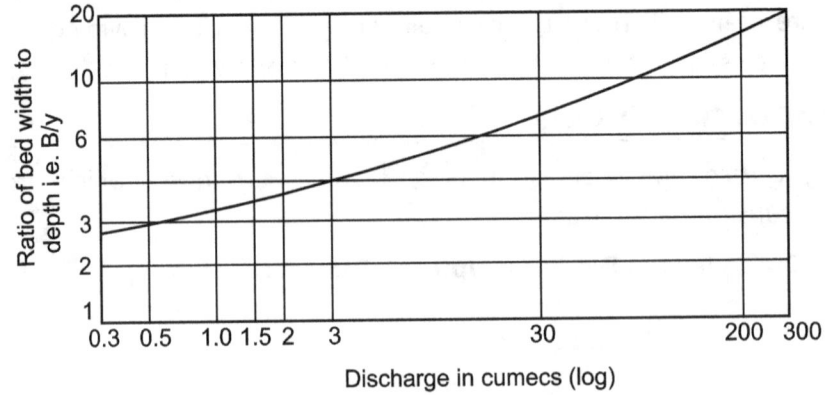

Fig. 3.8 : C.W.C. recommendations

3.9.2 Permissible Velocities in Unlined and Lined Drains

Table 3.16 shows values of permissible velocities in unlined and lined drains.

Table 3.16 : Values of Permissible Velocities in Unlined and Lined Drains

Sr. No.	Type of Soil	Maximum Permissible Velocity (m/sec)
A.	**Unlined Drains**	
1.	Rock and gravel	1.5
2.	Murum, hard soil etc.	1.0 – 1.1
3.	Sandy loam, black cotton soil	0.6 – 0.9
4.	Very light loose sand to average sandy soil	0.3 – 0.6
5.	Ordinary soils	0.6 – 0.9
B.	**Lined Drains**	
1.	Stone pitched	1.5
2.	Burnt clay tile lined	1.8
3.	Cement concrete lined	2 – 2.5

3.9.3 Common Shapes of Surface Drains

The different shapes of surface drains are shown in Fig. 3.9.

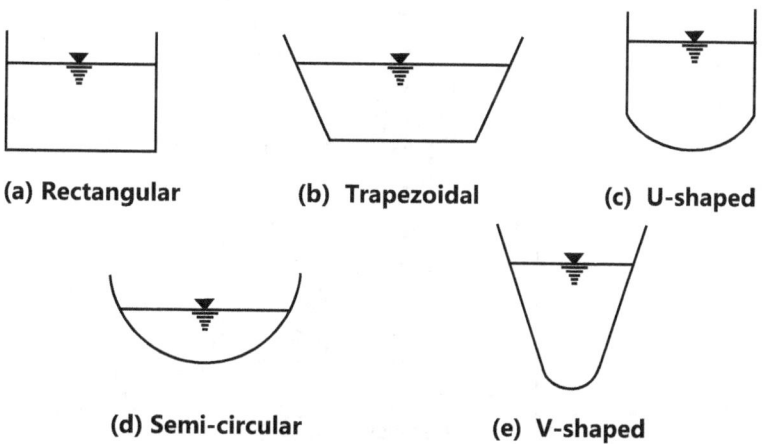

(a) Rectangular   (b) Trapezoidal   (c) U-shaped

(d) Semi-circular   (e) V-shaped

Fig. 3.9 : Different shapes of surface drains

CONSTRUCTION OF SEWERS

3.10 DIFFERENT SHAPES OF SEWERS

Table 3.17 shows different shapes of sewers.

Table 3.17 : Different Shapes of Sewers

Sr. No.	Shape of Sewer	Sketch of Sewer	Uses of Sewer
1.	Circular shaped sewer.		Used for all types of sewers.
2.	Standard egg-shaped sewer.		Preferred for combined sewers.
3.	New egg-shaped sewer.		Preferred for combined sewers.
4.	Parabolic shaped sewer.		Used for carrying smaller quantities of sewage.

Contd...

5.	Horse shoe shaped sewer.		Used for large sewers with heavy discharges like trunk and outfall sewers.
6.	Rectangular shaped sewer.		Used for covered storm water drains.
7.	Semi-elliptical shaped sewer.		Used for carrying large amounts of sewage.
8.	U-shaped sewer.		Used for larger sewers and especially in open cuts.

3.11 SEWER MATERIALS

The following are the most common materials used for constructing sewer pipes :

- Vitrified clay/stoneware/salt-glazed sewers.
- Cast iron sewers.
- Plain cement concrete and Reinforced cement concrete sewers.
- Asbestos cement sewers.
- Brick sewers.
- Lead sewers.
- Plastic sewers.

At the time of selecting a particular material for constructing sewer pipes, the following factors should be considered which are tabulated in Table 3.18.

Table 3.18

Sr. No.	Factors	Necessity of Consideration of Factors While Selecting
1.	Resistance to abrasion	The sewer material should be strong enough to withstand possible abrasions which may be due to presence of grit and sand particles.
2.	Resistance to corrosion	The sewers are likely to be corroded, due to the presence of gases, acids and other impurities in sewage. So the sewer material should be such as to be resistant to corrosion.
3.	Strength and durability	The sewer pipes should be strong enough to withstand all the forces that are likely to come on them.
4.	Imperviousness	To avoid seepage of sewage from sewer, the sewer material should be impervious.
5.	Light weight	To be handled and transported easily, the sewer material used for sewers should be light.

1. **Vitrified Clay / Stoneware / Salt-Glazed Sewers :**

Uses :

For carrying sewage and drainage, as house connections as well as lateral sewers.

Size :

- 50 mm increments from 100 to 300 mm.
- 75 mm increments from 300 mm to 900 mm.

Advantages :

- They are highly impervious.
- They are hydraulically very efficient because their interiors are very smooth.
- They are preferred for carrying polluted sewage and industrial wastes because they are highly resistant to sulphide corrosion.
- These pipes are quite cheap, easily available, durable and they can be easily laid and jointed.
- They are quite strong in compression and hence they are quite suitable for withstanding compressive stresses which are caused by traffic and back-fills.

2. **Cast Iron Sewers :**

Cast iron sewers are costlier compared to cement concrete or stone ware pipes.

They are structurally stronger and can bear greater tensile, compressive, as well as bending stresses.

Uses :

•   These sewers can be laid below heavy traffic loads.

•   For outfall sewers, inverted siphons, rising mains of pumping stations, all running under pressure.

•   For sewers which are to be 100% leak proof.

3. **Plain Cement Concrete and Reinforced Cement Concrete Sewers :**

Size : Plain cement concrete pipes

→   upto 450 mm diameter

→   R.C.C. pipes

→   upto 1800 mm diameter.

→   may be got manufactured upto 450 mm diameter on special orders.

Properties of Concrete : (a) Mix $: 1 : 1\frac{1}{2} : 3$ (b) W/C ratio : 0.5 to 0.7.

Fig. 3.10 shows reinforced pipes.

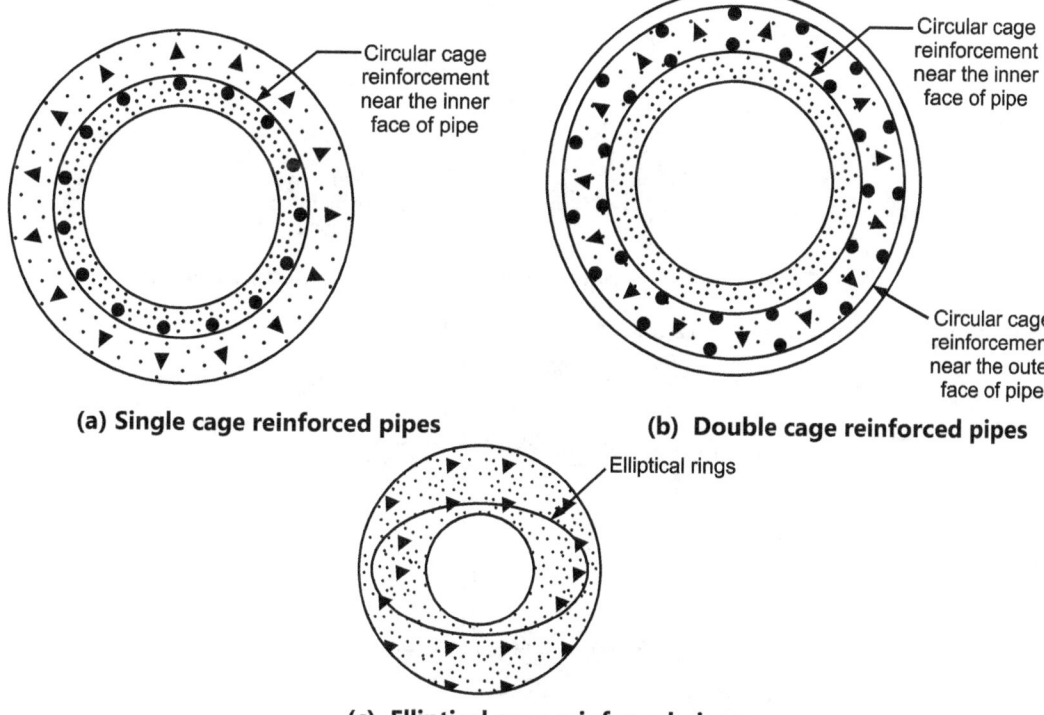

(a) **Single cage reinforced pipes**   (b) **Double cage reinforced pipes**

(c) **Elliptical cage reinforced pipes**

Fig. 3.10

Advantages :

- They are economical for medium and large size, therefore mostly used for main and branch sewers.

- These can be easily manufactured.

- These can be made of required strength by proper design of mix, thickness and reinforcement.

Disadvantages :

- They get easily corroded due to the corrosive action of the contents of the sewage.

- They are susceptible to erosion by sewage containing too much silt and grit.

The concrete sewers can be protected from above actions by lining vitrified clay linings inside the sewers as shown in Fig. 3.11.

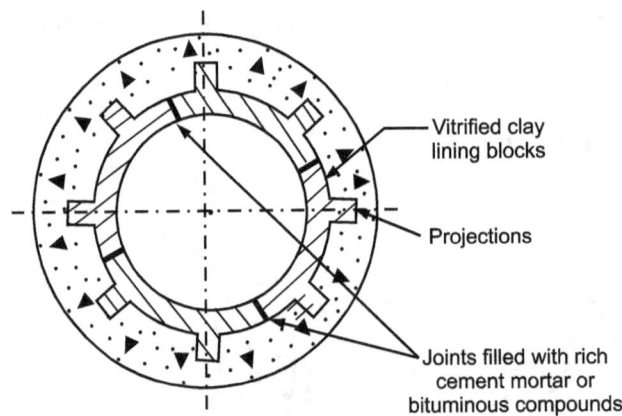

Fig. 3.11 : Cement concrete pipe, lined inside with vitrified clay lining

Jointing : Following Fig. 3.12 shows bell and spigot joint.

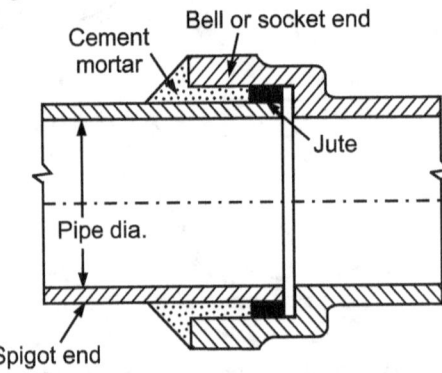

Fig. 3.12 : Bell and spigot joint

4.   **Asbestos Cement Sewers :**

Size : Diameter → 100 mm to 900 mm.

Length → 4 m.

Advantages :

- Their interiors are very smooth and they are hydraulically very efficient.
- They are easy to transport because they are light in weight.
- They can be easily cut and no need of skilled labour to assemble the same.

Disadvantage : They are not strong enough to bear compressive stresses.

Jointing : Fig. 3.13 shows simplex joint for A.C. pipes.

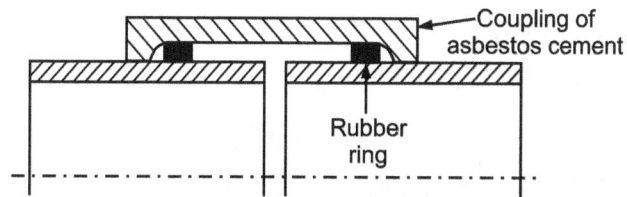

Fig. 3.13 : Simplex joint for A.C. pipes

5.   **Brick Sewers :**

Bricks had been used since olden days. Now-a-days they are almost replaced by cement concrete sewers. They are still be used for constructing large sized combined sewers. They are generally plastered on their outer surfaces.

6.   **Lead Sewers :**

Size : Smaller sizes : 300 to 400 mm.

Uses :

- In smaller length in the toilets.
- As a down take pipe of flushing cisterns.
- As a waste pipe from stall urinals and wash basins.

Advantages :

- They are smooth, soft and can be easily bent in odd shapes.
- They can resist sulphide corrosion and are also not affected by acid or alkaline sewage discharge.

Disadvantage : They are very costly.

7.   **Plastic Sewers :**

The use of plastic sewer pipes is recent in origin and is still in experimental stage. Their use has recently started in the form of domestic sewers.

Advantages :

- High hydraulic efficiency.
- They are corrosion resistant.
- They are easily jointed.
- Available in longer lengths.

MAINTENANCE, VENTILATION AND CLEANING OF SEWERS

3.12 MAINTENANCE OF SEWERS

The maintenance of sewers includes :

- Cleaning and flushing.
- Repairing the leaking joints / any other damaged portion, if any.
- Supervision. (d) Measuring the rate of flow. (e) Preventing explosions etc.

3.13 VENTILATION OF SEWERS

Ventilation of sewers is must due to the following reasons :

- Due to the decomposition and putrefaction of sewage inside the sewers, gases may be present, such as carbon dioxide, carbon monoxide, methane, hydrogen sulphide, ammonia, nitrogen etc. By suitable methods of ventilation, these gases are disposed off into the atmosphere.

- Another use of ventilation is to keep a continuous flow of sewage inside the sewer. Due to ventilation, surface of sewage can be kept in contact with free air and thus preventing the formation of air-locks in the sewage.

3.13.1 Methods of Ventilation

The following are the methods of ventilation :

- **Proper Design of Sewers :** The velocity in the sewer should be self-cleansing, so that sewage does not stay at one point for longer periods. Designing the sewers as running half or two third full, thus reserving the space above level of sewage for the sewer gases. Such proper design of sewers ensures enough ventilation.

- **Use of Ventilating Manhole Covers :** Due to perforated manhole covers, sewage gets exposed to the atmosphere. This will help in achieving some ventilation, but it will cause more nuisance, as the bad smells continue to erupt from them. Moreover, the perforated cover will permit admitting large quantities of storm water and other road dust etc. Thus, this method may be adopted in very isolated places.

- **Use of Ventilating Columns :** A typical vertical ventilating column is shown in Fig. 3.14. These columns or shafts are generally placed at intervals of 150 to 300 m along sewer lines for ventilation purpose. They are also provided at the upper end of every branch sewer.

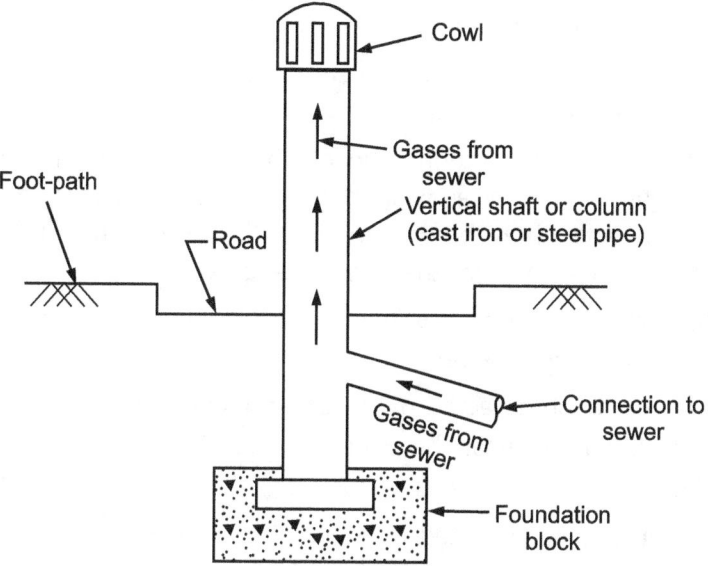

Fig. 3.14 : Ventilating column

The diameter of ventilating column is preferably kept equal to one third of the diameter of the sewer served by it. The height of ventilating column should be higher than the height of the nearby structures.

- **House Vent and Soil Pipes :** These pipes may directly help in ventilating house drains and public sewers.

- **Use of Mechanical Devices :** Forced draught is sometimes provided by exhaust fans to expel out the foul gases from the sewers.

3.14 CLEANING OF SEWERS

To avoid the clogging of sewers, they should be periodically cleaned.

Small Sewers : Flushing operations are essential as manual labour cannot enter in small sewer. A flexible fire hose with about 25 mm less sized nozzle can be inserted down and the water discharged under pressure. Flushing can also be carried by "flushing tanks".

Medium Size Sewers : They are generally cleaned by scraping instruments. A commonly used device consists of a steel cylinder of 200 to 250 mm diameter and 600 to 750 mm long and provided with sharp cutting teeth on the open forward end.

Large Size Sewers : These are generally cleaned by manual labour.

Precautions to be taken While Entering Sewers : When the sewage gets stale and septic, various poisonous and explosive gases are produced in sewers, they are hydrogen sulphide (H_2S), carbon dioxide (CO_2) and methane (CH_4) along with petrol vapours.

Ventilation of sewers is generally adopted to avoid the large scale presence of these poisonous and hazardous gases inside the sewers.

The following precautions should also be taken in addition of ventilation of sewers while allowing the workers to enter the sewers :

- First precaution before entering the manhole is to open the cover of manhole which is required to work as well as one on the upstream and the other on the downstream; half an hour before working. Due to this obtaining some ventilation and exposure of the sewer to the atmospheric oxygen.

- Now, the following tests may be carried out to detect the presence of any hazardous gases inside the sewer.

(a) **H_2S Gas :** It may be detected by exposing a sheet of paper moistened with lead acetate for 5 minutes near the sewer entry. H_2S gas is present in sewer, if paper turns black.

(b) **CH_4 Gas :** It may be detected by lowering the minor's safety lamp in the upper layers of the sewer (methane being lighter than air, is generally present in the upper layers of sewer). When the gas is present, it forms an explosive mixture with air and the gauge cylinder of the safety lamp gets filled with the flame.

(c) **CO_2 Gas :** It may be detected by lowering a minor's safety lamp near the level of sewage in the manhole. The CO_2 gas is present, if the flame extinguishes within 5 minutes.

Special breathing apparatus fitted with hose masks should be used by the workers entering the sewers, if any of these gases are found to be present.

(iii) A responsible officer should preferably be present to direct the operations. The workers going down for inspection must be tied with ropes to their waist.

(iv) Smoking inside the sewers should be strictly prohibited.

SOLVED EXAMPLES ON CIRCULAR SEWERS

Example 3.1 : A sewer of 0.4 m diameter having a gradient of 1 in 600 runs full. Calculate the velocity and the discharge. Use Crimp and Brug's formula.

Solution :

By using equation (3.5),

$$V = 83.47 \ R^{2/3} \ S^{1/2}$$

Now, for circular sewer running full,

$$R = \frac{D}{4} = \frac{0.4}{4} = 0.1 \text{ m}$$

(i) Velocity :

$\therefore$
$$V = 83.47 \times (0.1)^{2/3} \left(\frac{1}{600}\right)^{1/2}$$

$$= \mathbf{0.728 \text{ m/sec}} \qquad \qquad \text{... Ans.}$$

(ii) Discharge :
$$Q = \frac{\pi}{4} \times D^2 \times V$$

$$= \frac{\pi}{4} \times (0.4)^2 \times 0.728$$

$$= \mathbf{0.091 \text{ m}^3\text{/sec}} \qquad \qquad \text{... Ans.}$$

Example 3.2 : A sewer of 0.3 m diameter is to flow at 0.6 depth on a grade ensuring a degree of self-cleansing equivalent to that obtained at full depth at a velocity of 0.8 m/sec.

Determine :

(a) the required grade

(b) velocity

(c) the rate of discharge at this depth.

Given : $n = 0.013$, $a/A = 0.626$, $r/R = 1.110$, $p/P = 0.564$.

Solution :

(a) At full depth, $V = 0.8$ m/sec, $D = 0.3$ m, $N = 0.013$.

$$V = \frac{1}{N} R^{2/3} \cdot S^{1/2}$$

$$0.8 = \frac{1}{0.013} \times \left(\frac{0.3}{4}\right)^{2/3} \times S^{1/2}$$

$$S^{1/2} = 0.059$$

$\therefore$
$$S = 3.481 \times 10^{-3} = \frac{1}{287}$$

Also,
$$Q = \frac{\pi}{4} \times (0.3)^2 \times 0.8 = 0.0565 \text{ cumecs}$$

(b) For partial depth self cleansing flow,

At $\dfrac{d}{D} = 0.6$, $\dfrac{a}{A} = 0.626$, $\dfrac{r}{R} = 1.110$, $\dfrac{p}{P} = 0.564$.

Now,
$$s_S = \left(\frac{R}{r}\right) S = \frac{1}{1.110} \times \frac{1}{287}$$

$$= 3.14 \times 10^{-3}$$

$$= \frac{1}{319} \qquad \text{... Ans.}$$

Also,
$$\boxed{v_S = \frac{N}{n} \left(\frac{r}{R}\right)^{1/6} \cdot V}$$

$$= 1 \times (1.110)^{1/6} \times 0.8$$

$$v_S = \textbf{0.81 m/sec} \qquad \text{... Ans.}$$

and
$$\boxed{\frac{q_S}{Q} = \left(\frac{N}{n}\right) \cdot \left(\frac{a}{A}\right) \cdot \left(\frac{r}{R}\right)^{1/6}}$$

$$= (1) \times (0.626) \times (1.110)^{1/6}$$

$$\frac{q_S}{Q} = 0.637$$

$\therefore$
$$q_S = 0.637 \times 0.0565$$

$$= \textbf{0.036 cumecs} \qquad \text{... Ans.}$$

Example 3.3 : Design a sanitary sewer for the following data :

Population 100000 persons.

Rate of water supply = 200 litres/head/day.

Value of N = 0.013, Peak factor = 3, Slope = 1 in 700.

(6 Marks) [Pune University, Dec. 2000]

Solution :

Average rate of water supply

$$= 100000 \times 200$$

$$= 20 \times 10^6 \text{ litres/day}$$

$$= \frac{20 \times 10^6}{10^3 \times 24 \times 60 \times 60} = 0.23 \text{ cumecs}$$

$\therefore$ D.W.F. = 0.23 cumecs

Max. Q = $3 \times 0.23 = 0.69$ cumecs

Now,
$$Q = \frac{1}{N} A \cdot R^{2/3} \cdot S^{1/2}$$

$$0.69 = \frac{1}{0.013} \times \left(\frac{\pi}{4} \times D^2\right) \times \left(\frac{D}{4}\right)^{2/3} \times \left(\frac{1}{700}\right)^{1/2}$$

or $\quad D^{8/3} = 0.77$

∴ $\quad\quad\quad D = 0.90$ m

$$A = \frac{\pi}{4} D^2 = \frac{\pi}{4} \times (0.90)^2$$

$$= 0.64 \text{ m}^2$$

$$V = \frac{Q}{A} = \frac{0.69}{0.64} = \textbf{1.078 m/sec} \quad\quad \textbf{... Ans.}$$

Example 3.4 : Calculate the velocity and discharge through a sewer of 30 cm ϕ with invert bed slope of 1 in 100 with sewer flowing 0.3 and 0.6 of full depth. Assume n = 0.013 in Manning's formula. The hydraulic elements of circular sewer are as below.

Proportionate Depth d/D	Proportionate Velocity v/V	Proportionate Discharge q/Q
0.3	0.776	0.1956
0.6	1.072	0.6711

Is the velocity through the sewer within maximum and minimum velocity limits ?

(8 Marks) [Pune University]

Solution :

Maximum discharge, $\quad Q = \frac{1}{N} A \cdot R^{2/3} \cdot S^{1/2}$

$$= \frac{1}{N} \left(\frac{\pi}{4} D^2\right) \times \left(\frac{D}{4}\right)^{2/3} \times S^{1/2}$$

$$= \frac{1}{0.013} \times \frac{\pi}{4} \times (0.3)^2 \times \left(\frac{0.3}{4}\right)^{2/3} \times \left(\frac{1}{100}\right)^{1/2}$$

$$= 76.92 \times 0.071 \times 0.176 \times 0.1$$

$$= 0.096 \text{ cumecs}$$

Maximum velocity, $\quad V = \frac{Q}{A}$

$$= \frac{0.096}{\frac{\pi}{4} \times (0.3)^2} = 1.36 \text{ m/sec}$$

(i) Velocity and discharge for sewer flowing 0.3 of full depth.

From given table, for $\dfrac{d}{D}$ = 0.3

$$\frac{v}{V} = 0.776$$

$\therefore$ $v = 0.776 \times 1.36$

$= \mathbf{1.05\ m/sec}$ ... **Ans.**

Similarly, for d/D = 0.3

$$\frac{q}{Q} = 0.1956$$

$\therefore$ $q = 0.1956 \times 0.096$

$= \mathbf{0.019\ cumecs}$ ... **Ans.**

(ii)   Velocity and discharge for sewer flowing 0.6 of full depth.
From given table for d/D = 0.6

$$\frac{v}{V} = 1.072$$

$\therefore$ $v = 1.072 \times 1.36$

$= \mathbf{1.46\ m/sec}$ ... **Ans.**

Similarly, for d/D = 0.6

$$\frac{q}{Q} = 0.6711$$

$\therefore$ $q = 0.6711 \times 0.096$

$= \mathbf{0.064\ cumecs}$ ... **Ans.**

The velocity for 0.3 and 0.6 full depth are greater than self cleansing velocity.

Example 3.5 : Design a sanitary sewer main, to discharge a peak flow of 100 litres/sec, with a minimum velocity of 0.6 m/sec and a maximum velocity of 2 m/sec.

Sewer length between manholes = 100 m.

G.L. at upstream end of sewer = 50.500.

G.L. at downstream end of sewer = 50.200.

Depth of soil cover above sewer at upstream end = 1.5 m.

q/Q	U/V	Manning's n
0.838	1.120	0.013
0.671	1.070	0.013

Work out the invert level at the downstream end of the sewer.

(8 Marks) [Pune University]

Solution :

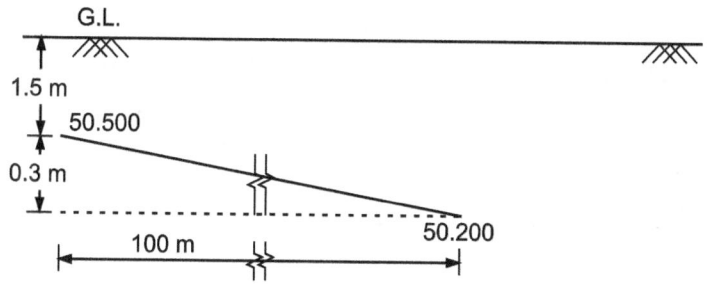

Fig. 3.15

$$\text{Slope} = \frac{0.3}{100} = \frac{1}{333.33}$$

(i) Determine size of sewer.

$$\text{Maximum Q} = 100 \; l/s$$

$$= \frac{100}{10^3}$$

$$= 0.1 \; \text{cumecs}$$

Now,

$$Q = \frac{1}{N} \cdot A \cdot R^{2/3} \cdot S^{1/2}$$

$$0.1 = \frac{1}{0.013} \times \left(\frac{\pi}{4} D^2\right) \times \left(\frac{D}{4}\right)^{2/3} \times \left(\frac{1}{333.33}\right)^{1/2}$$

$$D^{8/3} = 0.077$$

∴

$$D = 0.38 \; \text{m}$$

$$A = \frac{\pi}{4} D^2 = \frac{\pi}{4} \times (0.38)^2$$

$$= 0.11 \; \text{m}^2$$

and

$$V = \frac{Q}{A} = \frac{0.1}{0.11} = 0.9 \; \text{m/sec.}$$

This is within maximum velocity of 2 m/sec.

Assume

$$\frac{q}{Q} = 0.7$$

∴   From given table, $U/V = 1.08$

∴ $U = 1.08 \times V$

$$= 1.08 \times 0.9$$

$$= 0.972 \; \text{m/sec}$$

This is greater than the self cleansing velocity of 0.6 m/s.

As U is more than self cleansing velocity and V within maximum velocity of 2 m/sec, provide a sewer of 0.38 m.

(ii) Determine the invert level at the downstream end of the sewer.

Assume thickness of sewer is 10 mm.

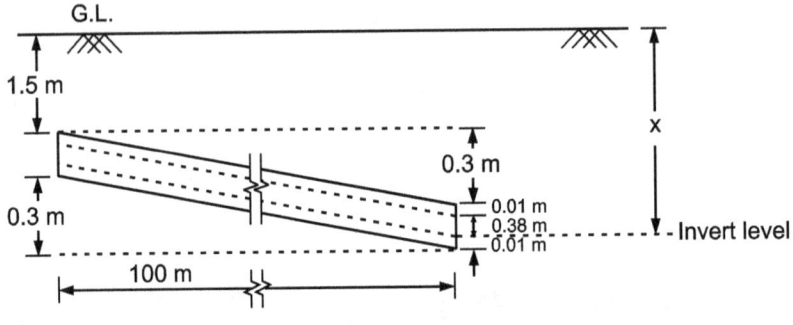

Fig. 3.16

The invert level at the downstream end of the sewer

$$= x = 1.5 + 0.3 + 0.01 + 0.38 \qquad = 2.19 \text{ m.} \qquad \text{... Ans.}$$

Example 3.6 : A 30 cm diameter sewer having an invert slope of 1 : 200 was flowing full. What would be velocity of flow and discharge ? (n = 0.013).

Is the velocity self-cleansing ? What would be velocity and discharge, when the same is flowing 0.2 and 0.8 of its full depth ?

Given :

Prop. Depth (d/D)	Prop. Velocity (v/V)	Prop. Discharge (q/Q)
0.2	0.615	0.088
0.4	0.902	0.3364
0.6	1.072	0.6711
0.8	1.140	0.9781

(8 Marks) [Pune University]

Solution :

$$Q = \frac{1}{N} A \cdot R^{2/3} \cdot S^{1/2}$$

$$= \frac{1}{0.013} \times \left(\frac{\pi}{4} \times (0.3)^2 \right) \times \left(\frac{0.3}{4} \right)^{2/3} \times \left(\frac{1}{200} \right)^{1/2}$$

$$= 76.92 \times (0.071) \times (0.176) \times (0.071)$$

$$= 0.067 \text{ cumecs}$$

Velocity, $V = \dfrac{Q}{A}$

$$= \dfrac{0.067}{\dfrac{\pi}{4} \times (0.3)^2}$$

$$= \dfrac{0.067}{0.071}$$

$$= 0.94 \text{ m/sec}$$

Assume $\dfrac{q}{Q} = 0.333$;   From given table $\dfrac{v}{V} = 0.898$

$\therefore$ $v = 0.898 \times V$

$$= 0.898 \times 0.94$$

$$= \mathbf{0.844 \text{ m/sec}} \qquad \text{... Ans.}$$

This is greater than self-cleansing velocity.

(i)   Velocity and Discharge for Sewer Flowing 0.2 of Full Depth.

For, $\dfrac{d}{D} = 0.2$

$$\dfrac{v}{V} = 0.615$$

$\therefore$ $v = 0.615 \times 0.94 = \mathbf{0.5781 \text{ m/sec}} \qquad \text{... Ans.}$

Similarly, for $\dfrac{d}{D} = 0.2$

$$\dfrac{q}{Q} = 0.088$$

$\therefore$ $q = 0.088 \times 0.067$

$$= \mathbf{0.0059 \text{ cumecs}} \qquad \text{... Ans.}$$

(ii) Velocity and Discharge for Sewer Flowing 0.8 of Full Depth.

For $\dfrac{d}{D} = 0.8$

$$\dfrac{v}{V} = 1.140$$

$\therefore$ $v = 1.140 \times 0.94$

$$= \mathbf{1.0716 \text{ m/sec}} \qquad \text{... Ans.}$$

Similarly, for $\dfrac{d}{D}$ = 0.8

$$\dfrac{q}{Q} = 0.9781$$

$\therefore$ q = 0.9781 × 0.067

= **0.066 cumecs**   ... **Ans.**

Example 3.7 : Determine the size of a circular sewer for a discharge of 650 lps running half-full. Assume S = 0.0001 and n = 0.015.

Solution :

$$d = 0.5\ D$$

$$\dfrac{d}{D} = 0.5$$

$$q = 650 \text{ litres/sec.}$$

$$= 0.65 \text{ cumecs}$$

$$S = 0.0001$$

$$n = 0.015$$

From Table 3.12,   at $\dfrac{d}{D}$ = 0.5.

We have $\dfrac{q}{Q}$ = 0.5

$$Q = \dfrac{q}{0.5}$$

$$= \dfrac{0.650}{0.5}$$

$$= 1.3 \text{ cumecs}$$

By using Manning's formula,

$$Q = \dfrac{1}{N} \cdot AR^{2/3} \cdot \sqrt{S}$$

or $1.3 = \dfrac{1}{0.015} \cdot \left(\dfrac{\pi}{4} \cdot D^2\right) \cdot \left(\dfrac{D}{4}\right)^{2/3} \cdot \sqrt{0.0001}$

or $\dfrac{1.3 \times 0.015 \times 4 \times 2.52}{\pi \times 0.01} = D^{8/3}$

$\therefore$ D = 1.98 m

Hence, the diameter of the sewer required = **1.98 m**   ... **Ans.**

Alternatively,　　　　　　　　$\dfrac{d}{D}$ = 0.5

$$= \dfrac{1}{2}\left(1 - \cos\dfrac{\beta}{2}\right) \qquad \text{... Refer equation (3.8)}$$

or　　　　　　　$\cos\dfrac{\beta}{2}$ = 0

or　　　　　　　$\dfrac{\beta}{2}$ = 90°

or　　　　　　　β = 180°

Now, using equation (3.9), we have

$$a = \dfrac{D^2}{4}\left[\dfrac{\pi\beta}{360°} - \dfrac{\sin\beta}{2}\right]$$

$$= \dfrac{D^2}{4}\left[\dfrac{\pi \cdot 180°}{360°} - \dfrac{\sin 180°}{2}\right]$$

$$= \dfrac{D^2}{4}\left[\dfrac{\pi}{2} - 0\right]$$

$$= \dfrac{\pi D^2}{8}$$

Now, using equation (3.11), we have

$$p = \pi D\,\dfrac{\beta}{360°}$$

$$= \pi D\,\dfrac{180°}{360°}$$

$$= \dfrac{\pi D}{2}$$

$\therefore$　　　　　$r = \dfrac{a}{p} = \dfrac{\pi D^2}{8} \cdot \left(\dfrac{1}{\dfrac{\pi D}{2}}\right) = \dfrac{D}{4}$

Using Manning's formula, we have

$$q = \dfrac{1}{n} \cdot a \cdot r^{2/3}\sqrt{S}$$

$\therefore$　　　　$0.65 = \dfrac{1}{0.015} \cdot \dfrac{\pi D^2}{8} \cdot \left(\dfrac{D}{4}\right)^{2/3} \cdot \sqrt{0.0001}$

or　　　　　$D^{8/3} = \dfrac{0.65 \times 0.015 \times 8 \times 2.52}{\pi \times 0.01}$

or　　　　　D = **1.98 m**　　　　　　　　　**... Ans.**

Example 3.8 : Calculate the velocity and discharge through a rectangular concrete lined smooth channel 2.4 m wide and 1.2 m deep built to a slope of 1 in 200, when running completely full. Use Bazin's coefficient in Chezy's formula as :

$$C = \frac{157.6}{1.81 + \dfrac{K}{\sqrt{r}}}$$

where, K = 0.3 for smooth concrete lined surface.   **(Engg. Services)**

Solution :

$$\text{Area of channel} = A = 2.4 \text{ m} \times 1.2 \text{ m}$$

$$= 2.88 \text{ m}^2$$

$$\text{Wetted perimeter} = P$$

$$= 2.4 + 1.2 + 1.2$$

(considering the sewer to be running completely full)

$$= 4.8 \text{ m}$$

$$R = \frac{A}{P}$$

$$= \frac{2.88}{4.8}$$

$$= 0.60 \text{ m}$$

Now,

$$C = \frac{157.6}{1.81 + \dfrac{0.3}{\sqrt{0.60}}}$$

$$= \frac{157.6}{1.81 + 0.387}$$

$$= \frac{157.6}{2.197}$$

$$= 71.72$$

Using, Chezy's formula, we have

$$V = C \cdot \sqrt{RS}$$

$$= 71.72 \sqrt{0.60 \times \frac{1}{200}}$$

$$= \textbf{3.93 m/sec} \qquad\qquad \textbf{... Ans.}$$

Discharge, $Q = A \cdot V$

$\qquad = 2.88 \times 3.93$

$\qquad = \mathbf{11.32\ cumecs}$ ... **Ans.**

Example 3.9 : Design an outfall circular sewer of the separate system for a town with a population of 1,00,000 persons with a water supply at 180 litres per head per day. The sewer can be laid at a slope of 10 in 10,000 with n = 0.012. A self-cleansing velocity of 0.75 m/sec is to be developed. The dry weather flow may be taken as 1/3 of the maximum discharge.

Given the following table :

Proportionate Depth	Proportionate Velocity	Proportionate Discharge
0.31	0.7901	0.2086
0.35	0.8430	0.2629
0.37	0.8675	0.2981
0.39	0.8909	0.3217
0.40	0.9022	0.3370
0.42	0.9299	0.3662

(Engg. Services)

Solution :

$\qquad$ Population $= 100000$

$\qquad$ Average rate of water supply $= 180$ litres/person/day

∴ $\quad$ Average rate of water supplied per day

$\qquad = 100000 \times 180$ litres

∴ $\quad$ Average rate of water supplied in cumecs

$$= \frac{100000 \times 180}{1000 \times 24 \times 60 \times 60}\ \text{cumecs}$$

$\qquad = 0.208$ cumecs

∴ $\qquad\qquad$ D.W.F. $= 0.208$ cumecs

∴ $\qquad$ Maximum discharge

$\qquad\qquad Q = 3 \times 0.208$ cumecs

$\qquad\qquad Q = 0.624$ cumecs

Let us design the sewer as running full at maximum discharge.

Using Manning's formula, we have

$$Q = \frac{1}{N} \cdot A \cdot R^{2/3} \cdot \sqrt{S}$$

Assuming that the sewer is laid at the available slope of 10 in 10000 i.e. 1 in 1000, we have

$$S = \frac{1}{1000}$$

∴

$$0.624 = \frac{1}{0.012} \times \left(\frac{\pi}{4} D^2\right) \times \left(\frac{D}{4}\right)^{2/3} \times \frac{1}{\sqrt{1000}}$$

or

$$D^{8/3} = \frac{0.624 \times 0.012 \times 4 \times 2.52 \times 31.6}{\pi}$$

or

$$D^{8/3} = 0.758$$

∴

$$D = 0.915 \text{ m}$$

Now, velocity of flow at full flow,

$$V = \frac{Q}{A} = \frac{0.625}{\frac{\pi}{4}(0.915)^2}$$

$$= 0.95 \text{ m/sec}$$

This is more than 0.75 m/sec, and hence O.K.

Let us check for the velocity at D.W.F.

At D.W.F.,

$$\frac{q}{Q} = \frac{1}{3} = 0.333$$

From the given table,

$$\frac{d}{D} = 0.40$$

$$\text{Velocity ratio} = \frac{v}{V} = 0.9022 \text{ (given)}$$

Hence, the velocity developed at D.W.F.

$$= 0.9022 \times 0.95 \text{ m/sec}$$

$$= 0.855 \text{ m/sec}$$

This is more than 0.75 m/sec and therefore, satisfactory.

Hence, Use 0.915 m Diameter Pipe as Worked Out.   **... Ans.**

Example 3.10 : Calculate the diameter and discharge of a circular sewer laid at a slope of 1 in 500 when it is running half full, and with a velocity of 2.0 m/sec. (n in Manning's formula = 0.012).

Solution :

When pipe is running half full,

The area of section, $\quad a \;=\; \dfrac{\pi D^2}{8}$

The wetted perimeter, $\quad p \;=\; \dfrac{\pi D}{4}$

The H.M.D. $\qquad\qquad r \;=\; \dfrac{D}{2}$

Using Manning's formula, we have

$$v \;=\; \frac{1}{n} \cdot r^{2/3} \cdot \sqrt{s}$$

$\therefore\qquad\qquad 2.0 \;=\; \dfrac{1}{0.012} \cdot \left(\dfrac{D}{4}\right)^{2/3} \cdot \dfrac{1}{\sqrt{500}}$

or $\qquad\qquad D^{2/3} \;=\; 2.0 \times 0.012 \times 2.52 \times 22.36$

$\therefore\qquad\qquad\quad D \;=\; \mathbf{1.57} \qquad\qquad\qquad \textbf{... Ans.}$

$\qquad$ Discharge, $Q \;=\; a.v$

$$=\; \frac{\pi \,(1.57)^2}{8} \times 2.0 \;=\; \mathbf{1.94 \; cumecs} \qquad \textbf{... Ans.}$$

IMPORTANT POINTS

- Different hydraulic formulae.
- Maximum velocity (non-scouring velocity) and minimum velocity (self cleansing velocity).
- Characteristics of circular sewer.
- Different shapes of sewers.
- Different sewer materials and their advantages.
- Ventilation and cleaning of sewers.

EXERCISE

1. Write short notes on :
   (1) Velocity in sewers
   (2) Design of sewers
   (3) Sewer ventilation
   (4) Design of storm water drains
   (5) Maximum and minimum permissible velocities in sewers.
2. State the importance of
   (i) Sewer velocities, (ii) Sewer ventilation.

3. Define self cleansing velocity and explain its importance in sewer design.

4. Compare the different materials of sewer pipes and mention their suitability.

5. Draw a neat sketch of a standard egg-shaped sewer. Under what circumstances it is more advantageous compared to a circular one ?

6. Derive an expression

$$V_s = \sqrt{\frac{8a}{f}\,(S_s - 1)\ g \cdot d_g}$$

7. Explain various factors considered while selecting material for sewer. Hence, compare R.C.C. and plastic pipes.

8. Enlist different types of sewers depending upon their shapes. Draw neat sketches for any two.

9. State various formulae used for computing velocity of flow in sewer. Explain any one with meanings of each term used.

UNIVERSITY QUESTIONS

1. Describe the procedure for laying and testing of sewers.   **(6 M) (May 2010)**

2. Differentiate between sanitary sewage and storm water runoff. **(4 M) (May 2011)**

3. Differentiate dry weather flow and wet weather flow.   **(6 M) (May 2010)**

4. Design a sanitary sewer for the following data :   **(6 M) (May 2010, 2011)**
    (i)   Population = 120000 persons.
    (ii)   Rate of water supply = 200 lpcd.
    (iii) Value of N = 0.013.
    (iv)   Peak factor = 3.
    (v)   Slope = 1 in 700.

5. Determine the size of a circular sewer for a discharge of 600 *lps* running half full. Assume s = 0.0001 and n = 0.015.   **(6 M) (Dec. 2010)**

6. Determine the size of a circular sewer for a discharge of 600 *lps* running half full. Assume i = 0.001 and n = 0.015.   **(6 M) (May 2009)**

Proportionate Depth (d/D)	Proportionate Area (a/A)	Proportionate Wetted Perimeter p/P	Proportionate HMD (r/R)	Proportionate Velocity (v/V)	Proportionate Discharge (q/Q)
0.50	0.500	0.500	1.000	1.000	0.500
0.40	0.373	0.444	0.857	0.902	0.337
0.30	0.252	0.369	0.684	0.776	0.196

✠ ✠ ✠

Chapter 4

SEWER APPURTENANCES AND SEWAGE PUMPING

SEWER APPURTENANCES

Sewer appurtenances are those structures which are constructed at suitable intervals along a sewerage system to assist in efficient operation and maintenance of the system. The following are the important sewer appurtenances.

1. Street inlets.
2. Clean-outs.
3. Catch pits (catch basins).
4. Manholes.
5. Drop manholes.
6. Lampholes.
7. Flushing tanks.
8. Grease and oil traps.
9. Inverted siphons.
10. Storm regulators.

4.1 STREET INLETS [MAY 2009]

Street inlets are called gullies or openings. These inlets are on the road surface at the lowest point for draining rain water from roads and allowed it into the underground storm water sewers or combined sewers. The inlets are located at an interval of 30 m to 60 m or so on straight roads. Fig. 4.1 shows the locations of storm sewer inlets at street intersections. The inlets are located in such a way that cross-walk will not be flooded. Inlets are connected to the nearby manholes by pipe lines.

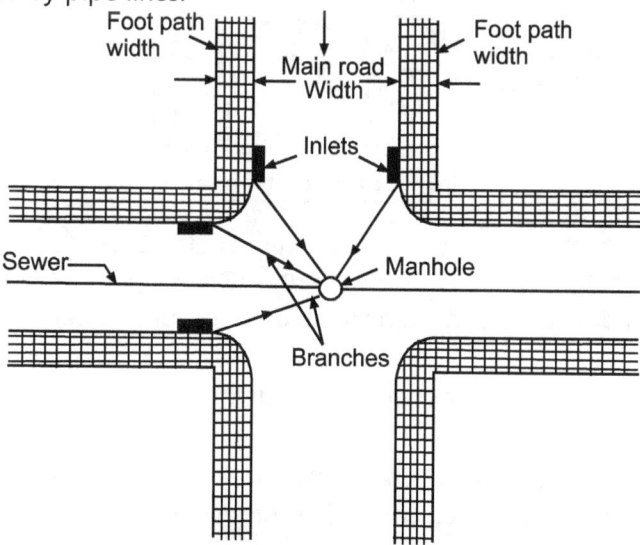

Fig. 4.1 : Showing the locations of storm sewer inlets at street intersections
[Note : The arrows shows the direction of storm runoff in the streets]

Fig. 4.2 and Fig. 4.3 shows vertical inlet or curb inlet and horizontal inlet or gutter inlet respectively. Both these types are of concrete boxes having gratings in vertical or horizontal direction.

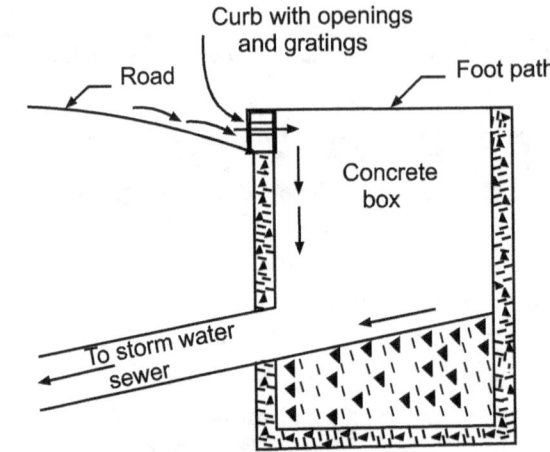

Fig. 4.2 : Vertical inlet or curb inlet

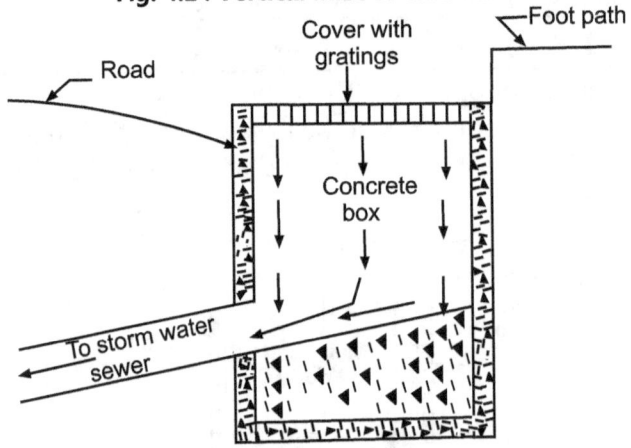

Fig. 4.3 : Horizontal inlet

4.2 CLEAN-OUTS

A clean-out is an inclined pipe. A clean-out is used for cleaning sewer pipes. (See Fig. 4.4) The one end of inclined pipe is connected to the underground sewer and the other end is at ground level.

In place of manholes, a clean-out is generally provided at the upper ends of lateral sewers.

Functioning of Clean-Out :

Firstly, removing the top cover and forcing water through the clean-out pipe to lateral sewers to remove obstacles in the sewer line. For removing larger obstructions, a flexible rod may be inserted through the clean-out pipe and pushed forward and backward to remove such obstacles.

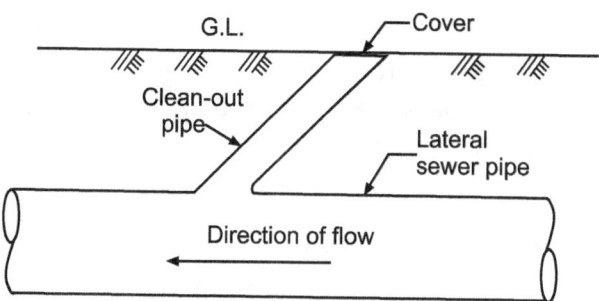

Fig. 4.4 : Clean-out

4.3 CATCH BASINS OR CATCH PITS

Catch basins are actually street inlets with provision of small settling basins to settle out grit, sand, debris etc., which are flowing in with storm water. To prevent the escape of foul gases, hood is also provided in basins. Catch basins need periodical cleaning to avoid decomposition of organic matter. (Fig. 4.5)

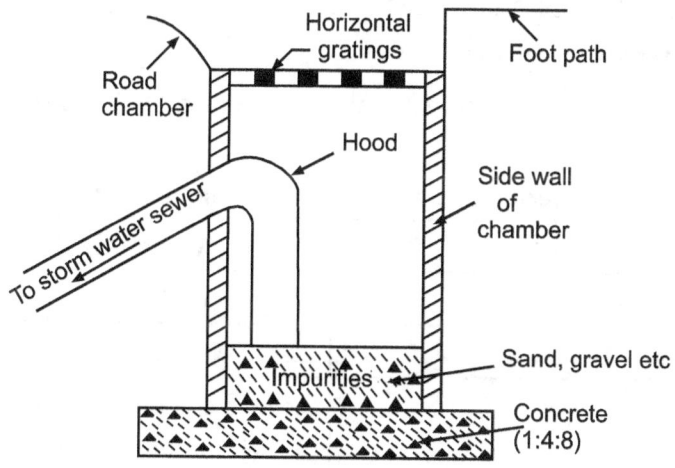

Fig. 4.5 : Catch basins or catch pits

4.4 MANHOLES

Manholes are masonry or R.C.C. chambers, constructed at suitable intervals along the sewer lines.

The purpose of manholes are for providing access into sewer lines thus, helps in joining sewer lines or in changing the direction or alignment. They also help in their inspection, cleaning and maintenance.

4.4.1 Location and Spacing of Manholes

The manholes are generally provided at every bend, junction, change of gradient or change of sewer diameter.

For sewer line running straight, the manholes are provided at regular intervals as per Table 4.1. The spacing of manholes are mainly depended upon the size of the sewer line. The larger is the diameter of the sewer, the greater will be the spacing between the manholes, because they can be entered easily by men for inspection.

Table 4.1 : Spacing of Manholes (IS 1742–1960)

Size of the Sewer	Recommended Spacing of Manholes on Straight Reaches of Sewer Lines
Diameter upto 0.3 m	45 m
Diameter upto 0.6 m	75 m
Diameter upto 0.9 m	90 m
Diameter upto 1.2 m	120 m
Diameter upto 1.5 m	250 m
Diameter greater than 1.5 m	300 m

4.4.2 Dimensions of Manholes

The minimum internal dimensions of manhole chambers, as per IS 1742–1960 are given in Table 4.2.

Table 4.2 : Minimum Internal Dimensions for Manhole Chambers (IS 1742–1960)

Sr. No.	Depth		Minimum Size Specified
1.	0.8 m or less		0.75 m × 0.75 m
2.	0.8 m and 2.1 m		1.2 m × 0.9 m
3.	Greater than 2.1 m		Circular chambers with minimum diameter of 1.4 m; or rectangular chambers with minimum dimensions of 1.2 m × 0.9 m.
	Minimum wall thickness		
	(a)	upto 1.5 m depth	20 cm
	(b)	> 1.5 m depth	30 cm

4.4.3 Classification of Manholes

Related to depth, the manholes may be classified as follows :

    (a)   Shallow manholes.

    (b)   Normal manholes or Medium manholes.

    (c)   Deep manholes.

(a) Shallow Manholes (Inspection Chamber) :

Depth   :   0.75 to 0.9 m

Location   :   Constructed at the start of a branch sewer or at places, which are not subjected to heavy traffic

Cover   :   Light cover at it's top.

(b) Normal or Medium Manholes :

Depth   :   1.5 m

Cross section   :   Square (1 m × 1 m) or

Rectangular (1.2 m × 1 m)

Cover   :   A heavy cover at it's top

Section   :   Not changed with depth.

(c) Deep Manholes :

Depth   :   More than 1.5 m.

Cover   :   A heavy cover at it's top (C.I. frame).

Section   :   Changed with depth. The upper portion is reduced by providing an offset as shown in Fig. 4.6.

Steps   :   Steps are provided in such a manhole to enable the workers to go upto the bottom.

4.4.4 Component Parts of a Manhole

The following are the parts of manhole (See Fig. 4.6):

(a) **Access Shaft :** The upper portion of a deep manhole is known as access shaft. For rectangular manhole, it's minimum size is about 0.75 × 0.6 m and for a circular manhole, the minimum diameter is about 0.6 to 0.75 m. It's depth depends upon the depth of manhole and the height required for the working chamber.

(b) **Working Chamber :** The lower portion of the manhole is called working chamber. This provides a working space for inspection and cleaning operations. The minimum size for a rectangular deep manhole is about 1.2 m × 0.9 m and for a circular manhole, the minimum diameter is about 1.2 m. The height of working chamber should not be less than 1.8 m.

(c) **The Benching** (the bottom or invert portion of manhole) : It is constructed in cement concrete. A semicircular or a U-shaped channel is generally constructed and the sides are made to slope towards it. The benching is facilitated by the entry of sewage into the main sewer. If the branch sewer and main sewer meet at the same level at the bottom of the manhole, channels connected with each other are constructed with easy curve.

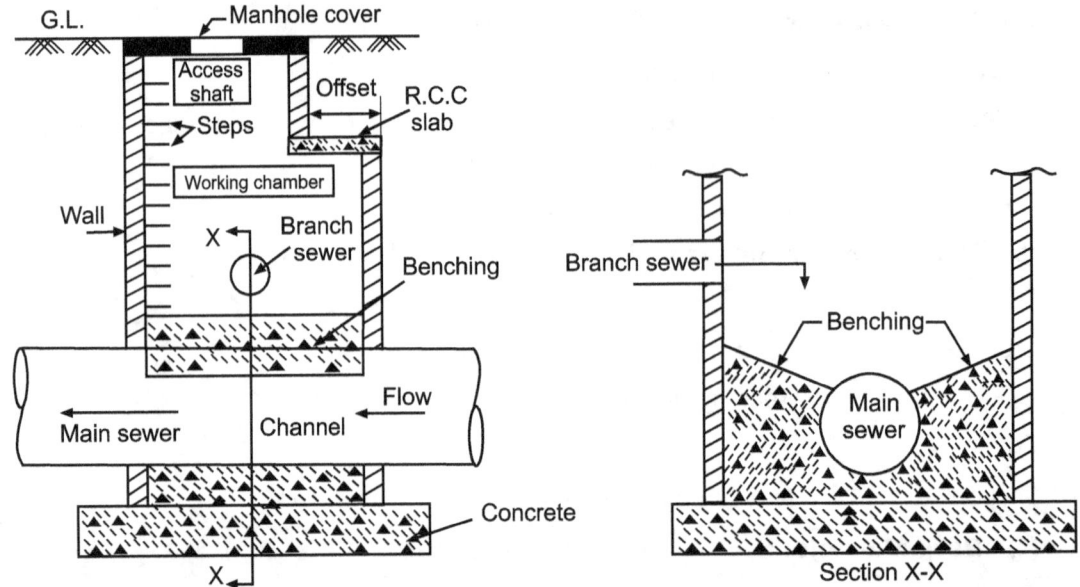

Fig. 4.6 : Deep manhole

(d) **Side Walls :** The side walls of the manhole are made of brick or stone masonry or R.C.C.

The brick masonry is quite common since construction is simple. The minimum thickness of brick wall should be 22.5 cm (9"). The approximate thickness may be computed by using the empirical thumb-rule.

$$t = 10 + 4D \quad \text{(for brick walls)} \qquad \text{... (4.1)}$$

where, t = Thickness of wall in cm

D = Depth of manhole in metres

(e) **Steps or Ladders :** Steps are generally provided for descending into the manhole. These are made of cast iron. These are placed staggered at a horizontal centre to centre distance of 20 cm. If the steps are made of double width, staggering is not required. The vertical distance between the steps may be about 30 cm. To avoid overturn of steps, they should be firmly embedded in wall. In case of deep manhole, the ladders are provided instead of steps. The first step or ladder may start from 40 cm below the ground level and last step or ladder end may be 30 cm above the bottom level of the manhole.

(f) **Top Cover and Frame :** The manhole is provided with a cast iron cover which set in suitable cast iron frame. The thickness of the frame is 20 to 25 cm and its base is about 10 cm wide. The cover rests in the groove which is kept inside the frame.

The size of rectangular cover is about 0.6 m × 0.45 m and that of circular cover diameter is 0.5 to 0.6 m. The cover is marked with an arrow and the cover is placed as to place in the direction of the arrow in the direction of the flow of sewage.

The weight of the cover and frame is between 90 to 270 kg.

4.5 DROP MANHOLES   [MAY 2009, DEC. 2010, MAY 2011]

It is constructed to provide a connection between a high level branch sewer to a low level main sewer. When a branch sewer enters a manhole by more than 0.5 to 0.6 m above the main sewer, the sewage is generally not allowed to fall directly into the manhole, but is brought into it through a vertical pipe (drop pipe) and if the drop is only a few metres, the drop pipe can be kept inclined at 45° to the ground.

When the vertical pipe is used, it is called a drop manhole and when the inclined pipe is used, it is called a ramp.

The following are the advantages of deep manholes over the ordinary manholes, related to high level branch sewer enters low levelled main sewer :

- In case of ordinary manholes, the sewage trickling into the manhole from the directly placed branch sewer is likely to fall on person's working in the manhole, which is avoided in manholes.

- In case of deep manholes, more earth work excavation can be avoided by avoiding steep gradients to the branch sewer.

A plug is provided at the end of branch sewer, (if branch sewer kept straight which intersects at the wall of manhole). The purpose of plug is to inspect and clean the branch sewer.

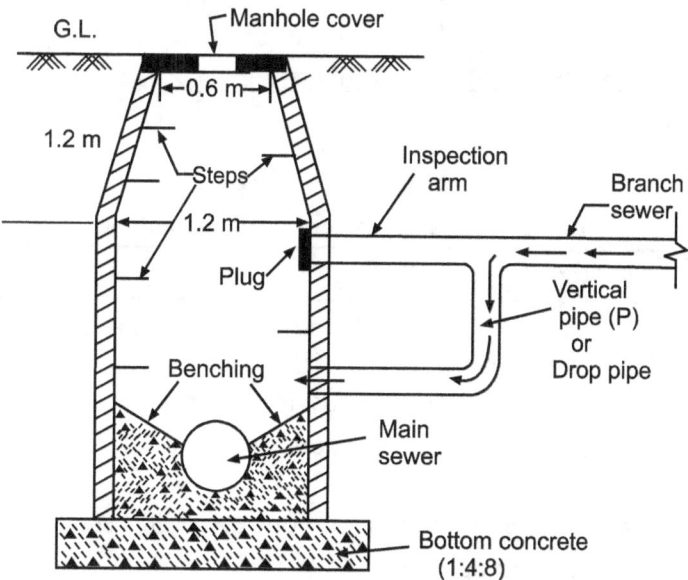

Fig. 4.7 : A typical section of circular drop manhole

4.6 LAMPHOLES

These are openings constructed to join a hole in the sewer and ground to permit the insertion of a lamp into the sewer. The lamp light is checked from upstream or downstream manholes. The obstructed light is the indication of obstruction in sewer.

It consists of a vertical cast iron or stone ware pipe (Fig. 4.8). This pipe is surrounded by concrete so as to make it stable and give it strength.

The lampholes are located when (i) a bend in a sewer is necessary, (ii) construction of manhole is difficult and (iii) the spacing of manholes is more than the usual.

Already we have seen that the lampholes are useful for inspection purpose. Lampholes are also useful for the following purposes :

- **Ventilation :** If its cover is kept perforated, it can be used for ventilation of sewers. In such a case, it is known as a fresh air inlet.
- **Flushing :** In some cases, it can be used as a flushing device.

Now-a-days, the use of lampholes have become obsolete.

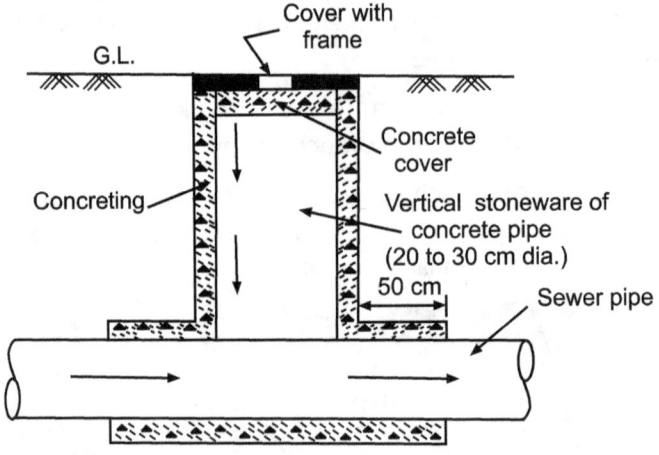

Fig. 4.8 : Typical cross-section of a lamphole

4.7 FLUSHING TANKS

These devices store water and throw it into the sewer for the purpose of flushing and cleaning the sewer. In case of sewers laid on flat gradients not producing self cleansing velocities, possibility of blockage is more. The flushing tanks are useful to clean such sewers.

The capacity of flushing tank is kept equal to about one-tenth of the cubical contents of the sewer line served by it.

The following are the two types of flushing operations generally used :

    (a)   Hand operated flushing operation.

    (b)   Flushing operation by using automatic flushing tank.

(a) **Hand Operated Flushing Operation :** In this method, the flushing action can be achieved by using one of the following methods.

- The inlet and outlet ends of the manhole are closed by sluice valves or gates. The manhole is now filled by water arranged from outside. After achieving sufficient head in the manhole, the sluice valves or gates of inlet and outlet ends are suddenly opened up for the flushing of sewer.

- The outlet end of the manhole is closed by sluice valve or gate and it allow the sewage from inlet end in the manhole to fill upto sufficient head, once the sufficient head of water is achieved, it suddenly opens the outlet sluice valve or gate for the flushing of sewer.

- For the flushing operation, join a hose pipe to nearby fire hydrant and other end of hose pipe is placed in the manhole.

(b) **Automatic Flushing Tanks :** In this flushing operation, flushing action may be achieved by automatic flushing tanks, which are operated automatically at regular intervals. The entry of water is so regulated as to fill the tank upto the discharge point in a period equal to the flushing interval. An overflow pipe is used to drain away water in case the tank overflows before the flushing action starts.

4.7.1 Operation of an Automatic Flushing Tank

- At empty condition of the tank, the water level stands at X –Y in the tube as shown in Fig. 4.9.

- As the water enters in the tank, water level in the tank goes on rising, but the water level in the U-tube remains at X-Y level until the water level in the tank below the level of sniff hole.

- But when the water goes above the sniff holes, the air is caught and compressed in the bell portion.

- Due to compressed air it exerts pressure on the surface X, thus the water level gets depressed in this long arm of U-tube.

- As the tank goes on filling, the water level goes on depressing more and more and when tank gets filled upto the discharge level, the water level of U-tube reaches the bend portion. When this happens, some compressed air gets released through the shorter arm of U-tube and a siphoning action starts releasing the water from the tank into the sewer through the enlarger pipe.

- When water level of the tank reaches below the sniff hole, air then enters the bell portion and it breaks the siphonic action.

- The water level in the two arms of the U-tube again assumes the position X-Y. This cycle goes on repeating and thus releasing water in the sewer through an automatic flushing tank at regular intervals.

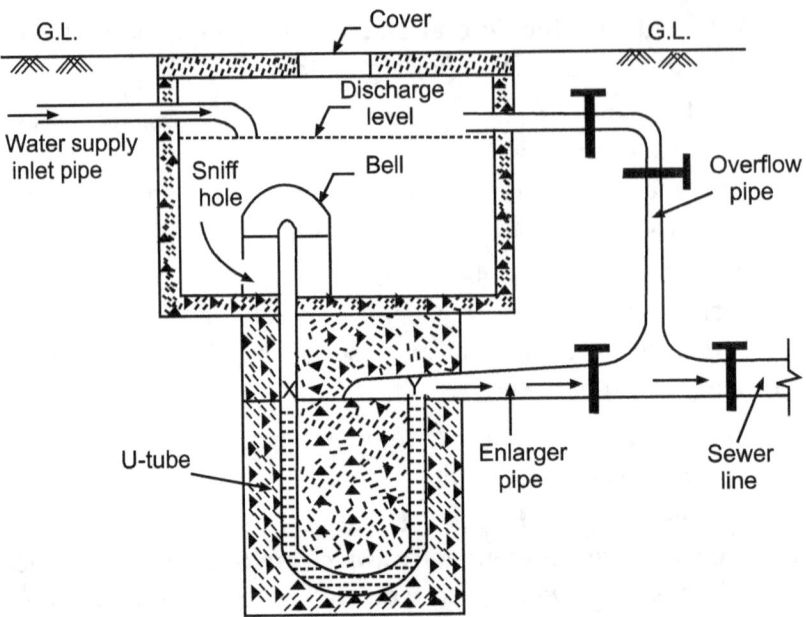

Fig. 4.9 : Automatic flushing tank

4.8 GREASE AND OIL TRAPS

These are constructed in a sewerage system to remove oil and grease from the sewage before they enter into the sewer line. Such traps are located near those sources which contribute grease and oil from their waste water, such as kitchens of hotels, oil and grease industries, automobile repair workshops, garages etc.

The removal of oil and grease is essential from the sewage before it enters into the sewer pipe because of the following reasons :

- Due to presence of oil and grease in the sewage, it increases possibilities of explosions in the sewers.

- Possibility of suspended matter of such sewage sticks to the interior surface of sewer, it leads to reducing sewer capacity.

- Difficulties in the treatment of waste water arises due to presence of oil and grease in the waste water.

- Due to presence of oil and grease on the surface of waste water, it is difficult to penetrate the oxygen, due to which aerobic bacteria will not survive and hence organic matter will not be decomposed. This will lead to bad odours.

As the oil and grease being lighter in weight, they float on the top surface of the sewage. Based on such principle, if outlet is located near the bottom of the chamber, oil and grease will be easily excluded. Fig. 4.10 shows a typical oil and grease trap.

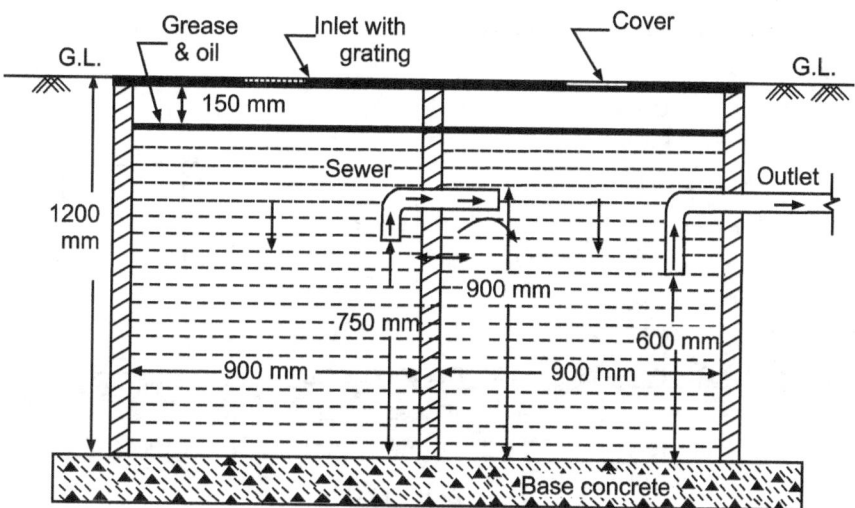

Fig. 4.10 : Grease and oil trap

Fig. 4.11 shows combined sand, grease and oil trap. This type of chamber is useful in case of waste water which is coming from garages, floor drains and wash racks, contains oil, mud and sand.

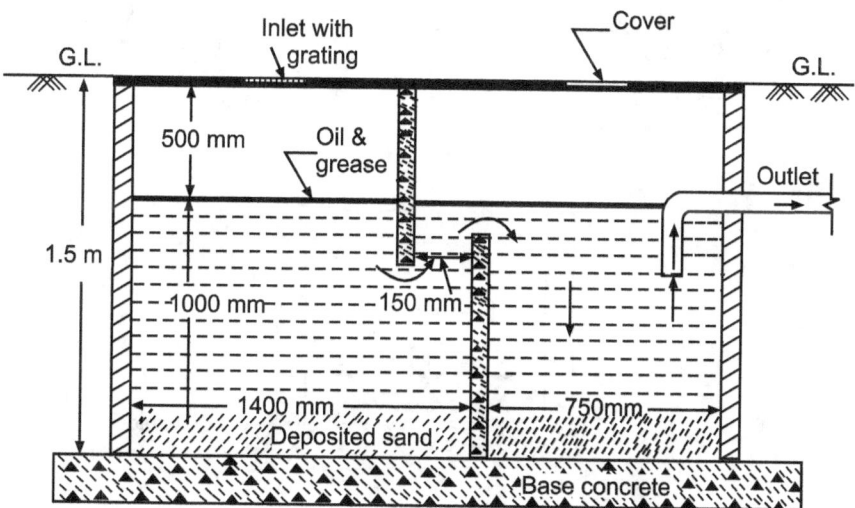

Fig. 4.11 : Combined sand, grease and oil trap

4.9 INVERTED SIPHONS (DEPRESSED SEWER OR SAG PIPE)

When a sewer pipe has to be dropped below the hydraulic gradient line, it is called an inverted siphon. The purpose is to carry the sewer pipe under the obstructions such as, railway, roadway, stream river etc. The sewage through such a pipeline or inverted siphon will be flowing under pressure which is greater than atmospheric.

It consists of siphon tubes or pipes made of cast iron or concrete. Fig. 4.12 shows a typical inverted siphon.

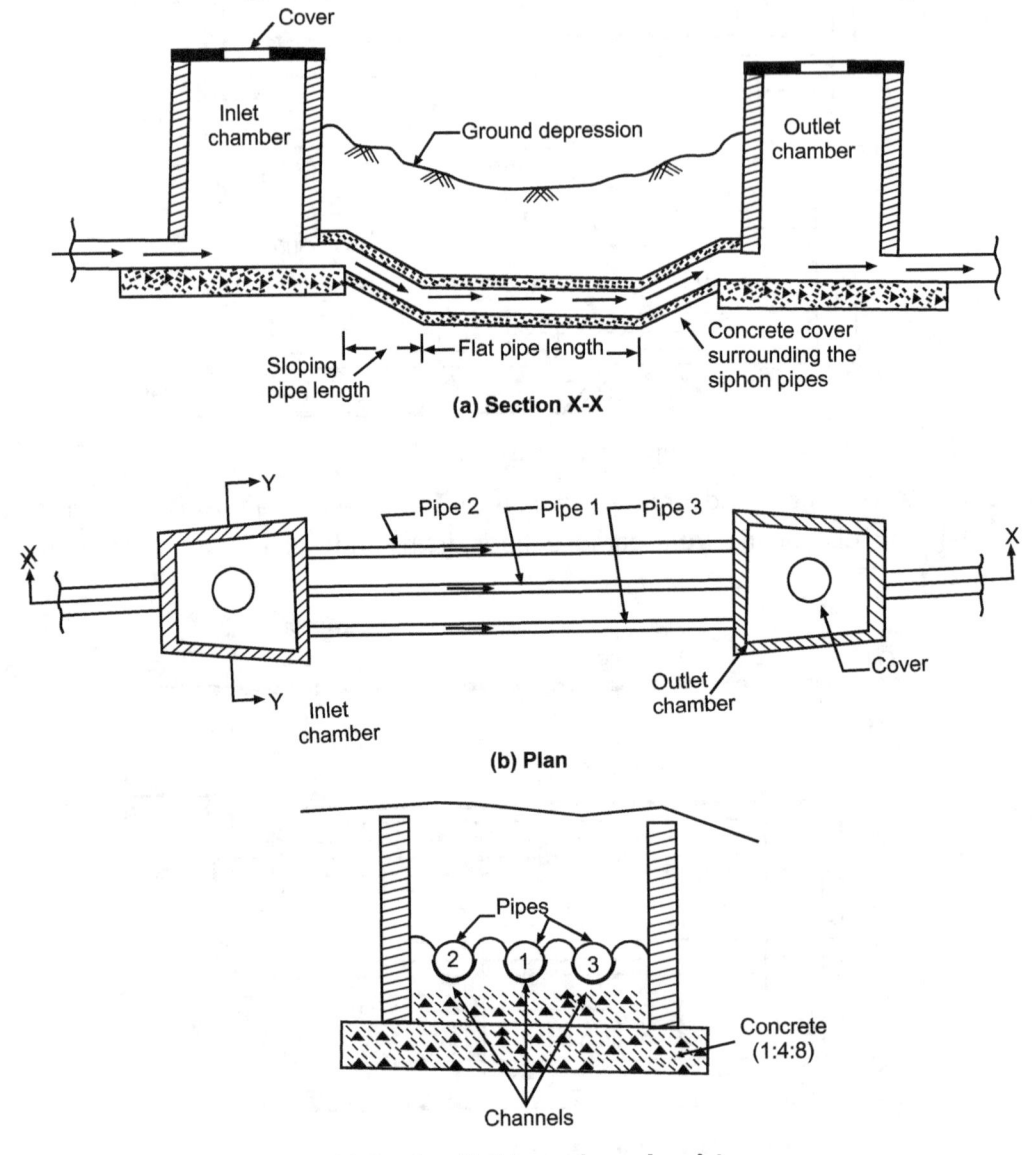

(a) Section X-X

(b) Plan

(c) Section Y-Y (on enlarged scale)

Fig. 4.12 : Inverted siphon

4.9.1 Design of an Inverted Siphon

- **Self Cleansing Velocity :** 0.9 m/sec, even during minimum discharge.
- **Minimum Siphon Pipe Diameter :** 150 to 200 mm.

- **Three Channels :**   1. One is for carrying minimum sanitary sewage.

                                   2. Other one is for carrying maximum sanitary sewage.

                                   3. Third one is for carrying combined flow during monsoons.

Note : Three channels, as given above, are provided for combined sewers. However, for sanitary sewage alone, two channels are sufficient, one is for minimum dry weather flow and the other is for maximum dry weather flow.

In Fig. 4.12 (c) three channels are shown, one for each pipe section. Channel no. 1 comes into operation first. When channel no. 1 overflows, the sewage enters channel no. 2 and pipe no. 2 starts functioning and lastly, when channel no. 2 overflows, the sewage enters channel no. 3 and pipe no. 3 starts functioning.

Besides above points of designing the inverted siphons, the following points should be considered while designing these inverted siphons :

- The changes of direction of inverted siphons should be easy and gradual.
- If the length of the siphon is more, hatch boxes at intervals of about 100 m should be provided for facility of rodding. There should be a vent pipe in the hatch box to prevent the formation of air-locks in the siphon.
- The design of siphons should be made on the basis of pipes running full under pressure. It is, therefore, essential to know the maximum available head.
- To remove the coarser silt, debris grit etc. from the sewage before it enters the siphon pipes, the inlet chamber should be provided with screens.
- Manholes should be provided at each end of the siphon to enable barrels to be cleaned.
- It is advisable to keep a diversion for the siphon. So when the siphon either overflows or gets chocked, the flow of sewage can be diverted.

4.9.2 Disadvantages of Inverted Siphons

Due to the following disadvantages, the inverted siphons should be avoided as far as possible.

- They are likely to get silted, as the down gradient is not continuous. Therefore, the proper design with self cleansing velocity at different discharges is very important. To stir and keep in suspension the deposited silt in the siphon, a chain extending from the inlet chamber to the outlet chamber is provided.
- The design of inlet chamber should be perfect, otherwise, floating matter present in the sewage will separate out, and will accumulate in this chamber, and seriously affecting the proper working of this chamber.
- It is not possible to give side connections to the inverted siphons.

SOLVED EXAMPLE ON THE DESIGN OF AN INVERTED SOPHON

Example 4.1 : Design a three barrel siphon for carrying sewage across a river stream. The total length of the siphon measured along the centre line including slopes is about 85 m. The invert levels at the inlet and the outlet ends of the sewer are 127.80 m and 127.18 m respectively. The average flow of the sewage is 190 litres per second, and the maximum and the minimum flows are 250% and 40% of the average respectively. Assume the minor losses to be about 0.065 m and self-cleansing velocity of 0.9 m/sec.

Solution :

(A) Discharges at Various Flows :

The average flow to be carried by the siphon

$$= \text{190 litres/second}$$
$$= \text{0.19 cumecs}$$

The maximum flow to be carried by the siphon

$$= \text{250\% of 0.19 cumecs}$$
$$= 2.5 \times 0.19$$
$$= \text{0.475 cumecs}$$

The minimum flow to be carried by the siphon

$$= \text{40\% of 0.19 cumecs}$$
$$= 0.4 \times 0.19$$
$$= \text{0.076 cumecs}$$

Maximum available head $= $ Difference in the invert levels at the inlet and outlet

$$= 127.80 - 127.18$$
$$= \text{0.62 m}$$

(B) Design for Flow at Minimum Discharge :

$$Q = A \cdot V$$

$$0.076 = \frac{\pi}{4} \cdot d^2 \cdot V$$

$$0.076 = \frac{\pi}{4} d^2 \cdot (0.9)$$

or $$\qquad d = \sqrt{\frac{0.076 \times 4}{\pi \times 0.9}}$$

$$= \text{0.328 m}$$

Use 30 cm diameter cast iron pipe.

$$\begin{bmatrix} \text{Actual velocity} \\ \text{through first barrel} \end{bmatrix} = \frac{0.076}{\frac{\pi}{4} \times (0.30)^2}$$

$$= 1.075 \text{ m/sec} > 0.9 \text{ m/sec}$$

∴   Safe and self cleansing.

The head loss in the siphon pipe can be calculated by using Manning's formula :

$$V = \frac{1}{n} \cdot R^{2/3} \cdot S^{1/2}$$

where,

$$R = \frac{d}{4} = \frac{0.30}{4} = 0.075 \text{ m}$$

$$V = 1.075 \text{ m/sec}$$

$$n = 0.013 \text{ (Assume)}$$

∴

$$1.075 = \frac{1}{0.013} (0.075)^{2/3} \cdot S^{1/2}$$

∴

$$\frac{1.075 \times 0.013}{(0.075)^{2/3}} = S^{1/2}$$

or

$$S^{1/2} = \frac{0.0139}{(0.075)^{2/3}} = 0.0785$$

∴

$$S = 0.0062$$

Now frictional head loss, $H_f = S \times L$

$$= 0.0062 \times 85$$

$$= 0.527 \text{ m}$$

∴   Total losses = Frictional head loss, H_f + Minor losses

$$= 0.527 + 0.065$$

$$= 0.592 \text{ m}$$

This is less than the available head of 0.62 m. Hence, the pipe diameter is satisfactory.

(C) Design for Flow at Average Discharge :

At average discharge, the excess discharge passing through the second pipe

$$= \text{Average discharge} - \text{Minimum discharge}$$

$$= 0.19 - 0.076$$

$$= 0.114 \text{ cumecs}$$

For self cleansing velocity of 0.9 m/sec, the diameter required,

$$d = \sqrt{\frac{0.114 \times 4}{\pi \times 0.9}}$$

$$= 0.4 \text{ m}$$

Use 380 mm diameter cast iron pipe.

Actual velocity through the second barrel

$$= \frac{0.114}{\frac{\pi}{4} \times (0.38)^2}$$

$$= 1.006 \text{ m/sec}$$

Using Manning's formula, we have

$$V = \frac{1}{n} R^{2/3} \cdot S^{1/2}$$

$$\therefore \quad 1.006 = \frac{1}{0.013} \times \left(\frac{0.38}{4}\right)^{2/3} \cdot S^{1/2}$$

or

$$S^{1/2} = \frac{1.006 \times 0.013}{(0.095)^{2/3}} = 0.063$$

$$\therefore \quad S = 0.0039$$

$$\therefore \quad H_f = 0.0039 \times 85$$

$$= 0.332 \text{ m}$$

$$\text{Total losses} = H_f + \text{Minor losses}$$

$$= 0.3315 + 0.065$$

$$= 0.397 \text{ m} < 0.62 \text{ m} \quad \text{Hence O.K.}$$

(D) Design for Flow at Maximum Discharge :

At maximum discharge, the excess discharge passing through the third pipe

$$= 0.475 - 0.19$$

$$= 0.285 \text{ cumecs}$$

Assuming the velocity as 1.5 m/sec, in this case.

$$\therefore \quad \text{The required diameter, } d = \sqrt{\frac{0.285 \times 4}{\pi \times 1.5}} = 0.492 \text{ m}$$

Use 500 mm diameter pipe.

Actual velocity through this third barrel

$$= \frac{0.285}{\frac{\pi}{4} \times (0.50)^2} = 1.45 \text{ m/sec}$$

Using Manning's formula, we have

$$1.45 = \frac{1}{0.013} \left(\frac{0.50}{4}\right)^{2/3} \cdot S^{1/2}$$

or $$S^{1/2} = \frac{1.45 \times 0.013}{0.250}$$

$\therefore$ $S = 0.0057$

$\therefore$ $H_f = 0.0057 \times 85$

$= 0.483$ m

Total losses $= 0.483 + 0.065$

$= 0.548$ m < 0.62 m   Hence O.K.

Hence, use barrels of the following sizes :

Barrel No. 1 = 300 mm diameter pipe   ... **Ans.**
Barrel No. 2 = 380 mm diameter pipe   ... **Ans.**
Barrel No. 3 = 500 mm diameter pipe   ... **Ans.**

4.10 STORM WATER REGULATORS OR STORM RELIEF WORKS

Storm water regulators are constructed for combined sewerage systems and allow the diversion of excess storm water into nearby natural stream or river.

Generally, a combined sewer is designed for a discharge equal to 3 to 6 times the dry weather flow (D.W.F.). Sometimes, the intensity of rain is more, in such cases, the quantity of sewer crosses its limit. This excess quantity is diverted to some natural stream or river. This excess quantity of sewage will be mainly composed of storm water and therefore it will not be foul in nature.

The following are three types of storm regulator:

- Leaping weir,
- Overflow weir, and
- Siphon spillway.

4.10.1 Leaping Weir   [May 2009]

The arrangement of leaping weir is shown in Fig. 4.13. This arrangement consists of an opening in the invert of the storm drain or combined sewer through which the normal storm flow is diverted into the intercepting sewer while the excess flow leaps over the combined sewer to flow into the nearby natural stream or river.

Sewage Discharge is Small : The sewage will fall directly into the intercepting sewer through the opening.

Sewage Discharge Exceeds a Certain Limit : The excess sewage leaps or jumps across the weir, and it is carried to the natural stream or river.

Silting Problems : In heavy storms, most of the flow may leap over the combined sewer and only small quantity may be left in the sewer, which may result in low velocity and thus creating silting problems.

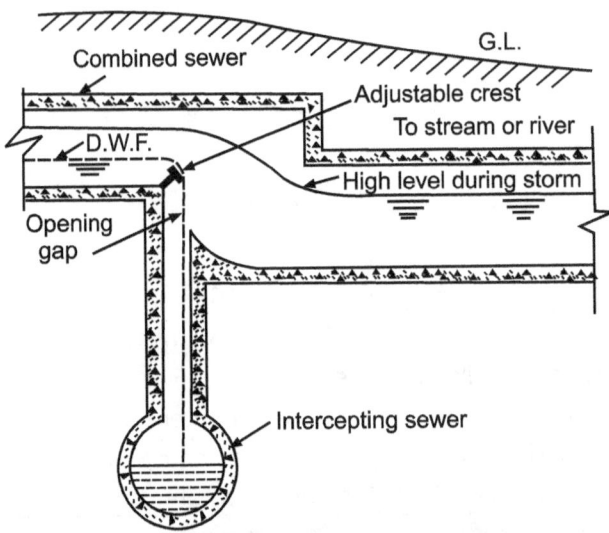

Fig. 4.13 : Leaping weir

4.10.2 Overflow Weir (or Side Flow Weirs)

Fig. 4.14 shows the arrangement of overflow weir.

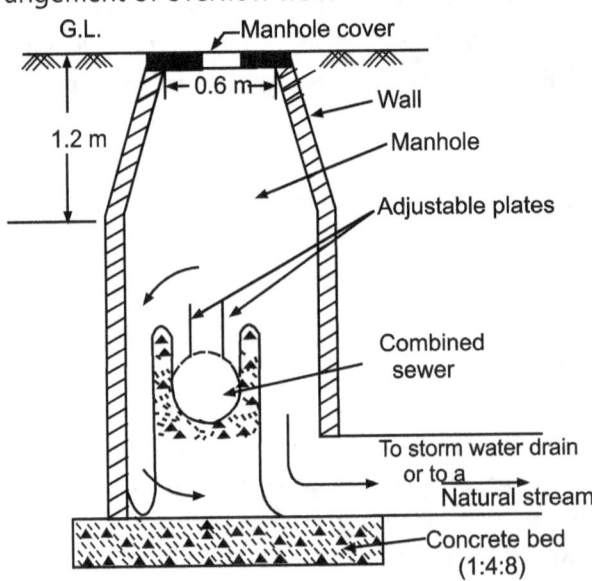

Fig. 4.14 : Overflow weir

In this system, excess sewage is allowed to overflow the combined sewer in the manhole, from where it enters into a channel carrying it into a storm water drain or directly into a stream or river. Adjustable plates may be used to avoid the escape of the floating matter from the combined sewer.

Fig. 4.15 shows another type of arrangement.

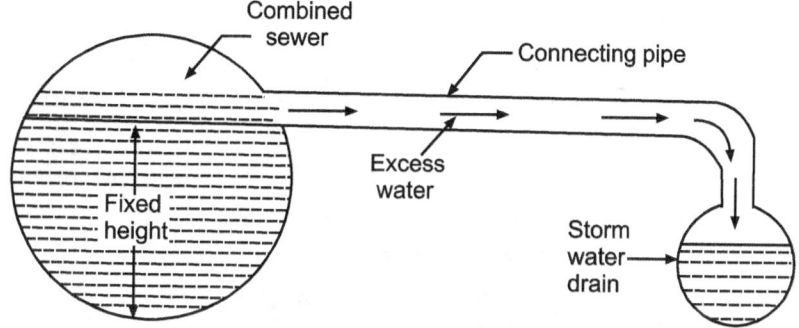

Fig. 4.15 : Overflow weir

In another system, openings at suitable height above the invert of the sewer are provided at suitable intervals along the length of the combined sewer. These openings are then connected to a storm water drain as shown in Fig. 4.16. Storm water drain is laid near the combined sewer. The excess sewage above this fixed height is thus diverted and conveyed to the stream, through the storm water drain.

4.10.3 Siphon Spillway

Fig. 4.16 shows the arrangement of siphon spillway. It is used for diverting excess sewage discharge from the combined sewer to the natural stream or river, through the storm water drain or overflow channel. This is an automatic process and works on the principle of siphonic action. The siphonic action starts when the level of the sewage in the combined sewer goes above the crest level of the siphon and stops when the level of sewage falls below this crest level.

The level of the crest of the siphon is fixed related to the level reached by the flow in the combined sewer during the period of maximum dry weather flow.

4.10.3.1 Operation of Siphon Spillway

When the sewage level in the combined sewer goes beyond the crest level, the mouth of the air pipe gets sealed, at the same time, the air contained in the siphon is removed by the flow. Thus, siphonic action starts and flow is immediately established in the siphon. When the sewage level of the combined sewer falls below the crest level, mouth of air pipe gets exposed, air enters the siphon pipe and thus breaking the siphonic action.

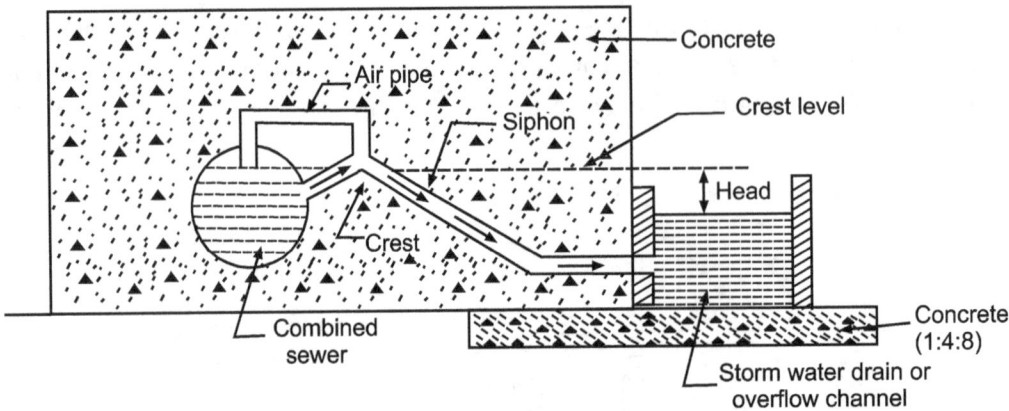

Fig. 4.16 : Siphon spillway type of storm regulator

SEWER PUMPING

4.11 NECESSITY OF PUMPING SEWAGE OR WASTEWATER

The necessity of pumping sewage or wastewater arises under the following circumstances :

- The sewage of a low-lying area of a town has to be pumped into branch or main sewer of town.

- In case if the area is flat, the laying of sewers at their designed gradients required deeper and deeper excavation. To avoid this, it may be advisable to lift the sewage at suitable intervals.

- In case if basements of large commercial buildings, sewage may have to be pumped, as the street sewer may be higher than the level of the basement floor.

- When outfall sewer is at a lower level than the body of water into which it is to be discharged or when the outfall sewer is lower than the level of the treatment plant, the sewage will have to be pumped.

- When a sewer has to go across a high ridge, it will be more economical to pump it into sewers laid across the slope of the ridge at reasonable depth, instead of driving a tunnel.

4.12 PUMPING STATIONS

Pumps and other accessories are installed in building for lifting sewage is called a sewage pumping station.

4.12.1 Proper Location of Pumping Stations

These pumping stations should be located near a disposal unit, such as a natural stream, a river or a lake etc. so that the accumulated sewage can overflow in such disposal units in case break-down of the pumping plant, failure of power occurs etc.

4.12.2 Component Parts of Pumping Stations

The following are the major component parts of pumping stations :

1.   Grit channel
2.   Coarse and fine screens
3.   Sump well or wet well
4.   Dry well or pump room
5.   Motor room
6.   Rising mains
7.   Emergency exit pipe and
8.   Other accessories like valves, flow recorders, starters etc.

Fig. 4.17 shows a typical sewage pumping station.

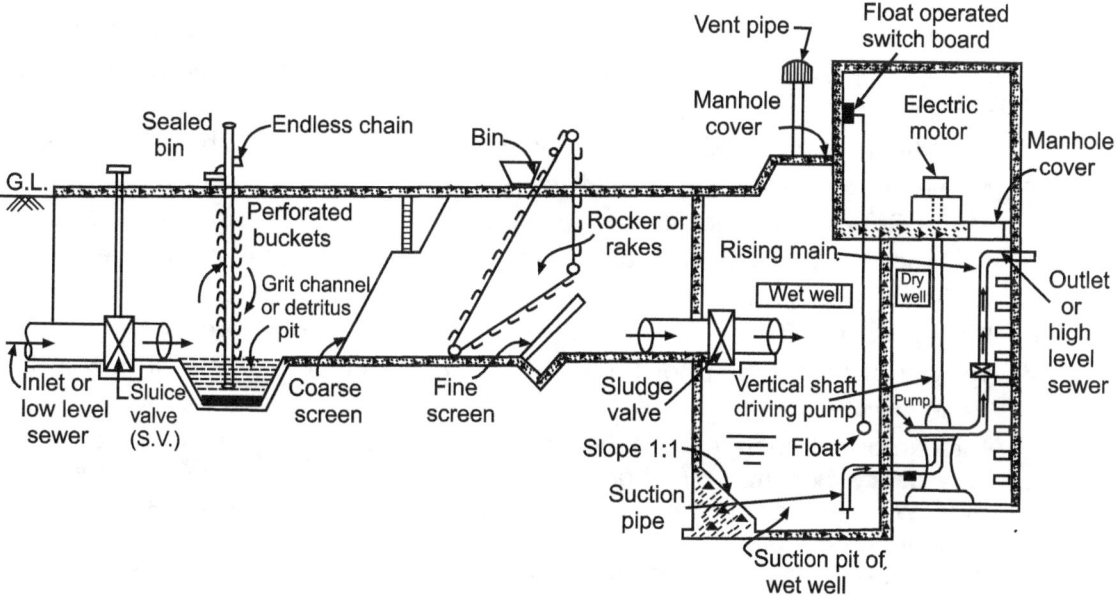

Fig. 4.17 : Typical sewage pumping station

1.   **Grit Channel :** To minimise the wear and tear of the pump impeller and of the rising main, remove indestructible solid matter, such as grit, sand, gravel etc., in addition to the solids in suspension like faeces, papers etc. before pumping.

   Grit channel or grit chamber is provided to achieve above purpose. So the sewage is first passed through grit channel where its velocity is reduced to the order of 0.15 to 0.3 m/sec. Due to the less velocity, the grit settles down and is removed by an endless chain to which perforated buckets are fixed.

   The minimum capacity of grit channel should have one per cent of the daily dry weather flow. In small installations, grit is removed once in a week whereas in larger installations, grit is removed daily.

2. **Screens :** Screens are generally provided after the grit channel or grit chamber for extracting excess of rags, sticks, papers etc.

    Generally two types of screens are used, one is coarse and other is fine. The sewage is first passed through coarse screens to intercept solids like scrubbing brushes, blocks of wood etc. The clear openings of coarse screens are 50 to 100 mm. The sewage is then passed through fine screens to intercept all except very fine particles of sewage. The clear openings of fine screens are 25 to 50 mm.

3. **Sump Well or Wet Well :** A sump well is provided to form a suction pit from which the pump may draw sewage through the suction pipe. A float is provided in this sump well which is connected to a switch. When sewage rises above the float level, the switch gets pressed and pump automatically starts functioning. To avoid the priming of pump, the designed level of the sewage in the sump well is kept above the pump level. Usually, a detention period of 15 to 30 minutes of peak flow is adopted for design. To avoid deposition of solids, the floor of the bottom should slope 1 : 1 or steeper.

4. **Dry Well or Pump Room :** In this room, pumps are installed. The end of suction pipe is located near the bottom of wet well.

5. **Motor Room :** The electric motor is situated in this room. Besides electric motor, this room also accommodates other appurtenances such as flow recorders, automatic starter etc.

6. **Rising Mains :** It may be of cast iron or asbestos cement pressure pipes. The velocity of flow should not be less than 0.75 m/sec at any time of flow in the rising main.

    The purpose of rising mains is the sewage led to high levelled gravity sewer.

7. **Emergency Exit Pipe :** This pipe is connecting the sump well with a stream or river. When the sump well overflows, the excess sewage can be easily directed through this exit pipe.

8. **Other Accessories :** Apart from above major parts, various other appurtenances such as automatic starters, flow recorders, check valves etc., are needed and installed suitably in the pumping station.

4.12.3 Types of Pumps

The following are various types of pumps that are commonly employed for pumping sewage :

1. Centrifugal pumps.
2. Reciprocating pumps.
3. Air pressure pumps or pneumatic ejectors.

1. **Centrifugal Pumps :** These are most widely used for lifting sewage and storm water, as they can be easily installed in pits and sumps and can be easily transported the suspended matter present in sewage without getting clogged so often.

The following are the component parts of centrifugal pump : (i) Impeller, (ii) Casing, (iii) Suction pipe and (iv) Delivery pipe.

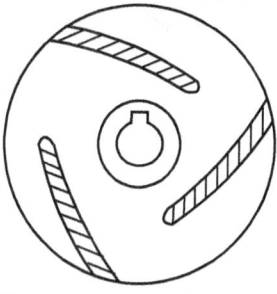

Fig. 4.18 : Three vane type impeller of a non-clog centrifugal pump

The impeller rotates with high speed inside the casing. The commonly used horizontal axial flow type pumps are fitted with either open or closed three vane type impellers (Fig. 4.18). The clearance between the vanes is kept large enough to allow any solid matter entering the pump to pass out with the liquid, thus preventing the clogging. Such pumps are therefore, called non-clog pumps.

In another type of centrifugal pumps, the solid matters are broken-up as they pass through the pump impeller. Such pumps are called disintegrating pumps.

To avoid the priming of the pump, the pump is installed in such a way that its suction pipe remains below the lowest sewage or wastewater level in the adjacent level. (Fig. 4.19).

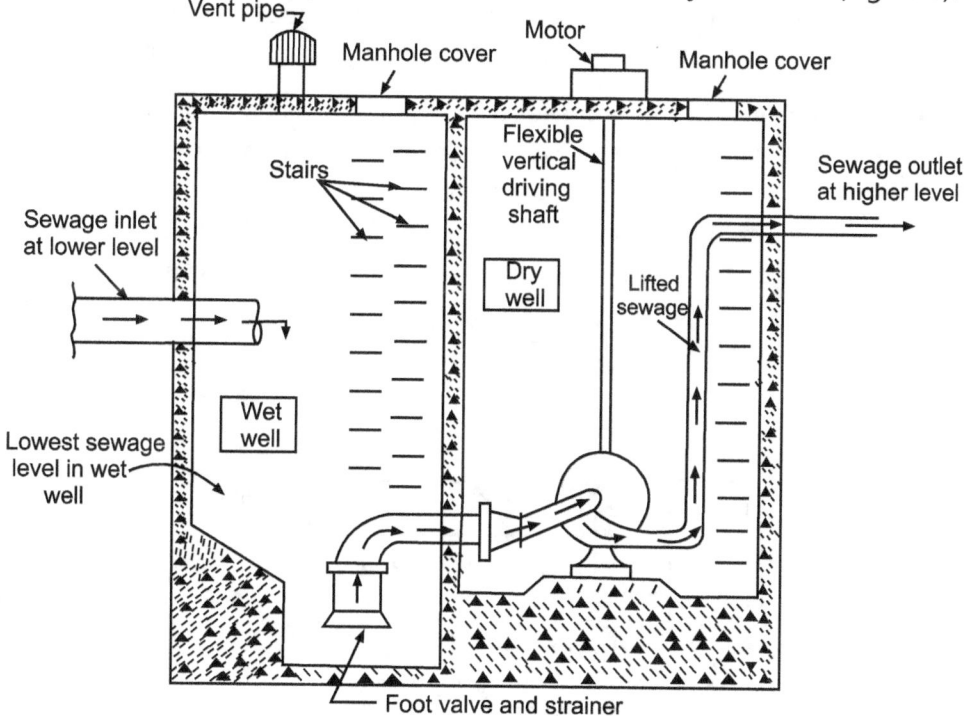

Fig. 4.19 : Typical centrifugal pump installation for sewage pumping

2. **Reciprocating Pumps :** In modern days, reciprocating pumps are obsolete, because of their high initial cost, difficulty in maintenance and greater wear and tear of their values (as they are liable to be clogged by solids or fibrous material).

These may sometimes be used for pumping difficult sludges and where large quantity is required to be pumped against low heads. These pumps may be used after passing the sewage through screen with 20 mm spacing.

Reciprocating pumps are generally of two types :

- **Ram Type :** In the ram type of a reciprocating pump, a piston or plunger moves through glands displacing liquid in a vessel. The delivery valve remains closed during intake stroke. A diaphragm pump is an example of this type.

Diaphragm Pump : The diaphragm pump is as shown in Fig. 4.20.

This is a ram type reciprocating pump. In this pump, a piston or plunger is attached to the centre of a circular rubber diaphragm. The outer edge of the rubber diaphragm is bolted to a flange on the pump.

Due to flexibility of the diaphragm the up and down motion of the plunger is permitted, thus increasing or decreasing the capacity of the pump casing, through the suction valve, on the upward movement of the plunger. When the piston moves downward, the suction valve closes and the liquid is forced through the delivery pipe by opening the delivery valve.

- **Propeller Type :** In the propeller type of a reciprocating pump, a multiple blade screw rotor or propeller moves vertically inside a pump casing causing the sewage to lift up. It draws water through inlet guide vanes and discharges through outlet guide vanes. This action is somewhat similar to that of ships propeller. The axial flow screw pump is an example of this type.

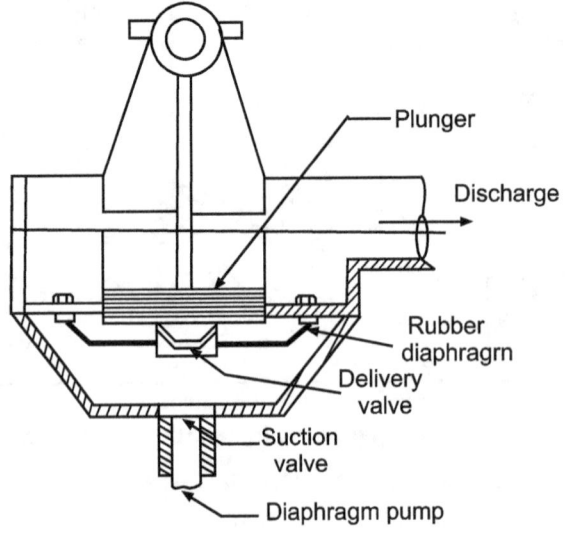

Fig. 4.20 : Diaphragm pump

3. **Air Pressure Pumps or Pneumatic Ejectors :** Fig. 4.21 shows Shone's air-ejector. These are used for pumping smaller quantities of waste water, such as for lifting wastewaters from basements of buildings and thus discharging it into street sewers. These are also helpful where centrifugal pumps of smaller capacity are likely to be clogged.

- It consists of a cast-iron chamber with a spindle having an upper and a lower cup as shown in Fig. 4.21.

- Two reflux or check valves, that open in one direction only, are provided at the entrance (V_1) and exit points (V_2). The ejector chamber rests on a seat.

- The compressed air inlet valve (V_3) is operated by a level arrangement having a counter weight at its end. The compressed air is supplied through this valve at a pressure of about 1.5 kg/cm² (0.147 N/mm²).

- The wastewater enters the ejector through the valve V_1 and slowly rises in the chamber. At this stage, valve V_2 and valve V_3 remain closed.

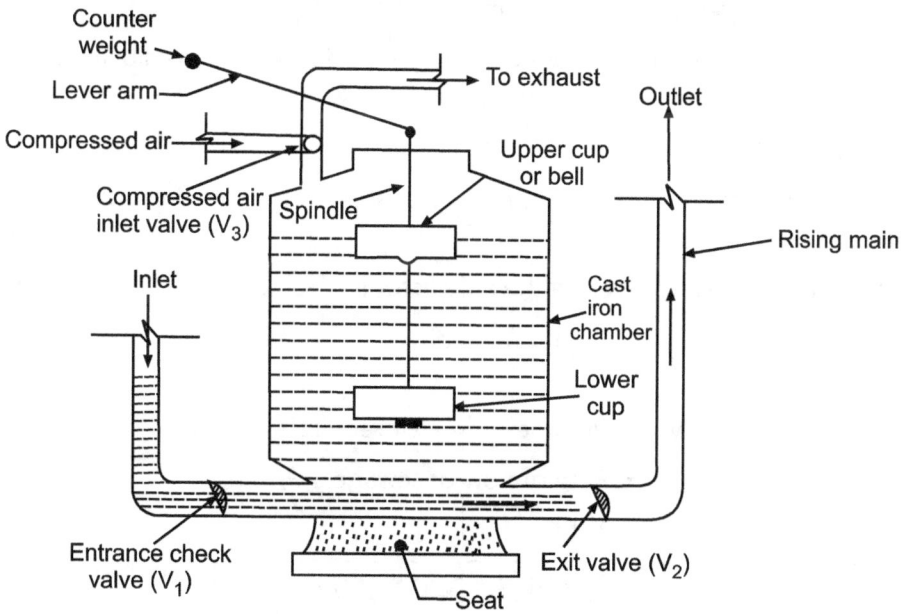

Fig. 4.21 : Shone's air ejector

- As the level rises, the air from the chamber escapes through the exhaust. The air inside the upper cup is entrapped, when the wastewater level in the chamber reaches the bottom of the upper cup. Due to this, the spindle to lift up and through the lever arrangement, it results in the closing of the exhaust and opening the valve V_3.

- The air under pressure entering the chamber from valve (V_3) forces the wastewater from inside the chamber to rise up in the outlet pipe by opening the valve V_2.

- At this stage V_1 is closed, thus the wastewater is lifted up and discharged from the outlet, when the sewage level in the chamber falls below the cup.

- At this stage, the lever arrangement opens the exhaust and closes the compressed air inlet valve (V_3), because of the entrapped air from the upper cup escapes.

- The entrance valve (V_1) opens and the exit valve (V_2) closes to repeat the process.

Merits of Air Ejectors :

- Require least supervision, as an automatic units.

- These are not likely to be clogged.

- These are economical, where the smaller quantities of wastewaters are required to be lifted.

- Screening is not required, as connecting lines and check valves or reflux valves will pass all the solids that enter the ejector compartments.

- These are useful over small capacity centrifugal pumps, as the possibility of clogging of small capacity centrifugal pumps is more.

Demerits of Air Ejectors :

The only one demerit of air ejectors is that they possess very low efficiency, of the order of 15 percent.

The quantity of air required to operate the air ejector is given by the following   expression :

$$V = \frac{Q(H + 10.3)}{12.2}$$

where, V = Volume of free air required, m^3/min

Q = Rate of flow of sewage, m^3/min

H = Total head, m

IMPORTANT POINTS

Sewer appurtenances and sewage pumping:

- Different sewer appurtenances and their functions.

- Types of storm water regulators and their uses.

- Different types of pumps and their advantages.

- Component parts of pumping stations.

EXERCISE

1. Write short notes on :

    (1) Drop manhole

    (2) Sewer appurtenances

    (3) Necessity of appurtenances

    (4) Street inlets

    (5) Catch basins

    (6) Clean-outs

    (7) Lampholes

    (8) Inverted siphons.

2. What is the necessity of appurtenances in sewerage system ? Explain with sketch of the 'Drop manhole'.   **(8 Marks) (Pune University)**

3. Write about the following with sketch (any two) :

    (i)   Automatic flushing tank

    (ii) Inverted siphon.

    (iii) Leaping weir.   **(8 Marks) (Pune University)**

4. Draw a neat sketch of a sewage ventilator.

5. Describe with the help of a neat sketch the components of a manhole.

6. Explain the necessity of providing a manhole in a sewer line.

7. Explain the purposes of lamphole.

8. Explain the working of an overflow weir.

9. Explain with a neat sketch, the working of any one type of storm regulator.

10. When is the necessity of pumping the sewage ?

11. Write various points that should be kept in mind while selecting the site for a sewage pumping station.

12. Draw a neat sketch of a typical pumping station. Describe in brief the function of each component.

13. Draw a neat sketch of automatic flushing tank and explain the operation of flushing.

UNIVERSITY QUESTIONS

1. Describe briefly and explain the functions of the following :

    (i)   Street inlet,

    (ii) Leaping weir,

    (iii) Drop manhole.   **(4 M) (May 2009)**

2. Write short notes on drop manhole.   **(4 M) (Dec. 2010, May 2011)**

✠ ✠ ✠

Chapter 5

WASTEWATER CHARACTERISTICS

5.1 INTRODUCTION

The biological world consists of more than 3,50,000 species of plants (algae, fungi, mosses and higher plants) and 10,75,480 species of animals (from unicellular protozoa to man). The different forces of nature which sustain the biological world are air, water, food and living space (habitat).

But environmental pollution has reached such alarming proportions that it now threatens the very existence of man. The food we eat, the air we breathe, the water we use, the land we live in are gradually becoming more and more polluted as man advances in the path of human civilization. If man has to survive, he has to devise ways of making his physical environment as less contaminated and as pure as possible.

5.2 BASIC PRINCIPLES

The problem of pollution of natural waters may be attributed largely to municipal and industrial waste-waters. The contamination of surface and ground water poses grave dangers for human health. Degradable pollutants i.e. those that can be reduced in quantity by natural processes, include organic and other water from domestic sewage and thermal discharges. Degradation process uses the dissolved oxygen in water and hence has its limitations. Non-degradable pollutants are salts, soluble gases, particulate matter which may include a wide range of toxic metals viz. cadmium, mercury, lead etc. arising from complex industrial processes. Paper, petroleum, chemical and steel industries account for a large amount of wastewater discharge. Release of city wastes into rivers is one of the main reasons for the spread of diseases like infective hepatitis, cholera, amoebic dysentery, bacillary dysentery and typhoid. Agricultural operations contribute considerably to water pollution through mixing of pesticides, herbicides and fertilizers in surface runoff. Another serious pollutant is the drainage of acids from mines, mostly abandoned coal diggings. Thermal pollution i.e. discharge of wastewater at a high temperature is hazardous.

To introduce a pollution control programme, the required steps are stream and waste sampling, laboratory and pilot plant investigation and process design and plant construction. The assessment, development and application of processes for the treatment of industrial wastes, and an understanding of what each can achieve, depends on a detailed knowledge of the *composition of the waste and its treated effluent.* This knowledge can be obtained by the proper application of suitable analytical methods. In addition, to carry out analyses in order to ensure that the treated effluent confirms to the discharge consent conditions, it is necessary to carry out many routine analyses each day to ensure the smooth and efficient operation of the treatment plant.

Industrial wastes are sampled and analysed both to determine the degree of contamination and to aid the selection of the proper treatment process. The following is an indication of the major characteristics of industrial wastewaters which will affect receiving water quality and consequently may have to be dealt with either by treatment or by some preventive, in plant measure.

- Organic matter (fats, sugars, proteins, detergents)
- Suspended solids (organic, inorganic)
- Dissolved solids (e.g. chlorides)
- Nutrients (Nitrate and Phosphate)
- Acids (Sulphuric, Nitric, Organic etc.)
- Alkalies (Lime, Sodium hydroxide)
- Toxic matter (Toxic to man, animals, plants, fish, micro-organisms e.g. heavy metals, pesticides, ammonia, cyanide, nitrate)
- Heat (not effluents)
- Colour (dyes, pigments)
- Volatile Organic Matter (petroleum products, solvents)
- Pathogens (Anthrax, Salmonella)
- Flow variation (Hourly, daily, seasonal).

5.3 SAMPLING

The value of any laboratory result depends on the **sampling** – integrity of the sample. The object of sampling is to collect a portion of the wastewater small enough in volume to be conveniently handled in the laboratory. The sample of waste should be still before examination. It must be collected in such a manner that nothing is added or lost in the portion collected and no change occurs during the time between collection and laboratory examination. Unless these conditions are met, laboratory results may be misleading and worse than no results.

The sampling for a physical and chemical examination of wastewaters forms an important feature. Samples should be taken in clean, colourless glass bottles provided with ground-in-glass stoppers. Certain determinations (e.g., D.O., Oil, Sulphides, Phenols) must be performed on a separate sample taken specifically for the purpose in another bottle.

In this context, the observations of Webber are of particular relevance :

"The actual collection of the sample is a matter of considerable importance, more especially as this is often done by laymen with little knowledge of such matters. There can be a few responsible chemists who have not received a grubby bottle filled with dirty water late on a

Friday afternoon, accompanied by a vague note dated the previous Saturday. On opening the "sample" it may reek to high heaven of cough mixture, "Evening in Paris" or gin. Such efforts are completely useless."

The label on the sample bottle should include information as to the type of sample (sewage, industrial waste, treated effluent etc.), source, date, time and temperature of the sample.

The location of the sampling points and collection of samples cannot be specified in all cases as conditions vary in different plants and suitable sampling procedures must be adapted to each plant. However, certain general principles can be listed.

- Individual or combined waste sample should be taken where the waste is well mixed. This is most easily accomplished if the sampling point is located where the waste flow is turbulent e.g. free fall from a pipeline, discharge from a pipe is against a baffle as at the inlet of a tank.

- Large particles should be excluded (greater than $\frac{1"}{4}$ in diameter). Wastewater should be sampled after screening where screens are used.

- No deposits, growths or floating material that have accumulated at the sampling point should be included.

- Samples should be examined as soon as possible. If held for more than one hour, they should be cooled by keeping them in ice box in order to avoid bacterial decomposition.

Normally two types of samples are collected depending on the time available. They are (1) "Grab or Catch" samples, (2) Integrated or Composite samples.

Grab sample consists of a portion of the wastewater all taken at one time. The composite sample consists of portions of wastewater taken at regular time intervals, the volume of each portion being proportional to the waste flow at the time of its collection. All the portions are mixed to produce a final sample representative of the wastewater. There are advantages and disadvantages in both types.

Grab Samples are not representative of the average wastewater since they reflect only the conditions at the time of sampling. Since, the time available in most cases is limited, grab samples are used for analysis which is not a good practice. Composite grab samples are sometimes collected in place of composite samples.

Composite or Integrated Samples indicate the character of the wastewater over a period of time. The effects of intermittent or batch discharges in strength and flow are eliminated. The portion used should be collected with sufficient frequency to obtain average results. If the strength and flow of the wastewater do not fluctuate rapidly, hourly samples over a period of 12 hours are satisfactory. In case, where fluctuations are rapid, 30 min. or 15 min. samples may be required. The period of sampling may be varied covering 8, 12 or 24 hours depending upon the use to be made of the results. Generally, composite samples are collected to determine the characteristics of the wastewater and to establish the water-pollution load for designing treatment plant.

Flow Measurement :

The rate of waste flow must be measured when each portion is taken and the volume of the portion adjusted to the flow by use of a factor. Variation in flow is also a very important factor which has to be taken into account for the designing of the treatment plant. It is possible to have one or two high peak flows followed by a constant or slightly varying flow. It is necessary to locate a suitable point or points in the waste drain and weirs have to be fixed and flow measured. Without flow data, it is not possible to collect integrated or composite sample.

5.4 WASTEWATER ANALYSIS

The analyses performed on wastewaters may be classified as physical, chemical and biological. The principal parameters used to characterise wastewater are listed in the following Table 5.1.

Table 5.1 : Characteristics of Wastewater and their Sources

Parameter	Source
	Physical
Solids	Carriage water, domestic and industrial wastes.
Temperature	Domestic and industrial wastes.
Colour	Domestic and industrial wastes.
Odour	Decomposing sewage, industrial wastes.
	Chemical
Organic	
Proteins	Domestic and commercial wastes.
Carbohydrates	Domestic and commercial wastes.
Fats, oils and grease	Domestic, commercial and industrial wastes
Surfactants	Domestic and industrial wastes.
Phenols	Industrial wastes.
Pesticides	Agricultural wastes.
Inorganic	
pH	Industrial wastes.

Contd...

Chlorides	Carriage water, domestic waters, ground water infilteration.
Alkalinity	Domestic wastes, carriage water, ground water infilteration.
Nitrogen	Domestic and agricultural wastes.
Phosphorus	Domestic and industrial wastes, natural run-off.
Sulphur	Carriage water and industrial wastes.
Toxic compounds	Industrial wastes, ground water infilteration.
Heavy metals	Industrial wastes.
Gases	
Oxygen	Carriage water, surface water infilteration.
Hydrogen sulphide	Decomposition of domestic wastes.
Methane	Decomposition of domestic wastes.
	Biological
Protista (bacteria, fungi, protozoa and algae)	Domestic wastes, treatment plants.
Viruses	Domestic wastes.
Plant (seed plants, ferns, mosses and liver worts)	Open watercourses and treatment plants.
Animals (Invertebrates and vertebrates)	Open watercourses and treatment plants.

The various parameters reported in Table 5.1, details concerning the exact method of analyses are not presented. These details may be found in *standard methods for examination of water and wastewater by American Water Works Association.*

Analytical results for wastewater samples are expressed in terms of physical and chemical units of measurement. Chemical parameters are usually expressed in the physical unit of (mg/litre) milligrams per litre.

5.5 PHYSICAL CHARACTERISTICS

- **Total Solids :** The most important physical characteristic of wastewater is its total solids content, which is composed of floating matter, matter in suspension, colloidal matter and matter in solution.

  Total solids = Suspended solids + Dissolved solids and colloidal solids.

  (Further classified on the basis of volatility at 600°C as volatile solids and fixed solids).

Classification and size range of particles are given in Table 5.2.

Table 5.2 : Classification and Size Range of Particles

Size of Particle, Microns	Size of Particle, Millimeters	Type of Particles or Solids
10^{-5} to 10^{-3}	10^{-8} to 10^{-6}	Dissolved
10^{-3} to 1	10^{-6} to 10^{-3}	Colloidal
1 to 100	10^{-3} to 10^{-1}	Suspended
10 to 100	10^{-2} to 10^{-1}	Settlable

- **Colour :** Due to dissolved matter, usually organic acids.
- **Turbidity :** Presence of colloidal solids which may be clay or silt particles or micro- organisms.
- **Taste and Odour :** Normally, due to dissolved solids or gases which may be natural in origin e.g. from algae or other micro-organisms or man-made e.g. phenol from gas liquors and tar spraying.
- **Temperature :** This has an influence on taste since warm water tastes flat and insipid, partly as a result of the decrease of oxygen and carbon dioxide at elevated temperature. Abnormally high temperatures can faster the growth of undesirable water plants and sewage fungus, increase in the rate of biochemical reactions.

5.6 CHEMICAL CHARACTERISTICS

- **pH :** The hydrogen ion concentration is an important quality parameter of wastewaters. It may alter the concentration in the natural waters.
- **Alkalinity :** Due to the presence of the hydroxides, carbonates and bicarbonates of elements such as calcium, magnesium, sodium, potassium or of ammonia.
- **Dissolved Oxygen (DO) :** Oxygen is a vital element in water since without it only the lowest form of life can survive-unfortunately, oxygen is only slightly soluble in water (9.1 mg at $20^{\circ}C$). Pollution of water by organic matter rapidly utilizes the D.O. by biological oxidation and thus the receiving water may become depleted of oxygen with consequent death of aquatic life.
- **Biochemical Oxygen Demand (BOD) : Definition :** "The amount of dissolved oxygen from wastewater required by heterotrophic micro-organisms to degrade biodegradable organic matter at $20^{\circ}C$ for 5 days period". Recently, the temperature and period is changed to $27^{\circ}C$ and 3 days respectively.

The sewage contains both suspended and dissolved matter. The portion of suspended and dissolved matter may be organic in nature. This organic matter is carbohydrates, proteins and fats present in sewage. This is called as carbonaceous organic matter or nitrogenous organic matter depending on presence of carbon and nitrogen.

This organic matter is the source of food for most of the micro-organisms present in sewage. As it is not possible for micro-organisms to ingest food in the form available outside the cell wall, it is necessary to convert it into such a form so that it will pass through it. Thus, conversion of complex organic matter into simpler one is degradation. The dissolved oxygen is used by micro-organisms to carry on this process of degradation.

More addition of organic matter through different sources leads to more degradation process resulting in more depletion of dissolved oxygen from wastewater. This is very important to note that minimum 2-4 mg/l of dissolved oxygen must be present for the survival of aquatic life. Thus, this parameter BOD gives us the idea of amount of organic matter and ultimately the pollutional strength of wastewater.

BOD is expressed in mg/l at 20°C for 5 days period.

$(BOD)_5$ at 20°C = D.O. consumed in the test by diluted sample × Dilution factor.

In fact, if the oxygen supply is made available for periods more than 5 days, it is found that the oxygen is consumed rapidly for 6 or 7 days, and then slows down until the end of about 20 days or so.

The demand for oxygen by micro-organisms is exerted in two stages. The initial demand is known as carbonaceous demand. The latter demand occurs due to biological oxidation of ammonia and is called nitrogenous demand or second stage demand.

The rate at which BOD is satisfied at any time (i.e. rate of deoxygenation) depends on temperature and also on the amount and nature of organic matter present in sewage at that time.

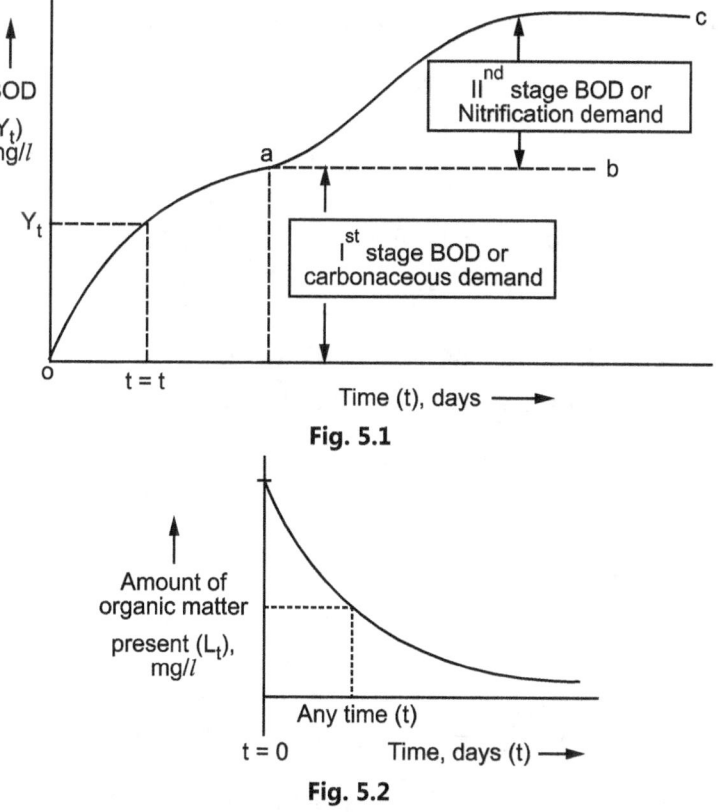

Fig. 5.1

Fig. 5.2

Thus, at a certain temperature, the rate of deoxygenation is directly proportional to amount of organic matter present in sewage at that time.

$$\frac{dL_t}{dt} = -KL_t \qquad\qquad ...(5.1)$$

(minus sign indicates, as time passes, L_t decreases)

where, L_t = Oxygen equivalent of oxidisable organic matter present in sewage after t days from start of oxidation in mg/L.

t = Time in days

K = Reaction rate constant

Integrating the above equation (5.1), we get

$$\int \frac{dL_t}{L_t} = \int -K \cdot dt \qquad\qquad ...(5.2)$$

$$\log L_t = -Kt + C \qquad\qquad C = \text{constant of integration}$$

In the initial stage of sewage, maximum organic matter

when t = zero

$L_t = L$ (L = organic matter at start)

Substituting in equation (5.2), we get

$$\log_e L = K(0) + C$$

i.e. $C = \log_e L$

But putting this value of C in equation (5.1), we have

$$\log_e L_t = -K \cdot t + \log_e L$$

i.e. $\log_e L_t - \log_e L = -K \cdot t$

i.e. $\log_e \left(\dfrac{L_t}{L}\right) = -K \cdot t$

i.e. $2.303 \log_{10} \left(\dfrac{L_t}{L}\right) = -K \cdot t$

i.e. $\log_{10} \left(\dfrac{L_t}{L}\right) = -\dfrac{K}{2.303} \cdot t = -0.434\, K \cdot t$

By putting 0.434 K = K_D, K_D = Deoxygenation constant or BOD rate constant, we get

$$\log_{10}\left(\frac{L_t}{L}\right) = -K_D \cdot t$$

i.e.
$$\frac{L_t}{L} = 10^{-K_D \cdot t} \qquad \ldots (5.3)$$

Here L is the organic matter present in the beginning of BOD reaction; and L_t is organic matter left after t days. This means that, the organic matter oxidised is $L - L_t$.

If we assume Y_t = organic matter oxidised in t days, then, we get

$$Y_t = L - L_t$$

i.e.
$$Y_t = L\left(1 - \frac{L_t}{L}\right)$$

i.e.
$$\frac{L_t}{L} = 1 - \frac{Y_t}{L}$$

Putting this value of $\frac{L_t}{L}$ in equation (5.3), we get

$$1 - \frac{Y_t}{L} = 10^{-K_D \cdot t}$$

i.e.
$$\frac{Y_t}{L} = 1 - 10^{-K_D t}$$

$$Y_t = L\left(1 - 10^{-K_D t}\right) \qquad \ldots (5.4)$$

where,
$$Y_t = \text{Amount of organic matter oxidised}$$
$$= \text{Amount of BOD exerted in mg/L}$$
$$L = \text{Amount of organic matter in beginning}$$
$$= \text{Ultimate BOD in mg/L}$$
$$K_D = \text{Deoxygenation constant}$$
$$t = \text{Time in days}$$

The value of K_D depends on temperature of oxidation reaction. The value of K_D at other temperatures is given by

$$K_{D\,(T)} = K_{D\,(20)}\,[1.047]^{T-20^\circ C}$$

where,
$$K_{D\,(T)} = \text{Deoxygenation constant at any temperature, } T^\circ C$$
$$K_{D\,(20)} = \text{Deoxygenation constant at 20}^\circ C$$

The value of $K_{D~(20)}$ for municipal wastewater is between $0.1 - 0.15$ and for treated wastewater is between $0.05 - 0.1$.

- **Chemical Oxygen Demand (COD) (Dec. 2010)** : A known quantity of wastewater is mixed with a known quantity of standard solution of potassium dichromate and the mixture is heated. The organic matter is oxidised in presence of H_2SO_4 by potassium dichromate. The resulting solution of potassium dichromate is titrated. The oxygen is used in oxidising the wastewater is known as COD. The COD of a waste is, in general, higher than the BOD because more compounds can be oxidised chemically than can be oxidised biologically.

- **Chlorides (May 2009)** : Chlorides are good indicators of sewage pollution since there is high chloride content in urine (an adult discharges about 6 gm of chloride each day).

Many other chemical characteristics may be of interest e.g. oil and grease, heavy metals, cyanides, phenolic compounds, organic gases, total organic carbon etc.

5.7 $\dfrac{BOD_5}{COD}$ RATIO

BOD is oxygen demand for oxidation of organic matter by micro-organisms.

COD is oxygen demand for oxidation of organic (biodegradable) and non-biodegradable organic matter by strong oxidising chemical. COD is always greater than BOD. Hence, BOD/COD ratio will be always less than one.

For $\qquad \dfrac{BOD_5}{COD} = 0.92 - 1.0$, the w/w is fully biodegradable

$\qquad\qquad \dfrac{BOD_5}{COD} =$ more than 0.63, amenable to biological treatment

For untreated domestic wastes, the $\dfrac{BOD_5}{COD}$ ratio varies from 0.4 to 0.8 and the

$\dfrac{BOD_5}{TOC} = 1.0$ to 1.6.

5.8 TREATABILITY INDEX   [DEC. 2010]

Treatability Index (TI) $= \dfrac{BOD}{COD - BOD}$

Sr. No.	Range of T.I.	Type of Treatment Required
1.	TI < 0.5	Chemical treatment
2.	0.5 < TI < 1.0	Biological treatment plus nutrient supplement
3.	TI > 1.0	Biological treatment

Significance of Treatability Index : BOD is a measure of only the carbonaceous component of biodegradable organic matter in waste, whereas COD measures nearly all the oxidizable matter in the waste. Therefore, COD is always greater than BOD value. Both BOD and COD values of any waste are important parameters as their inter-relationship decides the type of treatment to be adopted for the waste. This inter-relationship of BOD and COD shown in above equation is called treatability index.

5.9 BIOLOGICAL CHARACTERISTICS

- All natural waters and most wastewaters contain a variety of living micro-organisms. Micro-organisms are responsible for several water borne diseases and thus, the presence of such pathogenic microorganisms in water is something to be avoided. On the other hand, most micro-organisms are harmless to man. Micro-organisms are capable of stabilizing organic matter and this property is utilized by nature in self purification of polluted waters and by man in the more intensive activity of a wastewater treatment plant. The naming of biological organism is complicated but this is inevitable because of the vast number of different organisms. A specific type of organism is denoted by its species name and a collection of species with similar characteristics is given a generic name e.g. *Vibrio cholerae*, a member of the *Vibrio genus*, in fact the particular member responsible for cholera. Owing to their small size, identification and counting of micro-organisms is not possible with the naked eye. An optical microscope which has a maximum magnification of upto about 1000 times must be used and, to aid viewing, the micro-organisms are usually stained with dyes to make them contrast with the background. The smallest organisms cannot be identified by their physical features alone so that knowledge of their biochemical properties must also be used to make positive identifications possible.

- **Viruses :** Viruses that are excreted by humans may become a major hazard to public health. For example, from experimental studies, it has been found that from 10,000 to 1,00,000 infectious doses of hepatitis virus are emitted from each gram of faeces of a patient ill with this disease. It is known that some viruses will live as long as 41 days in water or sewage at 20°C and for 6 days in a normal river.

- **Coliform Organisms : (Non-Fecal and Fecal) :** The intestinal tract of man contains countless rod shaped bacteria known as coliform organisms. Each person discharges from 100 to 400 billion coliform organisms per day, in addition to other kinds of bacteria. Coliforms are harmless to man and are, in fact, useful in destroying organic matter in biological waste treatment processes.

The number of pathogenic organisms present in wastes and polluted waters are few and difficult to isolate. The coliform organism, which is more numerous and more easily tested for, is used as an indicator organism. The presence of coliform in wastewater is a warning signal that other dangerous germs may be present.

The usual procedure for determining the presence of coliforms consists of the presumptive and confirmed tests.

Methods Used :

(i)   Multiple tube fermentation (MPN test).

(ii) Membrane filter technique.

- **Bio-Assy Test :** The results of bio-assy tests are used to evaluate the toxicity of wastewaters to the biological life of the receiving waters.

Specific Objectives : (i) To determine the concentration of a given waste that kill 50% of the test organisms in a specified time period. (ii) To determine the maximum concentration causing no apparent effect on the test organisms in 96 hours.

5.10 OBJECTIVES OF WASTEWATER TREATMENT

Contamination of rivers, lakes, ground water and that of seas and oceans is one of the greatest dangers to human society. On an urgent basis there is a need to implement a series of measures to counteract the contamination of natural waters to conserve its quality.

The objectives of a wastewater treatment system are governed by a number of factors, the nature of the receiving system i.e. whether the discharge is to a sewer, river, lake or marine environment, the legal requirement of meeting any standards imposed by the regulating agency and the desire to protect the aquatic environment. Treatment objectives are largely related to alleviating adverse effects on the environment.

- The removal of organic matter to reduce BOD and COD.
- The removal of suspended matter.
- The removal of toxic matter, although prevention of discharge is generally better and easier than treatment at later stage.
- The removal of nitrates, phosphates.
- pH control.
- Disinfection.
- The plant must either treat the water before discharging or redesign the industrial process so as to remove certain pollutants before discharging into inland surface waters.
- Thermal pollution can be controlled by cooling the waters by cooling towers before discharging or storing the water for its reuse.
- Water reuse may be used for industrial and agricultural purposes, such as culturing fish and cultivating field crops.

Finally, environmental pollution has become a matter of grave importance to the whole world for the survival of humanity.

Albert Einstein rightly said "Two things are unlimited, one the universe, the other man's foolishness". It is certainly foolishness on our part to degrade the environment in order to become more and more civilized.

5.11 PROCESS FLOW DIAGRAM FOR SEWAGE TREATMENT

(Please Refer Appendix – B)

SOLVED EXAMPLES

Example 5.1 : The BOD of sewage incubated for one day at 30°C has been found to be 150 mg/lit. What will be 5 day BOD at 20°C ? Assume K = 0.12 (base 10) at 20°C.   **[May 2011]**

Solution :

Given : $y_1 (BOD_1)_{30°C}$ = 150 mg/lit

K_{20} = 0.12

First find out K_{30}

∴ K_{30} = $K_{20} (1.047)^{T - 20°C}$

= $0.12 (1.047)^{30 - 20}$

= 0.189

Again applying the BOD equation at 30°C,

$y_{t (30)}$ = $L (1 - 10^{-K_{30} \times t})$

150   = $L (1 - 10^{-0.189 \times 1})$

∴   L   = 425.1 mg/lit

This is the ultimate BOD. The value of ultimate BOD does not depend on temperature. Hence, applying BOD equation again at 20°C,

$y_{t (20)}$ = $425.1 (1 - 10^{0.12 \times 5})$

$y_{5 (20)}$ = **318.3 mg/lit**   ... **Ans.**

Example 5.2 : Determine ultimate BOD for a sewage having 5 day BOD at 20°C as 200 mg/lit. Assume the deoxygenation constant as 0.12 per day.

Solution :

$(BOD)_5$ = y_5 = $L - L_5$ = $L (1 - 10^{-K \times 5})$

$(BOD)_5$ = 200 mg/l

∴   200   = $L (1 - 10^{-0.12 \times 5})$

∴   L   = **267 mg/lit**   ... **Ans.**

Example 5.3 : The BOD_5 of a waste has been measured as 450 mg/lit. If rate constant is 0.12, find out ultimate BOD and 3 day BOD at 27°C.

Solution :

Given :

$$(BOD)_5 = 450 \text{ mg/lit}$$

$$K_{20} = 0.12$$

$$\therefore \quad y_5 = L(1 - 10^{-K \cdot t})$$

$$450 = L(1 - 10^{-0.12 \times 5})$$

$$L = 600.9 \text{ mg/lit}$$

To find 3 day BOD at 27°C,

$$K_{27} = 0.12(1.047)^{27 - 20}$$

$$= 0.165$$

$$\therefore \quad y_3 = 600.9(1 - 10^{-0.165 \times 3})$$

$$y_3 = 409.3 \text{ mg/lit}$$

$$\therefore \quad \text{Ultimate BOD, } L = \mathbf{600.9 \text{ mg/lit}} \qquad \text{... Ans.}$$

$$(BOD)_3 \text{ at } 27°C = \mathbf{409.3 \text{ mg/lit}} \qquad \text{... Ans.}$$

Example 5.4 : Calculate the B.O.D. of 5 days and ultimate BOD of the sample from following observations were made on 5% dilution of wastewater.

    (i)   Dissolved oxygen (D.O.) of original sample = 0.8 mg/lit.

    (ii) Dissolved oxygen of aerated water used for dilution = 4.0 mg/lit.

    (iii) Dissolved oxygen of diluted sample after 5 days incubation = 1.0 mg/lit.

Assume deoxygenation coefficient is 0.1.

Solution :

    1.   **5 days B.O.D. :**

        D.O. of diluted sample = D.O. of dilution water × its content

                            + D.O. of wastewater × its content

                         = 4.0 × 0.95 + 0.8 × 0.05

                         = 3.84 mg/lit

        D.O. consumed = D.O. of diluted sample – D.O. of diluted sample after

                                              5 days incubation

                         = 3.84 – 1.0

                         = 2.84 mg/lit

Albert Einstein rightly said "Two things are unlimited, one the universe, the other man's foolishness". It is certainly foolishness on our part to degrade the environment in order to become more and more civilized.

5.11 PROCESS FLOW DIAGRAM FOR SEWAGE TREATMENT

(Please Refer Appendix – B)

SOLVED EXAMPLES

Example 5.1 : The BOD of sewage incubated for one day at 30°C has been found to be 150 mg/lit. What will be 5 day BOD at 20°C ? Assume K = 0.12 (base 10) at 20°C.   **[May 2011]**

Solution :

Given : $y_1 (BOD_1)_{30°C}$ = 150 mg/lit

$$K_{20} = 0.12$$

First find out K_{30}

∴ K_{30} = $K_{20} (1.047)^{T - 20°C}$

$$= 0.12 (1.047)^{30 - 20}$$

$$= 0.189$$

Again applying the BOD equation at 30°C,

$$y_{t (30)} = L (1 - 10^{-K_{30} \times t})$$

$$150 = L (1 - 10^{-0.189 \times 1})$$

∴ L =   425.1 mg/lit

This is the ultimate BOD. The value of ultimate BOD does not depend on temperature. Hence, applying BOD equation again at 20°C,

$$y_{t (20)} = 425.1 (1 - 10^{0.12 \times 5})$$

$$y_{5 (20)} = \textbf{318.3 mg/lit} \qquad \text{... Ans.}$$

Example 5.2 : Determine ultimate BOD for a sewage having 5 day BOD at 20°C as 200 mg/lit. Assume the deoxygenation constant as 0.12 per day.

Solution :

$$(BOD)_5 = y_5 = L - L_5 = L (1 - 10^{-K \times 5})$$

$$(BOD)_5 = 200 \text{ mg/}l$$

∴ 200 = $L (1 - 10^{-0.12 \times 5})$

∴ L =   **267 mg/lit**   ... Ans.

Example 5.3 : The BOD_5 of a waste has been measured as 450 mg/lit. If rate constant is 0.12, find out ultimate BOD and 3 day BOD at 27°C.

Solution :

Given :

$$(BOD)_5 = 450 \text{ mg/lit}$$
$$K_{20} = 0.12$$

$\therefore$
$$y_5 = L\,(1 - 10^{-K \cdot t})$$
$$450 = L\,(1 - 10^{-0.12 \times 5})$$
$$L = 600.9 \text{ mg/lit}$$

To find 3 day BOD at 27°C,

$$K_{27} = 0.12\,(1.047)^{27-20}$$
$$= 0.165$$

$\therefore$
$$y_3 = 600.9\,(1 - 10^{-0.165 \times 3})$$
$$y_3 = 409.3 \text{ mg/lit}$$

$\therefore$ Ultimate BOD, L   = **600.9 mg/lit**   ... **Ans.**

       $(BOD)_3$ at 27°C   = **409.3 mg/lit**   ... **Ans.**

Example 5.4 : Calculate the B.O.D. of 5 days and ultimate BOD of the sample from following observations were made on 5% dilution of wastewater.

(i)   Dissolved oxygen (D.O.) of original sample = 0.8 mg/lit.

(ii)   Dissolved oxygen of aerated water used for dilution = 4.0 mg/lit.

(iii) Dissolved oxygen of diluted sample after 5 days incubation = 1.0 mg/lit.

Assume deoxygenation coefficient is 0.1.

Solution :

1.   **5 days B.O.D. :**

D.O. of diluted sample   =   D.O. of dilution water × its content
$$+ \text{ D.O. of wastewater} \times \text{its content}$$
$$= 4.0 \times 0.95 + 0.8 \times 0.05$$
$$= 3.84 \text{ mg/lit}$$

D.O. consumed   =   D.O. of diluted sample – D.O. of diluted sample after 5 days incubation
$$= 3.84 - 1.0$$
$$= 2.84 \text{ mg/lit}$$

$\therefore$ B.O.D. of 5 days   = D.O. consumed $\times$ Dilution factor

$$= 2.84 \times \frac{100}{5}$$

$$= \textbf{56.80 mg/lit} \hspace{4cm} \textbf{... Ans.}$$

2. Ultimate B.O.D. (L) :

$$Y_t = L [1 - (10)^{-k_D \cdot t}]$$

$\therefore$ Substituting $56.80 = L [1 - (10)^{-0.1 \times 5}]$

$$= L [1 - (10)^{-0.5}]$$

$$= L \left[1 - \frac{1}{(10)^{0.5}}\right] = L \left[1 - \frac{1}{3.16}\right]$$

$$= L [1 - 0.316] = L \times 0.684$$

or $L = \dfrac{56.80}{0.684}$

$$= \textbf{83.04 mg/lit} \hspace{4cm} \textbf{... Ans.}$$

IMPORTANT POINTS

- Bio-chemical Oxygen Demand (BOD).
- Chemical Oxygen Demand (COD).
- Ultimate BOD.
- Sampling analysis of sewage.
- Physical characteristics of sewage.
- Chemical characteristics of sewage.
- Biological characteristics of sewage.
- Objectives of wastewater sewage.

EXERCISE

1. Explain the importance of characterisation of wastewater in its treatment.
2. What are the different constituents of wastewater ? Explain.
3. What precautions should be taken during sampling of wastewater at treatment plant ?
4. What do you understand by Grab sampling and Composite sampling ?
5. What are physical, chemical and biological characteristics of wastewater ?
6. Define BOD. Deduce equation for first stage BOD.

7. Write a note on BOD/COD ratio and its importance.

8. Differentiate between BOD and COD.

9. What is the significance of treatability index ?

10. Differentiate between :

    (i)   DO and BOD (ii) BOD and COD   (iii) Settlable and non-settlable solids.

11. Why is 5 day BOD of a sample at 20°C determined as a standard practice ?

12. Define BOD. Explain in detail the procedure for BOD determination.

13. Explain the importance of the following :

    (i)   DO   (ii) BOD   (iii) COD   (iv) Total solids and its fraction.

14. What are the limitations in BOD determination ?

15. Define treatability index.

16. What is BOD ? What are the limitations of BOD ? Why COD is preferred to BOD ?

17. Derive the BOD equation with usual symbols

    $y_t = L_o (1 - 10^{-Kt})$.

UNIVERSITY QUESTIONS

1. Define and explain BOD and COD.   **(4 M) (May 2011)**

2. Explain how treatability index helps in deciding the types of treatment.
                                                                     (6 M) (Dec. 2010)

3. Explain the necessity of DO fixation while determining DO in water and state procedure for the same.   **(4 M) (May 2009, May 2010)**

4. State the formulae for sodium thiosulphate, ferrous ammonium sulphate and potassium dichromate.   **(6 M) (May 2009)**

5. Explain the use of various equipments used in the experiments of BOD, COD and solids in one sentence.   **(4 M) (May 2009)**

6. State the indicator used in COD test and the colour of end point of titration.
                                                                     (4 M) (May 2009)

7. What are the units of measurements for the following :

    (i) Solids, (ii) Colour, (iii) Test and odour, (iv) Turbidity.   **(6 M) (May 2009)**

8. The BOD_5 of a waste has been measured at 500 mg/l. The rate constant is 0.12. Determine ultimate BOD and 3 day BOD at 27°C.   **(6 M) (May 2010, Dec. 2010)**

9. The BOD of sewage incubated for one day at 30°C has been found to be 150 mg/lit. What will be 5 day BOD at 20°C ? Assume K = 0.12 (base 10 at 20°C).
                                                                     (6 M) (May 2011)

✠ ✠ ✠

Chapter 6

EFFLUENT DISPOSAL AND STREAM SANITATION

The sanitary engineer can design a treatment plant to accomplish as much removal of pollutants as may be required. Ultimate disposal of wastewater effluents will be by :

    (a)   Dilution i.e. disposal in larger bodies like lakes, rivers, estuaries or ocean; and

    (b)   disposal on land.

Disposal by dilution is most common method.

6.1 DISPOSAL BY DILUTION

Disposal by dilution is the process whereby the treated wastewater or effluent from treatment plants is discharged either in large static water bodies like lake or ocean or in moving water bodies like streams or rivers. The discharged sewage, in due course of time, is purified by what is known as *self purification process* of natural waters. The limit of effluent discharge and the degree of treatment of wastewater depend not only upon the quality of raw sewage but also upon the self purification capacity of the river-stream as well as the intended use of the water body.

6.1.1 Conditions Favouring Disposal by Dilution (Without Treatment)

The dilution method without treatment for disposing of the sewage can favourably be adopted under the following conditions :

- Where the wastewater is quite fresh, i.e. it is discharged within 2 to 3 hours of its collection.

- Where the diluting water has a high dissolved oxygen (DO) content.

- Where receiving water body has large volume in comparison to the volume of untreated wastewater.

- Where receiving water is not used for the purpose of navigation or water supply immediately to the downstream side.

- Where the wastewater does not contain industrial wastewater having toxic substances.

- Where the flow currents of the diluting waters are favourable, causing no deposition, destruction of aquatic life.

6.1.2 Conditions Essential for Treatment before Disposal by Dilution

The treatment is essential before disposal of wastewater in the following cases :

- Where the wastewater contain industrial wastes having toxic substances.

- Where the industrial wastewater is in warm condition.

- Where receiving water body has less volume in comparison to the volume of the untreated wastewater. i.e. the volume of diluting water is insufficient.
- Where receiving water is used for drinking purpose.
- Where the receiving water is used for inland navigation.

6.1.3 Standards of Dilution for Discharge of Wastewaters into Rivers

$$\text{Dilution factor} = \frac{\text{The quantity of the diluting water or receiving water}}{\text{The quantity of the wastewater or effluent discharge}}$$

Related to dilution factor, the Royal Commission Report on sewage disposal has laid down certain standards which are indicated in Table 6.1.

Table 6.1 : Standards of Dilution

Sr. No.	Dilution Factor	Standards of Purification Required
1.	Above 500	No treatment is required. The raw sewage or wastewater can be discharged directly in the receiving water.
2.	Between 300 to 500	Primary treatment such as plain sedimentation is essential, and the effluents should not contain suspended solids more than 150 ppm.
3.	Between 150 to 300	Treatment such as sedimentation, screening and chemical precipitation are required. The effluents should not contain suspended solids more than 60 ppm.
4.	Less than 150	The sewage should be treated thoroughly. The effluent should not contain suspended solids more than 30 ppm and its 5 days BOD at 18.3°C should not exceed 20 ppm.

6.2 STREAM AND EFFLUENT STANDARDS

Once the criteria necessary for the protection of the various beneficial uses have been established, it is possible to set standards for surface waters with stipulation that no discharge shall create conditions that violate them. These standards are known as receiving - water or stream standards.

The standards shown in Table 6.1 have been operated in England since 1912, and has also been followed in India without much variance.

As the increasing pollution of surface streams by discharging domestic and industrial wastewaters without bothering to look into the available dilution ratios, it has become essential to limit the concentrations of various pollutants being discharged into the surface water sources along with the sewage and industrial effluents. Therefore, the tolerance limits for such constituent pollutants have been prescribed by various countries, including India. These limits are dependent upon the treatment to domestic and industrial wastewater upto minimum level of "Secondary Treatment".

The Bureau of Indian Standards (BIS), previously known as Indian Standards of Institution (ISI), has therefore laid down its guiding standards for sewage effluents, vide **IS 4764 – 1973** and for industrial effluents vide **IS 2490, 1974** (Refer Table 11.3).

Column No. 4 of Table 11.3 shows tolerance limits for industrial effluents discharged into public sewers prescribed by **IS 3306 – 1974** and Column No. 5 of Table 11.3 shows tolerance limits for inland surface water, when used as raw water for public water supplies and bathing ghats prescribed by **IS 2296 – 1974.**

STREAM SANITATION

6.3 SELF PURIFICATION OF NATURAL STREAMS   [MAY 09, 10, 11]

When pollutants are discharged into a stream, a succession of changes in water quality take place, in the downstream side of the point of pollution. The resulting pattern of change along the stream establishes a well defined profile of pollution and self purification, which again changes with seasons and hydrography.

Whenever a single, heavy charge of putrescible organic matter is added into a clean stream, depending on the hydrography of the stream, the suspended matter is either settled at the bed near the point of discharge, or is carried along with the water to the downstream side.

If the wetted surface of the river bed is sufficiently large, a major portion of the organic load is also removed from the main stream by adsorption. At the same time, the aerobic micro organisms, which utilize the organic pollutants as the source of their food and energy, grow till the food supply is adequate for them, and thus the organic matter is stabilized under aerobic condition. The removal of organics are accomplished by (i) settling and adsorption, and (ii) micro-biological activities.

The intensity of the life activities of the micro-organisms is reflected by the biochemical oxygen demand (BOD). Due to the microbial activities, the oxygen resources of the water are heavily drawn upon; in an overloaded stream, the dissolved oxygen (DO) may be completely exhausted due to these activities.

In course of time and flow, the food supply gets exhausted. The life activities of the microbial population come to an end; and as such the BOD is decreased. The rate of reaeration or the absorption of oxygen from the atmosphere, which at first has lagged behind the rate of oxygen consumption by the micro-organisms, assumes a momentum and very soon takes the lead. The water becomes clear and the stream returns to its original condition. The self purification is thus complete.

In short, when the wastewater or the effluent is discharged into a natural stream, the organic matter is broken down by bacteria to ammonia, nitrates, sulphates, carbon dioxide, etc. In this process of oxidation, the dissolved oxygen content of natural water is utilised. Due to this, deficiency of DO is created. As the excess organic matter is stabilized, the normal cycle will be reestablished in a process known as *self-purification*.

As stated earlier, the self-purification is a very slow process. A heavily polluted stream may have to traverse quite a long distance for many days for the attainment of a significant degree of purification. It may also be noted that, besides the factor noted earlier, many other natural forces play an important role in the natural purification either in favour or against the process.

The various natural forces of purification which affect the process of self purification of stream are summarised below :

(A) Physical forces :

    1. Dilution and dispersion (due to currents),

    2. Sedimentation,

    3. Sunlight.

(B) Bio-chemical forces (chemical forces aided by biological forces)

    1. Oxidation,

    2. Reduction.

(A) Physical Forces :

    1. **Dilution and Dispersion :** When the wastewater is discharged into the large volume of water, it gets rapidly dispersed and diluted. Ofcourse, dispersion depends upon currents. Due to dispersion and dilution, preventing locally high concentration of pollutants and the potential nuisance of sewage is also reduced.

    High velocity of currents improves reaeration which reduces the concentration of pollutants.

    The concentration of the mixture (concentration of sewage and river) is given by

$$C_{Se} \cdot Q_{Se} + C_R \cdot Q_R = C (Q_{Se} + Q_R)$$

or
$$C = \frac{C_{Se} Q_{Se} + C_R Q_R}{Q_{Se} + Q_R} \qquad \ldots (6.1)$$

where,
C_{Se} = Concentration of sewage

C_R = Concentration of river

Q_{Se} = Rate of flow of sewage of concentration C_{Se}

Q_R = Rate of flow of river of concentration C_R

The equation (6.1) is applicable separately to concentrations of different impurities such as oxygen content, suspended solid, BOD and other characteristic content of sewage.

When the dilution ratio is high, large quantities of DO are always available which will reduce the chances of putrefaction and pollutional effects.

2. **Sedimentation :** The settlable solids, if present in sewage effluents, will settle down into the bed of the river (when the stream velocity is lesser than the scour velocity of particles). It will help in self-purification process.

3. **Sunlight :** In presence of sunlight, certain micro-organisms absorbing carbon dioxide and releasing oxygen by a process known as *photosynthesis*. Sunlight acts as a disinfectant and stimulates the growth of algae which produces oxygen during daylight but utilise the same at night. Due to evolution of oxygen in river water will help in the self purification process.

(B) Bio-Chemical Forces :

1. **Oxidation :** An aerobic bacteria oxidises the organic matter which is present in sewage effluent by utilising dissolved oxygen (DO) of the river. The process of oxidation will continue till the organic matter has been completely oxidised. This is the very important action to help in self-purification of rivers.

2. **Reduction :** Reduction occurs in the river or streams due to hydrolysis of the organic matter settled at the bottom either biologically or chemically. Anaerobic bacteria will split the organic matter into liquids and gases and thus paving the way for their ultimate stabilization by oxidation.

The following are the various factors on which these natural forces of purification depend :

- **Available Dissolved Oxygen :** If the larger amount of dissolved oxygen is available in water, then the self purification will occur in better manner.

- **The Amount and Type of Organic Matter Biological Growth Present :** Due to this also rate of self purification will affect. e.g. Algae.

- **Temperature :** At low temperature, the activity of bacteria is less and at higher temperature it is more. At higher temperature the DO concentration is low, so that the self purification takes lesser time and this will lead to anaerobic conditions.

- **Turbulence :** It will help in maintaining aerobic conditions in the river stream. But too much turbulence is not desirable, because it scours the bottom sediment, leads to increasing the turbidity and retards algae growth.

6.3.1 Zones of Pollution in the Stream   [May 2009, 2010; Dec. 2010]

The self-purification process of polluted stream can be divided into the following four zones :

- Zone of degradation or zone of pollution
- Zone of active decomposition
- Zone of recovery and
- Clear water zone.

Table 6.2 is itself explanatory about zones of pollution along a river stream.

Table 6.2 : Zones of Pollution along a Stream

1	2	3	4	5	6
Particulars	**Zones of Pollution**				
Zones	**Clear water**	**Zone of degradation**	**Zone of active decomposition**	**Zone of recovery**	**Clear water zone**
Dissolved oxygen sag curve	100% Saturation level 0%	40%			100% DO
	• No bottom sludge. • No colour. • Clear water	• This zone is just below the point where the sewage is discharged. • Dark and turbid. • Bottom sludge present. • DO is reduced to @ 40% of the saturation value. • Increase in CO_2 content. • Reoxygenation occurs, but slower than deoxygenation • Unfavourable to the development of aquatic life. • Algae dies out. • Fish life may be present. • Bottom worms Tubifex and Limondrilus appear with sewage fungi.	• Heavy polluted zone. • Darker and greyish colour. • DO concentration falls down to zero. • Active anaerobic organic decomposition takes place with the evolution of methane (CH_4), hydrogen sulphide (H_2S), carbon dioxide (CO_2), nitrogen (N_2), etc. • Lot of sludge coming to the surface forming an ugly scum layer at top. • Near the end of this zone, as the decomposition slackens, reaeration sets in and DO again rises to its original level of 40%. • Fish life will be absent. • Bacteria flora will flourish. • At the upper end → anaerobic bacteria present. • At the lower end → anaerobic bacteria present. • Algae and Tubifex will be absent. • Maggots and Psychoda larvae will present. • Protozoa and fungi will first disappear and then reappear.	• Algae reappears as water becomes clearer. • Fungi decreases. • BOD falls down. • DO content rises above 40% of the saturation value. • Protozoa, Rotifers, Crustaceans and large plants like sponges, bryozons etc. also reappear. • Mineralisation is active, with the resulting formation of products like nitrates (NO_4), sulphates (SO_4), carbonates (CO_3) etc.	• Water becomes clearer and attractive in appearance. • DO rises to the saturation level. • Oxygen balance is attained. • Aquatic life prevails. • Recovery is said to be complete in this zone. • Some pathogenic organisms may still survive and remain present, it means that once the river has been polluted, it will not be safe for drinking purpose, unless it is properly treated.

6.3.2 Oxygen Sag or Oxygen Deficit of a Polluted River Stream

[Dec. 2010, May 2010]

The oxygen sag or oxygen deficit (D) at any time in a polluted river stream is defined as *the difference between the actual DO content at that time and the saturation DO content at the water temperature.*

| Oxygen deficit (D) = Saturation DO – Actual DO | ... (6.2)

The normal saturation DO value for fresh water depends upon the temperature and its value varies from 14.62 mg/lit to 7.6 mg/lit for temperature varying between 0°C to 30°C.

Oxygen deficit must be nil to maintain a river-stream in clean conditions.

Oxygen deficit can be found out by knowing rates of deoxygenation and reoxygenation.

Fig. 6.1 shows oxygen deficit or oxygen sag curve.

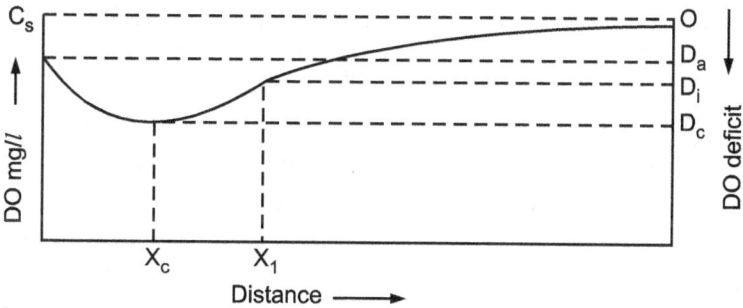

Fig. 6.1 : Oxygen sag curve

Deoxygenation curve :

Organic waste normally undergoes aerobic decomposition in the stream only when the rate of supply of oxygen cannot keep pace with the rate of oxygen demand, the condition within the stream becomes anaerobic. The anaerobic condition however not desirable, as while the aerobic receiving water look reasonably clean and is free from odour, the anaerobic condition makes it black, unsightly and malodourous. The biochemical reactions within the stream exert BOD, resulting in the deoxygenation of the stream. The rate of deoxygenation depends upon the amount of the organic matter remaining to be oxidised at the given time as well as on the temperature of reaction. Deoxygenation curve (refer curve I of Fig. 6.2) is similar to the first stage BOD curve.

Apart from the above, a certain portion of the biodegradable organics get deposited at the bed of the stream.

They undergo anaerobic and benthic decomposition. The products of such decomposition are organic acids and reduced gases. These are further stabilized by the aerobic microorganisms in the upper layer, thereby increasing the BOD of the stream. A small amount of oxygen is also utilized by the higher animals for their respirations.

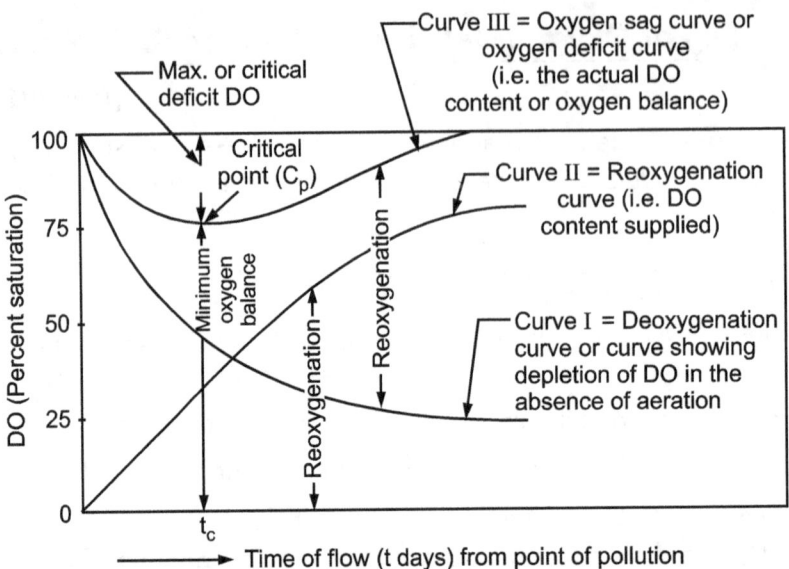

Fig. 6.2

Reoxygenation Curve :   **(Dec. 2010, May 2011)**

The simultaneous replenishment of oxygen in the stream occurs due to the absorption of oxygen from the atmosphere and also due to the release of oxygen by the green plants during photosynthesis. In other words, though the DO content of the stream is gradually consumed due to BOD load, atmosphere supplies oxygen continuously to the water and the process is known as *reaeration* or *reoxygenation of the stream*. The rate of reoxygenation depends upon :

- Depth of the receiving water (more for shallow depth).

- The temperature of water.

- The oxygen deficit below saturation DO.

- The velocity of flow in the stream (rate is more in running stream).

Fig. 6.2 shows curve II called reoxygenation curve. Depending on above factors, the rate of reoxygenation can also be expressed mathematically.

Oxygen Deficit Curve :

The interplay between deoxygenation and reaeration produces a well defined profile (oxygen deficit curve) of the dissolved oxygen in the stream as shown in Fig. 6.2. (Refer curve III). If deoxygenation is more rapid than the reoxygenation, an oxygen deficit results. While algebraically adding the deoxygenation and reoxygenation curves, the resultant curve so obtained is known as the *oxygen sag curve* or the *oxygen deficit curve*.

From Fig. 6.2, we have concluded that when the reoxygenation rate is less than the deoxygenation rate, oxygen deficit will increase and at the point CP (critical point) these two rates are equal and then finally the rate of reoxygenation increases, the oxygen deficit goes on decreasing till it becomes zero.

Streeter–Phelp's Equation :

The entire analysis of super-imposing the rates of deoxygenation and reoxygenation have been carried out mathematically, as suggested by Streeter-Phelp's analysis. This is the classic Streeter-Phelp's oxygen sag equation, which is most commonly used in river analysis. This equation is applied to channels of uniform cross section only, where effects of algae and sludge deposits are negligible.

The following is the form of well-known Streeter-Phelp's equation :

$$D_t = \frac{K_1 L_a}{K_2 - K_1} [(10)^{-K_1 \cdot t} - (10)^{-K_2 \cdot t}] + [D_a \times (10)^{-K_2 \cdot t}] \qquad \ldots (6.3)$$

(By using different values of t in above equation (6.3), the oxygen sag curve can be plotted easily.)

where,

D_t = DO deficit in mg/lit. at any time t

L_a = Initial BOD_L or ultimate first stage BOD of the mix at the point of discharge in mg/lit.

D_a = Initial DO deficit, mg/lit, at the point of waste discharge, at time t = 0.

K_1 = Deoxygenation constant per day; which can be considered as equal to the BOD rate constant.

Also K_1 varies with temperature as per the following relationship :

$$(K_1)_T = (K_1)_{20} \cdot (\theta_{K_1})^{T-20} \qquad \ldots (6.4)$$

Where,

$(K_1)_{20}$ = Deoxygenation constant at a temperature of T°C, and θ_{K_1} = A temperature coefficient = usually 1.047 for K_1 in the temperature range of 15°C to 30°C.

The value of K_1 may vary from 0.12 per day for treated wastewater to 0.39 per day for a strong waste; while values of $(K_1)_{20}$ vary between 0.1 to 0.2, generally taken as 0.1

K_2 = Reaeration or Reoxygenation coefficient per day. It can be calculated by the field tests by using equation :

$$(K_2)_{20} = 4.75 \, V/(H)^{3/2} \qquad \ldots (6.5)$$

where, $(K_2)_{20}$ = Reaeration coefficient at 20°C per day

V = Mean velocity in m/sec.

and H = Average depth of the stream in m.

K_2 varies with temperature as per the equation :

$$(K_2)_T = (K_2)_{20} \cdot \theta_{K_2}^{(T-20)} \qquad \qquad ... (6.6)$$

where, θ_{K_2} = Reaeration temperature coefficient, usually 1.0241.

Typical values of reaeration constants are given in Table 6.3.

Table 6.3 : Reaeration Constants at 20°C

Sr. No.	Type of Water Body	$(K_2)_{20}$ Per Day
1.	Small ponds and back waters	0.05 – 0.10
2.	Large lakes and sluggish streams	0.10 – 0.15
3.	Large streams of low velocity	0.15 – 0.20
4.	Large streams of normal velocity	0.20 – 0.30
5.	Swift streams	0.30 – 0.50
6.	Rapids and waterfalls	> 0.50

The Critical Time (t_c) :

The critical time is a time after which the minimum DO occurs and the same can be found by differentiating equation (6.3) and equating it to zero. Thus, we obtain

$$\therefore \qquad t_c = \left[\frac{1}{K_2 - K_1}\right] \log\left[\left\{\frac{K_1 \cdot L_a - K_2 D_a + K_1 D_a}{K_1 \cdot L_a}\right\} \frac{K_2}{K_1}\right] \qquad ... (6.7)$$

Critical or Maximum Oxygen Deficit :

The critical or maximum oxygen deficit is given by

$$D_c = \frac{K_1 L_a}{K_2} [10]^{-K_1 \cdot t_c} \qquad ... (6.8)$$

Self Purification Constant or Self Purification Ratio (f) :

It is the ratio of $\dfrac{K_2}{K_1}$ and represented as (f) and is called the self purification constant.

The values of self purification constant are given in Table 6.4.

Table 6.4 : Self Purification Constants

Sr. No.	Type of Water Body	$f = \dfrac{K_2}{K_1}$
1.	Small ponds and back waters	0.5 – 1.0
2.	Large lakes, sluggish streams and impounding reservoirs	1.0 – 1.5
3.	Large streams of low velocity	1.5 – 2.0
4.	Large streams of normal velocity	2.0 – 3.0
5.	Swift streams	3.0 – 5.0
6.	Rapids and waterfalls	above 5.0

By substituting $\dfrac{K_2}{K_1}$ = f in the equation (6.7), we obtain,

$$t_c = \frac{1}{K_1(f-1)} \log \left[\left\{ 1 - (f-1)\frac{D_a}{L_a} \right\} f \right] \qquad \ldots (6.9)$$

Also from equation (6.8), we obtain,

$$D_c = \frac{L_a}{f} [10]^{-K_1 \cdot t_c} \qquad \ldots (6.10)$$

Taking log of both sides, we obtain,

$$\log D_c = \log \frac{L_a}{f} - K_1 \cdot t_c \qquad \ldots (6.11)$$

Substituting the value of t_c from equation (6.9) in equation (6.11), we obtain,

$$\log D_c = \log \frac{L_a}{f} - \frac{K_1 \cdot 1}{K_1(f-1)} \log \left[f \left\{ 1 - (f-1)\frac{D_a}{L_a} \right\} \right]$$

or $$\log D_c = \log \frac{L_a}{f} - \frac{1}{(f-1)} \log \left[f \left\{ 1 - (f-1)\frac{D_a}{L_a} \right\} \right]$$

or $$(f-1) \left[\log \frac{L_a}{f} - \log D_c \right] = \log \left[f \left\{ 1 - (f-1)\frac{D_a}{L_a} \right\} \right]$$

or $$\log \left[\frac{\frac{L_a}{f}}{DC} \right]^{f-1} = \log \left[f \left\{ 1 - (f-1)\frac{D_a}{L_a} \right\} \right]$$

or
$$\left(\frac{L_a}{D_c \cdot f_a}\right)^{f-1} = f\left[1 - (f-1)\frac{D_a}{L_a}\right] \qquad \text{... (6.12)}$$

This is important equation, in which L_a is the first stage BOD of mixture of wastewater and stream. The self purification constant (f) corresponds to the temperature of mixture of wastewater and stream at the outfall.

The solubility of oxygen in water which affects the reoxygenation, is a function of temperature. Appendix A gives the values of DO in fresh water at various temperatures.

Distance at Which Oxygen Deficit Occurs :

The distance, at which the critical DO deficit will occur in the downstream, can be calculated by following equation :

$$\boxed{\text{Distance at which oxygen deficit occurs} \ = \ \text{Velocity of river} \times \text{Travel time}} \qquad \text{... (6.13)}$$

Limit of Dissolved Oxygen (DO) in the Stream :

To avoid anaerobic decomposition of the organic wastes and also to provide adequate support to the aquatic life, *the DO is not allowed to fall below about 3 mg/lit.* This information fixes the allowable maximum DO saturation deficit.

DISPOSAL INTO SEA

6.4 DISPOSAL OF WASTEWATER INTO SEA WATER

Sea disposal is typically accomplished by submarine outfalls that consists of a long section of pipe to transport the wastewater some distance from shore and in the best examples, a diffuser section to dilute the waste with wastewater. Diffusers are one of the most efficient methods of providing initial dilution of a waste in any waterway.

The saturation concentration of DO in water decreases with increasing salt content. Because of this, sea water normally contains 20% less oxygen than that contained in fresh water of a river stream.

Sleek :

The specific gravity of sea water is larger than that of sewage and temperature of sea water is lesser than the sewage temperature. Due to this reason, when the sewage is discharged into the sea water, the lighter and warmer sewage will rise upto the surface, this will result in spreading of the sewage at the top, surface of sea in a thin film or 'sleek'.

Sludge Banks :

Sea water contains a large amount of dissolved matter which chemically react with the sewage solids, when thrown into sea water, resulting in precipitating some of the sewage solids, giving a milky appearance to sea water and forming **Sludge Banks.**

These sludge banks and the thin milky layer produce offensive hydrogen sulphide (H_2S) gas by reacting with the sulphate rich water of the sea. The reaeration in sea water is slower, also we know that, the oxygen content of sea water is less than that of fresh water and the sea contains too larger volumes of water, most of these deficiencies can be overcome if the sewage is discharged deep into the sea much away from the coast line. To avoid the backing up and spreading of sewage on the sea shore, the sewage should not be disposed during high tides.

In such a case, to hold the sewage during high tides, the large sized tanks may therefore be constructed near the outfall.

The following points should be considered whole discharging sewage into the sea:

- The sewage should be discharged in deep sea (Generally 1 to 1.5 km away from the shore). As we have seen earlier, this is accomplished by outfall that consists of a long section of pipe to transport the wastewater some distance from the shore. Such outfalls are placed on a firm rocky foundation so it protects from wave action, floating debris, etc. Fig. 6.3 shows the cast iron pipe used for this purpose which is encased in thick special type of concrete. (For making such a special type of concrete, generally pozzolana cement is used).

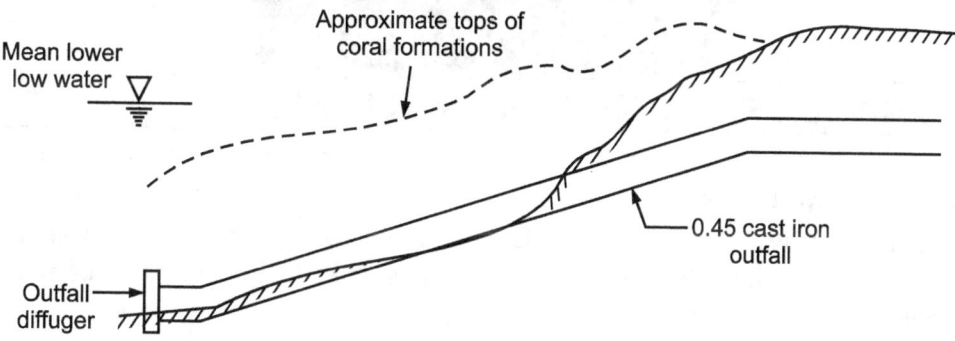

Fig. 6.3 : General layout of outfall

- The diffuser should be provided at the end of section for the proper dilution of waste with sea water.

- The sewage should be released at a minimum depth of 3 to 5 metres below the water level.

- At time of deciding the position of outfall point, the direction of wind, velocity, sea currents etc. should be carefully taken into consideration.

The following Table 6.5 shows standards for wastewater effluents to be discharged into marine coast. So while discharging industrial effluent into sea water the standards shown in the following table should be considered to control the effluent in respect of the quality of the effluents.

Table 6.5 : BIS (ISI) Standards for Wastewater Effluents to be Discharged into Marine Coasts (IS : 1968 – 1976)

Sr. No.	Constituent Pollutant Contained in the Wastewater Effluent	Tolerance Limit
1.	pH	5.5 to 9.0
2.	BOD_5	100 mg/lit
3.	COD	250 mg/lit
4.	Total suspended solids	100 mg/lit
5.	Oil and grease	20 mg/lit

Table 6.6 shows the comparison of sewage dilution by sea and stream.

Table 6.6 : Comparison between Sea and Stream Water Dilution

Sr. No.	Item	Sea Water	Stream Water
1.	DO	20% less than stream water	More DO
2.	Specific gravity	High	Low
3.	Quantity of solids in suspension	Large	Small
4.	Maximum sewage load	No limit	Depends on stream discharge.

DISPOSAL INTO LAKES

6.5 DISPOSAL OF WASTEWATER INTO LAKES

In many inland locations where nearby streams are not available, it may be necessary to discharge treated wastewater into lakes.

Actually, disposal of wastewaters in lakes is much more harmful than its disposal in flowing streams and rivers. So a study of the lake system is essential. The study of lake pollution is called *limnology*. The major lake pollutant is phosphorus which is largely contained in industrial as well as domestic wastewaters. As phosphorus is a major pollutant, there needs a special study of phosphorous in water quality management of lakes.

Stratification in Large Lakes :

For large lakes the complete mixing assumption cannot be applied. In such cases, a different model should be used based on the physical phenomena found to exist in the water system under study. Particularly significant is the vertical stratification common during certain seasons of the year. A complete mix model would not be a good representation of a stratified lake because waste would not normally distribute itself over the entire lake volume.

The water of a lake gets stratified during summers and winters in the following way :

During summer season, due to sunlight and warm air, the surface water of lake gets heated. Such heated water being lighter, therefore remains in upper layers near the surface, until mixed downward by turbulence from waves, winds, boats etc. Since, such turbulence is only to a limited depth from below the water surface, so the top layers of water in the lake becomes well mixed and aerobic. This top layer is called *epilimnion zone*. In other words, epilimnion zone is fairly uniform in temperature because of mixing by wind action. The lower depth, which remains cooler, poorly mixed and anaerobic, is called *hypolimnion zone*. The intermediate zone or a dividing line is called *thermocline*. The thermocline is a zone of significant temperature change and is extremely resistant to mixing. Fig. 6.4 shows summer stratification in a lake.

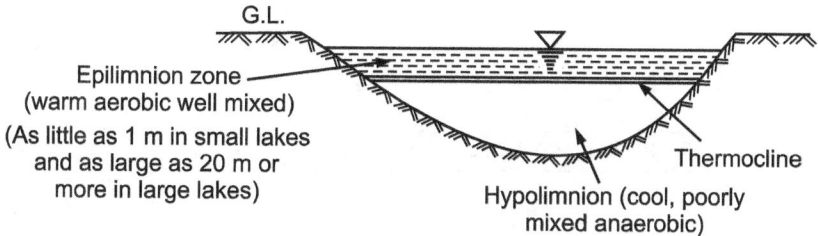

Fig. 6.4 : Summer stratification in a lake

In colder season, the epilimnion cools, until it is more dense than the hypolimnion. The surface water, then sinks, causing *'over turning or turn over'*. In other words, during the fall, temperatures drops, decreasing the amount of stratification until wind action may again completely mix the lake waters. This phenomenon is known as the fall turnover. In regions of freezing temperatures, when the temperature drops below 4°C, the above process of turnover stops, because water is most dense at this temperature. Fig. 6.5 shows winter stratification in a lake.

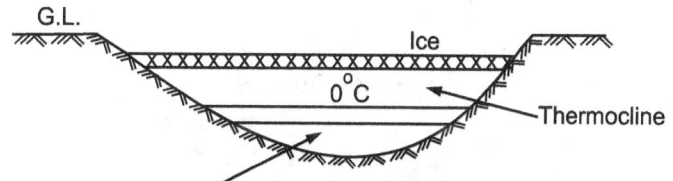

Fig. 6.5 : Winter stratification in a lake

DISPOSAL ON LAND

6.6 DISPOSAL BY LAND TREATMENT

In this method, the sewage effluent, either raw or partly treated is generally disposed on land, this method is called disposal by land treatment. The percolating water may either join the water-table or is collected below by a system of under drains. This method can then be used for irrigating crops. The sewage adds to the fertilising value of the land and crops can be profitably raised on such land. Due to this, the disposal by land treatment is also sometimes called as sewage farming.

Effluent Irrigation (Or Board Irrigation) :

The chief consideration in 'effluent irrigation' is the successful disposal of sewage. The raw or settled sewage is discharged on a vacant land, which is provided underneath, with a system of properly laid under-drains. These under-drains usually consist of 15 to 20 cm diameter porous tile pipes laid open jointed at a spacing of 12 to 30 m. The effluent filtered through the soil pores which is collected in these drains generally of small quantity and well stabilised, and can be easily disposed into some natural water courses, without any further treatment.

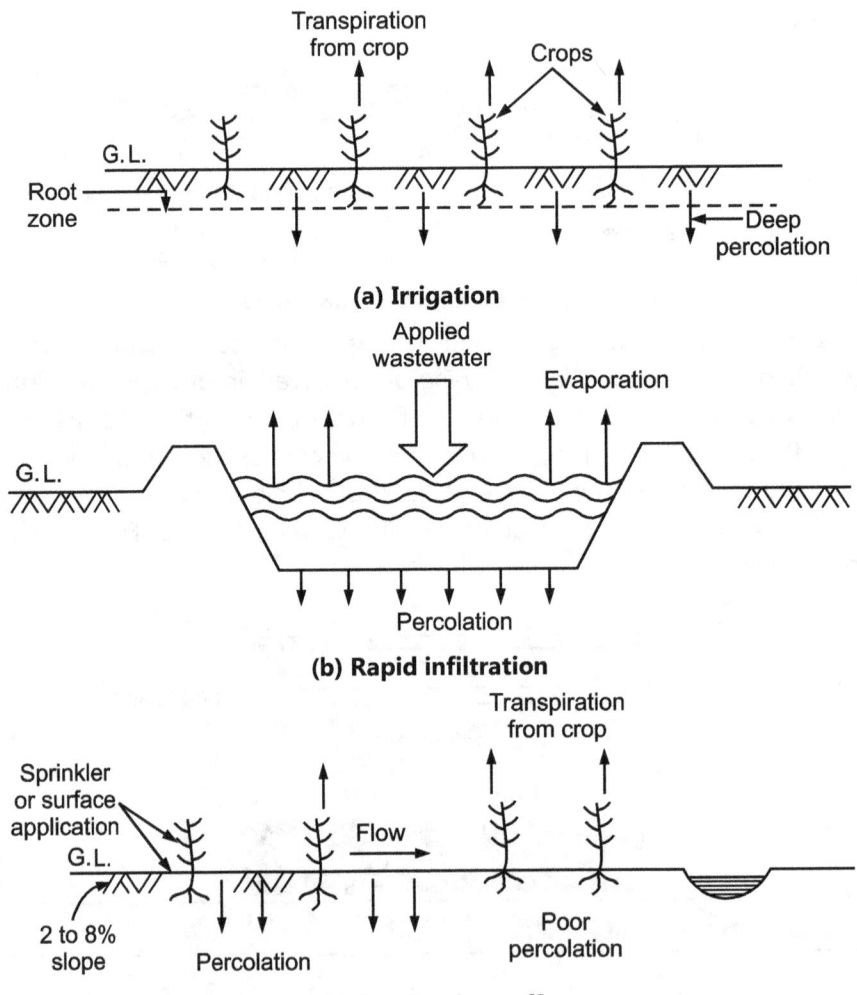

(a) Irrigation

(b) Rapid infiltration

(c) Overland runoff

Fig. 6.6 : Three principal processes of land treatment

Sewage Farming : The chief consideration in 'sewage farming' is the successful growing of the crops. In this case, the stress is laid upon the use of sewage effluents for irrigating crops and increasing the fertility of the soil. The pre-treatment in this case is necessary to remove ingradients which may prove harmful and toxic to the plants.

So for all practical purposes, both these terms (effluent irrigation and sewage farming) are used as synonyms.

The three principal processes of land treatment are as follows :

- Broad irrigation/sewage farming;
- Rapid infiltration and
- Overland runoff.

These three principal processes of land treatment are shown in Fig. 6.6.

Irrigation process is discussed in detail under article 6.6.2.

Rapid Infiltration : The rapid infiltration process involves spreading wastewater in shallow, unlined earthen basins and allowing the liquid to pass through the porous bottom and percolate towards the ground water. Rapid infiltration may be used for waste disposal, ground water recharge or both. Many of the rapid infiltration systems in current use were designed primarily to dispose of unwanted wastewater. But now-a-days, the process has been used as a means of aquifer recharge or as an advanced wastewater treatment, with the percolated wastewater being collected for reuse. Fig. 6.7 shows different techniques of rapid infiltration of wastewater. See rapid infiltration technique in Fig. 6.7 (a).

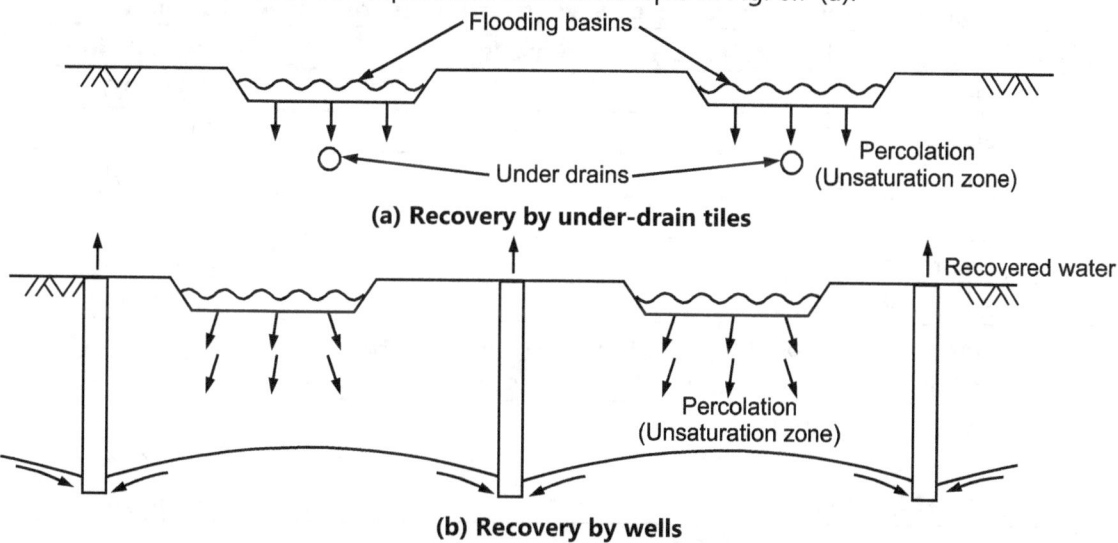

(a) Recovery by under-drain tiles

(b) Recovery by wells

Fig. 6.7 : Rapid infiltration of wastewater

Overland Runoff : This technique is applied when soils have poor permeability.

Recommended Doses for Sewage Farming : When raw or partly treated sewage is applied on to the land, a part of it evaporates, and the remaining portion percolates through the ground soil. While percolating through the soil, the suspended particles present in the sewage are caught in the soil voids. If proper aeration of these voids is maintained, the organic sewage solids get oxidised by aerobic process. Such aerobic condition will more likely prevail if the soil is sufficiently porous and if the soil is of sticky and fine grained materials, then the void spaces will soon get choked up and due to this developing anaerobic decomposition of organic matter and evolution of foul gases. So dosing of sewage depends on type of soil. Table 6.7 shows recommended doses for sewage farming.

Table 6.7 : Recommended Doses for Sewage Farming

Sr. No.	Type of Soil	Doses of Sewage in Cubic Metres per Hectare Per Day	
		Raw Sewage	Settled Sewage
1.	Sandy soil	120 – 150	220 – 250
2.	Sandy loam	90 – 100	150 – 200
3.	Loam	60 – 80	100 – 150
4.	Clayey loam	40 – 50	50 – 100
5.	Clayey	30 – 45	30 – 50

6.6.1 Quality Standards

IS : 3307 – 1965 laid down the standards of sewage effluents for their discharge on land for irrigation. Table 6.8 shows Indian Standards of sewage for sewage farming.

Table 6.8 : Indian Standards of Sewage Effluents for Sewage Farming

Sr. No.	Characteristics of Wastewater	Prescribed Limit
1.	pH	5.5 to 9.0
2.	BOD_5	500 mg/lit
3.	Total dissolved solids	2100 mg/lit
4.	Oil and grease	30 mg/lit
5.	Chlorides (as Cl)	600 mg/lit
6.	Sulphates	1000 mg/lit
7.	Percentage of sodium with respect to total content of sodium, calcium, magnesium and potassium	60%
8.	Radioactive materials (i) α-emitters (ii) β-emitters	$10^{-9}\,\mu C/ml$ $10^{-8}\,\mu C/ml$

Favourable Conditions for Land Treatment :

The effluent irrigation method for disposal of sewage can be adopted favourably under the following conditions :

• Land treatment is the only alternative, when natural rivers or streams are not located in the vicinity.

• Cash crops can be easily grown on sewage farms.

• The use of sewage for irrigating crops is good in case of irrigation where water is scarcely available.

• Land treatment is much favoured, when the land available for disposal is porous, such as sandy, loamy or alluvial soil, or soft moorum. Such soils are easily aerated and it is easy to maintain aerobic conditions in them. It should not be made of heavy retentive soils like clay, etc. which prevent easy aeration of the soil, voids, and thus creating anaerobic conditions.

- This method will prove useful in areas where rainfall is low. Due to this, it is easy to maintain good absorption capacity of the soil.
- Where large areas of open land are available, broad irrigation with the help of sewage effluent may be practised.
- This treatment is favoured when subsoil water table is low, where rate of percolation may be quite high.

6.6.2 Methods of Application of Sewage Effluent to Farms

Sewage effluent can be applied to land by the following methods :

1. Surface Irrigation (Broad Irrigation)
2. Sub-surface Irrigation.
3. Sprinkler or Spray Irrigation.

The sewage effluents can be used for irrigating farms similarly as irrigation water is used for farming. Fig. 6.8 shows different irrigation techniques.

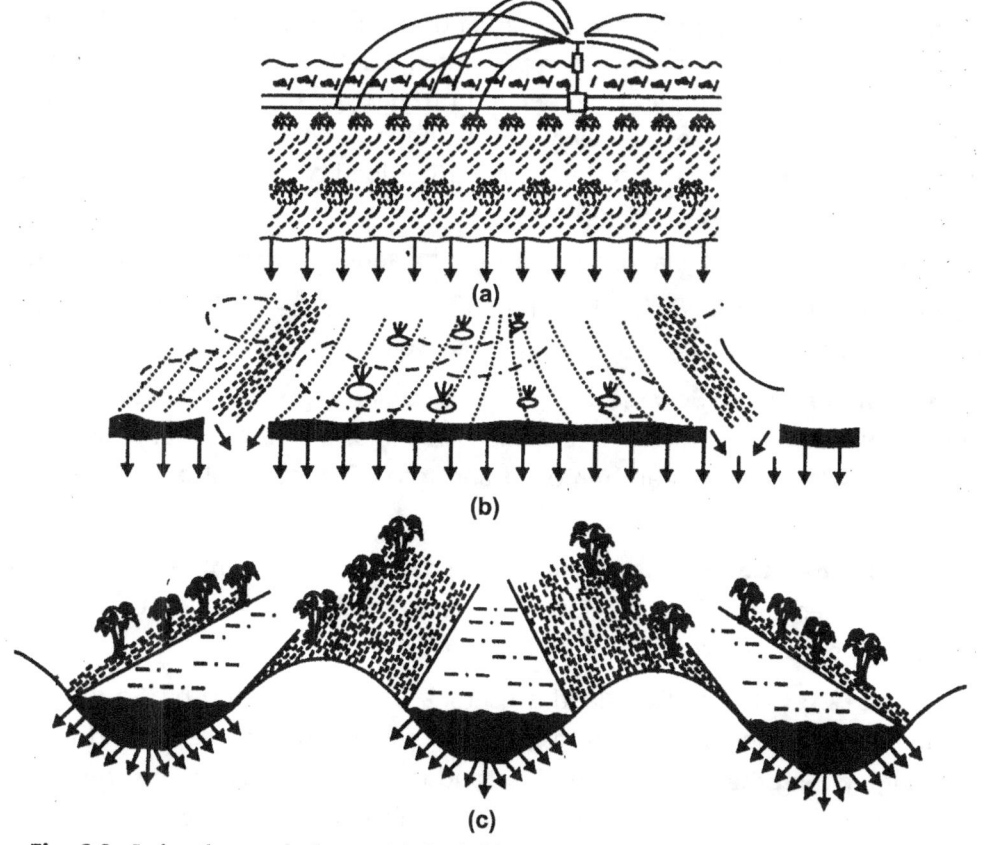

Fig. 6.8 : Irrigation techniques (a) Sprinkler, (b) Flooding, (c) Ridge and furrow

1. **Surface Irrigation or Broad Irrigation :** In this method, sewage is applied in different ways on the surface of the land. The following are the different types related to mode of application.

    - Free flooding
    - Border flooding
    - Check flooding
    - Furrow irrigation method and
    - Basin flooding.

2. **Sub-Surface Irrigation :** In this method, sewage effluent is applied through open-jointed pipes to root zone of crops.

3. **Sprinkler or Spray Irrigation :** In this method, sewage is spread over the land through nozzles, which are fixed at the tips of the pipe carrying sewage under pressure. This method generally not used in India, as this process is costly one.

6.6.3 Sewage Sickness

Due to continuous application of sewage on land, the total pores of the soil get clogged with sewage matter retained in them, thus preventing oxidation and causing noxious smells. The time taken for such a clogging will depend on the type of soil (Porous sandy soils will clog less as compared to heavy clayey soils) and on the load of sewage. So due to continuous loading land is unable to take any further load of sewage. This phenomenon of soil is called as 'sewage sickness' of land.

To avoid 'sewage sickness' of a land, the following preventive measures may be adopted :

- **Choice of Land :** The land that may be chosen should be having higher permeability such as sandy or loamy, clayey land should be avoided.

- **Primary Treatment of Sewage :** To avoid clogging of soil pores, sewage should be disposed of, only after primary treatment (screening, grit removal and sedimentation). Due to this settlable solids are removed and also BOD load will be reduced by about 30%.

- **Under Drainage of Soil :** The sewage is being disposed of, can be better drained, if a system of under-drains is laid below to collect the effluent. Due to this, minimise the possibility of sewage sickness.

- **Provision of Extra Land :** Extra land is useful as reserve or stand-by. So the land being used for disposal should be given rest, periodically and using reserve land for diverting the sewage during the period of the first land is at rest. During the rest period, the sick land should be properly ploughed so that it is broken up and aerated.

- **Rotations of Crops :** By planting different crops in rotation instead of growing single type of crop, minimise the chances of sewage sickness.

- **Applying Shallow Depths :** Sewage should be applied in thin layers. Greater depth of sewage on a land does not allow the soil to receive the sewage satisfactorily and therefore, chances of sewage sickness increases.

6.7 COMPARISON OF DILUTION AND LAND DISPOSAL METHOD FOR DISPOSAL OF SEWAGE

Sr. No.	Item	Dilution Method	Land Disposal Method
1.	Cost	In cities and urban areas which are generally situated near rivers or ocean, this method is economical, as cost of land is very high.	In rural areas, this method is economical as land value is less.
2.	Management	This is a simple method and does not require too much of management.	Good management is required in case if cost of land is high. Due to good management, some return may be available due to sewage farming.
3.	Pumping	Requires nil or small head pumping.	Requires high head pumping.
4.	Hot climatic areas	Not suitable, as DO content due to hot climate is reduced.	This method is generally suitable in hot climatic areas.
5.	Pollution	Rivers are polluted due to sewage.	This method saves rivers from pollution.

6.8 RIVER CLASIFICATION AS PER MOEF, GOVERNMENT OF INDIA

Classes	No Development Zone for Any Type of Industries	Only Green & Orange Category of Industries with Pollution Control Devices.	Any Type of Industries (Red, Orange, Green) with Pollution Control Devices
A-I Origin to Dam	3 km on the either side of river	From 3 km to 8 km from river (H.F.L.) on either side	Beyond 8 km from river (H.F.L.) on either side.
A-II	1 km on the either side of river.	From 1 km to 2 Km from (H.F.L.) on either side	Beyond 2 km from river (H.F.L.) on either side.

Contd...

A-III Fisheries and wildlife	1/2 km on the either side of river	From 1/2 km to 1 km from river (H.F.L.) on either side	Beyond 1 km from river (H.F.L.) on either side.
A-IV Agricultural and Industrial usages.	1/2 km on the either side of river	From 1/2 to 1 km from river (H.F.L.) on either side	Beyond 1 km from river (HFL.) High Flood Line on either side

6.9 EFFLUENT DISCHARGE STANDARDS

Please refer article 11.4.

SOLVED EXAMPLES ON SEWAGE DISPOSAL IN STREAM OR RIVER

Example 6.1 : The domestic sewage of a town is to be discharged into a river stream after treatment. Find out the BOD of the diluted water, if the quantity of sewage produced per day is 10 million litres, having BOD as 300 mg/lit, the discharge in the river is 210 litres/sec and it's BOD is 9 mg/lit.

Solution :

Given : Rate of flow of sewage, $Q_{Se} = 10 \times 10^6$ litres.

$$= \frac{10 \times 10^6}{24 \times 60 \times 60}$$

$$= 115.74 \text{ litres/sec.}$$

Rate of flow of the river,

$$Q_R = 210 \text{ litres/sec}$$

BOD of sewage, $C_{Se} = 300$ mg/lit

BOD of river, $C_R = 9$ mg/lit

BOD of diluted mixture can be calculated by using equation (6.1).

∴   BOD of diluted mixture,

$$C = \frac{C_{Se} \cdot Q_{Se} + C_R \cdot Q_R}{Q_{Se} + Q_R} = \frac{300 \times 115.74 + 9 \times 210}{115.74 + 210}$$

$$C = \textbf{112.4 mg/lit} \qquad \qquad \text{... Ans.}$$

Example 6.2 : The sewage of a town is to be discharged into a river stream. The population of town is 65000. Determine the maximum permissible effluent BOD and the percentage purification required in the treatment plant, given the following data :

D.W.F. of sewage : 160 lit/capita/day

BOD concentration per capita : 0.075 kg per day.

Minimum flow of stream : 0.23 m³/sec.

BOD of stream : 3 mg/lit.

Maximum BOD of stream on downstream : 5 mg/lit.

Solution :

Given : Rate of flow of sewage,

$$Q_{Se} = 160 \times 65000 \text{ litres/day}$$

$$= \frac{160 \times 65000}{24 \times 60 \times 60 \times 1000}$$

$$= 0.12 \text{ m}^3/\text{sec.}$$

Rate of flow of stream, $Q_R = 0.23$ m³/s.

BOD of sewage, $C_{Se} = ?$

BOD of stream, $C_R = 3$ mg/lit.

BOD of mixture, $C = 5$ mg/lit.

BOD of sewage can be calculated by using equation (6.1).

∴   BOD of the mixture on the downstream is

$$C = \frac{C_{Se}\,Q_{Se} + C_R\,Q_R}{Q_{Se} + Q_R}$$

$$5 = \frac{C_{Se} \times 0.12 + 3 \times 0.23}{0.12 + 0.23}$$

$$1.75 = 0.12\,C_{Se} + 0.69$$

∴ $C_{Se} = 8.83$ mg/lit

Now, BOD per capita per day = $0.075 \times 1000 \times 1000$

$$= 75000 \text{ mg/day}$$

Sewage D.W.F. $= 160$ litres/day

∴   Actual BOD of effluent $= \dfrac{75000}{160}$

$$= 468.75 \text{ mg/lit}$$

∴   Percentage purification required

$$= \frac{468.75 - 8.83}{468.75} \times 100$$

$$= \mathbf{98.12\%} \qquad\qquad \text{... Ans.}$$

Example 6.3 : A stream saturated with DO has a flow of 1.4 m³/sec, BOD of 5 mg/lit and rate constant of 0.3 per day. It receives an effluent discharge of 0.29 m³/s having BOD 25 mg/lit, DO 6 mg/lit and rate 0.12 per day. The average velocity of flow of the stream is 0.20 m/sec. Calculate the DO deficit at point 20 km and 50 km downstream. Assume that the temperature is 20°C throughout and BOD is measured at 5 days. Take saturation DO at 20°C as 9.17 mg/lit.

Solution :

Given : Rate of flow of stream, Q_R = 1.4 m³/sec.

BOD of stream, C_R = 5 mg/lit.

Rate of flow of effluent, Q_{Se} = 0.29 m³/sec.

BOD of effluent, C_{Se} = 25 mg/lit.

BOD of mixture can be calculated by using equation (6.1).

$\therefore$ BOD of the mixture, $C = \dfrac{C_{Se}\, Q_{Se} + C_R\, Q_R}{Q_{Se} + Q_R}$

$$= \frac{25 \times 0.29 + 5 \times 1.4}{0.29 + 1.4}$$

$$= 8.432 \text{ mg/lit}$$

Now, $Y_5 = C = L_a\, [1 - 10^{-K_1 \cdot t}\,]$

$8.432 = L_a\, [1 - 10^{-0.13 \times 5}]$

$L_a = 10.86 \text{ mg/lit}$

Again saturation DO of stream at 20°C, $(DO)_R$ = 9.17 mg/lit.

DO effluent, $(DO)_{Se}$ = 6 mg/lit

$\therefore$ $(DO)_{mix} = \dfrac{(DO)_{Se} \cdot Q_{Se} + (DO)_R \cdot Q_R}{Q_{Se} + Q_R}$

$$= \frac{6 \times 0.29 + 9.17 \times 1.4}{0.29 + 1.4}$$

$$= 8.63 \text{ mg/lit}$$

$\therefore$ Initial DO deficit (D_a) = 9.17 – 8.63 = 0.54 mg/lit

(a) DO deficit at a point 20 km downstream :

$$t = \frac{\text{Distance}}{\text{Velocity}} = \frac{20 \times 1000}{0.20 \times 60 \times 60 \times 24}$$

$$= 1.16 \text{ days}$$

Using Streeter-Phelp's equation (6.3),

$$D_t = \frac{K_1 \cdot L_a}{K_2 - K_1} \left[(10)^{-K_1 \cdot t} - (10)^{-K_2 \cdot t} \right] + \left[D_a \times (10)^{-K_2 \cdot t} \right]$$

$$= \frac{0.13 \times 10.86}{0.3 - 0.13} \left[(10)^{-0.13 \times 1.16} - (10)^{-0.3 \times 1.16} \right] + \left[0.54 \times (10)^{-0.3 \times 1.16} \right]$$

$$= 8.3 \left[0.71 - 0.448 \right] + \left[0.54 \times (-0.448) \right]$$

$$= 2.168 - 0.24$$

$$= \mathbf{1.93\ mg/lit} \qquad\qquad\qquad \text{... Ans.}$$

(b) DO deficit at a point 50 km downstream :

$$t = \frac{50 \times 1000}{0.20 \times 60 \times 60 \times 24}$$

$$= 2.894\ \text{days}$$

$$D_t = \frac{0.13 \times 10.86}{0.3 - 0.13} \left[(10)^{-0.13 \times 2.894} - (10)^{-0.3 \times 2.894} \right]$$

$$+ \left[0.54 \times (10)^{-0.3 \times 2.894} \right]$$

$$= 8.3 \left[0.42 - 0.135 \right] + \left[0.54 \times (-0.135) \right]$$

$$= 2.37 - 0.0729$$

$$= \mathbf{2.29\ mg/lit} \qquad\qquad\qquad \text{... Ans.}$$

Example 6.4 : A city discharges 1700 litres per second of sewage into a stream. The minimum rate of flow of stream is 7000 litres per second. The temperature of sewage as well as water is 20°C. The 5 day BOD at 20°C for sewage is 250 mg/lit and that of the stream is 90% of the saturation DO If the minimum DO to be maintained in the stream is 4.5 mg/lit, find out the degree of sewage treatment required. Assume the deoxygenation coefficient as 0.1 and reoxygenation coefficient as 0.3. Take saturation DO at 20°C as 9.17 mg/lit .

Solution :

Given :

Rate of flow of sewage, Q_{Se} = 1700 litres/sec.

Rate of flow of stream, Q_R = 7000 litres/sec

BOD of river, C_R = 1 mg/lit.

Deoxygenation constant (K_1) = 0.1

Reoxygenation constant (K_2) = 0.3

Minimum DO maintained in the stream = 4.5 mg/lit

Saturation DO at 20°C = 9.17 mg/lit.

DO content of the stream

$$= 90\% \text{ of the saturation DO}$$

$$= \frac{90}{100} \times 9.17$$

$$= 8.25 \text{ mg/lit}$$

DO of the mix at the start point

$$= \frac{(DO)_{Se} \times Q_{Se} + (DO)_R \times Q_R}{Q_{Se} + Q_R}$$

$$= \frac{0 \times 1700 + 8.25 \times 7000}{1700 + 7000} \qquad \text{(Assuming DO of sewage as zero)}$$

$$= 6.83 \text{ mg/lit}$$

∴   Initial DO deficit,

$$D_a = \text{Saturation DO} - \text{DO of mix.}$$

∴ $$D_a = 9.17 - 6.83$$

∴ $$D_a = 2.34 \text{ mg/lit}$$

Minimum DO to be maintained in the stream

$$= 4.5 \text{ mg/lit}$$

∴   Maximum permissible saturation deficit (critical DO deficit),

$$D_c = 9.17 - 4.5$$

$$= 4.67 \text{ mg/lit}$$

The first stage BOD of mixture of sewage and stream (L_a) can be calculated by using equation (6.12).

$$\left[\frac{L_a}{D_c \cdot f}\right]^{f-1} = f\left[1 - (f-1)\frac{D_a}{L_a}\right]$$

$$f = \frac{K_2}{K_1} = \frac{0.3}{0.1} = 3$$

Now, $$\left[\frac{L_a}{4.67 \times 3}\right]^{3-1} = 3\left[1 - (3-1)\frac{2.34}{L_a}\right]$$

$$\left[\frac{L_a}{14.01}\right]^{2} = 3\left[1 - \frac{4.68}{L_a}\right]$$

Solving by hit and trial, we get

$$L_a = 21 \text{ mg/lit}$$

Now using
$$Y_t = L_a [1 - 10^{-K_1 \cdot t}]$$

∴ Maximum permissible 5 day BOD of the mix at 20°C,

$$Y_5 = 21 [1 - 10^{-0.1 \times 5}]$$

$$= 14.36 \text{ mg/lit}$$

The permissible BOD_5 of discharged wastewater can be calculated by using equation (6.1).

∴
$$C = \frac{C_{Se} Q_{Se} + C_R Q_R}{Q_{Se} + Q_R}$$

$$14.36 = \frac{C_{Se} \times 1700 + 1 \times 7000}{1700 + 7000}$$

∴
$$C_{Se} = 69.37 \text{ mg/lit}$$

∴ Degree of treatment required

$$= \frac{\text{Original BOD of sewage} - \text{Permissible BOD}}{\text{Original BOD}} \times 100$$

$$= \frac{250 - 69.37}{250} \times 100$$

$$= \textbf{72.25\%} \hspace{3cm} \textbf{... Ans.}$$

Example 6.5 : A town discharges 90 cumecs of sewage into a stream having a rate of flow of 1400 cumecs during its lean days with a velocity of 0.12 m/sec. The BOD_5 of sewage at the given temperature is 290 mg/lit. Find when and where the critical DO deficit will occur in the downstream portion of the river and what is its amount ? Assume coefficient of self purification (f) as 3.5 and coefficient of deoxygenation (K_1) as 0.1. Assume saturation DO at given temperature as 9.2 mg/lit.

Solution :

	Given :	Rate of flow of sewage, Q_{Se}	= 90 cumecs

Given :

Rate of flow of sewage, Q_{Se}	= 90 cumecs
Rate of flow of stream, Q_R	= 1400 cumecs
Velocity of stream	= 0.12 m/sec
BOD_5 of sewage	= 290 mg/lit
Coefficient of self purification (f)	= 3.5
Deoxygenation coefficient (K_1)	= 0.1

Saturation DO $= 9.2$ mg/lit

$$(DO)_{mix} = \frac{9.2 \times 1400 + 0 \times 90}{1400 + 90} \quad \text{(Assuming DO of sewage as zero)}$$

$$= 8.64 \text{ mg/lit}$$

∴   Initial DO deficit, $D_a = 9.2 - 8.64 = 0.56$ mg/lit

BOD₅ of the mixture can be calculated by using equation (6.1).

$$C = \frac{C_{Se} Q_{Se} + C_R Q_R}{Q_{Se} + Q_R}$$

$$= \frac{290 \times 90 + 0 \times 1400}{90 + 1400}$$

$$= 17.52 \text{ mg/lit}$$

The ultimate BOD of mix can be calculated by

$$Y_5 = L_a [1 - 10^{-K_1 \cdot t}]$$

∴ $$17.52 = L_a [1 - 10^{-0.1 \times 5}]$$

∴ $$L_a = 25.62 \text{ mg/lit}$$

Now, critical deficit, D_c can be calculated by using equation (6.12).

$$\left[\frac{L_a}{D_c \cdot f}\right]^{f-1} = f\left[1 - (f-1)\frac{D_a}{L_a}\right]$$

$$\left[\frac{25.62}{D_c \times 3.5}\right]^{3.5-1} = 3.5\left[1 - (3.5-1)\frac{0.56}{25.62}\right]$$

$$\frac{7.32}{D_c} = (3.31)^{1/2.5} = 1.61$$

∴ $$D_c = 4.53 \text{ mg/lit}$$

The critical time can be calculated by using equation (6.9).

$$t_c = \frac{1}{K_1(f-1)} \log_{10}\left[\left\{1 - (f-1)\frac{D_a}{L_a}\right\}f\right]$$

∴ $$t_c = \frac{1}{0.1(3.5-1)} \log_{10}\left[\left\{1 - (3.5-1)\frac{0.56}{25.62}\right\}3.5\right]$$

$$= \frac{1}{0.25} \log_{10} [3.31]$$

$$= \textbf{2.08 days} \hspace{4cm} \textbf{... Ans.}$$

Now,   Distance = Velocity of stream × Travel time

= 0.12 × (2.08 × 24 × 60 × 60)

= 21551.5 m

= **21.55 km**   ... **Ans.**

Example 6.6 : The population of town is 40,000 and the domestic sewage is 150 litres/capita/day having per capita BOD of 75 gm/day.

Dairy wastes of 4 million litres per day with BOD of 1200 mg/lit and sugar mill waste of 2.6 million litres per day with BOD of 1600 mg/lit are produced. An overall expansion factor of 12% to be provided. The sewage effluents are to be discharged to a river stream with a minimum dry weather flow of 4900 litre per second and a saturation dissolved oxygen content of 9.0 mg/lit. It is necessary to maintain a dissolved oxygen content of 4 mg/lit in the stream. For design of the treatment plant, determine the degree of treatment required to be given to the sewage. $(K_1 = 0.1, \ K_2 = 0.3)$.

Solution :

   Given :   Population = 40,000

Domestic sewage = 150 lit/capita/day

Quantity of dairy waste = 4 million litres

BOD of dairy waste = 1200 mg/lit

Quantity of sugar mill waste = 2.6 million litres

BOD of sugar mill waste = 1600 mg/lit

Rate of flow of stream = 4900 mg/lit

Per capita sewage = 150 litres/day

Amount of domestic sewage

= 40000 × 150

= 6 million litres/day

Per capita BOD of domestic sewage

= 75 gm/day

= 75 × 1000 mg/day

BOD per litre of the domestic sewage $= \dfrac{75 \times 1000}{150} = 500$ mg/lit.

Net BOD of all wastewaters

$$= \left[\frac{6 \times 500 + 4 \times 1200 + 2.6 \times 1600}{6 + 4 + 2.6} \right] = 949.21 \text{ mg/lit}$$

Total wastewater discharge in litres/sec

$$= \text{Volume of wastewaters entering per day}$$

$$= \frac{6 \times 10^6 + 4 \times 10^6 + 2.6 \times 10^6}{24 \times 60 \times 60}$$

$$= 145.83 \text{ litres/sec}$$

Using an expansion factor of 12%,

Total wastewater $= 1.12 \times 145.83$

$$= 163.33 \text{ litres/sec}$$

Initial DO of stream $= 9.0$ mg/lit

$\therefore$ DO of the mixture $= \dfrac{(DO)_{Se} \times Q_{Se} + (DO)_R \times Q_R}{Q_{Se} + Q_R}$

$$= \frac{0 \times 150 + 9 \times 4900}{150 + 4900} \qquad \text{(Assuming DO of sewage as zero)}$$

$$= 8.73 \text{ mg/lit}$$

$\therefore$ Initial DO deficit, $D_a = 9 - 8.73$

$$= 0.27 \text{ mg/lit}$$

Critical DO deficit, $D_c = 9 - 4$

$$= 5.0 \text{ mg/lit}$$

Now, L_a can be calculated by using equation (6.12).

$$\left[\frac{L_a}{D_c\, f}\right]^{f-1} = f\left[1 - (f-1)\frac{D_a}{L_a}\right]$$

Here, $f = \dfrac{K_2}{K_1} = \dfrac{0.3}{0.1} = 3$

$\therefore$ $\left[\dfrac{L_a}{5 \times 3}\right]^2 = 3\left[1 - (3-1)\dfrac{0.27}{L_a}\right]$

Solving by hit and trial,

$$L_a = 25.5 \text{ mg/lit}$$

Maximum permissible BOD_5 of mix can be calculated by

$$Y_5 = L_a\,[1 - 10^{-K_1 \cdot t}]$$

$$= 25.5\,[1 - 10^{-0.1 \times 5}]$$

$$= 17.44 \text{ mg/lit}$$

Now, maximum permissible BOD_5 of wastewaters can be calculated by using equation (6.1).

$$C = \frac{C_{Se}\, Q_{Se} + C_R\, Q_R}{Q_{Se} + Q_R}$$

$$17.44 = \frac{C_{Se} \times 150 + 0 \times 4900}{150 + 4900} = 587.02 \text{ mg/lit}$$

∴   Degree of treatment required

$$= \frac{\text{Original BOD of city wastewaters – Permissible BOD}}{\text{Original BOD of city wastewaters}} \times 100$$

$$= \frac{949.21 - 587.02}{949.21} \times 100 = \textbf{38.16\%} \qquad \textbf{... Ans.}$$

Example 6.7 : In the previous example, no treatment is provided. Determine the dilution ratio and river discharge.

Solution :

When no treatment is provided, the value of maximum permissible BOD_5 should be 949.21 mg/lit. Q_R can be calculated as :

$$17.44 = \frac{949.21 \times 150 + 0 \times Q_R}{150 + Q_R}$$

∴ Q_R = **8014.08 litres/sec**   **... Ans.**

$$\text{Dilution ratio} = \frac{Q_R}{Q_{Se}} = \frac{8014.08}{150} = \textbf{53.43} \qquad \textbf{... Ans.}$$

Example 6.8 : A waste water effluent of 560 litres/sec with a BOD = 50 mg/lit, DO = 3.0 mg/lit and temperature of 23°C enters a river where the flow is 28 m³/sec, and BOD = 4.0 mg/lit, DO = 8.2 mg/lit, and temperature of 17°C. K_1 of the waste is 0.10 per day at 20°C. The velocity of water in the river downstream is 0.18 m/sec and depth of 1.2 m. Determine the following after mixing of waste water with the river water :

(i)   Combined discharge; (ii) BOD; (iii) DO; and (iv) Temperature.   **(Civil Services)**

Solution :

Particulars of Sewage thrown	Particulars of River
Q_{Se} = 560 litres/sec	Q_R = 28 m³/sec
= 0.56 m³/sec	
Concentrations (C_{Se}) :	**Concentrations (C_R) :**
BOD = 50 mg/lit	BOD = 4.0 mg/lit
DO = 3.0 mg/lit	DO = 8.2 mg/lit
Temperature = 23°C	Temperature = 17°

$$K_1 \text{ at } 20°C = 0.1 \text{ per day}$$

(i)   Combined discharge $= Q_{Se} + Q_R$

$$= 0.56 + 28$$

$$= \textbf{28.56 m}^3\textbf{/sec.} \qquad ... \textbf{Ans.}$$

Now, using equation (6.1), for concentration of mix as

$$C = \frac{C_{Se} \cdot Q_{Se} + C_R \cdot Q_R}{Q_{Se} + Q_R}$$

(ii)   BOD of mix $= \dfrac{50 \times 0.56 + 4.0 \times 28}{0.56 + 28}$

$$= \frac{140}{28.56} = \textbf{4.9 mg/lit} \qquad ... \textbf{Ans.}$$

(iii)   DO of mix $= \dfrac{3.0 \times 0.56 + 8.2 \times 28}{0.56 + 28}$

$$= \textbf{8.098 mg/lit} \qquad ... \textbf{Ans.}$$

(iv)   Temperature of mix $= \dfrac{23 \times 0.56 + 17 \times 28}{0.56 + 28}$

$$= \textbf{17.12°C} \qquad ... \textbf{Ans.}$$

Example 6.9 : 125 cumecs of sewage of a city is discharged in a perennial river which is fully saturated with oxygen and flows at a minimum rate of 1600 cumecs with a minimum velocity of 0.12 m/sec. If the 5 day BOD of the sewage is 300 mg/lit, find out where the critical DO will occur in the river. Assume

(i)   the coefficient of purification of the river as 4.0,

(ii)   the coefficient of DO as 0.11, and

(iii)   the ultimate BOD as 125% of the 5 day BOD of the mixture of sewage and river water.   **(Engg. Services)**

Solution :

Assume saturation DO concentration of the given river $= 9.2$ mg/lit

The DO of the river at the mixing point after disposal of sewage (D)

$$= \frac{125 \times 0 + 1600 \times 9.2}{125 + 1600}$$

$$= 8.53 \text{ mg/lit}$$

Initial DO deficit $(D_a) = D_S - D$

$$= 9.2 - 8.53$$

$$= 0.67 \text{ mg/lit}$$

BOD$_5$ of the river at the mixing point after disposal of sewage (Y$_5$)

$$= \frac{125 \times 300 + 1600 \times 0}{125 + 1600}$$

$$= 21.74 \text{ mg/lit}$$

The ultimate BOD of river (mix) at mixing point (L$_a$)

$$= 125\% \text{ BOD}_5 \qquad \text{[as per given in assumption (iii)]}$$

$$= 1.25 \times 21.74$$

$$= 27.17 \text{ mg/lit}$$

Now, $$\text{BOD}_5 = L_a [1 - (10)^{-K_1 \times 5}]$$

or $$21.74 = 27.17 [1 - (10)^{-K_1 \times 5}]$$

or $$0.8 = [1 - (10)^{-5K_1}]$$

or $$(10)^{-5K_1} = 0.20$$

or $$-5K_1 \log 10 = \log 0.20$$

or $$K_1 = 0.14$$

The coefficient of DO or BOD (K$_1$) is given in assumption No. (ii) to be 0.11, as against its value of 0.14 computed above on the basis of assumption (iii). Eventually, there is some inconsistency in the given data, and the Examiner should have given only one of the two assumptions, i.e. either (ii) and (iii), which would have suffice the purpose.

Under such a difficult situation, we may solve the example by using both the values of K$_1$, i.e. 0.11 as well as 0.14. The K$_1$ value of 0.14 will, however, give more DO deficit and will displace the critical point upstream; and will thus provide more conservative design values :

Case 1 : When K$_1$ = 0.11 : Using equation (6.9) as

$$t_c = \frac{1}{K_1 (f - 1)} \log \left[\left\{ 1 - (f - 1) \frac{D_a}{L_a} \right\} f \right]$$

We get $$t_c = \frac{1}{0.11 \ (4 - 1)} \log \left[\left\{ 1 - (4 - 1) \frac{0.67}{27.17} \right\} 4 \right]$$

$$= 1.723 \text{ days}$$

The distance along the river, where the critical DO deficit will occur

$$S = \text{Velocity} \times \text{Time}$$

$$= 0.12 \times (1.723 \times 24 \times 3600)$$

$$= 17.86 \text{ km}; \quad \text{Say 18 km}$$

Hence, critical DO deficit will occur at **18 km downstream of the sewage disposal point.**   ... **Ans.**

Case 2 : When $K_1 = 0.14$:

$$t_c = \frac{0.11}{0.14} \times 1.723 = 1.354 \text{ days}$$

$$S = 17.86 \times \frac{1.354}{1.723} = 14.04 \text{ km}$$

Hence, **critical DO deficit will occur at 14 km downstream of sewage disposal point.**   ... **Ans.**

Example 6.10 : A wastewater treatment plant disposes its effluents into a stream at a point A. Characteristics of the stream at a location fairly upstream of A and of the effluent are as below :

Item	Units	Effluent	Stream
Flow	m³/s	0.20	0.50
Dissolved oxygen	mg/lit	2.00	8.00
Temperature	°C	26	22
BOD$_5$ at 20°C	mg/lit	40	3

Assume that the deoxygenation constant K_1 at 20°C (base e) = 0.20 d^{-1} and the reaeration constant K_2 at 20°C (base e) = 0.40 d^{-1} for the mixture. Equilibrium concentration of dissolved oxygen (C_S) for the fresh water is as follows :

Temperature, °C	18	20	22	23	24	25	26
C$_S$ (mg/lit)	9.54	9.17	8.99	8.83	8.53	8.38	8.22

The velocity of the stream downstream of the point A is 0.2 m/sec. Determine the critical oxygen deficit and its location.

[Use temperature coefficients of 1.04 for K_1 and 1.02 for K_2]   **(Civil Services)**

Solution :

K_1 at 20°C (base e) = 0.2 d^{-1}

                    = 0.2 per day

∴ K_1 at 20°C (base 10) = $\dfrac{K_1}{2.3}$ = 0.434 K_1

                    = 0.434 × 0.2 per day

                    = 0.087 per day

Similarly, K_2 at 20°C $= 0.434 \times 0.4$ d^{-1}

$= 0.174$ per day

The formulae to be used in this example for converting K_1 and K_2 at any other temperature (T°C) will be

$$K_{1\,(T°)} = K_{1\,(20°)}\,[1.04]^{T°-20°}$$

and $$K_{2\,(T°)} = K_{2\,(20°)}\,[1.02]^{T°-20°}$$

(i)   We will now determine DO, BOD and temperature of mixture as below :

$$\text{DO of mixture} = \frac{\text{DO of sewage} \times Q_{se} + \text{DO of river} \times Q_R}{Q_{se} + Q_R}$$

$$= \frac{2 \times 0.20 + 8 \times 0.50}{0.20 + 0.50}$$

$$= 6.29 \text{ mg/lit}$$

BOD$_5$ of mixture

(i.e. 5 day BOD at 20°C) $$= \frac{40 \times 0.20 + 3 \times 0.50}{0.20 + 0.50}$$

$$= 13.57 \text{ mg/lit}$$

$$\text{Temperature of mixture} = \frac{26 \times 0.20 + 22 \times 0.50}{0.20 + 0.50}$$

$$= 23.14°C$$

(ii)   Ultimate BOD of mixture (L_a)

$$L_a = \frac{Y_5 \text{ (i.e. 5 day BOD of mixture at 20°C)}}{1 - (10)^{-K_1 \times 5}}$$

where, K_1 is at 20°C $= 0.087$ per day

$$= \frac{13.57}{1 - (10)^{-0.087 \times 5}}$$

$$= \frac{13.57}{0.633} = 21.45 \text{ mg/lit}$$

(iii)   Initial DO deficit of mixture,

DO of mixture $= 6.29$ mg/lit

Saturation DO at mixture temperature of 23.14°C

$= 8.79$ (interpolated from given values)

$\therefore$ $\quad D_a$ = DO deficit

$\quad$ = 8.79 – 6.29

$\quad$ = 2.50 mg/lit

(iv) Corrected values of K_1 and K_2 are :

$$K_{1\,(23.14°)} = K_{1\,(20°)}\,[1.04]^{T-20}$$

$$= 0.087\,[1.04]^{3.14}$$

$$= 0.098$$

$$K_{2\,(23.14°)} = K_{2\,(20°)}\,[1.02]^{T-20}$$

$$= 0.174\,[1.02]^{3.14}$$

$$= 0.185$$

(v) The time (t_c) after which critical DO deficit (D_c) occurs is given by equation (6.9) as,

$$t_c = \frac{1}{K_1(t-f)}\,\log_{10}\left[\left\{1-(f-1)\,\frac{D_a}{L}\right\}f\right]$$

where, $\quad K_2 = 0.185$

$\quad K_1 = 0.098$

$\therefore$ $\quad f = \dfrac{K_2}{K_1} = \dfrac{0.185}{0.098} = 1.888$

$\quad L_a = 21.45$ mg/lit

$\quad D_a = 2.5$ mg/lit

$\therefore$ $\quad t_c = \dfrac{1}{0.098\,(1.888-1)}\,\log_{10}\left[\left(1-\dfrac{0.888\times2.5}{21.45}\right)1.888\right]$

$$= \frac{1}{0.098\,(0.888)} \times 0.228$$

$$= 2.625 \text{ days}$$

(vi) Now, $\quad$ Distance = Velocity × Travel time

$\quad$ = 0.2 × (2.625 × 24 × 60 × 60)

$\quad$ = **45.36 km** $\hspace{3cm}$ ... **Ans.**

(vii) D_c is now given by equation (6.12) as

$$\left(\frac{L_a}{D_c\cdot f}\right)^{f-1} = f\left(1-(f-1)\,\frac{D_a}{L_a}\right)$$

or $\qquad \left(\dfrac{21.45}{D_c \times 1.888}\right)^{0.888} = 1.888 \left(1 - \dfrac{0.888 \times 2.5}{21.4}\right)$

or $\qquad \dfrac{21.45}{1.888\, D_c} = (1.692)^{\frac{1}{0.888}} = (1.692)^{1.126} = 1.808$

or $\qquad D_c = \dfrac{21.45}{1.888 \times 1.808} = \mathbf{6.28\ mg/lit}$

Hence, the critical DO deficit equal to 6.28 mg/lit occurs at 45.36 km downstream of A, after 2.625 days. ... **Ans.**

SOLVED EXAMPLES ON SEWAGE DISPOSAL ON LAND

Example 6.11 : A town having population of 70000 dispose sewage by land treatment. The water supply from the waterworks is 150 lit/capita/day. The land used for sewage disposal can absorb 70 m^3 of sewage per hectare per day. Determine the land area required.

Solution :

Given :

Population = 70000

Rate of water supply = 150 lit/capita/day

Total water supplied per day

= 70000 × 150

= 10.5 × 10^6 litres

= 10500 cu.m.

Assuming that sewage generation is 80% of this water,

∴ The quantity of sewage generated per day

$= \dfrac{80}{100} \times 10500 = 8400$ cu.m.

∴ Area of land required for disposing of sewage

$= \dfrac{8400}{70} = 120$ hectares

Providing 50% extra land for rest and rotation, we have

Total land area required = 1.5 × 120 = **180 hectares** ... **Ans.**

Example 6.12 : A town having a population of 45000 and the rate of water supply as 140 lit/capita/day, disposes sewage by land treatment. The area of sewage farm is 160 hectares. The area included an extra provision of 50% for rest and rotation. If 80% of the water is converted into sewage, determine the consuming capacity of soil.

Solution :

Quantity of water produced per day

= 45000 × 140

= 6.3 × 10^6 litres = 6300 cu.m.

Quantity of sewage produced per day

$$= \frac{80}{100} \times 6300 = 5040 \text{ cu.m./day}$$

Area of farm land provided

$$= 160 \text{ ha (including 50\% for rest and rotation)}$$

∴   Actual available land for application

$$= \frac{160}{1.5} = 106.67 \text{ ha}$$

∴   Consuming capacity of soil

$$= \frac{5040}{106.67}$$

$$= \textbf{47.25 cu.m/ha/day} \qquad \text{... Ans.}$$

IMPORTANT POINTS

- Plant disposal and stream sanitation.
- Disposal of sewage by dilution and its conditions.
- Purification of natural stream and forces required to complete it.
- Oxygen-sag curve and Stricter-Phelp's equation.
- Disposal of sewage by sea, lake and land treatment.
- Application of sewage effluent to farms.
- Sewage sickness.

EXERCISE

1. What are the factors affecting self-purification of polluted streams ? What measures would you recommend to control stream pollution in India ?

2. What is meant by "Environmental Pollution" ? Describe what happens when untreated sewage from a town is discharged into a nearby stream.

3. Sewage disposal systems are to be provided for :
    (i)   an isolated residential building with ten users
    (ii)   a small town of 2000 persons located on the bank of a river
    (iii) a town with 10,000 persons located on the bank of a small river.
    Describe the possible methods of sewage disposal for each case and bring out the advantages and disadvantages of the various methods listed.

4. Write a detailed note on land treatment of sewage dealing with the chemical as well as the engineering aspects of the process.

5. What do you understand by self-purification property of a stream ? Explain the factors affecting this property.

6. Explain clearly the methods, problems, and limitations of land disposal of sewage.

7. Explain how domestic sewage is different from industrial waste.

8. Explain in details the methods of self purification in a stream.

9. Enlist the factors governing the reoxygenation and deoxygenation of stream.

10. Write short notes on :

    (a)   Stream standards and effluent standards.

    (b)   Oxygen sag curve. (Pune University, A.M.I.E.)

    (c)   Disposal of sewage by dilution.

    (d)   Dilution factor.

    (e)   Sewage farming.

    (f)   Irrigation farming.

    (g)   Zones of pollution in a stream.

    (h)   Sewage sickness.

    (i)   Broad irrigation.

    (j)   Self purification constant.

    (k)   Disposal of sewage in sea water.

    (l)   Minimum DO content in polluted stream for survival of aquatic life.

11. Explain the importance of effluent standards and stream standards in controlling water pollution.

12. Explain the terms with sketch :

    (i)   Self purification of stream.

    (ii)   Importance of critical DO deficit.

13. Discuss in details the disposal of sewage on land.

14. Give effluent standards for the following (W/W to be discharged in river).

    (i)   BOD, (ii) COD, (iii) Temperature, (iv) Total suspended solids.

15. Mention various methods of wastewater disposal. Discuss their merits and demerits. Explain the conditions favourable for their adoption.

16. Explain the difference between dilution process if the wastewater effluents are disposed of in stream water and sea water.

17. A city discharges 2000 litres per second of sewage into a stream whose minimum rate of flow is 7500 litres per second. The temperature of sewage as well as water is 20°C. The BOD_5 at 20°C for sewage is 300 mg/lit and that of the stream is 90% of the saturation DO If the minimum DO to be maintained in the stream is 5 mg/lit, find out the degree of sewage treatment required. Assume the deoxygenation coefficient as 0.1 and reoxygenation coefficient as 0.3.

UNIVERSITY QUESTIONS

1. What are the natural forces acts for the purification of streams.

(6 M) (May 2009, 2010, 2011)

2. Discuss the following zones of a stream which is undergoing self purification

   (i)   Zone of degradation   (ii) Zone of active decomposition

   (iii) Zone of recovery   (iv) Zone of clear water.

(6 M) (May 2009; Dec. 2010)

3. Draw a figure showing different zones of stream pollution and discuss in detailed about zone of active decomposition.   **(6 M) (May 2010)**

4. Give the Streeter – Phelp's equation and explain each term in equation.

(6 M) (Dec. 2010, May 2011)

5. Write short note on oxygen say curve.   **(6 M) (Dec. 2010, May 2010)**

✠ ✠ ✠

Chapter 7

SEWAGE TREATMENT – PRELIMINARY AND PRIMARY TREATMENT

7.1 INTRODUCTION

The preliminary treatment consists of
- Screening – for removal of floating matter.
- Grit chamber – for removal of sand and grit.
- Skimming tank – for removal of oil and grease.

The primary treatment consists of
1. Settling tanks – for removal of suspended solids.

The possible arrangements of these units are shown in Fig. 7.1.

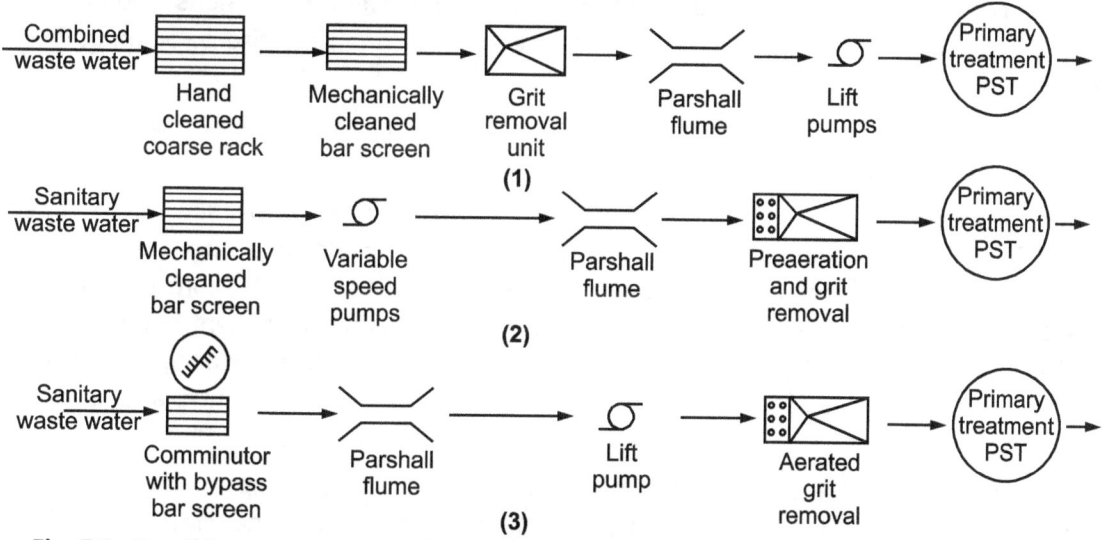

Fig. 7.1 : Possible arrangements of preliminary and primary treatment units in wastewater processes

SCREENS

7.2 SCREENING OF SEWAGE

Screening of sewage normally removes large floating solids from the sewage.

Screening of sewage has to be done in the sewerage system also, e.g., in a pumping station, coarse screens are normally provided before the pumps. Screens are provided as a common unit in sewage treatment plants to avoid the following troubles that the floating solids may cause :

1. They may clog the pumps.
2. They may interfere with the secondary treatment by clogging the trickling filter media or by obstructing aeration in activated sludge process.

Sometimes, when the sewage is to be disposed off without any treatment, the gross solids have still to be removed to avoid their floating on the receiving water, thus preventing the reaeration and giving an ugly appearance.

7.3 CLASSIFICATION OF SCREENS

The screens are normally classified in number of ways as follows :

- Based on the size of opening – such as coarse, medium and fine screens.
- Depending on the shape – such as disc, drum, band etc.
- The mode of settling such as fixed, movable or moving types.
- The method of cleaning such as manual or mechanical types.

The classification based on sizes of opening normally divides the screens as follows :

Coarse screens when the size of opening is above 80 mm, **medium screens** when the size of opening is between 20 mm – 50 mm and **fine screens** when the size of opening is less than 20 mm.

The disc, band and cage screens are very commonly used in the case of industrial waste treatment and in chemical engineering operations.

In normal practice, medium bar screens or racks are used in municipal sewage treatment plants. Thus, in a screening chamber, bars, rectangular or circular in shape, are kept at an inclination to the horizontal. Normally, sharp edged rectangular bars (10 mm × 40 mm) set about 25 mm apart are used. The inclination of these bars is normally kept between 30° to 45° for manual cleaned types and 45° to 60° in such cases where the cleaning is done by using mechanical means. Normal practice in municipal sewage treatment plants is to use fixed screens.

As the velocity inside the chamber is reduced below the value in the approach channel, the transition should be as far as possible smooth to avoid undue headloss and related problems.

The velocity through the screen opening is normally kept at 0.6 m per second at 50% clogging of the screens. Thus, on knowing the velocity to be provided, the requisite area of opening can be calculated; on the basis of which the width of screen chamber should be arrived at. As far as possible, the depth of flow inside the screening chamber is maintained at the same level as that in the approach channel. As the sewage flows through the screens, head loss occurs and to maintain the continuity of the flowline, normal practice is to depress the invert of the channel on the downstream side of the screen by an equal amount as shown in Fig. 7.2.

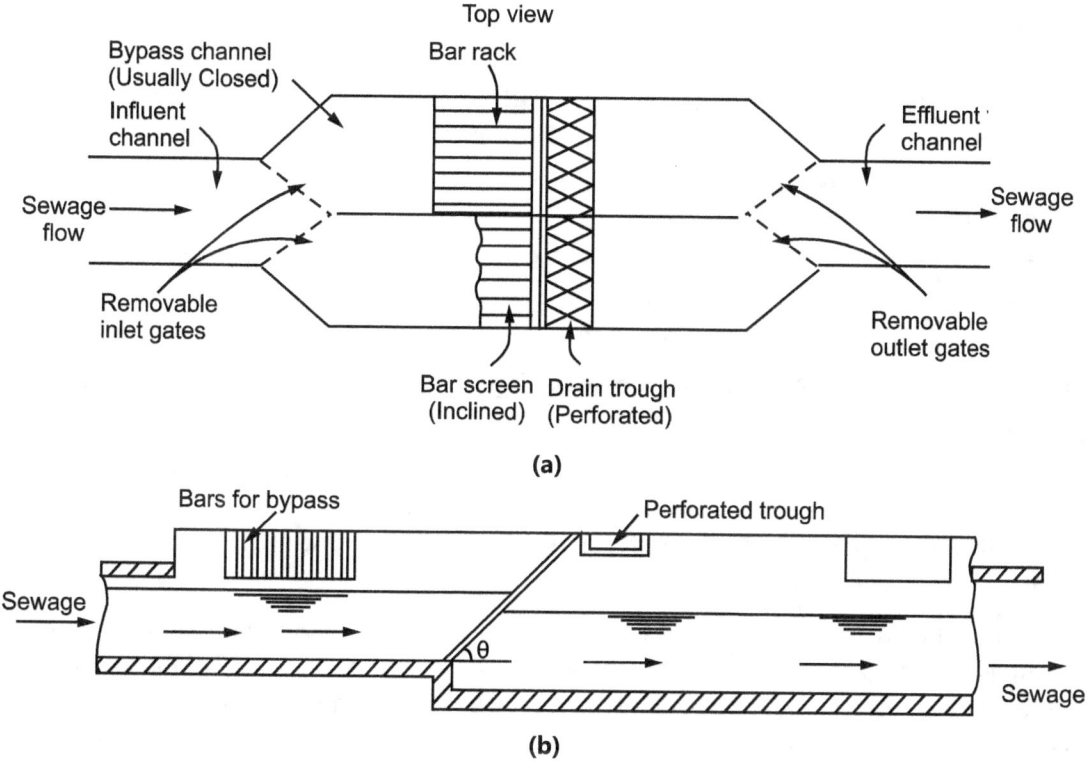

Fig. 7.2 : Screen chamber

The head loss through the screens can be calculated in the following ways :

(i) $\qquad$ $h = (V^2 - v^2) \times 0.0729$

where, $\qquad$ h = Head loss in m

$\qquad$ V = Velocity through screens in m/sec

$\qquad$ v = Velocity before screens in m/sec.

(ii) **O' Kirschmer (1926) Formula :**

$$h = \beta \left(\frac{W}{b}\right)^{1.33} h_v \sin\theta$$

where, $\qquad$ β = 2.42 for sharp edged rectangular bars

$\qquad$ = 1.79 for circular bars

$\qquad$ $h_v = \dfrac{v^2}{2g}$ where, v = Approach velocity in m/sec

and $\qquad$ θ = Inclination of bars to horizontal.

As the material goes on getting accumulated on the face of the screens, the liquid level in the chamber starts rising. When the liquid level rises sufficiently high, the mechanical cleaning devices are put into operation. The mechanical cleaning device can be either the time operated switch or float operated switch type. However, regulations make it mandatory that a float operated switch must be provided even in such cases where time switch operated cleaning mechanism is used. As can be easily guessed, the float operated switch is sturdier and hence more reliable. The manual cleaning of the screens is normally done once in a day in the case of flows less than 5 ml/d.

If the cleaning devices fail and the sewage is likely to overflow the channels, an overflow weir is normally provided, which is equipped with bars set 0.6 m apart, which take the liquid to downstream side of the screen through a channel.

The material removed from against the screening surface is normally found to contain a high moisture content (70 – 80%) which can be reduced by drying on a draining platform.

The amount of screenings removed normally depend upon the type of sewage and the size of openings in the screens. In municipal practice, the amount of screenings normally vary between 0.0015 m³ per million litre with screen sizes of 10 cm and 0.015 m³ per million litre in case of 2.5 cm size.

These screenings as they are removed from the screening chamber are found to contain a large moisture content of about 90%. Hence, it is desirable to reduce this moisture content to at least 60% for proper disposal. This is normally done in India, by sun drying. After the moisture content is reduced to 60%, it can be disposed off by either composting it, burying in pits or by burning them.

Sometimes when the sewage has to be disposed off without any treatment, fine screening is done which removes most of the floating and lighter solids. The material that is removed, however, also contains a large proportion of organic matter and hence its disposal poses a problem. Also its efficiency is hardly 1/5 of what would be obtained in a sedimentation tank and in addition it entails a high maintenance cost. Now-a-days, hence, these are replaced by cutting devices known as **Comminuters or Shredders.** These normally consist of a revolving slotted drum with a number of cutters mounted on its surface which shear the material retained against a brush. The liquid can flow to the downstream side, only by passing through opening of 0.5 to 1 cm size in the drum surface. Thus, the retained particles when reduced to this size escape to the downstream side.

7.4 OPERATION AND MAINTENANCE OF SCREENS

- Regular cleaning of hand cleaned screens to prevent backing up of sewage.
- Lubrication of mechanical screens as per instructions of manufacturers.
- Painting of entire mechanism once in a year.
- Visual inspection to check whether screenings are retained between bars or being pushed through them due to more velocity.

- Volume of screening collected should be recorded regularly.
- Prompt and hygienic disposal of screenings.
- Daily record of operation and maintenance should be maintained.

7.5 DISPOSAL OF SCREENINGS

Screenings are disposed off by the following methods :

- Burial
- Digestion
- Incineration
- Grinding.

SOLVED EXAMPLES

Example 7.1 : Design a bar screen for a peak flow 50 million litres per day.

Solution :

Assume manual cleaning.

Keep the bars at inclination of 45° with horizontal.

Assume the rectangular bars of size 10 mm × 50 mm with 10 mm dimension facing the flow.

Assume clear spacing of 40 mm between the bars.

Assume the velocity through the screen as 0.8 m/s at peak flow.

$$\text{Maximum rate of flow} = 50 \text{ mld} = \frac{50 \times 10^6}{24 \times 60 \times 60 \times 1000}$$

$$= 0.578 \text{ m}^3/\text{sec}$$

$$\therefore \quad \text{Net area of screen} = \frac{0.578}{0.8} = 0.7225 \text{ m}^2$$

$$\therefore \quad \text{Gross area of screen} = 0.7225 \times \frac{50}{40} = 0.903 \text{ m}^2$$

(For 40 mm opening, net area is 0.7225 m². Therefore, for 50 mm, gross area is $0.7225 \times \frac{50}{40}$)

As the screen is inclined at 45° with the horizontal,

$$\text{Gross area of screen} = \frac{0.903}{\sin 45°} = 1.277 \text{ m}^2$$

Also velocity of flow above screen $= 0.8 \times \frac{40}{50} = 0.64 \text{ m/s}$

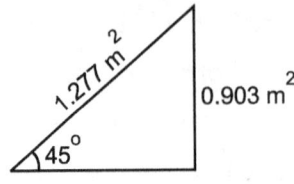

Fig. 7.3

Thus, we have   V = 0.8 m/s,   v = 0.64 m/s

∴ h_L = 0.0729 $(V^2 - v^2)$

                                    = 0.0729 $[(0.8)^2 - (0.64)^2]$

                                    = 0.017 m = 1.7 cm

This will be the head loss when the screen is clean.

If, however, the screen is half clogged,

                                 V = 2 × 0.8 = 1.6 m/s

∴ h_L = 0.0729 $[(1.6)^2 - (0.64)^2]$

                                    = 0.157 m

                                    = 15.7 cm

Example 7.2 : Design the screen chamber of a ETP to treat a peak flow of 60 mld of sewage.

Solution :

Assume manual cleaning.

Keep the bars at inclination of 60° with horizontal.

Assume the rectangular bars of size 10 mm × 70 mm; 10 mm dimension facing the flow.

Assume clear spacing between bars as 50 mm.

Assume the velocity through the screen as 0.8 m/s at peak flow.

Maximum rate of flow = 60 mld = 60,000 m^3/day

                                    = 0.694 m^3/sec

∴   The net area of screen openings required

                                    = $\dfrac{0.694}{0.8}$

                                    = 0.87 m^2

∴   Gross area of screen = 0.87 × $\dfrac{60}{50}$ = 1.044 m^2

As the screen is inclined at 60° with the horizontal,

$$\text{Gross area of screen} = \frac{1.044}{\sin 60°} = 1.205 \text{ m}^2$$

$$\text{Also velocity of flow above screen} = 0.8 \times \frac{50}{60} = 0.67 \text{ m/s}$$

Thus, we have   V = 0.8 m/s,   v = 0.67 m/s

$$\therefore \quad \text{Head loss, } h_L = 0.0729 (V^2 - v^2)$$

$$= 0.0729 [(0.8)^2 - (0.67)^2]$$

$$= 0.014 \text{ m}$$

$$= 1.4 \text{ cm}$$

Thus, provide the screen of area = 1.205 m²

$$\text{Dimensions of bars} = 10 \text{ mm} \times 70 \text{ mm}$$

$$\text{Clear spacing between bars} = 50 \text{ mm}$$

Example 7.3 : A screen consisting of 10 mm diameter bars, at a clear spacing of 40 mm, treats a maximum hourly flow of 1275 m³, velocity of flow through the screen chamber = 75 cm/sec. Work out :

   (i)   Length and number of bars.

   (ii) Head loss in the chamber.   **(8 Marks, Pune University)**

Solution :

$$\text{Maximum flow} = 1275 \text{ m}^3/\text{hr}$$

$$= \frac{1275}{60 \times 60}$$

$$= 0.35 \text{ m}^3/\text{sec}$$

$$V = 75 \text{ cm/sec}$$

$$= 0.75 \text{ m/sec}$$

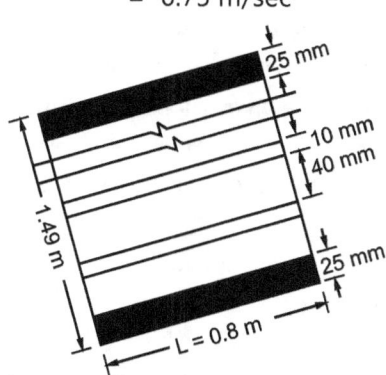

Fig. 7.4

$$Q_{max} = A \times V$$
$$0.35 = A \times 0.75$$
$$\therefore \quad A = 0.466 \text{ m}^2$$

Keeping 100% as excess openings,

$$\therefore \quad A = 2 \times 0.466 = 0.933 \text{ m}^2$$

Assuming length of screen 800 mm,

$$\therefore \quad \text{Effective width of the screen} = \frac{0.933}{0.800}$$
$$= 1.17 \text{ m}$$

Size of opening is 40 mm,

$$\therefore \quad \text{Number of openings} = \frac{1.17}{0.04}$$
$$= 29$$
$$\therefore \quad \text{Number of bars} = 28$$

Let the angle thickness at both ends be 25 mm (diameter of bars is 10 mm).

$$\therefore \quad \text{Total width of screen} = (29 \times 0.04) + (28 \times 0.01) + (2 \times 0.025)$$
$$= (1.16) + (0.28) + (0.05)$$
$$= 1.49 \text{ m}$$

For calculation of head loss please refer example 7.1.

GRIT CHAMBER

7.6 INTRODUCTION   [MAY 2010]

Grit includes sand, ash, cinder, egg shells, silt, clay, glass pieces, broken crockery pieces, etc. The diameter of grit is less than 0.2 mm. The specific gravity of grit is 2.0 to 2.6. Grit is non-putrescible and has more settling velocity than organic solids. This property of difference in settling is utilised in removing non-putrescible grit of more specific gravity and putrescible organic solids in two separate tanks by differential sedimentation.

Sand and grit enters into sewerage system :

- Through the open manhole covers in the case of separate sewerage system.
- Due to habit of Indian housewives of washing utensils by sand, grit, brickbats and such other materials.
- Through unauthorised connection of courtyards of the houses to the sewerage system.

The grit causes large number of problems such as :

- Erosion of pump impellers.
- Settling in conveying conduits.
- It settles along with the sludge, which when digested does not undergo any stabilisation with the result that the final product is of a poorer quality.

- If sewage is being disposed off without any treatment, it tends to settle out in the receiving water resulting in sludge bank formation with consequent problems.

Thus, the objectives of the grit removal are :

- Protection of pumps, valves, piping etc.
- Minimising chances of chocking of pipes and conduits with grit.
- Preventing the grit from occupying the volume in biological treatment units.

It is desirable to remove this grit in the case of municipal sewage treatment plants before further treatment is given. The removal of this material is normally done by using channels known as grit chambers which are based on the **'Differential sedimentation'** principle. The channels which are normally 0.9 m – 1.2 m deep are designed in such a manner that particles of settling velocity equal to or greater than 0.25 – 0.3 m/sec are only removed and those particles which are having a lesser settling velocity are carried ahead by the scouring velocity of the sewage flow. This horizontal velocity ensures the removal of sand and grit with diameter 0.2 mm or above specific gravity of 2.65.

7.7 TYPES OF GRIT CHAMBERS

1.   Horizontal Flow Grit Chambers : (Fig. 7.5)

These are designed to maintain a velocity as to 0.3 m/s as practical. Such a velocity will carry most organic particles through the chamber and will tend to resuspend any particle that settle; but will permit heavier particle to settle out. Fig. 7.5 shows the grit chamber, consisting of long narrow open channel with a liquid depth between 0.9 to 1.2 m.

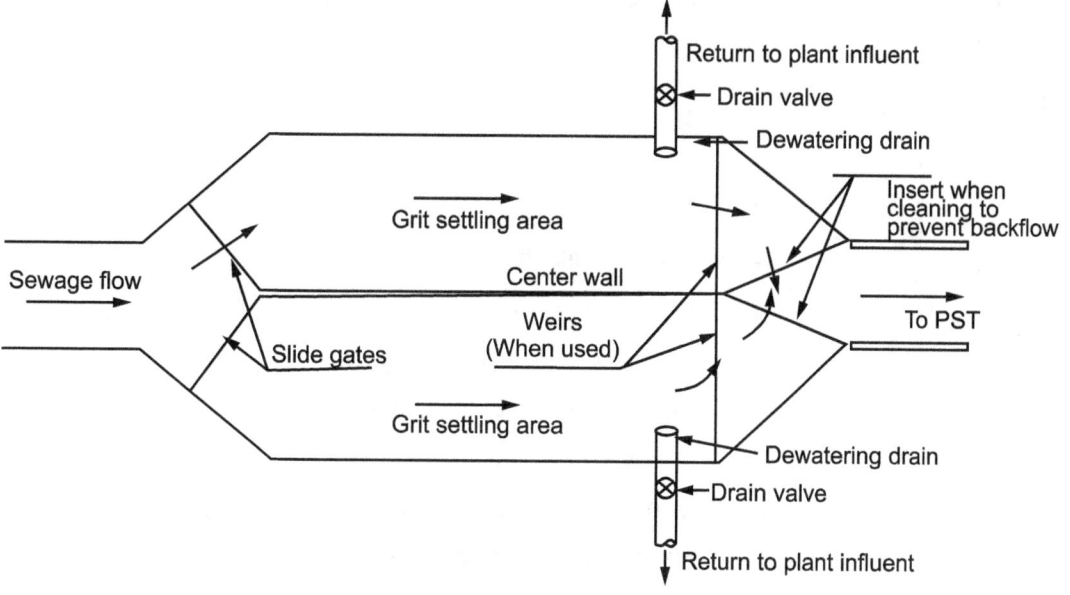

Fig. 7.5 : Grit chamber

2. Aerated Grit Chambers : (Fig. 7.6)

These are designed to provide detention periods of about 3 min at the maximum rate of flow. The cross-section of the tank is similar to that provided for oxidation ditch; except that a grit hopper of about 0.9 m deep with steeply sloping sides is located along one side of the tank under the air diffusers. The diffusers are located about 0.45 m or 0.6 m above the normal plane of the bottom.

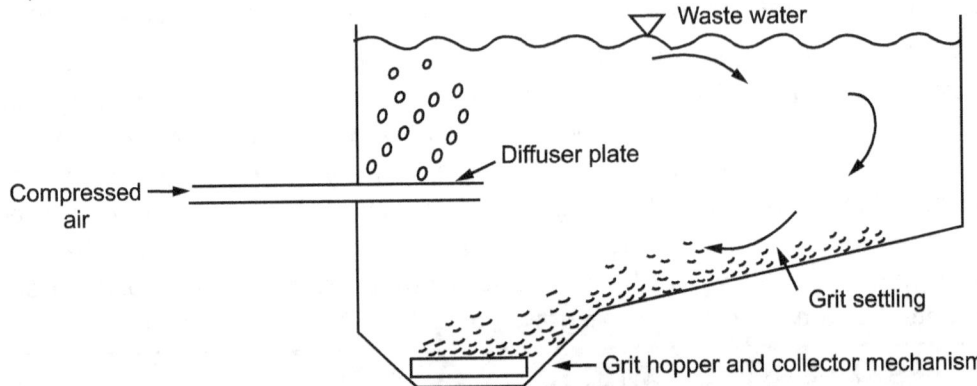

Fig. 7.6 : Aerated grit chamber

7.8 DESIGN OF GRIT CHAMBER

Grit chamber can be designed on a rational basis by considering it as a sedimentation basin having discrete settling.

The settling velocity is given by the Stoke's law, applicable for the particles of 0.1 mm diameter and less.

Settling velocity, $V_s = \dfrac{g}{18\,\mu}\,(\rho_s - \rho)\,d^2$

$V_s = \dfrac{g}{18\,v}\,(S_s - 1)\,d^2$

where,

V_s = Settling velocity (cm/sec)

d = Diameter of particle (cm)

μ = Absolute viscosity (centipoise)

v = μ/ρ = Kinematic viscosity (centistokes)

ρ_s = Density of particle (gm/cm³)

ρ = Density of water (gm/cm³)

S_s = Specific gravity of particle

g = Gravitational acceleration (cm/sec²)

For particles of diameter more than 1 mm,

$$V_s = \sqrt{3.33\,g\left(\frac{\rho_s - \rho}{\rho}\right)d}$$

Hazen's modified equation to determine settling velocity is

$$V_s = 60.6\,(S_s - 1)\,d\left[\frac{3t + 70}{100}\right]$$

where, t = Temperature of liquid in °C

By putting the value of S_s = 2.65 for grit, we get

$$V_s = d\,(3t + 70)$$

Table 7.1 : The Settling Velocities and Overflow Rates for Grit Chambers at 10°C

Diameter of Particles in mm	Settling Velocity cm/sec		Overflow Rate in an Ideal Grit Chamber, m³ld/m²	
	S_s = 2.65	S_s = 1.2	S_s = 2.65	S_s = 1.2
0.2	2.5	0.54	2160	467
0.15	1.8	0.39	1555	337

(Ref. : Manual on Sewerage and Sewage Treatment, 2nd Edition)

7.8.1 Design Criteria for Horizontal Flow Grit Chamber

- Detention time → 45 – 90 sec (Typical 60 sec)
- Horizontal velocity → 0.25 – 0.4 m/s (0.3 m/sec)
- Settling velocity for 65 mesh material → 1 – 1.3 m/min (1.15 m/min).
- Head loss in control section as % depth in channel → 30 – 40% (36%).
- Allowance for inlet and outlet turbulence → 2 × Ma × depth in channel.

7.8.2 Design Information for Aerated Grit Chamber

- Dimensions :

    Depth = 2 – 5 m
    Length = 7.5 – 20 m
    Width = 2.5 – 7.0 m

- Width/depth ratio → 1 : 1 → 5 : 2 (2 : 1).
- Detention time at peak flow → 2 – 5 min (3 min)
- Air supply, m³/m/min of length → 0.5 – 0.45 (0.3).

7.9 VELOCITY CONTROL

Theoretically, for obtaining a constant velocity of flow irrespective of fluctuation in sewage flow, a parabolic channel having an equation w = $\frac{3}{2}$ Q/nv has to be constructed. However, in normal practice, it is rather difficult to construct such channels of parabolic shape. Hence, a common practice is to use a rectangular channel and to ensure a proper control over the horizontal velocity of flow with the aid of outlet control devices such as :

1. A proportional flow weir or a Sutro weir. [Fig. 7.7 (a) and (b)].

2. Parabolic grit chamber. [Fig. 7.7 (c)]

3. A Parshall flume. [Fig. 7.7 (d)].

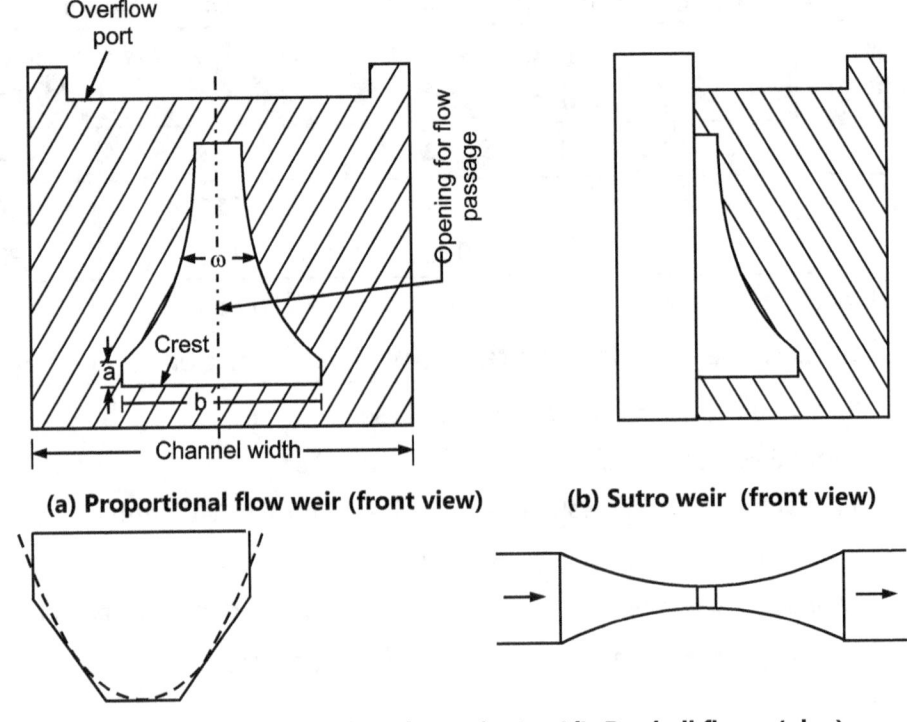

(a) Proportional flow weir (front view)   (b) Sutro weir (front view)

(c) Parabolic grit chamber (front view)   (d) Parshall flume (plan)

Fig. 7.7 : Velocity control devices

Thus, a normal grit chamber consists of a channel or a number of channels in parallel designed on the following basis :

*   It will have such a cross-sectional area, as it will give a horizontal velocity of flow of 0.25 to 0.3 m per second.

*   It's surface area gives a surface loading 22.50 m³/day/sq.m.

The design is thus based on the above two criteria and checked for the detention time which should fall between 45 to 90 seconds. The outlet control devices are then designed by following specific methods for each case. In normal practice, the invert of the proportional weir is provided at least 10 cm and normally about 30 cm above the invert of the channel.

- In order to avoid or bring down to a minimum value, the turbulence caused in the grit chamber due to momentum of incoming liquid and by drag of the outgoing liquid, smooth transition must be provided both at the inlet as well as at the outlet of the channel.
- Infact in normal practice, the actual length of the grit chamber is about 50% more than theoretically necessary, to compensate for the above factors.
- The grit collected at the bottom of these grit chambers is normally allowed to flow by gravity to a specific location from where it is then removed under hydraulic head. In such cases, where manual cleaning is practiced, the units have to be always in duplicate so that while one unit is being cleaned, the other can be used.
- The storage space for the grit at the bottom of the channels should be adequate for one day's storage for grit.
- The head loss, that will occur in the grit chambers, mostly depends upon the type of the outlet control device used and varies between 0.06 m to 0.6 m. The head losses are maximum in the case of the weir controlled sections and one lesser in cases where parshall flume is used.

In case parshall flume is used as a control device, it is necessary to use a parabolic cross-section of the grit chamber. However, in normal practice, it is difficult to construct such units and hence commonly a rectangular channel with chamfered sides are used. It will easily be appreciated, such compromises naturally result in sub-standard performance of the grit chamber.

7.10 WASHING OF GRIT

As known, it is very difficult to obtain a completely ideal performance of the grit chambers with the result that some of the lighter organic solids also settle to its bottom. Also some organic solids deposited on inorganic particles will settle at a faster rate and hence will be removed. Thus, it has been observed that in normal practice, grit contains a minimum of 5% of organic solids. It is hence necessary to remove these organic solids before the grit can be properly disposed off. The most common mechanism for doing this is by the use of grit washing equipment. In these devices, by some means, either mechanical or by supply of diffused air, sufficient shear is created between the interface of the organic and inorganic fractions so that the organic portion gets sheared off and is removed. This lighter material is then carried away by the flow of either water or the sewage flowing through the chamber.

The amount of grit removed is normally about 0.025 – 0.075 m³ per million litre of sewage flow and is normally used in the treatment plant itself for filling low lying areas or for laying minor roads.

Thus, the grit washing equipment is normally provided alongwith the grit chamber and hence some authorities feel that if inspite of providing the velocity control devices, if a washing arrangement is required, the cost can be brought down and also construction is simplified if no special control device is used. Such tanks which are normally referred to as Detritus tanks do not have any velocity control device and the only control that is exercised is to ensure that the grit particles which might have settled to the bottom are not scoured off. The net result is that a larger percentage of organic solids settle to the bottom, but then the design and construction becomes much easier. These tanks are normally designed for a detention time of 3 to 4 minutes and for an average horizontal velocity of flow of 0.3 m per second. These tanks are normally rectangular or square in cross-section and are provided with scrapers at the bottom for removal of collected matter and the grit washing equipment is also provided as in the case of grit chambers.

Sometimes, grit chambers are also provided with compressed air supply from bottom which enables a better control of grit removal, obviates need of separate grit washing, gives good efficiency even with improperly designed outlet control devices, and helps to remove oily materials here only. The air supply also helps to freshen the flowing sewage.

7.11 PROPORTIONAL FLOW WEIR   [MAY 1011]

For the efficient removal of grit, the velocity through the grit chamber should be constant inspite of change in flow. The proportional flow weir is most satisfactory type of automatic velocity control device. This is provided at the outer end of chamber. It consists of a rectangular plate, with an opening with curved sides for flow to pass through. This helps in maintaining the constant velocity in grit chamber by varying the cross-sectional area of flow through the weir so that the depth is proportional to the flow.

The shape of the opening between the plates of the proportional flow weir is made in such a way that the chamber depth will vary directly as the discharge, as a result of which the chamber velocity will remain constant for all flow conditions. The sides are so curved that the area decreases as the three half power of the increasing depth (h) of the flow over the weir.

The discharge Q in litres/sec over the weir –

$$Q = 1570 \, c \sqrt{2g} \, (Wh^{1/2}) \, h$$

where,

h = Depth of flow (m) above crest

W = Width of opening (m) at height h

g = Gravitational acceleration (m/sec^2)

c = Discharge coefficient

If we take $c = 0.6$ for sharp edged weir, we get

$$Q = 4170 \, (Wh^{1/2}) \, h$$

This shows that if $Wh^{1/2}$ is made constant, then the depth h will vary directly with the discharge. For different values of h, the corresponding values of width W can be determined and hence the parabolic curvature of the sides of weir could be worked out.

7.12 DISPOSAL OF GRIT

After separating grit from the sewage, it is washed to remove organic content from it. Washed grit may resemble particles of sand and gravel, which is total inorganic in nature. This may be disposed off by dumping or burying or by sanitary landfill. Unwashed grit, when mixed with soil, is valuable as soil conditioner and will give good yield of garden crops like tomatoes, cucumbers, etc.

7.13 EXAMPLES ON DESIGN OF GRIT CHAMBER

Example 7.4 : Design a grit chamber for the following data :

1. Maximum flow : 20 mld.
2. Diameter of particle to be removed : 0.2 mm and more.
3. Specific gravity of particle : 2.65.
4. Average temperature : 20°C.

Solution :

Assume a grit chamber of rectangular section and also assume that proportional flow weir is provided as velocity control device. Settling velocity as per Hazen's modified equation :

$$V_s = 60.6 (S_s - 1) \frac{3t + 70}{100} \cdot d$$

$$= 60.6 (2.65 - 1) \frac{3 \times 20 + 70}{100} \times \frac{0.2}{10}$$

$$= 2.6 \text{ cm/sec}$$

Assume flow through velocity (V_h) as 0.23 m/sec

Hence,   Cross sectional area $= \dfrac{\text{Flow (m}^3\text{/sec)}}{\text{Flow through velocity (m/sec)}}$

$$= \frac{20 \times 10^6}{24 \times 3600 \times 10^3 \times 0.23}$$

$$= 1.006 \text{ m}^2$$

Providing width of 1.2 m, liquid depth required $= \dfrac{1.006}{1.2} = 0.838$ m

Provide freeboard of 0.3 m and a space of 0.25 m for sludge accumulation.

∴   Total depth, $H = 1.388$ m   say 1.4 m

Now, $\dfrac{H}{L} = \dfrac{V_s}{V_h} = \dfrac{2.6}{23} = \dfrac{1}{8.84}$

∴ $L = 8.84\ H$ ∴ $L = 7.4$ m

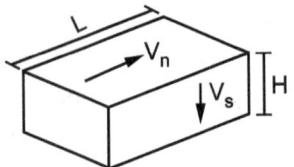
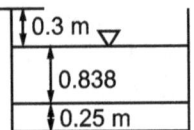

Fig. 7.8 (a)	**Fig. 7.8 (b)**

Example 7.5 : Design a grit chamber for the following data :

1. Flow : 15,000 m³/day.
2. Settling velocity of particle : 0.016 to 0.022 m/sec.
3. Flow through velocity : 0.3 m/sec.

Solution :

Let us provide a rectangular channel with a proportional flow weir.

Now horizontal velocity, $V_h = 0.3$ m/sec.

Assuming settling velocity as 0.02 m/sec (between 0.016 – 0.022 m/sec)

Now, $Q = 15000$ m³/day

$= \dfrac{15000}{24 \times 3600}$ m³/sec

$= 0.1736$ m³/sec

∴   Cross sectional area $= \dfrac{\text{Flow}}{\text{Velocity}} = \dfrac{0.1736}{0.3} = 0.578$ m²

Assuming a depth of 1 m, we have width of basin,

$W = \dfrac{0.578 \text{ m}^2}{1 \text{ m}} = 0.578$ m say 0.6 m

Now settling velocity, $V_s = 0.02$ m/sec

∴   Detention time $= \dfrac{\text{Depth}}{V_s} = \dfrac{1 \text{ m}}{0.02 \text{ m/sec}} = 50$ sec

∴   Length of tank $= V_h \times$ Detention time

$= 0.3 \times 50 = 15$ m

Hence, provide a grit chamber of size $L = 15$ m, $W = 0.6$ m, $H = 1$ m.

Example 7.6 : Design a proportional flow weir for a flow of 0.99 m³/sec.

Solution :

$$Q_{max} = 0.99 \text{ m}^3/\text{sec} = 990 \text{ lit/sec.}$$

$$\text{Assume, } h = 1.56 \text{ m}$$

Formula :

$$Q_{max} = 4170 \, bh^{1/2} \cdot h$$

$$990 = 4170 \, (b) \, (1.56)^{3/2}$$

∴

$$b = 0.12 \text{ m}$$

$$b = \text{Width of weir at crest level} = 12 \text{ cm}$$

If flow through velocity is to be constant for changing discharges, Q/a is to maintain constant. (a = cross sectional area of channel)

$$\frac{Q}{a} = \frac{Q}{bh} \quad (h = \text{depth of flow})$$

From this, we can have $\dfrac{Q}{h}$ = constant.

∴

$$\frac{Q}{h} = 4170 \, bh^{1/2} \cdot h = 4170 \, bh^{1/2} = \text{constant}$$

This constant is found from peak flow values.

i.e. b = 0.12 m and h = 1.56

∴

$$bh^{1/2} = 0.12 \times (1.56)^{1/2}$$

$$= 0.15$$

Thus, widths of weir for different depths of flow are calculated.

For $\quad h_1 = 0.035$ m,

For $\quad h_2 = 0.5$ m,

For $\quad h_3 = 0.75$ m,

For $\quad h_4 = 1.0$ m,

For $\quad h_5 = 1.25$ m,

$$b = \frac{0.15}{(0.035)^{1/2}} = 80 \text{ cm}$$

$$b = \frac{0.15}{(0.5)^{1/2}} = 21.2 \text{ cm}$$

$$b = \frac{0.15}{(0.75)^{1/2}} = 17 \text{ cm}$$

$$b = \frac{0.15}{(1.0)^{1/2}} = 15 \text{ cm}$$

$$b = \frac{0.15}{(1.25)^{1/2}} = 13.4 \text{ cm}$$

Now assume sill of weir at 30 cm from bottom.

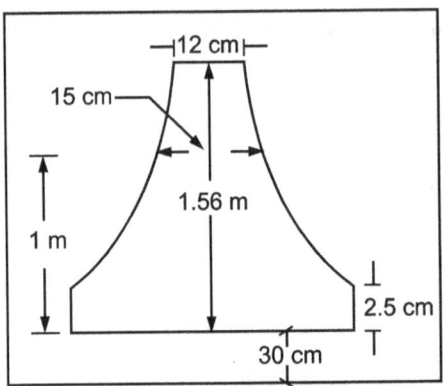

Fig. 7.9 : Proportional flow weir

SEDIMENTATION / SETTLING / CLARIFICATION

7.14 INTRODUCTION

Sedimentation is the separation from water, by gravitational settling, of suspended particles that are heavier than water. It is one of the most widely used unit operations in wastewater treatment. (Fig. 7.10).

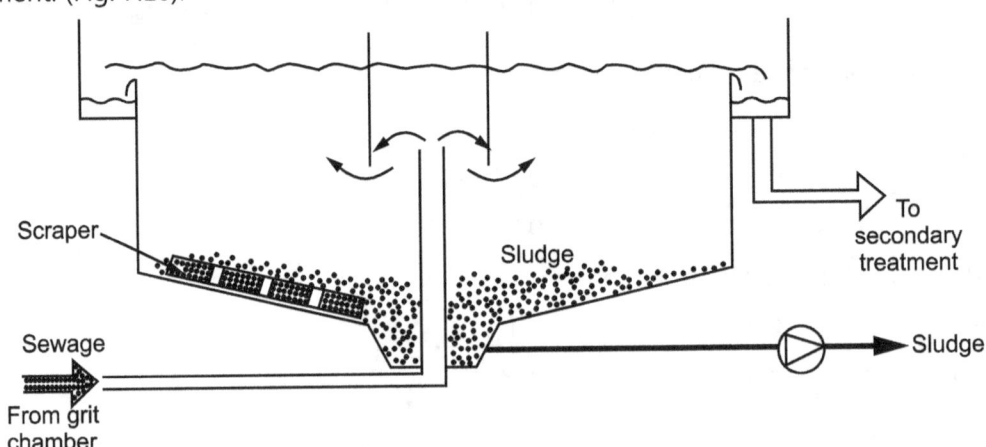

Fig. 7.10 : Schematic sketch of PST

This is used to remove grit and particulate matter in primary settling basin, to remove biological floc in secondary settling basin of ASP and to remove chemical floc when the chemical coagulation process is used. It is also used for solids concentration in sludge gravity thickeners.

7.15 DESCRIPTION

Depending on the concentration and nature of the suspended solids, discrete type, flocculant type or zone type settling will occur.

In the discrete type settling, which normally occurs in water supply practice, the solids are of such a nature that they do not change their size, shape and weight while settling. In the case of flocculant type of settling which normally occurs in the case of industrial waste treatment, the solids tend to increase their settling velocity due to coalescence during settling. When the concentration of suspended solids becomes too high, the particles are held in fixed position relative to each other by the Van der Waal's force of attraction and the mass settles as a whole. As the interface between the solid blanket and the clear liquid moves down, it encounters resistance from already settled particles and hence a transition zone comes into picture. Ultimately, when the solids reach the bottom, they come in direct contact with already settled sludge and the compression zone occurs. Thus in zone settling, the settling velocity decreases with time.

In the normal sedimentation practice, the Stoke's law is used to calculate the settling velocity of the particles. In designing continuous flow sedimentation basins, the following assumptions are normally made :

- Settling in a settling tank occurs exactly as it would occur in a quiescent container of liquid.

- The concentration of suspended solids at right-angles to the direction of flow is constant throughout.

- A particle that enters the sludge zone stays and is removed.

The normal sedimentation basins are designed on the basis of surface loading and detention time. The normal values of surface loading are between 25 to 45 $m^3/d/m^2$ and the detention time between 2 to 8 hours. The exact values of the surface loading and the detention times are normally selected depending on the specific purpose of use.

The normal practice is to use circular sedimentation tanks mainly because of their structural stability and due to their lesser cost for the same volume. They are also found to behave reasonably well from hydraulic point of view. Theoretically, a long narrow rectangular tank should give the best performance. Thus, in actual practice, either circular settling tanks having a diameter of 30 to 60 m, a side-water depth of 2.7 to 5 m with a bottom slope of 8% or rectangular tanks having a length to width ratio of 2 to 4, a maximum width of 20 m and a bottom slope of 1%; or square tanks having a bottom slope of 8% and the maximum side length of 20 m are used.

7.16 FACTORS AFFECTING SEDIMENTATION

(a) Characteristics of Solids :

- Size of particles
- Specific gravity of settling particles
- Concentration of suspended matter.

(b) Characteristics of Liquid :

- Temperature

- Viscosity

- Specific gravity of liquid.

(c) Physical Characteristics of Clarifier :

- Detention period.

- Shape of basins.

- Depth of the basin.

- Baffling and operation of basin.

- Viscosity and length of flow through basin.

7.17 CLASSIFICATION OF SETTLING TANKS

(a) According to the Shape of Tank :

- Rectangular tank. (Fig. 7.11)

- Circular tanks. (Fig. 7.12)

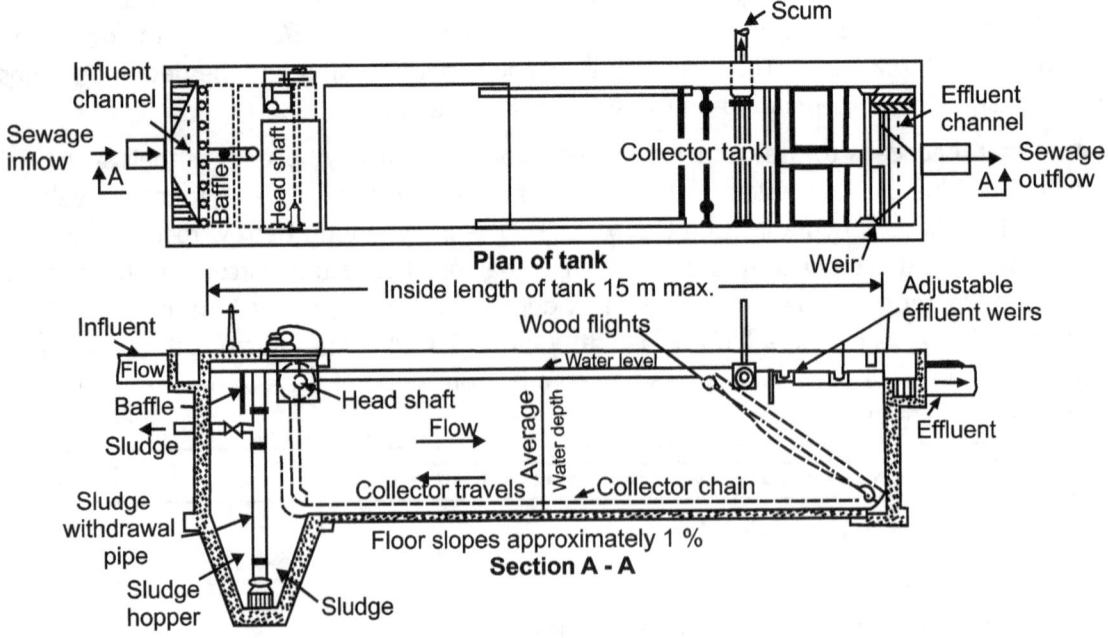

Fig. 7.11 : Rectangular settling tank

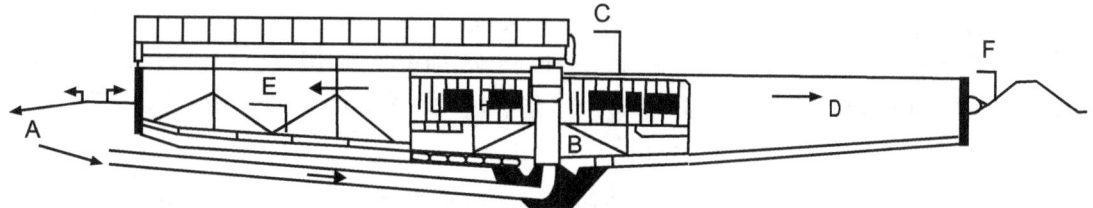

Sedimentation with flocculating compartment.

A = wastewater input, B = flocculation, C = stirrer, D = sedimentation, E = sludge scraper, F = outflow

Fig. 7.12 : Circular clarifiers

(b) According to Direction of Flow :

- Horizontal flow tanks – Longitudinal and radial flow.
- Vertical flow tanks.

(c) According to Method of Sludge Collection and Removal :

- Flat bottom tanks - without scraper.
- Hopper bottom tanks.
- Flat bottom tanks with mechanical scraper.

(d) According to Nature of Working :

- Fill and draw type.
- Continuous flow type.

(e) According to its Location :

- Preliminary settling tank (Grit chamber).
- Primary settling tank.
- Secondary settling tank.
- Sludge thickener.

7.18 INLET AND OUTLET ARRANGEMENTS

Inlet : The inlet to the tank can be of any of the following types :

1. **An Over-Flow Weir :** This type of inlet suffers from the drawback that it cannot give a uniform discharge over the whole weir length. But it is simple in construction.

2. **Baffle Type Inlet :** In this type of inlet, a number of pipes are provided along the width and the momentum of the incoming water is normally broken down by impact on a baffle kept against it. If a solid baffle is used, it is normally taken about 1 m below the water level. However, this sort of inlet is not much preferred now-a-days.

3. **Slotted Baffle Inlet :** The common practice now-a-days is to go in for the use of slotted baffle infront of the inlet. Thus, two slotted baffles are normally used one after another and the total area of the slots is normally kept from 7 to 20% of the cross-sectional area of the tank.

4. **Stengel Type of Inlet :** This is very commonly used in European countries.

In normal practice, the inlet zone, where inefficient settling occurs, is taken to extend for a length equal to depth of tank.

Outlet :

The outlet invariably consists of a weir. The rate of overflow over unit length of this weir is normally termed as the weir loading. In water supply practice, this weir loading is restricted to a maximum of 250 m³/d/m. While in the case of settling tanks for the activated sludge process etc., it is kept below 20,000 gpd/ft. Due to the flow occurring over the weir, an area in the form of a cylindrical sector having its axis along the outlet weir and a volume of KQ^2/V^2 is ineffective for settling. In this formula, given by the National Research Council of U.S.A., the value of K is normally between 0.35 to 0.55; Q is the weir loading and V is the settling velocity of the design particle. Obviously, the larger the weir loading, the larger will be the ineffective area.

The bottom slope provided to the tank provides sufficient space for the storage of sludge, which is normal practice, is continuously removed by a system of scrappers which complete one cycle over 15 to 30 minutes time.

7.19 DESIGN OF SETTLING TANKS

Size of the settling tanks is decided based on

- Overflow rate, m³/d/m²
- Detention time, hrs.
- Weir loading, m³/d/m.
- Solids loading rate, kg/day/m².

$$\text{Detention time (hrs)} = \frac{\text{Tank volume in m}^3}{\text{Flow (m}^3/\text{day)}} \times 24 = \frac{V}{Q}$$

$$\begin{bmatrix}\text{Surface loading or} \\ \text{overflow rate}\end{bmatrix} = \frac{\text{Flow (m}^3/\text{day)}}{\text{Area (m}^2)} = \frac{Q}{A}$$

$$\text{Weir loading rate} = \frac{\text{Flow (m}^3/\text{day)}}{\text{Length of weir (m)}}$$

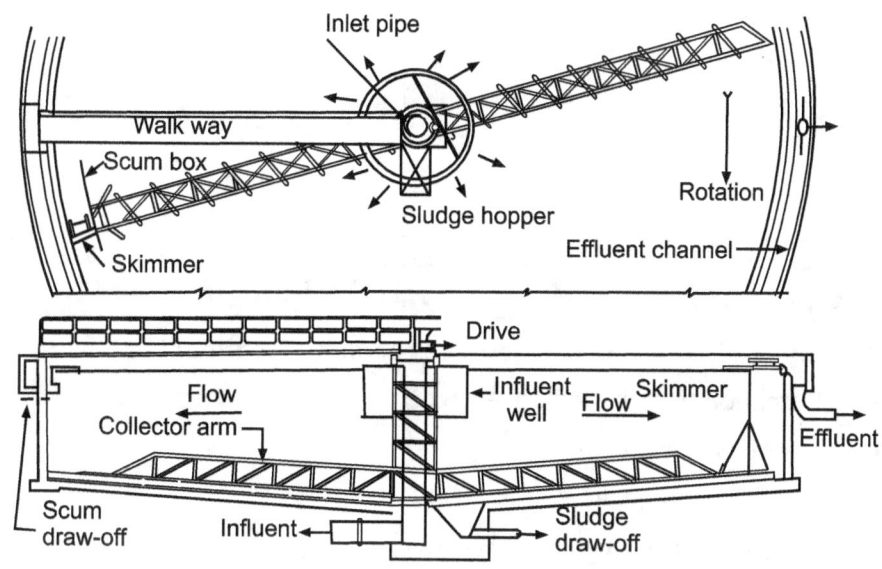

Fig. 7.13 : Circular primary clarifier with a

pier-supported center drive and peripheral effluent weir

Fig. 7.14 : Final clarifier designed for use with biological aeration

Table 7.2 : Design information for settling tanks

Tank Type	Value	
	Range	**Typical**
Rectangular		
Depth, m	2.5 – 4.5	3.6
Length, m	15 – 90	25 – 40
Width, m	3 – 21	6 – 10
Flight travel speed, m/min	0.6 – 1.2	1.0

Contd...

Circular		
Depth, m	2.5 – 4.5	4.5
Diameter, m	3.6 – 60.0	12 – 45
Bottom slope, mm/m	60 – 160	80
Flight travel speed, m/min	0.02 – 0.05	0.03

7.20 DESIGN CRITERIA FOR VARIOUS TYPES OF SETTLING TANKS

(a) Primary Settling Tank Followed by Secondary Treatment :

- Detention time, hrs → 2.0 – 2.5 (2)
- Overflow rate, m³/d/m²

    For average, flow → 35 – 50

    For peak flow → 80 – 120 (100)

- Weir loading, m³/d/m → 125 – 500 (250).

(b) Primary Settling with Activated Sludge Return :

- Detention time, hrs → 2.0 – 2.5 (2)
- Overflow rate, m³/d/m²
- For average flow → 25 – 35

    For peak flow → 50 – 60 (60)

- Weir loading, m³/d/m → 125 – 500 (250)

7.21 SLUDGE COLLECTION AND REMOVAL

Sludge collected at the bottom has to be removed from time to time. Now-a-days, sludge collection is invariably carried out with the help of mechanical scrapers.

- The floors of the mechanically scraped tanks should have gentle slopes. It should be around 2% for circular tanks and 8% for rectangular tanks.
- Slope of sludge hoppers without mechanical scraper is 2 to 1 (vertical to horizontal).
- Scraper velocity should be between one revolution in 45 min to one revolution in 80 min.
- Power required for driving scraping mechanism may vary from 0.5 to 1.5 H.P. for tanks of 3 m diameter or length.

The sludge collected at the bottom is taken out under hydrostatic pressure through an outlet pipe controlled by a sluice valve.

SOLVED EXAMPLE

Example 7.7 : Design a ciruclar PST with following data :

(i)   Average flow = 10 mld.

(ii) Surface loading = 50 m³/d/m² of tank area.

(iii) Effluent weir loading = 180 m³/d/m length of weir (only design of PST and outlet channels).

Solution : Assume detention time = 2 hrs.

$$\text{Depth of tank} = 3 \text{ m.}$$

$$Q_{avg} = \frac{10 \times 10^6 \times 10^{-3}}{24} = 416.67 \text{ m}^3/\text{hr}$$

$$\text{Volume of PST} = Q_{avg} \times T$$

$$= 416.67 \times 2$$

$$= 833.33 \text{ m}^3$$

$$\text{Plan area} = \frac{\text{Volume}}{\text{Depth}} = \frac{833.33}{3} = \mathbf{277.78 \text{ m}^2}$$

$$A = \frac{\pi}{4} d^2$$

$$277.78 = \frac{\pi}{4} \times d^2$$

$$\therefore \qquad d = 18.80 \text{ m}$$

$$\therefore \qquad \text{Diameter of tank} = \mathbf{18.80 \text{ m}}$$

$$\text{Surface loading} = \frac{Q}{A} = \frac{416.67}{277.78} \times 24$$

$$= 36 \text{ m}^3/\text{m/day} < 50 \text{ m}^3/\text{m/day} \quad \text{... Hence O.K.}$$

$$\text{Weir loading} = \frac{416.67 \times 24}{\pi \times D}$$

$$= 169.3 \text{ m}^3/\text{d/m} < 180 \text{ m}^3/\text{m/day ... Hence O.K.}$$

Design of outlet : Total flow in the outlet is

$$10 \text{ mld} = \frac{10 \times 10^6 \times 10^{-3}}{24 \times 60 \times 60} = 0.116 \text{ m}^3/\text{sec}$$

$$\text{Discharge is half one} = \frac{0.116}{2} = 0.058 \text{ m}^3/\text{sec}$$

Assume width $= 0.5$ m and $v = 1$ m/sec

$$\text{Depth} = \frac{\text{Discharge}}{\text{Width} \times \text{Velocity}} = \frac{0.058}{0.5 \times 1} = 0.116$$

$$= \mathbf{0.12 \text{ m}}$$

Slope of channel, $R = \dfrac{A}{P} = \dfrac{0.116 \times 0.5}{0.74} = 0.078$

Assume, $n = 0.015$

$$V = \frac{1}{n} R^{2/3} S^{1/2}$$

$$1 = \frac{1}{0.015} (0.078)^{2/3} S^{1/2}$$

$\therefore$ $S^{1/2} = 0.081$

$\therefore$ $S^{1/2} = \dfrac{1}{149}$

Say $S = 1$ in 160

$$L = \frac{\pi D}{2} = \frac{\pi \times 18.8}{2} = \mathbf{29.53 \text{ m}}$$

Difference between levels $= L \times \text{Slope} = 29.53 \times \dfrac{1}{160} = \mathbf{0.185 \text{ m}}$

EXERCISE

1. Explain the different treatment units in preliminary treatment of wastewater.

2. Describe in detail the working of screen chamber.

3. What are the different types of screens ? In what conditions each of them is used ?

4. How do you determine the head loss through screens ?

5. Write a short note on – Disposal of screenings.

6. What is the necessity of grit chamber in sewage treatment ?

7. Explain with sketch the working of grit chamber.

8. What is differential settling ? Explain with respect to grit chamber.

9. What is necessity of velocity control in grit chamber ? What are the different types of velocity control devices provided in grit chamber ?

10. What do you understand by proportional flow weir ? How do you determine the geometry of such a weir ?

11. Write a note on – Disposal of grit.

12. Design a grit chamber for the following data :

    (i)   Maximum flow : 12000 m³/day

    (ii)   Minimum size of grit to be removed : 0.18 mm

    (iii) Average temperature : 22°C

    (iv)   Specific gravity of particle : 2.65.

13. Design a screen chamber for the following data :

    (i)   Maximum flow : 12,000 m³/day.

    (ii)   Size of bar : 10 mm × 50 mm.

    (iii) Clear spacing between bars : 8 mm.

    (iv)   Velocity through screen at peak flow : 0.8 m/sec.

14. What is the necessity of PST in sewage treatment ?

15. Explain with sketch the working of PST.

16. Explain inlet and outlet arrangements in PST.

17. Give the design criteria for various types of settling tanks.

18. Discuss in brief various types of settling tanks.

19. Write a note on – Removal of suspended solids and BOD in PST.

UNIVERSITY QUESTIONS

1. Explain the purpose of providing grit chamber and give design criteria for grit chamber.   **(6 M) (May 2010)**

2. What is the difference between preliminary and primary treatment to waste water ?

                                                        (6 M) (May 2010, Dec. 2010)

3. Write a short note on proportional flow weir.   **(4 M) (May 2011)**

4. Explain different treatment units in preliminary treatment of wastewater.

                                                                    (4 M) (May 2009)

5. A screen consisting of 10 mm diameter bars, at a clear spacing of 40 mm, treats a maximum hourly flow of 1200 m³. Velocity of flow through the screen chamber is 0.75 m/sec.

    (i)   Length and number of bars.

    (ii)   Head loss in the chamber.   **(6 M) (May 2010)**

6. Design the screen chamber of an ETP to treat peak flow of 80 mld of sewage.

Assume inclination of bars 45° with horizontal, size of bars : 10 mm × 70 mm; 10 mm dimension facing the flow, clear spacing between bars as 50 mm and the velocity through the screen as 0.8 m/sec at peak flows.   **(6 M) (Dec. 2010)**

7. Design a grit chamber for the following data :

  (i)   Maximum flow   : 20 mld

  (ii)   Specific gravity of particle   : 2.65

  (iii) Diameter of particle to be removed   : 0.2 mm and above

  (iv)   Average temperature   : 20°C

  (v)   Flow through velocity   : 0.23 m/sec

  (vi)   Width of grit chamber   : 1.2 m

  (vii) Freeboard   : 0.3 m

  (viii) Space for sludge accumulation   : 0.25 m **(6 M) (Dec. 2010)**

8. Design a grit chamber for the following data :

  (i)   Maximum flow : 30 mld.

  (ii)   Diameter of particle to be removed : 0.2 mm and more.

  (iii) Specific gravity of particle : 2.65.

  (iv)   Average temperature : 20°C.   **(6 M) (May 2011)**

9. Design bar screen for a peak flow of 60 million litres per day.

          (6 M) (May 2009, 2011)

10. Design a grit chamber for the following data :

  (i)   Flow = 15000 m^3 per day,

  (ii)   Settling velocity of particle 0.016 to 0.022 m/sec

  (iii) Flow through velocity 0.3 m/sec.   **(6 M) May 2009**

✠ ✠ ✠

Chapter 8

WASTEWATER TREATMENT - SECONDARY

UNIT PROCESS AND UNIT OPERATIONS FOR SECONDARY TREATMENT

8.1 INTRODUCTION

8.1.1 Biological Unit Processes

In biological treatment processes, the removal or conversion of organic solids is brought about by the biological activities. They remove colloidal or dissolved biodegradable organic substances in wastewater. Organic substances are converted into gases that can escape to the atmosphere and as biological cell tissues that can be removed by settling.

The removal of dissolved and suspended carbonaceous BOD and the stabilization of organic matter found in wastewater is accomplished using a variety of microorganisms, principally bacteria. Microorganisms are used to oxidize the dissolved and suspended carbonaceous organic matter into simple end products and additional biomass. This is achieved by providing the favourable environment to microorganisms with food, DO, pH, temperature etc. The organic solids present in the wastewater serve as food for the aerobic microorganisms. The only thing to be provided is the DO, which is essential for the respiration of the aerobic organisms. In the biological treatment processes, the DO is supplied either through natural means or by mechanical means by agitation.

Anaerobic organisms can multiply in the absence of DO and do the decomposition, but the end products are undesirable fowl smelling gases like H_2S, CH_4, etc. Hence, anaerobic decomposition process is not generally preferred. However, anaerobic treatments are also adopted in certain situations because of certain specific advantages. Examples of anaerobic treatment processes are Septic tanks, UASB, Anaerobic sludge digesters.

8.1.2 Secondary Treatment

The secondary treatment is designed to remove soluble organics from the wastewater. Secondary treatment consists of a biological process and secondary settling is designed to substantially degrade the biological content of the sewage such as are derived from human waste, food waste, soaps and detergent. The majority of municipal and industrial wastewater plants treat the settled sewage liquor using aerobic biological processes. For this to be effective, the microorganisms require both oxygen and a substrate on which to live. There are number of ways in which this can be done. In all these methods, the bacteria and protozoa consume biodegradable soluble organic contaminants (e.g. sugars, fats, organic short chain carbon molecules etc.) and bind much of the less soluble fractions into floc particles.

8.1.3 Classification of Biological Treatment System

The biological treatment systems are classified as follows :

(a) Attached growth system and

(b) Suspended growth system.

(a) Attached Growth System :

In attached growth biological treatment systems, the biomass is attached. Trickling filters and biological towers are examples of systems that contain biomass adsorbed to rocks or plastic. Wastewater is sprayed over the top of the rocks or plastic and allowed to trickle down and over the attached biomass, which removes materials from the waste through sorption and biodegradation. A related type of attached growth system is the rotating biological contactor, where biomass is attached to a series of thin, plastic wheels that rotate the biomass in and out of the wastewater. This coating of microorganisms is able to trap and consume BOD and ammonia in the wastewater.

In attached growth or fixed film systems, the microorganisms responsible for conversion of organic matter are attached to an inert packing material. Packing material used in attached growth processes include rock, gravel, sand and wide range of plastic and other synthetic material. Attached growth system can be operated as aerobic or anaerobic processes. The packing materials can be completely submerged in liquid or not submerged, with air space above the biofilm liquid layer.

Fixed film systems are more able to cope with shocks in biological loading and provide higher removal rates for BOD and suspended solids than suspended growth systems.

(b) Suspended Growth System :

In suspended growth systems, the microorganisms responsible for treatment are maintained in liquid suspension by appropriate mixing methods. Typically, suspended growth systems require smaller footprints than fixed film systems for an equivalent capacity. There are a number of biological processes. The most common is activated sludge process in which microbes, also known as biomass, are allowed to feed on organic matter in the wastewater and remain in suspension. The make-up and dynamics of the microbial population is a function of how the ASP is operated.

Types of Biological Treatment based on Process :

There are two types of biological treatment process; aerobic and anaerobic. Aerobic process means that dissolved oxygen (DO) is present for the microbes for respiration. Anaerobic process means that the process proceeds in the absence of DO.

The effluent from primary treatment units is further treated generally using aerobic biological processes. For these processes to be effective, the microorganisms require both dissolved oxygen and a substrate on which to live. Oxygen can be supplied either through natural process or artificial mechanical means. In both cases, the bacteria and protozoa consume biodegradable soluble organic contaminants and bind much of the less soluble fractions into floc particles. The oxidization of organic substances can be achieved by anaerobic process also by anaerobic organisms, which do not need DO. They take their oxygen requirement from complex organic substances, such as sulphate (SO_4), phosphate (PO_4), etc.

The end products of aerobic and anaerobic processes are different. Under aerobic conditions, if completely oxidized, organic matter is transformed into non-hazardous products such as CO_2 and H_2O and cell tissues. But an anaerobic process, apart from CO_2 and H_2O and cell tissues, can also produce methane (CH_4), which is explosive, and ammonia (NH_3) and hydrogen sulfide (H_2S), which are toxic. Some materials are better degraded under anaerobic conditions than under aerobic conditions. In some cases, the combination of anaerobic and aerobic systems in a series provides better and more economical treatment than either system could alone provide.

8.1.4 Treatment Units in the Biological Processes

The following optional treatment units are used for the treatment of domestic sewage :

Conventional treatment processes :

1. Activated Sludge Process (ASP) and
2. Trickling Filter (TF).

Low cost methods :

1. Oxidation Ditch (OD),
2. Aerated Lagoon (AL),
3. Waste Stabilization Ponds (WSP) and
4. Up-flow Anaerobic Sludge Blanket System (UASB).

Emerging technologies :

1. Moving Bed Biological Reactor (MBBR) and
2. Membrane Biological Reactor (MBR).

(1) Activated Sludge Process :

The Activated Sludge Process (ASP) is an aerobic biological wastewater treatment process that uses microorganisms, including bacteria, fungi, and protozoa, to speed up decomposition of organic matter requiring oxygen for treatment. In this process, microorganisms are thoroughly mixed with organics under conditions that stimulate their growth and waste materials are removed. Activated sludge plants use a variety of mechanisms and processes to use dissolved oxygen to promote the growth of biological floc that substantially removes organic material. A portion of the settled sludge is returned to the aeration tank (and hence is called return sludge) to maintain an optimum concentration of acclimated microorganisms in the aeration tank to break down the organics. It also traps particulate material and can, under ideal conditions, convert ammonia to nitrite and nitrate and ultimately to nitrogen gas.

(2) Trickling filters :

Trickling filters are intended to treat particularly strong or variable organic loads. They are typically circular filters filled with open stone or synthetic filter media to which wastewater is applied at a relatively high rate. The design of the filters allows high hydraulic loading and a high flow-through of air. On larger installations, air is forced through the media using blowers. The resultant liquor is usually within the normal range for conventional treatment processes.

(3) Oxidation Ditch :

Oxidation ditch is an extended aeration ASP. It is a large holding tank in a continuous ditch with oval shape similar to that of a race-track. The ditch is built on the surface of the ground and is lined with an impermeable lining. With a detention time of more than 24 hours, the wastewater has plenty of exposure to the open air for the diffusion of oxygen. The liquid depth in the ditches is very shallow, 0.9 to 1.5 in, which helps to prevent anaerobic conditions from occurring at the bottom of the ditch.

(4) Aerated Lagoon :

An aerated lagoon is a suspended-growth process treatment unit. The aerated lagoon system consists of a large earthen pond or basin that is equipped with mechanical aerators to maintain an aerobic environment and to prevent settling of the suspend biomass. Initially, the population of microorganisms in an aerated lagoon is much lower than that in an ASP because there is no sludge recycle. Therefore, a significantly longer residence time is required to achieve the same effluent quality.

(5) Waste Stabilization Ponds :

Waste Stabilization Ponds (WSPs), often referred to as oxidation ponds or lagoons, are holding basins where decomposition of organic matter is taking place naturally. A WSP is a relatively shallow body of wastewater contained in an earthen man-made basin into which wastewater flows and from which, after certain retention time a well-treated effluent flows out. The activity in the WSPs is a complex symbiosis of bacteria and algae, which stabilizes the waste and reduces pathogens. The algae produce oxygen during photosynthesis by utilizing carbon dioxide and solar energy derived from sun light. The bacteria utilize oxygen for the biological process to convert the organic content of the wastewater to more stable and less offensive forms and release carbondioxide.

(6) Up-flow Anaerobic Sludge Blanket (UASB) Reactor

UASB reactor is an anaerobic treatment system. In a UASB reactor, the accumulation of influent suspended solids and bacterial activity and growth lead to the formation of a sludge blanket near the reactor bottom, where all biological processes take place. Two main features influencing the treatment performance are the distribution of the wastewater in the reactor and the "three-phase-separation" of sludge, gas and water.

(7) Moving Bed Biological Reactor :

Moving Bed Biological Reactor (MBBR) involves the addition of inert media into existing activated sludge basins to provide active sites for biomass attachment. This conversion results in a strictly attached growth system.

(8) Membrane Biological Reactors :

Membrane Biological Reactors (MBR) includes a semi-permeable membrane barrier system either submerged or in conjunction with an activated sludge process. This technology guarantees removal of all suspended and some dissolved pollutants. The limitation of MBR systems is directly proportional to nutrient reduction efficiency of the activated sludge process. The cost of building and operating a MBR is usually higher than conventional wastewater treatment.

The final step in the secondary treatment stage is to settle out the biological floc or filter material in a secondary sedimentation tank (SST) or secondary clarifier and produce sewage water containing very low levels of organic material and suspended matter

8.2 BIOLOGICAL PRINCIPLE

The natural process of microbiological metabolism in aquatic environment is capitalized in the biological treatment of waste water. Under proper environmental conditions, the soluble organic substances of the waste are completely destroyed by biological oxidation, part of it is oxidized while rest are converted into biological mass, in the biological reactors. The end products of the metabolism are either gas or liquid; one the other hand, the synthesised biological mass can flocculate easily, particularly with increasing mean age of the cells and are separated out in a clarifier. Therefore, the biological treatment system usually consists of (1) a biological reactor, and (2) a settling tank to remove the produced biomass or sludge.

The application of the above concept of biodegradation in the biological treatment designs, needs an adequate knowledge of the process kinetics. The following sections describe the process kinetics in brief.

8.3 IMPORTANT MICROORGANISMS IN WASTEWATER

Microorganisms are unicellular microscopic living things. They multiply by binary division of cells within 10 to 20 minutes. They require oxygen for their respiration. They decompose the organic matter and convert them into cells. Examples of microorganisms are Bacteria, Fungi, Virus etc.

There are two types of microorganisms :

1. Aerobic bacteria, and

2. Anaerobic bacteria.

Aerobic bacteria use dissolved oxygen (DO) from the water bodies for their respiration. They oxidize organic matter under aerobic conditions. The end products of the decomposition are water, CO_2 and cell tissues. Anaerobic bacteria use oxygen derived from chemical substances for their respiration. They multiply in the absence of DO in the water bodies. They oxidize the organic matter under septic conditions. The end products include fowl smelling gases like H_2S, CH, etc.

The Role of Microorganisms in Wastewater :

Bacteria may be aerobic, anaerobic or facultative. Aerobic bacteria require oxygen for life support whereas anaerobes can sustain life without oxygen. Facultative bacteria have the capability of living either in the presence or in the absence of oxygen. In the typical sewage treatment plant, oxygen is added to improve the functioning of aerobic bacteria and to assist them in maintaining superiority over the anaerobes. Agitation, settling, pH and other controllable are carefully considered and employed as a means of maximizing the potential of bacterial reduction of organic in the wastewater.

Single celled organisms grow and when they have attained a certain size, divide, becoming two. Assuming an adequate food supply, they then grow and divide again like the original cell. Every time a cell splits, approximately every 20 to 30 minutes, a new generation occurs. This is known as the exponential or logarithmic growth phase. At the exponential growth rate, the largest number of cells are produced in the shortest period of time. In nature and in the laboratory, this growth cannot be maintained indefinitely, simply because the optimum environment of growth cannot be maintained. The amount of growth is the function of two variables : environment and food. The pattern which actually results is known as the bacterial growth rate curve. Initially dehydrated products (dry) must first re-hydrate and acclimate in a linear growth phase before the exponential rate is reached.

Microorganisms and their enzyme systems are responsible for many different chemical reactions produced in the degradation of organic matter. As the bacteria metabolize, grow and divide they produce enzymes. These enzymes are high molecular weight proteins.

It is important to recognize the fact that colonies of bacteria are literally factories for the production of enzymes. The enzymes which are manufactured by the bacteria will be appropriate to the substrate in which the enzyme will be working and so you have automatic production of the right enzyme for the biological reduction of any waste material, provided you have the right bacteria to start with. Enzymes do not reproduce whereas as bacteria do.

Enzymes in biochemical reactions act as organic catalysts. The enzymes actually become a part of the action, but after having caused it, split off from it and are themselves unchanged. After the biochemical reactions are complete and products formed, the enzyme is released to catalyze another reaction. The rate of reaction may be increase by increasing the quantity of the substrate or temperature up to a certain point , but beyond this, the rate of reaction ceases to increase because the enzyme concentration limits it.

All treatment plants should be designed to take advantage of the decomposition of organic materials by bacterial activity. This is something you can equate to lower costs, increased capacity and an improved quality of effluent; even freedom from bad odours which may typically result when anaerobic bacteria become dominant and in their decomposition process, produce hydrogen sulfide gas and similar by-products.

Consider the fact that the total organic load of wastewater or sewage is composed of constantly changing constituent, it would be quite difficult to degrade all of these organics by the addition of one enzyme, or even several enzymes. Enzymes are specific catalysts and do not reproduce. What is needed is the addition of an enzyme manufacturing system right in the sewage that can be pre-determined as to its activity and performance and which has the initial or continuing capacity to reduce waste.

8.4 BACTERIAL GROWTH

General Growth Pattern :

Whenever a microorganism is inoculated in a suitable substrate it grown in number by multiplication and the process of growth continues till the substrate is exhausted or any other factor hinders the growth. In a batch reactor such growth of microorganisms may be schematically shown as in Fig. 8.1. The growth pattern follows three distinct phases viz.

- log or exponential growth phase,
- declining or retarded growth phase and
- endogenous growth phase or death phase.

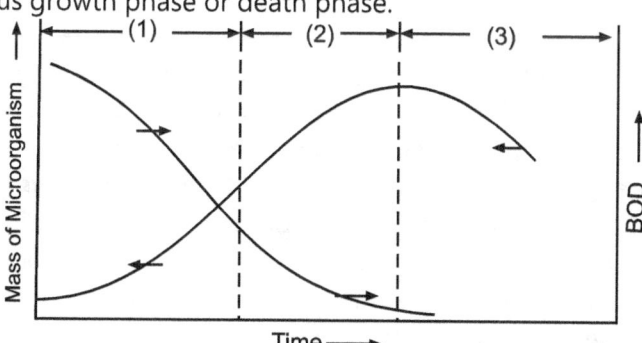

Fig. 8.1 : Microorganism growth pattern in batch reactors : (1) log growth phase, (2) declining growth phase, (3) endogenous growth phase

Growth in Terms of Bacterial Numbers and Mass :

In the log growth phase, the supply of the substrate is always adequate and the rate of metabolism is only dependent on the ability of the microorganism to utilize the substrate. In the declining growth phase, the rate of metabolism decreases due to the limitations in substrate supply. In the endogenous growth phase, the microorganisms are forced to oxidize their own protoplasms for energy (endogenous respiration) and thereby decrease in number.

The growth pattern as shown in Fig. 8.1 is not applicable in a continuous biological reactor, where the substrate or food for the microorganism is continuously supplied.

The rate of substrate supply and the mass of active microorganisms set the growth phase of microorganisms or the rate of metabolism in such a reactor. In other words, the "Food-to-microorganisms" ratio controls the rate of metabolism in a continuous biological reactor as shown in Fig. 8.2. Low food-to-microorganism ratio, i.e. relatively scanty supply of food results in an endogenous growth of microorganisms; on the other hand log growth phase of metabolism is observed when the supply of food is abundant, i.e. when the food-to-microorganism ratio is higher. The sludge produced at log phase is of very poor settling characteristics and that in the endogenous phase not only settles well but it is also more stable in nature. As such, in all biological reactors, the system is so adjusted as to create a rate of metabolism ranging in between endogenous and declining growth phase as shown in Fig. 8.2.

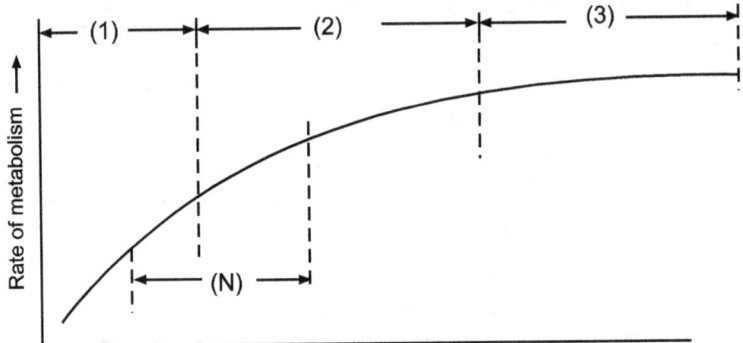

Fig. 8.2 : Rate of microbiological metabolism in continuous biological reactors :
(1) Endogenous growth phase, (2) Declining growth phase, (3) Log growth phase, (N) normal range of operations in most of the biological reactors

As evident from Fig. 8.1, the formulation of a biological process is possible either in terms of changes in the substrate concentration or in terms of microbiological growth. In the analyses and design of a biological treatment system, any such formulations can be relied upon, depending on the availability of relevant data. However, the microbiological growth kinetics offer a more rational method of designing the biological treatment units.

8.5 KINETICS OF BIOLOGICAL GROWTH

Normally the biological treatment units are operated in the declining growth phase of the microorganisms. At declining growth phase, the BOD removal rates are observed to be concentration dependent and are expressed by the following relationship :

$$-\frac{dS}{dt} = KS \qquad \qquad \text{... (8.1)}$$

where,   S = Amount of BOD remaining in the reactor after time t, mg/l(ML^{-3})

                t = Contact time, day (T)

and   K = 1st order BOD removal rate constant, per day (T^{-1})

It may be noted that the value of K may be based on either overall BOD$_5$ or only soluble BOD$_5$. Soluble BOD$_5$ removal rate constants are always higher than the overall BOD$_5$ removal rate constants. The value of K may vary with different types of wastes and environmental conditions. But for normal domestic waste it may be assumed to be equal to 0.23/day.

Integration of the equation (8.1) between the limits S = S$_0$ at t = 0 and S = S$_1$ at t = t yields :

$$\frac{S_1}{S_0} = e^{-Kt} \qquad \qquad \text{... (8.2)}$$

where S$_0$ = initial concentration of BOD and S$_1$ = final concentration of BOD.

The equation (8.2) is a normal 1st order BOD removal rate equation and is applicable for a batch operation only.

The equation (8.1) is sometimes written in the following form, which takes into account of the mass of microorganisms in the batch reactor :

$$-\frac{dS}{dt} = k \, X \, S \qquad \qquad \text{... (8.3)}$$

where,   k = specific BOD (overall or soluble, as the case may be removal coefficient, l/mg/day, which equal to K/X,

and   X = microorganism concentration in the reactor, mg/l

In most of the biological reactor designs, the concentration of the Volatile Suspended Solids (VSS) in the reactor is taken as the concentration of the microbial mass. This assumption is true only when the waste under treatment is soluble in nature; but the estimate with such assumption may be two fold to five fold in anaerobic treatment and upto two fold in anaerobic treatment, with domestic waste water, because of a large amount of inactive (i.e. non-biomass) volatile suspended solids present in it. However, since only the settled waste waters are treated, in most of the biological treatment units, the above approximation may not give rise to an identifiable error.

The value of k and K are generally reported for a standard reactor temperature of 20°C. These values at other temperatures may be calculated using the following relationship.

$$k_T = k_{20} \, \theta^{T-20} \qquad \qquad \text{... (8.4)}$$

where,   T = Temperature in °C,

and   θ = Temperature coefficient.

Different values of θ have been reported by different workers for different temperature ranges. Unless otherwise stated, for temperature not below 20°C, θ may be assumed as 1.047, in batch processes. In continuous flow biological reactors, however, the following values may be assumed for θ :

(i)   Activated sludge process   –   1.00 – 1.03

(ii) Trickling filter   –   1.02 – 1.04

(iii) Aerated lagoon   –   1.06 – 1.09

8.5.1 Cell Growth and Substrate Utilization

In any low-substrate-concentration system, under proper environmental conditions, the mass of microorganisms will tend to increase due to cell synthesis and decrease due to the endogenous respiration; the net rate of growth of bio-mass, dX/dt, may be given the following relationship :

$$\frac{dX}{dt} = Y\frac{dF}{dt} - k_d X \qquad \qquad \text{... (8.5)}$$

where, X = Concentration of the microorganisms in the reactor, mg/l (ML^{-3})

t = Time of contact in the reactor, days (T),

dX/dt = Growth of microorganisms in unit time per unit volume, (ML^{-3} T^{-1}), mg/l/day

$\dfrac{dF}{dt}$ = Rate of substrate utilization, mg/l/day (ML^{-3} T^{-1})

Y = Growth yield coefficient, mg/mg

and k_d = Microorganisms decay coefficient, per day, (T^{-1})

Now, if S is concentration of a soluble substrate in the reactor, for a normal biological reactor, where the substrate removal is mediated through the microorganisms only, the rate of reduction of substrate concentration can closely the approximated to the rate of substrate utilization.

i.e. $$\frac{dS}{dt} = \frac{dF}{dt} \qquad \qquad \text{... (8.6)}$$

The equation (8.5) may be modified in the following form :

$$\frac{dX/dt}{X} = Y\frac{dF/dt}{X} - k_d \qquad \qquad \text{... (8.7)}$$

In equation (8.7), the term (dX/dt)/X is referred to as the "specific growth rate" and is often symbolized as μ and the term (dF/dt)/X is referred to as the "specific substrate utilization rate".

Now in a batch process, if the substrate is supplied to the microorganisms in excess, the specific substrate utilization rate remains constant under a particular set of substrate type, microorganisms and environmental conditions. However, when the concentration of the substrate becomes growth limiting, i.e. when the substrate supply falls short, the specific utilization and hence specific growth of microorganisms declines. The relationship between the substrate concentration and the specific utilization rate is usually given by the following continuous hyperbolic function and is shown graphically in Fig. 8.3.

$$\frac{dF/dt}{X} = \frac{k_m S}{K_s + S} = \frac{dS/dt}{X} \qquad \qquad \text{... (8.8)}$$

where, k_m = Maximum rate of specific substrate utilization per day (T^{-1})

and K_s = Substrate concentration at the utilization rate of $k_m/2$, mg/l (ML^{-3})

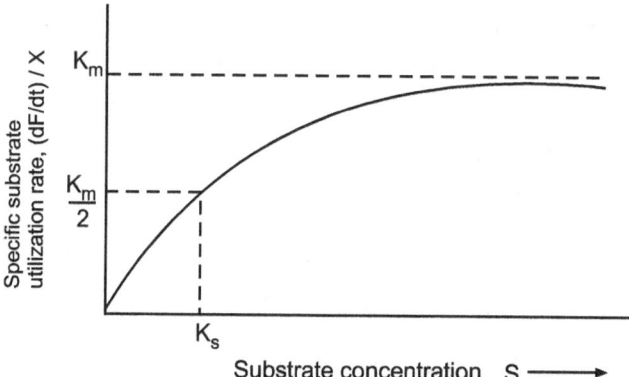

Fig. 8.3 : Effect of the substrate concentration on the specific substrate utilization rate

8.5.2 Effects of Endogenous Metabolism

In normal biological reactors where the substrate concentration is usually low, i.e. $S << K_s$, the specific utilization rate approaches to $k_m S/K_s$.

i.e.
$$\frac{dF/dt}{X} = \frac{dS/dt}{X} = \frac{k_m S}{K_s}$$

or
$$\frac{dS}{dt} = \frac{k_m}{K_s} XS \qquad\qquad\qquad ... (8.9)$$

Hence, comparing equation (8.3) and (8.9), when the substrate concentrations are given by soluble BOD, in a low-BOD-process,

$$k = \frac{k_m}{K_s} \qquad\qquad\qquad ... (8.10)$$

For any general case, using equation (8.8), the equation (8.7) may be rewritten as follows :

$$\frac{dX/dt}{X} = \frac{Yk_m S}{K_s + S} - k_d \qquad\qquad ... (8.11\ a)$$

$$= \frac{\mu_m \cdot S}{K_s + S} - k_d \qquad\qquad ... (8.11\ b)$$

where, μ_m = Maximum specific growth rate $(\mu) = Y k_m$.

For the analysis of any biological process any one of the equations (8.5), (8.7) and (8.11) may be used.

8.6 OXYGEN REQUIREMENT IN AEROBIC PROCESSES

The BOD removal in a biological reactor is accomplished not entirely by oxidation – a part of the BOD is removed from the system, without being oxidized, in the form of wastage of excess sludge (synthesized biomass) from the system.

So, the oxygen requirement will be equal to the amount that would have been required, if all the BOD was removed by oxidation only (i.e. the ultimate BOD removed), less, a credit for the fraction of BOD removed by sludge wasting. Therefore one can write :

Rate of oxygen usage = (Rate of BOD_L removal) – f(Rate of excess sludge wasted) in which, f is a function that denotes the amount of oxygen "saved" per unit weight of sludge removed from the system. Based on the stiochiometry of cell oxidation, it has been shown that f has a constant value of 1.42 kg of O_2 per kg of cells.

Therefore, an a finite time and mass basis :

$$O_2 \text{ requirement/day} = \text{Ultimate BOD removed/day}$$

$$- 1.42 \text{ (Excess sludge wasted per day)} \quad \quad \text{... (8.12)}$$

Now assuming BOD rate constant = 0.23/day at 20°C,

$$\frac{\text{Ultimate BOD}}{\text{5 day 20°C BOD}} = \frac{1}{1 - e^{0.23 \times 5}} = 1.47 \quad \quad \text{... (8.13)}$$

Using equation (8.13), the equation (8.12) may be modified in the following form :

Weight of oxygen required/day

$$= \text{(5 day 20°C BOD removed/day) } 1.47 - 1.42$$

$$\text{(excess sludge wasted/day)}$$

$$= 1.47 \ Q(S_0 - S_1) - 1.42 \ V \ (X/\theta_c) \quad \quad \text{... (8.14)}$$

where,   Q = Rate of inflow of waste

S_0, S_1 = Substrate concentration at the inlet and outlet of the system respectively, BOD_5 in mg/l

V = Volume of the reactor

X = Microorganism concentration in the reactor

and θ_c = Mean cell residence time

The equation (8.14) may be used directly to calculate the theoretical oxygen requirement of the system. It may be noted that, the above expression is not materially different from that given by Eckenfelder and O'Connor, as presented below :

Oxygen requirement/day = $Q \ (S_0 - S_1) \ a' + VXb'$ \quad \quad ... (8.15)

The equation (8.14) may be rewritten in the following form :

Weight of oxygen required/day

$$= 1.47 \ Q \ (S_0 - S_1) - 1.42 \ V \left(Y \frac{dF}{dt} - k_d X \right)$$

$$= Q \ (S_0 - S_1) \ (1.47 - 1.42 \ Y) + 1.42 \ k_d \ XV \quad \quad \text{... (8.16)}$$

in which Y is expressed in mg of cell per mg of 5 day BOD. The terms $(1.47 - 1.42 \ Y)$ and $1.42 \ k_d$ of the equation (8.16) are referred to as a' and b' respectively in the equation (8.15).

ACTIVATED SLUDGE PROCESS

8.7 INTRODUCTION   (MAY 2011)

Aerobic treatment processes utilise a mixed population of micro-organisms. The wastewater is first treated in preliminary and primary treatment units like screen chamber, grit chamber, oil and grease removal tank. Here the floating solids, bigger size material, settleable solids, oil and grease are removed. In these treatment units, around 50 to 60% suspended solids and about 40% of BOD is removed. Then the waste water is treated biologically. The objectives of biological treatment of wastewater are to coagulate and remove the non-settleable colloidal solids and to stabilize the organic matter with the help of mixed population of micro-organisms. Many different types of organisms, including bacteria, fungi, protozoa, rotifers, and other higher forms of life can be found in the system. At any particular time the various forms present, bacteria are the most important as they represent the major functional unit of biological system.

The biological treatment techniques used are of three types :

1. Attached growth processes.
2. Suspended growth processes.
3. Combined processes.

In the suspended growth process, all the contents of wastewater from the reactor are maintained in suspension with the liquid by employing either natural or mechanical mixing.

The suspended growth processes are :

1. Activated sludge process.
2. Aerated lagoons.
3. Digestion of sludge.

In this chapter, the various aspects of activated sludge process are discussed. One should understand that, the micro-organisms convert the soluble organic matter into gaseous form and cell mass. And then the insoluble cell mass is removed in the subsequent treatment units.

The treated effluent obtained from a well operated ASP is of high quality. As compared to trickling filter effluent, the ASP effluent will have low BOD values. BOD removal from 70% to 99.9% can be obtained in this biological treatment process. The advantage of ASP is it requires less land area and quality of sludge is also good.

8.8 PROCESS DESCRIPTION   (MAY 2010)

The process consists of (a) rapid adsorption of waste substrate by sludge, (b) progressive oxidation of adsorbed organics and synthesis of biomass, (c) separation of biomass and recirculation. Operationally, biological waste treatment with an ASP is typically accomplished using a typical flow diagram as shown in Fig. 8.4.

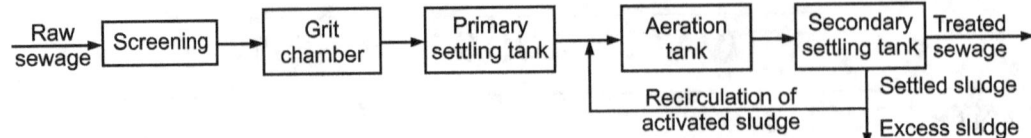

Fig. 8.4 : Flow diagram of ETP with conventional activated sludge process

- In activated sludge process, settled wastewater from primary settling tank is introduced into a reactor (aeration tank) where an aerobic bacterial culture is maintained in suspension.
- The agitated wastewater is known as mixed liquor.
- In the reactor, the micro-organisms convert soluble organic matter into energy, new cell mass and carbon dioxide gas.
- The aerobic environment into the reactor is maintained with the help of diffused or mechanical aerators.
- These aerators also keep the mixed liquor in suspension, after some specific period of time (hydraulic retention time), the mixture of new cell mass and old cells is transferred into secondary settling tank where the cells (biomass) are separated from treated effluent. A portion of biomass (sludge) is recirculated to maintain the desired concentration of micro-organisms in the reactor, and remaining sludge is either wasted or stabilised.

In activated sludge process, the bacteria are the most important micro-organisms because they are responsible for decomposition of organic material present in wastewater. In general, the bacteria in ASP are gram negative and include Pseudomonas, Achromobacter, Flavobacterium, Nocardia, Mycobacterium and two nitrifying bacteria Nitrosomonas and Nitrobacter. Also filamentous forms like Thiothrix, Beggiatoa, Geotrichum. In ASP, the bacteria degrade the organic waste in the influent, while other micro-organisms like protozoa and rotifers act as effluent polishers. Protozoa consume dispersed bacteria that have not flocculated and rotifers consume small biological floc particles that have not settled. The details of activated sludge process are given in Fig. 8.5.

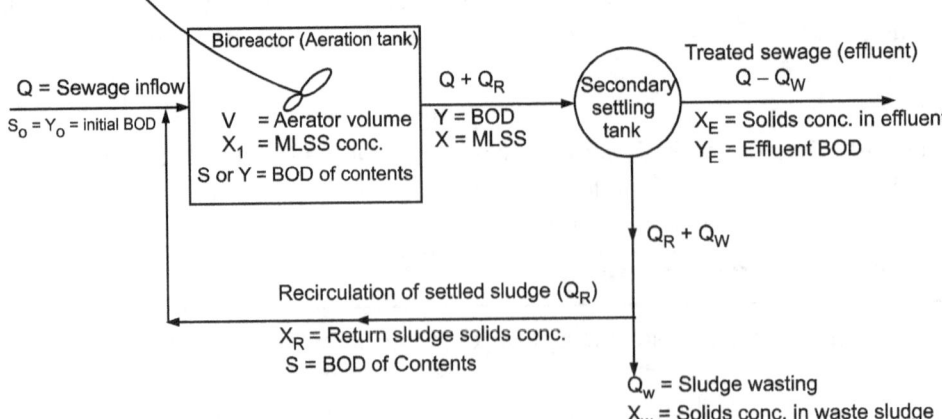

Fig. 8.5 : Flow diagram of conventional activated sludge process

8.9 ACTIVATED SLUDGE PROCESS VARIABLES

(DEC. 2010; MAY 2009, 2010)

The variables of importance in ASP are loading rate, the mixing regime and the flow scheme.

Loading rate : Loading rate is the rate at which wastewater is applied to the aeration tank. The loading parameter here is the hydraulic retention time (HRT) which is expressed as :

$$\text{HRT (hours)} = (V \times 24)/(Q)$$

where,

V = Volume of aeration tank, m^3

Q = Wastewater inflow (sludge recycle excluded), m^3/day

The organic loading in ASP should be such that the micro-organisms exhibit flocculant characteristics which will result in efficient separation of sludge from wastewater.

Volumetric loading (organic loading) is the kg of BOD applied for unit volume of aeration tank or kg of BOD applied per day.

To calculate kg of BOD to be applied, please see the following example.

e.g. BOD of given wastewater is 800 mg/lit. The daily flow rate is 10,000 m^3/day (10 mld). Calculate daily organic loading in kg.

$$\text{Organic loading} = \text{BOD in mg/lit} \times \text{flow lit/day}$$
$$= 800 \text{ mg/lit} \times 10,000 \text{ m}^3/\text{day} \times 1000 \text{ lit/m}^3$$
$$= 8 \times 10^9 \text{ mg/day}$$
$$= 8000 \text{ kg/day}$$

So,   Volumetric loading = $(\text{kg of BOD})/m^3/d$ = $(Q \times L_a \text{ or } S_o)/V$

where, L_a or S_o = Influent BOD to aeration tank

This organic loading is also referred as **Food to micro-organisms (F/M) ratio**. This is the ratio of BOD of kg BOD applied per day (representing microbial food) to kg MLSS in aeration tank (representing microbial mass), expressed as under,

$$\text{F/M} = \frac{[(Q \times L_a)/V]}{1000 \times X_t} \quad \text{or} \quad = \frac{Q \cdot S_o}{1000 \times V \times t}$$

where, X_t = MLSS (Mixed liquor suspended solids) or

MLVSS (Mixed liquor volatile suspended solids) in mg/lit

also, $\text{F/M} = \dfrac{\text{Daily BOD load applied to the aerator system in gm}}{\text{Total microbial mass in the system in gm}}$

Food to micro-organisms ratio is the main factor controlling BOD removal. F/M can be varied by varying MLSS concentration in the aeration tank.

Solids Retention Time (SRT) : This is also called as **Mean Cell Residence Time (MCRT)** or sludge age. It indicates the time period for which the solids are in the system.

$$\text{Sludge age or SRT} = \frac{\text{Total weight of solids in biological system (i)}}{\text{Total weight of solids leaving the system per day (i) + (ii)}}$$

The solids are lost from the reactor through treated effluent and through sludge wasting of SST (Secondary settling tank).

(1) Total weight of solids in the reactor = Volume of reactor × MLSS

(i) Mass of solids removed with wasted sludge per day

$$= Q_W \times X_W$$

(ii) Mass of solids removed with the effluent per day

$$= (Q - Q_W) \, X_E$$

∴ Total weight of solids leaving the system per day = (i) + (ii)

$$= (Q_W \times X_W) + (Q - Q_W) \, X_E$$

∴ Sludge age or SRT or MCRT, $\theta_c = \dfrac{V \times X_t}{(Q_W \times X_W) + (Q - Q_W) \, X_E}$

where,

X_t = MLSS in mg/lit

V = Volume of reactor, m^3

Q_W = Volume of wasted sludge per day

X_W = Solids concentration in wasted sludge (mg/lit)

Q = Waste water flow per day

X_E = Effluent solids concentration (mg/lit)

Sludge production and process control :

To design the sludge handling and disposal facilities, it is very important to know the quantity of sludge to be produced per day.

The quantity of sludge wasted daily can be estimated by the following equation :

Wasted sludge, $P_X = \dfrac{XV}{\theta_c}$

where,

P_X = Net wasted activated sludge produced each day, as volatile suspended solids, kg/day

Oxygen Requirements : To determine the theoretical requirements the following two factors are required :

(i) BOD_5 of the waste, and (ii) the amount of organisms wasted from the system per day.

The reasoning is as follows. If we will consider that all the BOD_5 were converted to end products, the total oxygen demand would be determined by converting BOD_5 to BOD_L using an appropriate conversion factor.

The amount of oxygen that must be supplied to the system = Total BOD – BOD_L of the wasted cells.

The following equation shows the BOD_L of a mole of cells.

$$C_5H_7NO_2 + 5O_2 \rightarrow 5CO_2 + 2H_2O + NH_3$$

$$113 \text{ cells} \qquad 5(32)$$

$$\frac{kg\ O_2}{kg\ cells} = \frac{160}{113} = 1.42$$

where, $\qquad BOD_L = 1.42$ (mass of cells, g/m^3)

Therefore, the theoretical oxygen requirements for the removal of carbonaceous organic matter in waste water can be determined by the following equation :

$$kg,\ O_2/day = \left(\begin{array}{c} \text{Total mass} \\ BOD_L \text{ utilized,} \\ \text{kg day} \end{array} \right) - 1.42 \left(\begin{array}{c} \text{Mass of organisms} \\ \text{wasted, kg/day} \end{array} \right)$$

$$\therefore \qquad kg,\ O_2/day = \frac{Q(S_0 - S)}{f} - 1.42(P_x)$$

where, $\qquad f =$ Conversion factor for converting BOD_5 to BOD_L

Table 8.1 : Design parameters for Conventional Activated Sludge Process

Sr. No.	Parameter	Design values
1.	Organic loading rate	0.3 – 0.5 kg BOD per day
2.	MLSS	1500 – 3000 mg/lit
3.	MLVSS	$0.8 \times$ MLSS
4.	F/M ratio	0.3 to 0.4
5.	Hydraulic retention time (HRT) θ	4 to 6 hrs.
6.	SRT or MCRT or θ_c	5 to 8 days
7.	Oxygen requirement	0.8 to 1 kg per kg of BOD removed
8.	Recirculation ratio, Q_R/Q	0.25 to 0.5
9.	BOD removal efficiency	85 – 92%
10.	Air required	40 – 100 m^3 per kg of BOD_5
11.	Excess sludge	0.55 to 0.6 kg per kg BOD removed
12.	Surface loading for SST	30 m^3/m^2/day
13.	Detention time for SST	2 hrs.

(Ref. Manual on Sewerage and Sewage Treatment, 2nd Edition)

8.10 SLUDGE VOLUME INDEX, SLUGE RECYCLE AND RATE OF RETURN SLUDGE

- **Sluge Volume Index :**

This parameter is used to understand the quality of sludge produced in the aeration tank. The degree of treatment achieved in an aeration process depends directly on settleability of activated sludge in the secondary settling tank. A biological floc that agglomerates and settles by gravity leaves a clear supernatant for discharge. Conversely, poorly flocculated particles or buoyant filamentous growths that do not separate by gravity contribute to BOD and suspended solids in the treated effluent. Excessive carry over of floc resulting in inefficient operation is referred to as sludge bulking.

- **Sludge Volume Index** (SVI) is defined as the volume occupied in ml by one gm of dried solids in mixed liquor after settling for 30 minutes. This can be determined in the laboratory. For this the sample is collected from outlet of the aeration tank of ASP. The collected one litre sample is poured in Imhoff cone and allowed to settle for 30 minutes. The settled volume of sludge is recorded. Then the sample is remixed, and is further tested for mixed liquor suspended solids concentration. The SVI is determined by the equation :

$$SVI = \frac{\text{Volume of settled sludge in ml}}{\text{MLSS concentration in mg/lit}} \times 1000$$

The usual adopted range of SVI is between 50 – 150 ml/gm and such a value indicates good settling sludge. SVI values of 100 – 150 are considered satisfactory in plants operating with MLSS of 1000 – 3500 mg/lit.

- **Sludge bulking** is due to

    1. Inadequate air supply.

    2. Low pH.

    3. Septicity.

    4. Growth of filamentous organisms.

Sludge bulking is controlled by eliminating the above causes. In addition to this **chlorine** or **hydrogen peroxide** can be applied to wastewater or return sludge for control of filamentous growth. Limited dissolved oxygen has been noted more frequently than any other cause of bulking. The minimum DO should be 2 mg/lit. The food to micro-organisms ratio should be checked to make sure that it is within the range of generally accepted values.

Table 8.2 : Operational Parameters for ASP

SVI, ml/g	Process	MLSS, mg/lit	F/M, d^{-1}	Aeration Time, h	Average Sludge Age, d	BOD removal efficiency, %	Quality of Sludge
150–200	High Rate	500 – 1000	0.5–1.0	3 – 4	5	60 – 75	Poor
50–(100)–150	Conventional	2000 – 3000	0.2–0.5	6 – 10	10	80 – 90	Good, as indicated by the median value 100 ml/g
25–50	Extended Aeration	4000 – 6000	0.05–0.2	24 – 36	25	90 – 98	Excellent

- **Sludge Recycle and Rate of return sludge :**

Sludge recirculation ratio,

$$\frac{Q_R}{Q} = \frac{X_t}{X_R - X_t}$$

where,

Q_R = Sludge recirculation rate in m³/day

X_t = MLSS in the aeration tank in mg/lit

X_R = MLSS in the returned or wasted sludge in mg/lit

$$X_R = \frac{10^6}{SVI}$$

Now,

$$\frac{Q_R}{Q} = \frac{X_t}{X_R - X_t} = \frac{X_t}{\left(\dfrac{10^6}{SVI} - X_t\right)}$$

The value of return sludge ratios for conventional sludge plant varies between 0.25 to 0.50.

8.11 MIXING REGIME

The mixing regime provided in the aeration tank may be completely mixed flow or plug flow. Completely mixed flow involves the rapid dispersal of incoming wastewater throughout the tank. Plug flow implied that the wastewater moves down progressively along the aeration tank, essentially unmixed with the contents of rest of tank.

8.12 FLOW PATTERN

This involves the method of wastewater addition and sludge return to the aeration tank and also the method of aeration. Sewage addition may be at the single point at the inlet or it may be at more points along the aeration tank. The sludge return may be from settling tank or through sludge reaeration tank. Aeration is done either with mechanical aerators or diffused aerators. Air is applied uniformly with either of the aerators along whole length of tank or it may be tapered from inlet end to outlet end of aeration tank.

8.13 AERATION SYSTEMS

Understanding of aeration processes in wastewater treatment needs greater knowledge of biology. The generalised biological process that takes place in the aeration tank is shown in Fig. 8.6.

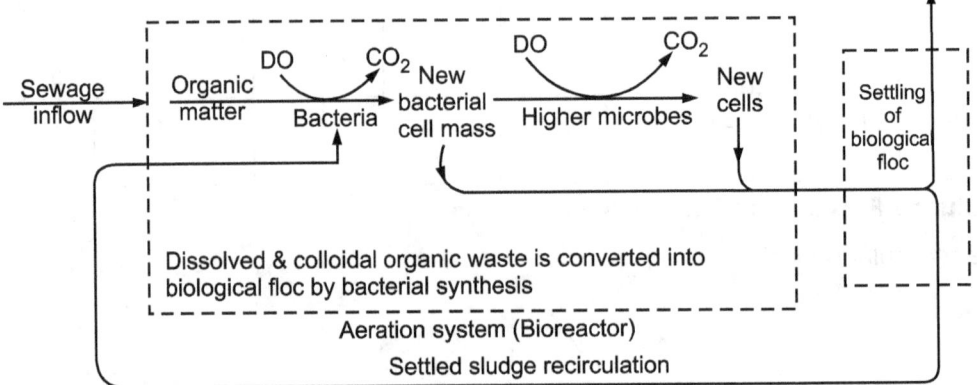

Fig. 8.6 : System biology of ASP

Here raw sewage contains organic matter. It enters into aeration tank in the form of food. The micro-organisms present in raw sewage metabolize waste organics, producing new cell mass while taking dissolved oxygen and releasing carbon dioxide. After the addition of large population of micro-organisms, aerating raw wastewater for a few hours removes organic matter from solution by synthesis into microbial cells. Mixed liquor is continuously transferred to settling tank for separation of biological floc and discharge of settled effluent. Settled sludge is recirculated into the system as per requirement.

Oxygen is supplied to the mixed liquor in an aeration tank by dispersing air bubbles through submerged diffusers or by entraining air into the liquid by mechanical aerators. Porous plates, tubes or nozzles are provided as air diffusers. Compressed air forced through the porous material is released as fine bubbles. Mechanical aerators are horizontal paddle, vertical turbine and vertical turbine draft tube.

8.14 MODIFICATIONS OF ACTIVATED SLUDGE PROCESS

The main limitations of conventional ASP are
1.   Higher aeration tank volume requirement.
2.   Lack of operational stability.

In order to overcome such difficulties and to meet specific treatment objectives, several modifications in conventional ASP have been suggested.

1.   Step Aeration :

It is a process in which wastewater is introduced at several points in the aeration tank while the return sludge is introduced at the head as shown in Fig. 8.7.

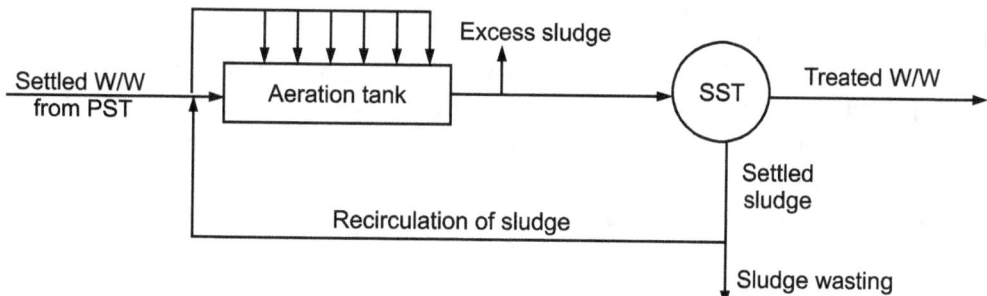

Fig. 8.7 : Flow diagram of step aeration process

Because of this type of arrangement, there is uniform demand of oxygen along the length of tank. This results in effective use of uniform supply of oxygen in conventional ASP. This method has the following advantages :

1.   Multiple entry of substrate thereby increasing removal of soluble organics by adsorption and higher BOD loading per unit volume.

2.   Oxygen demand is more evenly spread over entire length of tank resulting in better utilisation of oxygen supplied.

2.   Tapered Aeration :

Air is supplied at different rates along the length of tank according to need. It ensures higher air supply at inlet and in the initial length of tank, as compared to downstream length. In the aeration tank, as mixed liquor progresses through, its requirement for oxygen goes on decreasing. Therefore in this method oxygen is supplied at the higher rates at the inlet and gradually decreased as sewage move towards the outlet end of tank. The aerators are spaced close together at the inlet end to achieve higher oxygenation rate and spaced farther away at outlet end where oxygen demand is less.

The following are the advantages of this method :

1.   Less air requirement.

2.   Lower cost.

3.   Avoidance of over aeration.

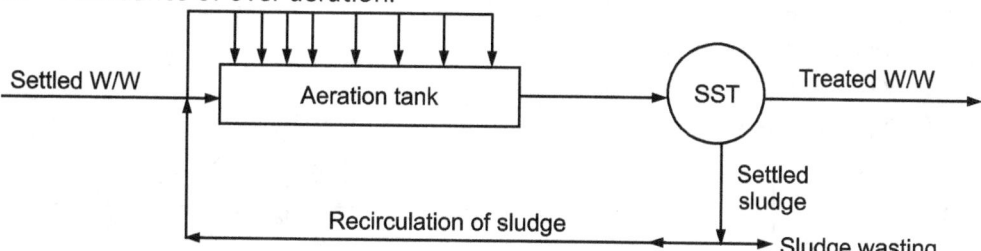

Fig. 8.8 : Flow diagram of tapered aeration process

3.   Contact Stabilization :

•   This process is also known as **Biosorption**. In this method, the settled wastewater is mixed with recirculated sludge and aerated in a contact tank for 30 to 90 minutes.

•   During this period, the organics are absorbed by the sludge floc.

- The sludge is then separated from the treated effluent by sedimentation and the returned sludge is aerated from 3 to 6 hours in a sludge aeration tank.
- During this period the absorbed organics used for energy and production of new cells. A portion of return sludge is wasted prior to recycle, to maintain a constant MLVSS concentration in the tanks.
- It is suitable for wastewaters where a great part of BOD is present in suspended or colloidal form.

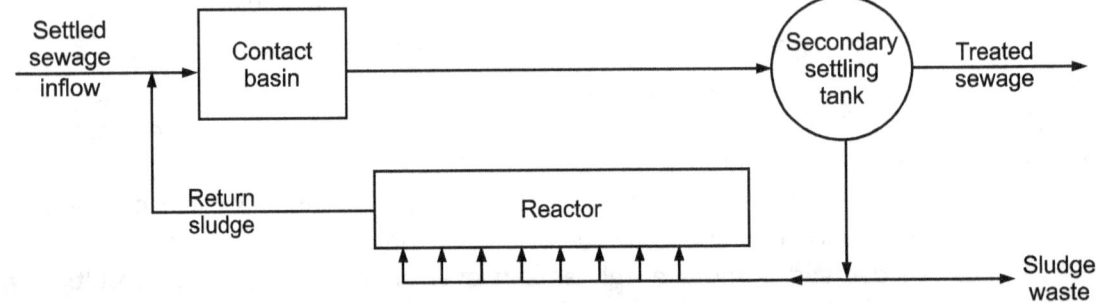

Fig. 8.9 : Flow diagram of contact stabilization process

Advantages of this method are as follows :
- It can be loaded higher.
- If toxic conditions occur, the system can be returned to normal condition easily as only a minor fraction of biological organisms is in direct contact with waste flow.

4.   Complete Mix :

In this process, plug flow regime of conventional ASP is replaced by a completely mixed flow regime. The influent wastewater and sludge flow are introduced at several points in the aeration tank from a central channel. The aerated sewage is withdrawn uniformly along the opposite side. Mechanical aerators are installed in the centre of the aeration tank. The collected mixed liquor is settled in the secondary clarifier. This process possesses capacity to hold much higher MLSS concentration level in aeration tank. (3000 mg/lit to 6000 mg/lit).

The following are the advantages of this process :
- Higher volumetric loading.
- Low residence time of liquid.
- Complete mixing.

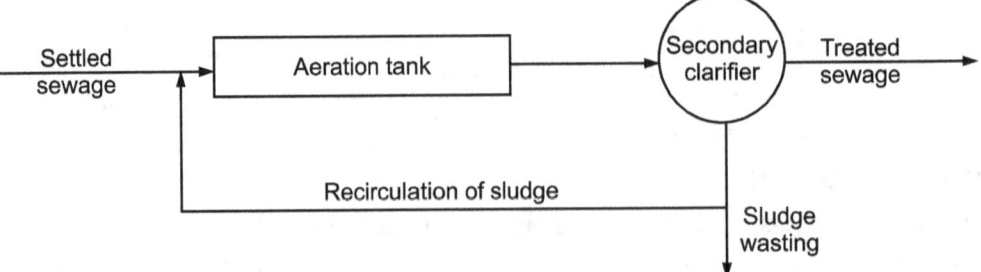

Fig. 8.10 : Flow diagram of complete mix process

Table 8.3 : Characteristics and design parameters of different activated sludge systems

Process type	F/M	HRT (hr)	Volumetric loading (kg BOD/m^3)	SRT (days)	$\dfrac{\text{kg } O_2}{\text{kg BOD}}$
1. Conventional	0.4 – 0.2	4 – 8	0.3 – 0.7	5 – 15	0.8 – 1.1
2. Tapered aeration	0.4 – 0.2	4 – 8	0.3 – 0.8	5 – 15	0.7 –1.0
3. Step aeration	0.4 – 0.2	3 – 5	0.7 – 1.0	5 – 15	0.7 – 1.0
4. Contact stabilization	0.5 – 0.2	3 – 6	1.0 – 1.2	5 – 15	0.7 – 1.1
5. Complete mix	0.6 – 0.2	3 – 5	0.8 – 2.0	5 – 15	0.7 – 1.0
6. Modified aeration	5.0 – 1.5	1.3 – 3.0	1.2 – 2.4	0.2 – 0.5	0.4 – 0.6
7. Extended aeration	0.15 – 0.05	18 – 36	0.2 – 0.4	20 – 30	1.2 – 2.0

5.   Extended Aeration : This process operates in the endogenous respiration phase of the growth curve. The process employs low organic loading, long aeration time, high MLSS concentration and low F/M. Thus, it is generally applicable only to small treatment plants with capacities of less than 4000 m^3/d. Continuous complete mixing is either by diffused air or by mechanical aerators and aeration periods are 24 to 36 hours. Because of these conditions, as well as low BOD loading, the biological process is very stable and can accept intermittant loads without upset. The advantages of this process are :

- Excess sludge production is low.
- MLSS undergo endogenous respiration and get well stabilised.
- The excess sludge does not require separate digestion.
- Operation is simple due to elimination of primary settling and separate sludge digestion.

8.15 PROBLEMS IN ACTIVATED SLUDGE PROCESS   (DEC. 2010)

The problems associated with operation of activated sludge process are given in the Table 8.4.

Table 8.4 : Problems and remedies in ASP

Problem	Probable cause	Remedy
1. Sludge floating at the surface of SST.	(a) Denitrification in SST resulting in nitrogen gas bubbles bouying up sludge. (b) More growth of filamentous organisms.	(a) Increasing rpm of scraper, sludge wasting, return sludge and DO. (b) Chlorine application.
2. Low return sludge concentration.	(a) Filamentous micro-organisms growth. (b) High return sludge rate.	(a) Add chlorine and increase pH and DO. (b) Reduce return sludge rate.

...Contd.

3.	Foam	Detergents	Sprinkle water on foam.
4.	Dead spots in aeration tank	(a) Less aeration and less DO. (b) Air diffusers plugged.	(a) Increase rate of aeration. (b) Clean or replace air diffusers.
5.	Small floc particles in settled effluent.	(a) More disturbance in aeration tank. (b) System devoid of oxygen.	(a) Reduce aeration and increase sludge washing. (b) Increase aeration rate.

Advantages and Disadvantages of Activated Sludge Process :   **(Dec. 2010, May 2009)**

Advantages :

- No problem of odours.
- No fly nuisanse.
- Removal of SS and BOD around 90% each.
- Non-putrescible effluent.
- Relatively low cost of installation.
- Area required is small as compared to other conventional treatment methods.
- Excess sludge has good fertilizer value.

Disadvantages :

- No variation in quality of influent is allowed.
- Operation and maintenance cost is high.
- Skilled supervision is required.
- Large quantity of sludge is produced.

EXAMPLES ON DESIGN OF ACTIVATED SLUDGE PROCESS

Example 8.1 : Data given :

1.	Municipal waste water flow rate,	Q	= 10,000 m³/day
2.	BOD of settled effluent,	S_o	= 150 mg/lit
3.	BOD of treated effluent,	S_e	= 5 mg/lit
4.	Yield coefficient,	Y	= 0.5 kg/kg
5.	Endogenous decay coefficient,	K_d	= 0.05 d⁻¹
6.	MLVSS concentration,	X	= 3000 mg/lit
7.	Return sludge solids concentration,	X_r	= 10,000 mg/lit
8.	Mean cell residence time,	θ_c	= 10 days.

Determine :

(a) The volume of the reactor.

(b) F/M ratio.

(c) Volumetric loading rate.

(d) Oxygen requirement.

(e) Recycle ratio.

(f) BOD removal efficiency.

Solution :

(a) The volume of the reactor :

$$V = \frac{Y Q\, \theta_c\, (S_o - S_e)}{X\, (1 + K_d\, \theta_c)} = \frac{0.5 \times 10000 \times 10\, (150 - 5)}{3000\, (1 + 0.05 \times 10)}$$

$$= \mathbf{1611\ m^3} \qquad \text{... Ans.}$$

(b) F/M ratio :

$$\text{F/M} = \frac{Q\, S_o}{V\, X} = \frac{10000\ m^3/day \times 150\ mg/lit}{1611\ m^3 \times 3000\ mg/lit} = \mathbf{0.31\ day^{-1}} \quad \text{... Ans.}$$

(c) Volumetric loading rate $= \dfrac{Q\, S_o}{V} = \dfrac{10000 \times 150}{1611} = 931.08\ gm/m^3 \quad$ **... Ans.**

(d) Oxygen requirement :

$$O_2\ \text{demand} = 1.47\, Q\, (S_o - S_e) - 1.42\, P_x,\ kg/day$$

$$Q = 10 \times 10^6\ lit/day$$

$$S_o - S_e = 150 - 5 = 145\ mg/lit$$

Wasted sludge, $\qquad P_x = \dfrac{XV}{\theta_c} = \dfrac{3000 \times 1611 \times 10^3}{10} = 4.83 \times 10^8\ mg/day$

$\therefore \qquad O_2\ \text{demand (kg/day)} = [1.47 \times 10 \times 10^6 \times 145 - 1.42 \times 4.83 \times 10^8]\, 10^{-6}$

$$= \mathbf{1445.64\ kg/day} \qquad \text{... Ans.}$$

(e) Recycle ratio, $(Q + Q_r)\, X = Q_r\, X_r$

where, $\qquad Q = $ Wastewater flow rate $= 10000\ m^3/day$

$\qquad X = $ Aerator MLSS concentration $= 3000\ mg/lit$

$\qquad X_r = $ Return sludge solids concentration

$$= 10000\ mg/lit$$

also, $\qquad Q_r = \dfrac{Q\, X}{X_r - X}$

$$= \dfrac{10000 \times 3000}{10000 - 3000} = 4286\ m^3/day$$

Recycle ratio, $R = \dfrac{Q_r}{Q} = \dfrac{4286}{10000}$

$\therefore \qquad$ Recycle ratio $= \mathbf{0.4286} \qquad\qquad\qquad\qquad$ **... Ans.**

(f) BOD removal efficiency $= \dfrac{S_o - S_e}{S_o} \times 100 = \dfrac{150 - 5}{150} \times 100 = \mathbf{96.60\%}$ **... Ans.**

Example 8.2 : Given the following data of operating ASP :

1. Wastewater flow, Q = 35000 m³/day
2. Influent total solids = 600 mg/lit
3. Influent suspended solids = 120 mg/lit
4. Influent BOD, S_o = 175 mg/lit
5. Effluent total solids = 495 mg/lit
6. Effluent suspended solids = 22 mg/lit
7. Effluent BOD, S_o = 20 mg/lit
8. MLVSS concentration, X = 2500 mg/lit
9. Return sludge solids concentration, X_r = 9800 mg/lit
10. Volume of aeration basins = 10000 m³

Determine :

(a) Aeration period.

(b) BOD load in kg/m³/day.

(c) F/M ratio.

(d) Total solids, suspended solids and BOD removal efficiency.

(e) Recirculation ratio.

Solution :

(a) Aeration period $= \dfrac{\text{Volume of reactor, m}^3}{\text{Wastewater flow, m}^3/\text{day}} \times 24 = \dfrac{10000 \text{ m}^3}{35000 \text{ m}^3/\text{day}} \times 24$

$= \textbf{6.85 hrs}$ ... **Ans.**

(b) BOD load $= \dfrac{Q \cdot S_o}{V} = \dfrac{35000 \text{ m}^3/\text{day} \times 175 \text{ mg/lit} \times 10^3}{10000 \text{ m}^3 \times 10^6}$

$= \textbf{0.6125 kg/m}^3\textbf{/day}$ ... **Ans.**

(c) F/M ratio $= \dfrac{Q \cdot S_o}{V\,X} = \dfrac{35000 \times 175}{10000 \times 2500} = \textbf{0.245 d}^{-1}$ ... **Ans.**

(d) Total solids removal efficiency $= \dfrac{600 - 495}{600} \times 100 = \textbf{17.5\%}$

Suspended solids removal efficiency $= \dfrac{120 - 22}{120} \times 100 = \textbf{81.6\%}$ ... **Ans.**

BOD removal efficiency $= \dfrac{175 - 20}{175} \times 100 = \textbf{88.6\%}$

(e)   Recirculation ratio = R

$$\therefore \qquad Q_r = \frac{Q\,X}{X_r - X} = \frac{35000 \times 2500}{9800 - 2500} = 11986 \text{ m}^3/\text{day}$$

and $$R = \frac{Q_r}{Q} = \frac{11986}{35000} = 0.34 \qquad \text{... Ans.}$$

Example 8.3 :

Raw sewage @ 5000 m³/day and having a BOD of 450 mg/lit is treated in an activated sludge plant where the aeration tank is 1200 m³ in volume and the MLVSS is 2500 mg/lit. Find the loading F/M based on solids in tank only.

Solution :

As MLVSS is 2500 mg/lit, the system is conventional.

Assume primary settling tank removes 33% BOD

$\therefore$ Incoming BOD to aeration tank (F) $\cong$ 300 mg/lit

$$= \frac{300 \times 5000 \times 1000}{1000 \times 1000}$$

$$= 1500 \text{ kg/day}$$

MLVSS in aeration tank (M) = 2500 mg/lit

= 2500 kg/1000 m³ vol

$$= 2500 \times \frac{1200}{1000} = 3000 \text{ kg}$$

$\therefore$ $$F/M = \frac{1500}{3000} = \textbf{0.5 kg of BOD/kg of MLVSS} \qquad \text{... Ans.}$$

Example 8.4 :

If the above aeration tank was operated as an extended aeration system and primary settling done away with, find the flow of sewage that can be treated @ F/M = 0.2 and MLVSS = 5000 mg/lit.

Solution :

MLVSS in aeration tank (M) = 5000 mg/lit

= 5000 kg/1000 m³

$$= 5000 \times \frac{1200}{1000} = \textbf{6000 kg} \qquad \text{... Ans.}$$

At F/M = 0.2,

$$\frac{F}{M} = \frac{\text{BOD allowable per day}}{\text{MLSS in aeration tank}}$$

$$0.2 = \frac{\text{BOD allowable per day}}{6000}$$

$\therefore$ BOD allowable per day = 0.2 × 6000 kg

= 1200 kg/day

$$\text{Incoming BOD (without settling)} = 450 \text{ mg/lit}$$
$$= 450 \text{ kg/1000 m}^3$$

$\therefore \quad$ Permissible flow $= \dfrac{1200}{450} = \textbf{2700 m}^3\textbf{/day only}$ ... **Ans.**

Example 8.5 :

If raw sewage of 300 mg/lit BOD is treated in a conventional activated sludge plant of 5000 m³/day capacity with an overall efficiency of 90%, find the kg of BOD discharged in treated effluent per day to river.

Solution :

$$\text{Incoming BOD} = 300 \text{ mg/lit} = 300 \text{ kg/1000 m}^3$$

$$= 300 \times \frac{5000}{1000} = 1500 \text{ kg/day}$$

$\therefore \quad$ BOD in effluent $= 0.1 \times 1500 = 150 \text{ kg/day}$

If the same sewage was treated in an extended aeration plant of 95% efficiency, the BOD in effluent would be

$$= 0.05 \times 1500$$
$$= \textbf{75 kg/day} \qquad\qquad \text{... \textbf{Ans.}}$$

Note : Pollution of river is reduced to half for only 5% increase in overall efficiency.

Example 8.6 :

Design a **conventional activated sludge** plant to treat 5000 m³/day of municipal sewage having BOD of 350 mg/lit. Assume BOD removal in primary settling at a slightly above 40% so that raw settled BOD is 200 mg/lit. Final BOD to be 30 mg/lit.

Solution :

Settled sewage BOD to aeration tank (F) $= 200 \text{ mg/lit} = 200 \text{ kg/1000 m}^3$

$$= 200 \times \frac{5000}{1000} = 1000 \text{ kg/day}$$

$$\text{Assume F/M} = 0.5 \text{ kg/kg of MLVSS at 23°C}$$
$$\text{(Refer table 8.2)}$$

$$\frac{1000}{M} = 0.5$$

$\therefore \quad$ MLVSS required in the system (M) $= \dfrac{1000}{0.5} = 2000 \text{ kg}$

Assume that only 80% of MLVSS are in aeration tank at any given time. The rest being in settling and sludge return system.

$\therefore \quad$ MLVSS in aeration $= 0.8 \times 2000 \text{ kg} = 1600 \text{ kg}$

Assume MLSS concentration in aeration tank $= 2500 \text{ mg/lit} = 2500 \text{ kg/1000 m}^3$

(Refer table 8.2)

$\therefore$ Aeration tank volume required $= \dfrac{1600 \times 1000}{2500} = 640 \text{ m}^3$

Hence,   Aeration time $= \dfrac{640 \text{ m}^3}{5000 \text{ m}^3/\text{d}} \times 24 \cong 3 \text{ hrs.}$

Return sludge : Assume it is 50% of inflow $= 5000 \text{ m}^3/\text{d} \times \dfrac{50}{100} \times \dfrac{1}{24} = 104.17 \text{ m}^3/\text{hr.}$

Hence, provide 3 pumps of 50 m³/hr capacity so that 2 pumps may work and 1 pump may be stand-by.

Aeration requirements :

For conventional activated sludge plants, it is customary to assume 0.8 kg O_2/kg BOD_5 removed.

$$\text{BOD to aeration } = 1000 \text{ kg/day as above}$$

$$\text{BOD in effluent } = 30 \text{ mg/lit} = \dfrac{30 \times 5000 \times 1000}{1000 \times 1000} = 150 \text{ kg/day}$$

$\therefore$ $\text{BOD removed } = 850 \text{ kg/day}$

$\therefore$ $\text{Oxygen required, } (N_o) = \dfrac{850 \times 0.8}{24} = 28 \text{ kg/hr}$

This is at the actual working conditions. Therefore, it has to be converted to equivalent value in tap water at standard conditions (20°C and zero DO).

$\therefore$ Oxygen transfer under field conditions,

$$N = \dfrac{N_o}{\alpha \left[\dfrac{C_{SW} - C_L}{C_S} \right] \cdot (1.025)^{T-20}}$$

where, N_o = oxygen transfer in water at 20°C and zero DO

Assume : $\alpha = 0.9$ = Oxygen transfer ratio of waste to water

Assume : $C_L = 1.5$ mg/lit = Dissolved oxygen to be maintained in the waste

Assume : $C_S = 9.17$ mg/lit = Oxygen saturation value for tap water at 20°C

Assume : $T = 23$°C = Temperature of waste in tank

Assume : C_{SW} = 0.9 to 0.98 of oxygen saturation value for tap water at T°C. (Adjust for barometric pressure also if necessary depending on plant site).

$= 0.9 \times 8.68 = 7.812$ mg/lit

$\therefore$ Substituting $N = \dfrac{28}{0.9 \left[\dfrac{7.812 - 1.5}{9.17} \right] \times 1.077}$

We get, $= \dfrac{28}{0.9 \times 0.69 \times 1.077} = 42 \text{ kg/hr}$

Assuming Aerator capacity   = 1.6 kg/HP-hr (= 3.5 lbs O_2/HP-hr)

$$\text{Total HP required} = \frac{42}{1.6} = 26 \text{ BHP}$$

Assuming 90% efficiency geared drive,

$$\text{Provide} \frac{26}{0.9} = 30 \text{ HP (say) totally}$$

(**Note** : If no corrections for temperature and nature of waste were done, the HP required would be $\frac{28}{1.6}$ = 18 HP only.)

Example 8.7 : Given the following data of operating ASP :

1. Wastewater flow $\qquad$ = 20,000 m^3/day
2. Influent BOD_5 $\qquad$ = 250 mg/lit
3. Effluent BOD_5 $\qquad$ = 18 mg/lit
4. Temperature $\qquad$ = 25°C
5. Influent volatile suspended solids to reactor are negligible
6. Ratio of MLVSS to MLSS $\qquad$ = 0.9
7. Return sludge concentration $\qquad$ = 12,000 mg/lit of suspended solids
8. MLVSS $\qquad$ = 3500 mg/lit
9. Mean cell residence time, θ_c $\qquad$ = 10 days
10. Effluent contains 25 mg/lit of biological solids, of which 65 percent is biodegradable
11. Value of BOD_5 $\qquad$ = 0.68 × BOD_L
12. Yield coefficient, Y $\qquad$ = 0.5 kg/kg
13. K_d $\qquad$ = 0.05 d^{-1}

Determine :

(a) Treatment efficiency.
(b) Reactor volume.
(c) Quantity of wasted sludge.
(d) Oxygen requirements based on BOD_L.

Solution :

1. Concentration of soluble BOD_5 in the effluent

$\qquad$ Effluent BOD_5 = Influent soluble BOD_5 + BOD_5 of effluent suspended solids

(i) BOD_5 of the effluent suspended solids :

(a)   Biodegradable portion of effluent biological solids

$$= 0.65 \times 25 = 16.25 \text{ mg/lit}$$

(b) BOD_L of the biodegradable effluent solids

$$= 0.65 \times 25 \times 1.42 = 23.1 \text{ mg/lit}$$

(c) BOD_5 of effluent suspended solids

$$= 23.1 \times 0.68 = 15.71 \text{ mg/lit}$$

(ii) Influent BOD_5, $18 = S_e + 15.71$

$$S_e = 2.29 \text{ mg/lit}$$

2.   Treatment efficiency,

$$E = \frac{S_o - S_e}{S_o} \times 100$$

(i)   The efficiency depends on soluble BOD_5

$$E_s = \frac{(250 - 2.29)}{250} \times 100 = \mathbf{99.10\%} \qquad \text{... Ans.}$$

(ii) The overall efficiency,

$$E_{overall} = \frac{(250 - 18)}{250} \times 100 = \mathbf{92.80\%} \qquad \text{... Ans.}$$

3.   Reactor volume, $V = \dfrac{YQ\theta_c (S_o - S_e)}{X (1 + K_d \theta_c)}$

$$= \frac{0.5 \times 2000 \times 10 (250 - 2.29)}{3500 (1 + 0.05 \times 10)}$$

$$= \mathbf{471.83 \text{ m}^3} \qquad \text{... Ans.}$$

4.   Quantity of wasted sludge

$$P_x = \frac{XV}{\theta_c}$$

$$= \frac{3500 \times 471.83}{10} = \mathbf{1.65 \times 10^8 \text{ mg/day}} \qquad \text{... Ans.}$$

5.   Oxygen requirements based on BOD_L :

$$Q = 20{,}000 \text{ m}^3/\text{day} = 20 \times 10^6 \text{ lit/day}$$

$$O_2 \text{ demand} = 1.47 \, Q \, (S_o - S_e) - 1.42 \, P_x$$

$$= [1.47 \times 20 \times 10^6 (250 - 2.29) - 1.42 \times 1.65 \times 10^8) \times 10^{-6}]$$

$$= \mathbf{7048.37 \text{ kg/day}} \qquad \text{... Ans.}$$

TRICKLING FILTER

8.16 INTRODUCTION

The objective of the biological treatment of wastewater is to coagulate and remove the non-settleable colloidal solids and to stabilise the organic matter. In biological treatment system, the living micro-organisms break down the waste organics and use it as food for them. The end product of this process are gases and formation of new cells. Thus, soluble and colloidal organic matter is converted into gases and insoluble biomass.

The suspended growth systems are discussed in earlier sections. In this section, the attached growth systems will be discussed.

The attached growth biological systems are those that contact wastewater with microbial growths attached to the surfaces of supporting media. Supporting media is an inert medium, such as rock, slag, redwood or specially designed ceramic or plastic materials. Such processes include : (i) Intermittant sand filters, (ii) Trickling filters, (iii) Rotating biological contactors, (iv) Packed bed reactors.

8.17 BIOLOGICAL PROCESS   (MAY 2009, 2010, 2011)

The trickling filter consists of the filter medium, wastewater distribution system, inlet pipe and wastewater collection system. The settled wastewater from PST is sprayed through the nozzles of distributor. The wastewater sprinkled over the media produces biological slimes that coat the surface. The films consist primarily of bacteria, protozoa and fungi that feed on waste organics. Sludge worms, fly larvae, rotifers and other biota are also found. As the wastewater flows over the slime layer, organic matter and dissolved oxygen are extracted and metabolic end products such as CO_2 are released (Fig. 8.11). Dissolved oxygen in the liquid is replenished by absorption from the air in the voids surrounding the filter media. Eventhough the film is very thin, the biological layer is anaerobic at bottom and aerobic at top. In the outer portion of biological film, the organic matter is degraded by aerobic micro-organisms.

Organisms attached to the media in the upper layer grow rapidly, feeding on the abundent food supply. As the micro-organisms at the outer surface grow, the thickness of the slime layer increases and the diffused oxygen is consumed before it can penetrate the full depth of layer. Hence, the lower (bottom) portion which is near the medium, is in a state of starvation, due to which anaerobic environment is established. As a result of having no external organic source available for cell carbon, the micro-organisms near the media surface enter into endogenous phase of growth and lose their ability to cling to the media surface. Eventually there is scouring of slime layer due to flowing liquid and a fresh slime layer begins to grow on the media. This phenomenon of scouring of the slime is called **sloughing** of the filter. Excess microbial growth sloughing off of the media is removed from the filter effluent by a final clarifier.

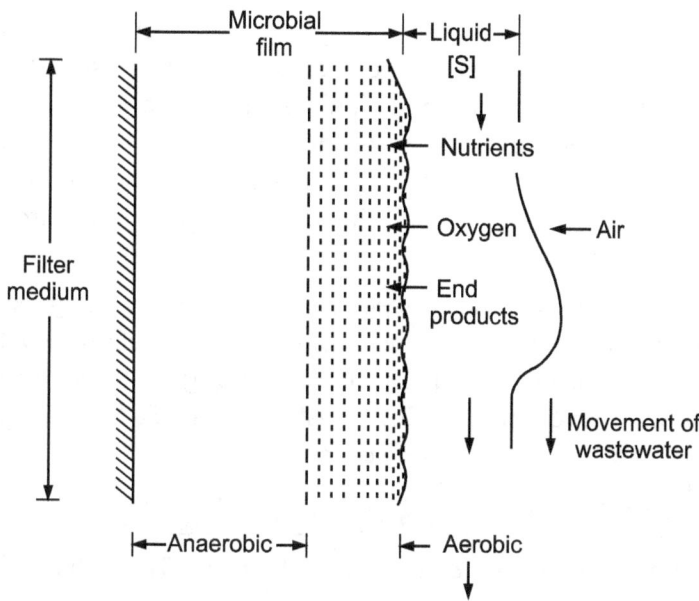

Fig. 8.11 : Schematic representation of exchanges taking place along surfaces biological slimes in trickling filters

8.18 FILTER MEDIA

The ideal filter medium is a material that has a high surface area per unit of volume, is low in cost and has a high durability and does not clog easily. The physical properties of filter media are shown in Table 8.5.

Table 8.5 : Physical properties of trickling filter media

Medium	Nominal size (mm)	Mass/unit bulk volume (kg/m^3)	Specific surface area (m^2/m^3)	Void space (%)
River rock				
Small	30–50	1200–1500	55–70	40–50
Large	100–130	800–1000	40–50	50–60
Blast furnace slag				
Small	40–80	800–1000	50–80	45–55
Large	80–130	800–1000	50–65	55–65
Plastic				
Conventional	600 × 600 × 1200	30–100	80–100	96–97
High specific surface	600 × 600 × 1200	30–100	100–200	95–97
Redwood	1200 × 1200 × 500	150–175	40–50	75–80

Plastic media fulfils the requirements except clogging. The most common media in existing filters are crushed rock, slag or field stone that are durable, insoluble and resistant to spalling. The size range preferred for stone media is 21.5 cm to 8 cm. If these materials are used, structural problems caused by their weight tend to restrict the bed depth to about 3 m. Although smaller stones provide more surface area for biological growth, the voids tend to plug and limit passage of air and liquid. Bed depths range from 1.5 m to 3 m, greater depths do not materially improve BOD removal efficiency.

Lightness of plastic media allows much deeper beds. They can be designed to be less prone to plugging by the accumulating slime and higher rates of BOD removal is possible. The popularity of plastic media is increasing. Crushed stone or gravel has a specific surface area of 50 – 100 m^2/m^3 and void volume 30 – 50%. Plastic filter media have a high surface area of greater than 100 m^2/m^3 and high void space of more than 95%.

8.19 ADVANTAGES OF RECIRCULATION

- High loading rate increases the sloughing of biomass. Thus, thin layer of biomass is maintained.
- The filter influent is freshened due to which odour problems are minimised.
- Self propelled distributors run continuously even at the time of reduced flows.
- The organic loading is reduced because of dilution.
- The applied sewage is seeded with active enzymes.

Recirculation ratio of 0.5 to 3 usually is maintained. For industrial wastewater, the ratio of more than 5 have been used.

Recirculation of sewage more than 3 times is not economical because there is less response for BOD removal.

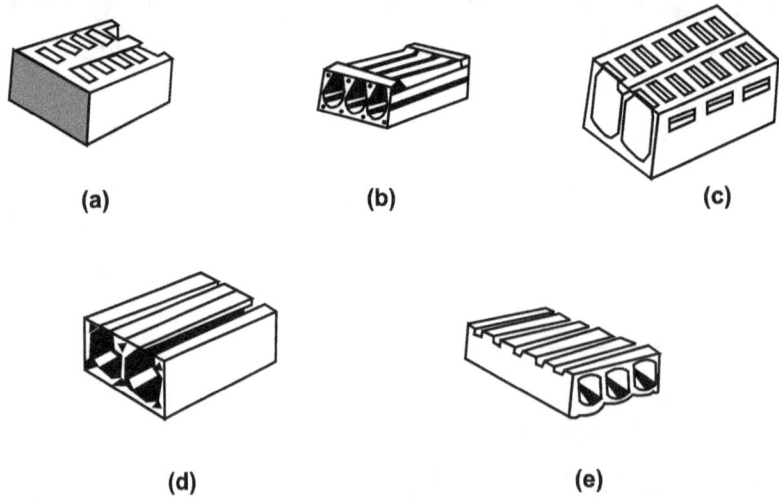

(a)   (b)   (c)

(d)   (e)

Fig. 8.12 : Blocks for under-drainage system

8.20 DISTRIBUTION SYSTEM

The rotor distributor used consists of two or more arms mounted in a pivot the center of filter which revolves in horizontal plane. The arms are hollow and contain nozzles through which the wastewater is sprayed over the bed. This can be done either from fixed sprays or moving sprays. In case of fixed sprays, pipe systems, placed evenly over the bed, distribute the wastewater uniformly.

Among the moving types, the present practice is to provide circular tanks to use only reaction type rotary distributors.

The reaction type rotary distributor consists of a feed column at the center of the filter, a turn table assembly at the top and two or more hollow radial distributor arms with orifices. The distributor should ensure that the entire surface is wetted and no area is left dry. This type of distributor requires a hydraulic head of 1 to 1.5 m measured from the center line of the distribution arm to the lower water level in the distribution well.

The rate of rotation may vary from 2 rpm for small distributors to less than 1/3 to 1/2 for large distributors.

8.21 UNDERDRAINAGE SYSTEM

This is provided with two objectives : (i) to collect treated wastewater and sloughed biological solids and (ii) to circulate or distribute air through the bed. The underdrains consists of semicircular or equivalent inverts. They are formed of precast vitrified clay or concrete blocks, complete with perforated cover. Fig. 8.9 shows the variety of commercially available underdrains. The underdrains have a slope towards the common collecting point or channel. The drains shall be so sized that flow occupies less than 50% of the cross-sectional area with velocity not less than 0.75 m/s at peak instantaneous hydraulic loading.

8.22 VENTILATION

This may be natural or forced. For natural ventilation, proper design of underdrains and effluent channels are must. The holes are provided in the walls of filter. Vertical vents along the periphery also improves the natural ventilation.

Forced ventilation is required in case of deep filters. It consists of forcing the air vertically upwards through the filters by the use of fans or other suitable equipments. The air required is 0.1 to 1 $m^3/min/m^2$ of floor area.

8.23 TYPES OF FILTERS

On the basis of hydraulic and organic loading rates, the filters are classified as

- Low rate trickling filter.
- High rate trickling filter.

In low rate trickling filters, the hydraulic loading rate is in the range of $1 - 4$ m³/m²/d and organic loading rate of $80 - 320$ gm BOD/m³/d. In high rate filters, hydraulic loading rate is $10 - 30$ m³/d/m² (including recirculation) and organic loading rate is 1000 to 4000 gm BOD/m³/day. Height is 3 to 6 m, sludge production is 0.4 kg/kg BOD removed and BOD removal efficiency is $40 - 70\%$. Hydraulic loading rate is the total flow including recirculation, when the organic loading rate is $5 -$ day 20°C   BOD, excluding the BOD of recirculant applied for unit volume per day.

8.24 RECIRCULATION

Filter plants return sufficient flow from the final clarifier hopper to the wet well for removal of accumulated settled solids and to prevent stalling of the distributor arm during low wastewater flow. Also in plant recirculation of wastewater increases liquid flow through the filter bed to allow greater organic loading without filling the bed voids with biological growths that would inhibit aeration. BOD removal efficiency is enhanced by passing wastewater through a filter more than once.

8.25 COMPONENTS OF TRICKLING FILTER

It consists of : (See Figs. 8.13 and 8.14)

1. Water tight holding tank.
2. Distribution system.
3. Filter media.
4. Underdrainage system.
5. Filter floor.
6. Filter walls.
7. Recirculation system.

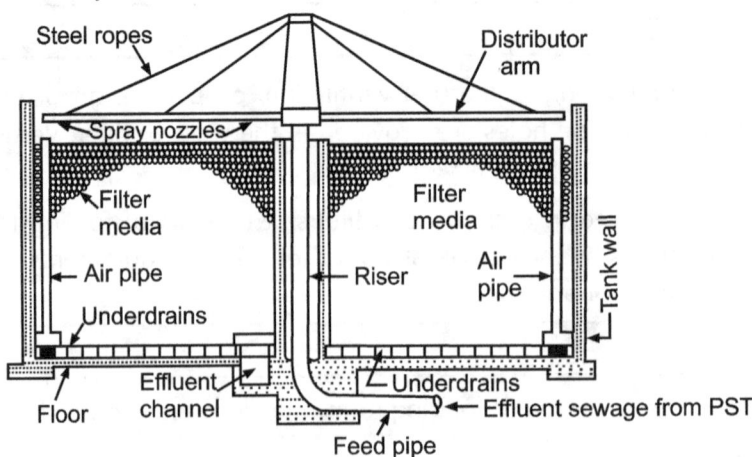

(a) Typical cross-section

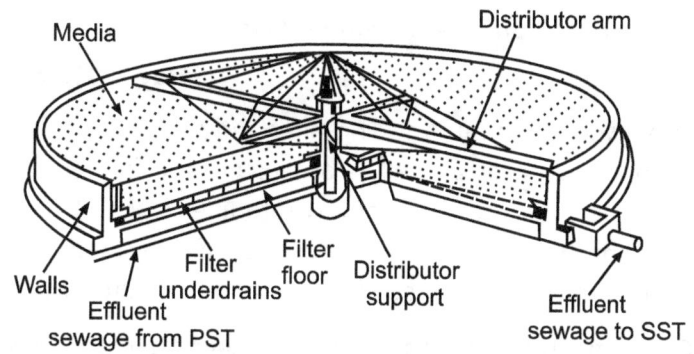

(b) Pictorical section

Fig. 8.13 : Trickling filter

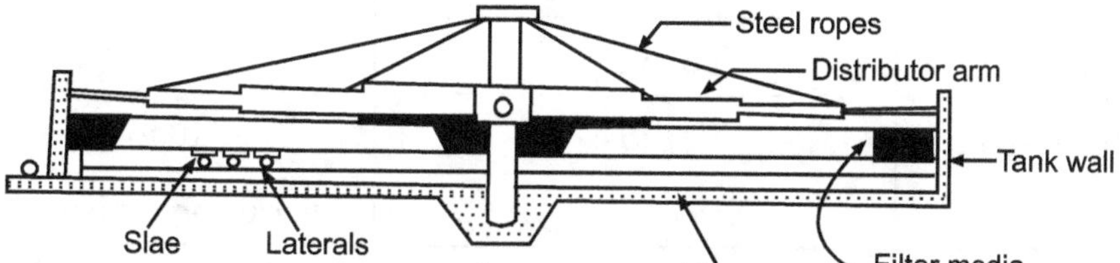

Section

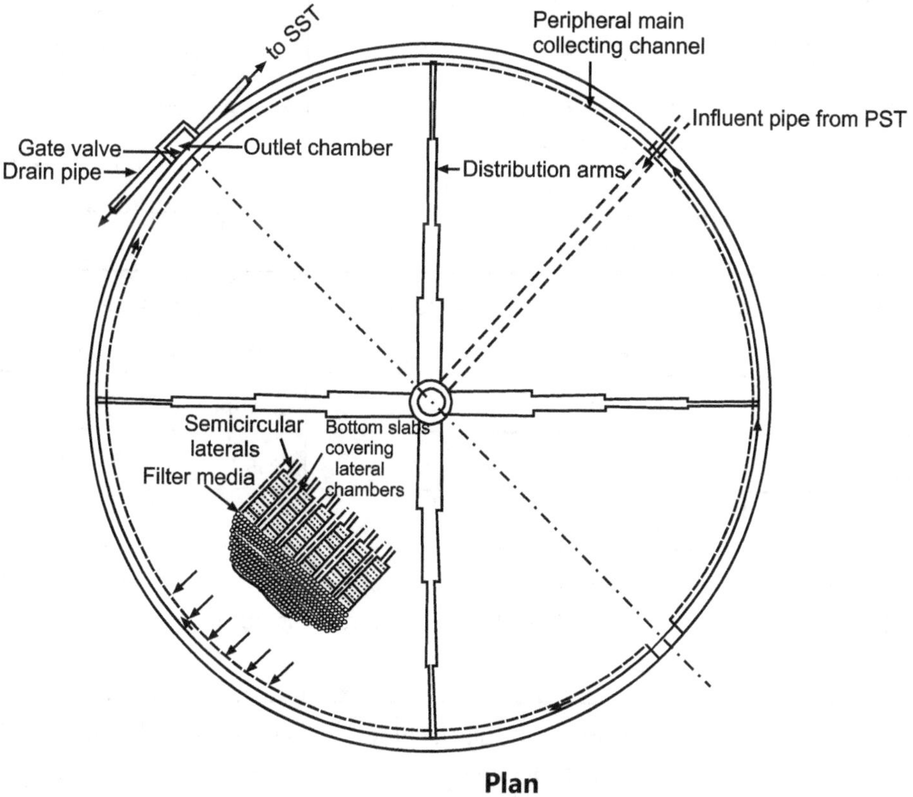

Plan

Fig. 8.14 : Typical details of trickling filter

Comparison of low rate and high rate trickling filters :

(May 2009, Dec. 2010, May 2011)

The basic difference between high rate trickling filter and slow rate trickling filter is that the rate of filter loading (both hydraulic as well as organic) of the former is several times more than that of the latter. The main drawback of low rate filter is that it has high initial cost, it requires larger area of construction and larger quantity of filter media. Table 8.6 gives the detailed idea about the comparison between low rate and high rate trickling filters.

Table 8.6 : Comparison between conventional and high rate trickling filters

Sr. No.	Characteristics	Conventional or low rate filter	High rate filter
1.	Depth of media	1.8 to 3.0 m	0.9 to 2.5 m
2.	Hydraulic loading $(m^3/d/m^2)$	1 to 4	10 to 40 (including recirculation)
3.	Organic loading as 5 day BOD in $g/d/m^3$	80 to 320	320 to 1000 (excluding recirculation)
4.	Recirculation system	Usually not provided, but can be provided if the hydraulic load does not exceed the limit.	Always provided. Recirculation ratio 0.5 – 3.0
5.	Volume of bed	5 times	1
6.	Interval of dosing	≯ 5 minutes. The sewage is applied at intervals.	≯ 15 seconds. Sewage is thus applied continuously.
7.	Sloughing	Intermittent	Continuous
8.	Cost of operation	More	Less
9.	Land required	More	Less
10.	Characteristics of final effluent	Contains BOD $\leq$ 20 mg/lit; it is highly nitrified into nitrate stage.	Contains BOD $\geq$ 30 mg/lit; it is not fully nitrified.
11.	Secondary sludge	Highly oxidized, black colour, having light fine particles.	Not fully oxidized; brownish black colour, containing fine particles.

(Ref. Manual on sewerage and sewage treatment, 2nd edition.)

High rate trickling filter :

Because of many drawbacks in low rate filter, many studies were conducted to increase the rate of filtration. Following are the observations :

- The thickness of biofilm reduces with increase in flow rate.

- The film is continuously washed away.

- Thinner biofilm is more active and supplies more nutrients to bacteria.

- The biomass quality collected in secondary settling tank is good.

- Because of less contact period, less degree of treatment and more putrescible organic material reaching to SST.

- The initial cost is less.

Because of above mentioned favourable reasons, the high rate filters are becoming more popular.

In high rate filters, better filtering media, with high surface area is provided. The filtering depth is reduced to 1.5 to 2.0 m to provide better aeration. The underdrains are provided of bigger size and steeper slope is given to filter bottom.

8.26 SINGLE STAGE AND TWO STAGE PLANTS

In single stage plant, the sewage is passed through single filter. Sewage may be recirculated to single stage filters.

In two stage filters, two filters in series are provided. It consists of primary settling tank and intermediate settling tank. Recirculation is provided to each stage. The treated effluent from first stage filter is applied on second stage filter either after settlement or without settlement.

The flow diagrams of high rate trickling filter with single stage and two stage are shown in Fig. 8.15.

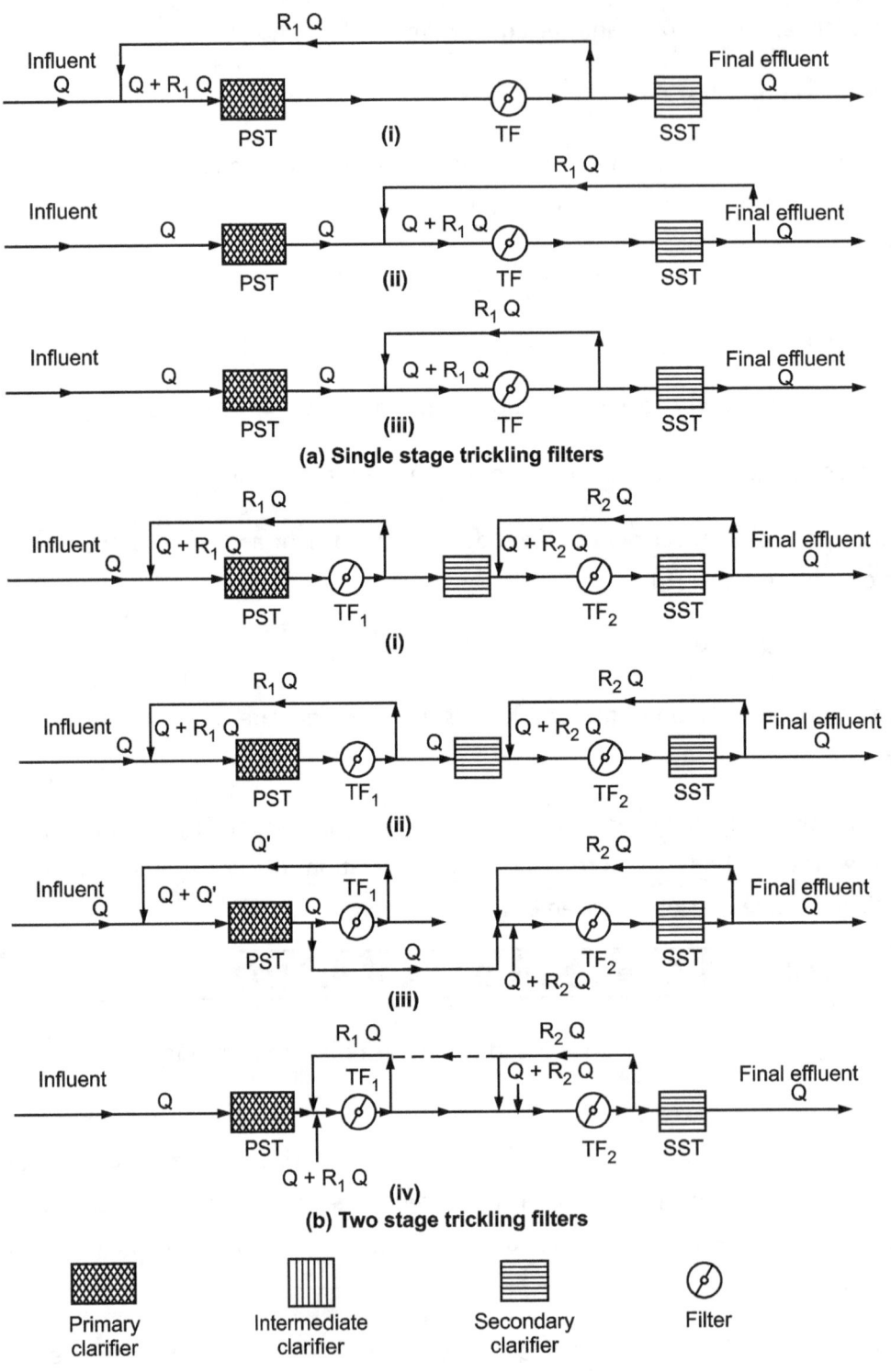

Fig. 8.15 : Flow sheets for high rate trickling filters

8.27 DESIGN OF TRICKLING FILTERS

The important considerations in the design of trickling filters are : (See Table 8.7).

    (a) Organic loading rate.   (b) Recirculation ratio.

Table 8.7 : Typical design criteria for trickling filters

Item	Low-rate	Intermediate	High-rate	Super-rate
HLR[a] $(m^3/m^2\text{-day})$	1 – 4	4 – 10	10 – 40	40 – 200
OLR[a] $(kg\ BOD_5$ per $m^3/day)$	0.08 – 0.32	0.2 – 0.5	0.32 – 1.0	0.8 – 6
Depth (m)	1.8 – 3	1 – 3	0.9 – 2.5	4.5 – 12
Recirculation ratio	0	0 – 1	0.5 – 3	1 – 4
Filter media	Rock, slag, gravel etc.	Rock, slag, etc.	Rock, slag, synthetics	Plastic media
Power $(kW/10^3\ m^3)$	2 – 5	2 – 5	5 – 10	10 – 20
Filter flies	Many	Intermediate	Few larvae are washed away	Few or none
Sloughing	Intermittent	Intermittent	Continuous	Continuous
Dosing intervals	Not more than 5 min	10 – 50 sec	< 15 sec	Continuous
Effluent	Usually fully nitrified	Partially nitrified	Nitrified at low loadings	Nitrified at low loadings.

    (Ref. Manual on sewerage and sewage treatment, 2nd edition).

[a]Based on surficial area, HLR – Hydraulic loading rate, OLR – Organic loading rate.

Once the organic loading rate is selected, the filter volume can be calculated. The depth and surface area are suitably chosen to secure hydraulic loading rates within the prescribed limits.

A number of equations are available for the determination of plant efficiencies based on organic loading rates and recirculation ratios.

The National Research Council (NRC) and Rankine have developed the empirical equations for trickling filter performance.

NRC equations :

The equations are applicable for both low rate and high rate trickling filters.

The efficiency of single stage or first stage of two stage filter is given by

$$E = \frac{100}{1 + 0.44 \sqrt{\dfrac{W}{VF}}}$$

or

$$E = \frac{100}{1 + 0.44 \sqrt{U}}$$

For the second stage of two stage filter, the efficiency is given by

$$E' = \frac{100}{1 + \dfrac{0.44}{1-e} \sqrt{\dfrac{W'}{V' F'}}}$$

or

$$E' = \frac{100}{1 + \dfrac{0.44}{1-e} \sqrt{U'}}$$

where,

E = Percentage BOD removal efficiency

$e = \dfrac{E}{100}$

E' = Percentage BOD removal efficiency for second stage of two stage filter.

W = BOD loading of settled sewage in single stage T.F. (kg/day)

V = Volume of first stage filter (m³)

F = Recirculation factor

$= \dfrac{1 + R}{(1 + 0.1 R)^2}$

R = Recirculation ratio, $\dfrac{Q_R}{Q}$

W', V', F' = BOD loading, volume and recirculation factor of second stage of two stage T.F.

$\dfrac{W}{VF} = U$ = Unit organic loading (kg/m³/day)

8.28 OPERATIONAL PROBLEMS IN TRICKLING FILTER

Chocking, ponding, fly nuisance, poor efficiency of BOD removal, tilting or stoppage of arms, odour are some of the problems faced. Media deterioration and loss, steel arm support corrosion are other problems.

8.28.1 Fly Nuisance

Filter flies, Psychoda, are nuisance problems near filter during warm weather. They breed in the sheltered area of the media, and on the inside surfaces of the retaining walls. Although wind can carry these small flies considerably long distances, their greatest irritation is to operating personnel.

Remedial Measures :

- Flooding the filter at regular intervals.
- Chlorinating the filter influent at two weeks interval.
- Periodic spraying of the peripheral area and walls of the filter with an insecticide.
- Continuous hydraulic loading to hamper the flies and larvae.
- Sprinkling lime at the site.

8.28.2 Ponding Nuisance

When all the voids of trickling filter are filled up due to chocking by heavy fungus and suspended solids, the problem of ponding of effluent arises. Ponding decreases ventilation, reduces effective volume of filter.

Remedial Measures :

- Flushing of filter with water.
- Reduce strength of filter influent by increasing recirculation.
- Chlorinate the influent.
- Stopping the distributor on ponded area.
- Allow the fungus to dry by keeping them out of operation for 12 to 48 hours.

Example 8.8 : A trickling filter plant has the following :

1. A primary clarifier with 17 m diameter, 2.5 m side water depth, and a single peripheral weir.
2. A trickling filter 25 m diameter, 2.5 m deep stone filled bed.
3. Final settling tank with 15 m diameter, 2.5 m side water depth and single peripheral weir.
4. Normal operating recirculation ratio = 0.5
5. The daily w/w flow = 6.2 mld
6. Average BOD of w/w = 180 mg/lit.

Calculate the loading on all units :

Solution :

[A] Primary clarifier :

$$A = \frac{3.14}{4} \times (17)^2 = 227 \text{ sq.m.}$$

$$V = 227 \times 2.5 = 567.5 \text{ m}^3$$

$$\text{Surface overflow rate} = \frac{6.2 \times 1000 \text{ m}^3/\text{d}}{227 \text{ m}^2}$$

$$= 27.31 \text{ m}^3/\text{d}/\text{m}^2$$

$$\text{Detention time} = \frac{\text{Volume}}{\text{Flow}} = \frac{567.5 \text{ m}^3}{6200 \text{ m}^3/\text{d}} \times 24 = 2.19 \text{ hrs.}$$

$$\text{Weir loading} = \frac{\text{Flow}}{\text{Weir length}} = \frac{\text{Flow}}{\pi D}$$

$$= \frac{6200 \text{ m}^3/\text{d}}{3.14 \times 17} = \textbf{116 m}^3/\textbf{d/m} \qquad \text{... Ans.}$$

[B] Trickling filter :

$$A = \frac{3.14 \times (25)^2}{4} = 490.6 \text{ sq.m.}$$

$$V = 490.6 \times 2.5 = 1226.5 \text{ m}^3$$

$$\text{Hydraulic loading} = \frac{Q + (R \times Q)}{A}$$

$$= \frac{6200 \text{ m}^3/\text{d} + (0.5 \times 6200) \text{ m}^3/\text{d}}{490.6 \text{ m}^2}$$

$$= \textbf{18.95 m}^3/\textbf{d/m}^2 \qquad \text{... Ans.}$$

BOD / Organic loading :

Assume 40% BOD removal by primary settling

∴ Settled wastewater BOD $= 0.6 \times 180 = 108 \text{ mg/lit}$

$$\text{BOD/Organic load} = \frac{6.2 \text{ m}l/\text{d} \times 108 \text{ mg/lit}}{1226.5 \text{ m}^3}$$

$$= \frac{669.6 \text{ kg/day}}{1226.5 \text{ m}^3}$$

$$= 0.546 \text{ kg/day/m}^3$$

$$= \textbf{546 gm/day/m}^3 \qquad \text{... Ans.}$$

[C] Final settling tank :

$$A = \frac{3.14 \times (15)^2}{4}$$

$$= 176.6 \text{ m}^2$$

$$V = 176.6 \times 2.5 \text{ m} = 441 \text{ m}^3$$

$$\text{Surface overflow rate} = \frac{6200 \text{ m}^3/\text{d}}{176.6 \text{ m}^2} = 35 \text{ m}^3/\text{d/m}^2$$

$$\text{Detention time} = \frac{\text{Volume}}{\text{Flow}} = \frac{441 \text{ m}^3}{6200 \text{ m}^3/\text{d}} = 1.7 \text{ hrs}$$

$$\text{Weir loading} = \frac{\text{Flow}}{\text{Weir length}} = \frac{6200 \text{ m}^3/\text{d}}{3.14 \times 15} = \mathbf{131.6 \text{ m}^3/\text{d/m}} \qquad \text{... Ans.}$$

Example 8.9 : Design a high rate trickling filter plant to treat settled domestic sewage having BOD of 200 mg/lit for an average flow of 20 mld **to satisfy an effluent BOD of 10 mg/lit**. Adopt peak factor as 2.25.

Solution :

As the effluent BOD_5 required is less than 30 mg/lit, **a two stage filtration plant shall be provided**. The filter will be designed for average flow. The distribution arms, underdrainage system and other pipelines etc. shall be for peak flow.

Taking an organic loading of 750 gm/d/m³,

$$\text{Volume of first stage filter} = 20 \times 10^6 \text{ l/d} \times \frac{200}{10^3} \text{ gm/lit} \times \frac{1}{750} \frac{\text{d/m}^3}{\text{gm}}$$

$$= 5333.3 \text{ m}^3$$

Adopting a depth of 1.5 m, filter area required $= \dfrac{5333.3}{1.5} = 3555.5 \text{ m}^2$

$$\therefore \qquad \text{Diameter of circular filter} = \sqrt{\frac{4 \times 3555.5}{\pi}} = 67.30 \text{ m}$$

As the diameter is too much high, two units shall be provided.

$$\therefore \qquad \text{Area of each unit} = 1777.75 \text{ m}^2$$

$$\text{Diameter of each unit} = \sqrt{\frac{4 \times 1777.5}{\pi}} = 47.60 \text{ m}$$

$$\text{Assume effluent BOD} = 30 \text{ mg/lit}$$

Filter dimensions for second stage filter :

Let us choose an organic loading rate of 500 gm/d/m³.

$$\text{Volume of second stage filter} = \frac{(20 \times 10^6) \ (30 \times 10^{-3})}{500}$$

$$= 1200 \text{ m}^3$$

Let us adopt a depth of 1 m.

$$\therefore \qquad \text{Area of filter} = \frac{1200 \text{ m}^3}{1 \text{ m}} = 1200 \text{ m}^2$$

and $\qquad$ Filter diameter $= \sqrt{\dfrac{1200 \times 4}{\pi}} = $ **39 m** $\qquad$ ... **Ans.**

Note : This problem can be solved by using NRC equation.

Example 8.10 : Design the high rate trickling filter for the following data :

1. Sewage flow = 10 mld
2. Recirculation ratio, R = 1.5
3. BOD of raw sewage = 250 mg/lit
4. BOD removal in primary clarifier = 30%
5. Final effluent BOD desired = 30 mg/lit.

Solution :

Q = 10 mld. BOD concentration = 250 mg/lit.

$\therefore$ $\qquad$ Total BOD present $= (10 \times 10^6)\,(250 \times 10^{-3}) \times 10^{-3}$

$\qquad\qquad = 2500$ kg/day

BOD removal in primary tank = 30%

$\therefore$ $\qquad$ BOD left in settled sewage $= 2500 - 0.3 \times 2500$

$\qquad\qquad = 1750$ kg/day

Desired BOD concentration in effluent = 30 mg/lit.

$\therefore$ $\qquad$ Total BOD left in effluent $= 10 \times 30 = 300$ kg/day

Hence, $\qquad$ BOD removed by filter $= 1750 - 300$

$\qquad\qquad = 1450$ kg/day

$\therefore$ $\qquad$ Efficiency of filter $= \dfrac{\text{BOD removal}}{\text{Total BOD present}} \times 100$

$\qquad\qquad = \dfrac{1450}{1750} \times 100 = 82.86\%$

But efficiency, given by NRC equation is

$$E = \dfrac{100}{1 + 0.44\,\sqrt{\dfrac{W}{VF}}}$$

where, $\qquad$ W = Total BOD applied to filter = 1750 kg/day

$\qquad\qquad$ V = Volume of filter (m³)

$\qquad\qquad$ F = Recirculation factor

$$= \frac{1 + R}{(1 + 0.1\,R)}$$

$$= \frac{1 + 1.5}{1 + (0.1 \times 1.5)^2}$$

$$= 1.89$$

$$82.86 = \frac{100}{1 + 0.44\,\sqrt{\dfrac{1750}{V \times 1.89}}}$$

Substituting

$$1 + 0.44\,\sqrt{\frac{1750}{V \times 1.89}} = \frac{100}{82.86} = 1.21$$

$$0.44\,\sqrt{\frac{1750}{V \times 1.89}} = 1.21 - 1 = 0.21$$

$$\sqrt{\frac{1750}{V \times 1.89}} = \frac{0.21}{0.44} = 0.48$$

$$\frac{1750}{V \times 1.89} = (0.48)^2 = 0.23$$

$$\frac{1750}{0.23} = V \times 1.89$$

$$7608.70 = 1.89 \times V$$

$$\therefore \qquad V = \frac{7608.70}{1.89}$$

$$\therefore \qquad V = 4026 \text{ m}^3$$

Let us assume the depth of filter as 1.8 m.

$$\therefore \qquad \text{Surface area of filter} = \frac{4026 \text{ m}^3}{1.8 \text{ m}} = 2236.67 \text{ m}^2$$

Provide two units.

$$\therefore \qquad \text{Area of each unit} = 1118.33 \text{ m}^2$$

$$\text{Hence, diameter of each filter} = \sqrt{\frac{1118.33 \times 4}{\pi}}$$

$$= \textbf{37.74 m} \cong \textbf{38 m} \qquad \text{... Ans.}$$

Hence, provide two single stage high rate filters of 38.5 m and 1.8 m deep filter media with a recirculation factor of 1.5.

Example 8.11 :

A single stage filter is designed for an organic loading of 10,000 kg of BOD in raw sewage per 10^4 sq.m. per day with a recirculation ratio of 1.2. This filter treats a flow of 10 m*l*d of raw sewage with a BOD of 250 mg/lit. Using NRC equation, determine the strength of effluent.

Solution :

$$\text{Total BOD of raw sewage} = (10 \times 10^6) \times (250 \times 10^{-6})$$

$$= 2500 \text{ kg/day}$$

$$\text{Required filter area} = \frac{\text{Total BOD of raw sewage, kg/day}}{\text{Permissible BOD loading, kg/m}^2\text{/day}}$$

$$= \frac{2500}{10000} \times 10^4 = 2500 \text{ m}^2$$

$\therefore$ $\quad\quad\quad\quad$ Volume of tank $= 2500 \times 1.8 = 4500 \text{ m}^3$

Assume depth of tank is 1.8 m.

Let us assume that primary clarifier removes 40% of BOD.

$\therefore$ $\quad\quad$ BOD of influent applied to filter $= 0.6 \times 2500$

$$= 1500 \text{ kg/day}$$

The efficiency of filter, $\quad\quad\quad\quad$ $E = \dfrac{100}{1 + 0.44 \sqrt{\dfrac{W}{V \times F}}}$

Here, $\quad\quad\quad\quad\quad\quad\quad\quad$ $W = 1500 \text{ kg/day}$

$\quad\quad\quad\quad\quad\quad\quad\quad\quad\quad$ $V = 4500 \text{ m}^3$

$\quad\quad\quad\quad\quad\quad\quad\quad\quad\quad$ $F = \dfrac{1 + 1.2}{1 + (0.1 \times 1.2)^2} = 2.169$

$\therefore$ $\quad$ Substituting $\quad\quad\quad\quad$ $E = \dfrac{100}{1 + 0.44 \sqrt{\dfrac{1500}{4500 \times 2.169}}}$

$\therefore$ $\quad\quad\quad\quad\quad\quad\quad\quad\quad\quad$ $E = 85.29\%$

$\therefore$ $\quad\quad\quad$ Total BOD of effluent $= (1 - 0.8529) \times 1500$

$$= 220.65 \text{ kg/day}$$

$$\text{BOD concentration of effluent} = \frac{\text{Total BOD}}{\text{Sewage volume}}$$

$$= \frac{220.65 \times 10^6}{10 \times 10^6}$$

$$= \textbf{22.07 mg/lit} \quad\quad\quad \textbf{... Ans.}$$

8.29 ROTATING BIOLOGICAL CONTACTORS

A rotating biological contactor (see Fig. 8.16) consists of a number of closely spaced circular disks made of polypropylene (PP) or polystyrene or polyvinyl chloride. The disks are partially submerged in wastewater and rotating slowly through it. Normally, the distance between the disks is 18 mm, in nitrification steps or in special cases the distance is 10 mm. The disks are lined upon an innox shaft.

Fig. 8.16 : Rotating biological contractor

The "biomass" will settle on the surface of the disks and form a slime layer over the wetted surface area of the disks. The disks alternately contact the biomass with the organic material in the wastewater and biomass getting oxygen from the atmosphere for decomposition during rotation. Due to rotation the biomass is maintained in an aerobic condition.

In average, the biomass will have a lifetime of about 80 days. When it gets too old, it will automatically fall down from the disks into the tank. This "excess sludge" will swim in the water flow, thus leaving the biological step and reaching the next module, the clarifier.

The colour of biomass is usually reddish-brown. In a high load process the biomass gets thicker and colour is dark brown to black, partially also slimy white. In case of under load, the biomass is very thin.

EXERCISE

1. Explain suspended growth processes.

2. What do you understand by MLSS concentration ? Differentiate between MLSS and MLVSS.

3. Discuss the importance of recirculation of sludge in ASP.

4. Write a note on : Sludge Volume Index.

5. Differentiate between step aeration and tapered aeration in ASP.

6. Explain system biology of ASP.

7. What is the necessity of modifications in conventional ASP ? Discuss different modifications with advantages and disadvantages of each.

8. Explain contact stabilisation process in ASP.

9. Write a note on : Extended aeration system.

10. Mention the design criteria for oxidation ditch.

11. What are the problems associated with ASP ? Explain.

12. Design a conventional activated sludge process for the following data :

    (i)   Flow = 15000 m³/day

    (ii)   Settled influent, BOD = 320 mg/lit

    (iii) Decay coefficient, K_d = 0.06.

    (iv) Yield coefficient, Y = 0.6

    (v)   MCRT, θ_c = 10 days

    (vi) MLSS,   X = 2700 mg/lit

13. What do you understand by attached growth process ? Explain various attached growth processes.

14. Explain with sketch construction and working of a conventional trickling filter.

15. Write a note on : Filter media in T.F.

16. Explain the importance of recirculation in T.F.

17. Explain : (a) Distribution system.

    (b) Underdrainage system.

18. What are low rate and high rate filters ? Differentiate them.

19. Explain with sketch single stage and two stage T.F.

20. Discuss the organic loading and hydraulic loading rate in the design of T.F.

21. What do you understand by efficiency of T.F. ? How do you determine the efficiency by using NRC equation ?

22. Give various flow diagrams used in single stage and two stage T.F.

23. Explain causes and remedies of various operational problems in trickling filter.

24. Determine the size of high rate trickling filter for the following data :

Sewage flow = 5 m*l*d.

Recirculation ratio = 1.5

BOD of raw sewage = 300 mg/lit.

BOD removed in primary clarifier = 40%

Final effluent BOD desired = 30 mg/lit

25. A single stage high rate T.F. is to treat a flow of 4 m*l*d with loading of 11000 kg of BOD in raw sewage per 10^4 sq.m. and the recirculation ratio is to be 1.2. What will be the strength of the effluent ? Use NRC equation. Assume that 30% BOD is removed in primary clarifier.

26. Calculate the effluent BOD of two stage trickling filter with the following data :

Q = 4700 m³/day.

BOD_5 = 300 mg/lit

Volume of filter No. 1 = 850 m³

Volume of filter No. 2 = 850 m³

Filter depth = 2m

Recirculation ratio (filter No. 1) = 1.25

Recirculation ratio (filter No. 2) = 1.00

Use NRC equation.

UNIVERSITY QUESTIONS

1. What is meant by activated sludge ? Describe with sketch the treatment of sewage by ASP.   **(6 M) (May 2011)**

2. Explain activated sludge process. Describe advantages and disadvantages of ASP.

    (6 M) (Dec. 2010, May 2009)

3. Explain the following terms with respect to ASP :

    (i)   F/M ratio   (iii) SRT

    (iii)   HRT (θ) (iv) MCRT ($θ_c$).   **(5 M) (May 2011, May 2009)**

4. Explain with sketch the biological process in trickling filter.

    (4 M (May 2011, May 2010)

5. What are the advantages of high rate T.F. over conventional or low rate T.F. ?

    (6 M) (May 2011, Dec. 2010, May 2009)

6. Explain activated sludge process. What are the advantages and disadvantages of activated sludge process ?   **(6 M) (Dec. 2010)**

7. What do you understand by "Trickling Filter" ? Explain with the help of neat sketch in detailed. Explain regarding biological process involved in the working of trickling filter. **(6 M) (May 2009, May 2011)**

8. (a) Explain with the help of a flow diagram, the essentials of activated sludge process. **(6 M) (May 2010)**

   (b) Design an activated sludge process for the following data : **(12 M) (May 2010)**

   (i) Municipal wastewater flow rate = 12,000 m³/day.

   (ii) BOD of settled effluent = 150 mg/lit.

   (iii) BOD of treated effluent = 5 mg/lit.

   (iv) Yield coefficient, Y = 0.5 kg/kg.

   (v) Endogenous decay coefficient, k_d = 0.05 d⁻¹.

   (vi) MLSS, X = 3000 mg/lit.

   (vii) Return sludge solids concentration, X_r = 15,000 mg/lit.

   (viii) Mean cell residence time, θ_c = 10 days.

   Determine :

   (a)   Volume of reactor.   (b)   F/M ratio.

   (c)   Volumetric loading rate.   (d)   Oxygen requirement.

   (e)   Recycle ratio.   (f)   BOD removal efficiency.

9. Design an activated sludge process for the following data :   **(12 M) (Dec. 2010)**

   (i)   Municipal wastewater flow rate   = 10,000 m³/day

   (ii)   BOD of settled effluent   = 150 mg/lit

   (iii)   BOD of treated effluent   = 5 mg/lit

   (iv)   Yield coefficient, Y   = 0.5 kg/kg

   (v)   Endogenous decay coefficient, k_d = 0.05 d⁻¹

   (vi)   MLSS, X   = 3500 mg/lit

   (vii) Return sludge solids concentration, X_r = 15,000 mg/lit

   (viii) Mean cell residence time, θ_c = 10 days

   Determine :

   (1)   Volume of reactor.

(2)   F/M radio.

(3)   Volumetric loading rate.

(4)   Oxygen requirement.

(5)   Recycle ratio.

(6)   BOD removal efficiency.

10. Design a high rate trickling filter using N.R.C. equation for the following data :

(10 M) (Dec. 2010)

(i)   Sewage flow   = 10 mld

(ii)   Recirculation ratio   = 1.5

(iii)   BOD of raw sewage   = 150 mg/lit

(iv)   BOD removal in primary clarifier   = 30%

(v)   Final effluent BOD desired   = 30 mg/l

11. (a) Design a high rate trickling filter using N.R.C. equation for the following data :

(10 M) (May 2010)

(i)   Sewage flow = 8 mld.

(ii)   Recirculation ratio = 1.5.

(iii)   BOD of raw sewage = 300 mg/lit.

(iv)   BOD removal in primary clarifier = 30%.

(v)   Final effluent BOD desired = 30 mg/l.

12. Given the following data of operating Activated Sludge Process.

(6 M) (May 2009, 2011)

(i)   Waste water flow = 30,00m m^3/day.

(ii)   Influent total solids = 600 mg/lit.

(iii)   Influent suspended solids = 120 mg/lit.

(iv)   Influent BOD = 170 mg/lit.

(v)   Effluent total solids = 480 mg/lit.

(vi)   Effluent suspended solids = 20 mg/lit.

(vii) Effluent BOD = 20 mg/lit.

(viii) MLVSSS concentration = 3000 mg/lit.

(ix)   Return sludge solid concentration = 9800 mg/lit.

Calculate :

(1)   Volume of reactor

(2)   F/m ratio

(3)   Oxygen required per day

13. A single stage filter is to treat a flow of 3.79 mℓd of raw sewage with BOD of 240 mg/ℓ. It is to be designed for a loading of 11086 kg of BOD in raw sewage per hectare metre and the recirculation ratio is to be 1. What will be the strength of the effluent, according to the recombination of NRC ?

✠ ✠ ✠

Chapter 9

LOW COST TREATMENT METHODS

9.1 INTRODUCTION

In previous chapter, we have studied the conventional biological treatment methods (trickling filters or activated sludge process). The installation and running cost of these methods is very high. The past experience with such treatment plant shows that many of them are performing poorly due to the lack of maintenance or due to the lack of skilled operational supervision. On the other hand, the low cost treatment systems like stabilisation ponds, aerated lagoons, oxidation ditches, etc. are very simple to construct, require little or no skilled supervision for operation and mechanization is least. In our country, the low cost treatment systems are achieved good degree of treatment as compared to the conventional systems under certain conditions.

9.2 OXIDATION PONDS (STABILISATION PONDS)

9.2.1 General

A **stabilisation pond** is simply a shallow body of water contained in an earthen basin, open to sun and air. The **oxidation pond**, often used is synonymous. The detention period of these ponds is long. These ponds may be considered to be completely mixed biological reactors without solids return. Due to their low construction and operating cost, these ponds are widely used in rural areas. Now-a-days, these ponds are also used for treatment of various industries like dairies, oil refineries, poultry-processing plants etc.

9.2.2 Classification of Ponds   (May 2010, 2011)

The ponds are classified according to the nature of the biological activity which takes place within the pond as :

1. Aerobic
2. Facultative (aerobic – anaerobic) and
3. Anaerobic.

9.2.2.1 Aerobic Stabilisation Ponds (Algae Ponds)

General : These are large shallow earthen basins that are used for the treatment of wastewater by natural processes involving the use of algae and bacteria. Therefore these ponds are also called as **algae ponds.**

Applications : This type of ponds are used for nutrient removal, treatment of soluble organic wastes, conversion of wastes etc.

Process Description : As per the name of the pond, aerobic condition is prevailed throughout the depth of pond. This pond contains algae and bacteria in suspension.

The following Table 9.1 shows depth of aerobic ponds related to different uses.

Table 9.1

Sr. No.	Uses	Depth
1.	Treatment of irrigation return water or any other industrial waste (Remove the nitrogen by algal growth).	Shallow depth of 0.15 m to 0.45 m.
2.	Treatment of domestic waste water.	1 m to 1.2 m

The length to width ratio is generally kept as 3 : 1.

For better results, their contents must be mixed periodically using pumps or surface aerators.

Process Microbiology : In aerobic stabilisation pond, the oxygen is supplied by natural surface aeration and by algal photosynthesis. Except for the algal population, the microbiological population present in the ponds are similar to that in activated sludge system.

Bacterial-Algal-Symbiosis (May 2011, 2010, Dec. 2010, May 2009) : The sewage containing organic material is a necessary food for aerobic population like bacteria which stabilises the putrescible matter by oxidising it and releases carbon dioxide (CO_2) which is taken up by the algal for their growth, algae produce more algal cells and oxygen which help in maintaining the aerobic condition of the pond. This cycle is known as **'bacterial-algal-symbiosis'**. This cyclic symbiotic relationship is shown in Fig. 9.1.

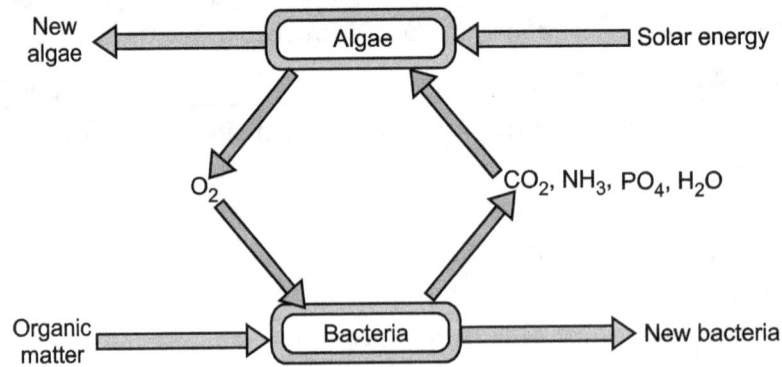

Fig. 9.1 : Symbiotic relationship between algae and bacteria

As we have seen that micro-organisms like bacteria and algae are predominating in this system. Also protozoa and rotifers are present under certain loading conditions. The main function of protozoa and rotifers is to polish the effluent.

The presence of these micro-organisms in aerobic pond depends on pH, nutrients, temperature, degree of pond mixing, sunlight etc.

9.2.2.2 Facultative (Aerobic – Anaerobic) Stabilisation Ponds

General : The stabilisation of wastes in facultative ponds is brought about by a combination of aerobic, anaerobic and facultative bacteria.

Process Description : Three zones exist in this type of ponds :

1. **The Top Zone :** This is an aerobic zone in which the algal photosynthesis and aerobic biodegradation takes place.

2. **The Bottom Zone :** This is an anaerobic zone, the wastewater settle and undergo anaerobic decomposition.

3. **The Intermediate Zone :** This is partly aerobic and partly anaerobic zone, the decomposition of organic wastes are done by the facultative bacteria.

Fig. 9.2 shows elevation diagram of facultative pond.

The nuisance associated with the anaerobic reactions are eliminated due to the presence of top aerobic zone, the end products of anaerobic decomposition are foul smelling one which are carried to the top zone by mixing currents and are oxidized, hence the maintenance of an aerobic layer in the facultative pond is important. The aerobic condition in top layer is maintained by the presence of algae or by surface aerators. When surface aerators are used to maintain aerobic condition in upper layer, algae are not required.

The depth of pond is generally 1 to 1.5 m.

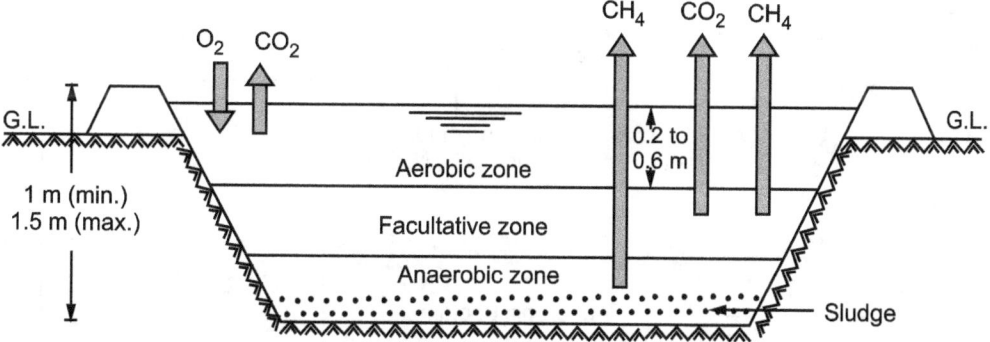

Fig. 9.2 : Elevation diagram of facultative pond

Process Microbiology : The micro-organisms present in upper aerobic layer are similar to that of an aerobic pond i.e. giving rise to bacterial algae symbiosis and in the bottom layer of the pond are facultative and anaerobic bacteria. The treatment effected by this type of pond is comparable to that of conventional secondary treatment processes. So facultative ponds are most commonly used for treatment of sewage.

In this pond, the organic matter is stabilised by bacterial oxidation in top layer and by methane fermentation in the bottom zone. In facultative zone, facultative bacteria oxidize incoming organics as well as the end products of anaerobic decomposition of the bottom anaerobic zone. When the sewage is loading in the pond, the suspended organic matter and bioflocculated organic matter settle down to the bottom of the pond. The settled sludge of the bottom undergoes anaerobic fermentation in absence of the dissolved oxygen. Due to the anaerobic fermentation it librates the methane (CH_4), this indicates the removal of BOD (Generally, 0.25 gm of methane is being liberated for every gramm of ultimate BOD utilized.) In the liquid layers (above bottom sludge layer), algae are present under favourable conditions. During day light, algae utilizes CO_2 for photosynthesis, and liberating oxygen, which helps to maintain aerobic condition in the top layer of the pond. In presence of this oxygen, aerobic bacteria oxidise organic matter. So it means that there is an interdependence between algae and bacteria. This is shown in Fig. 9.3.

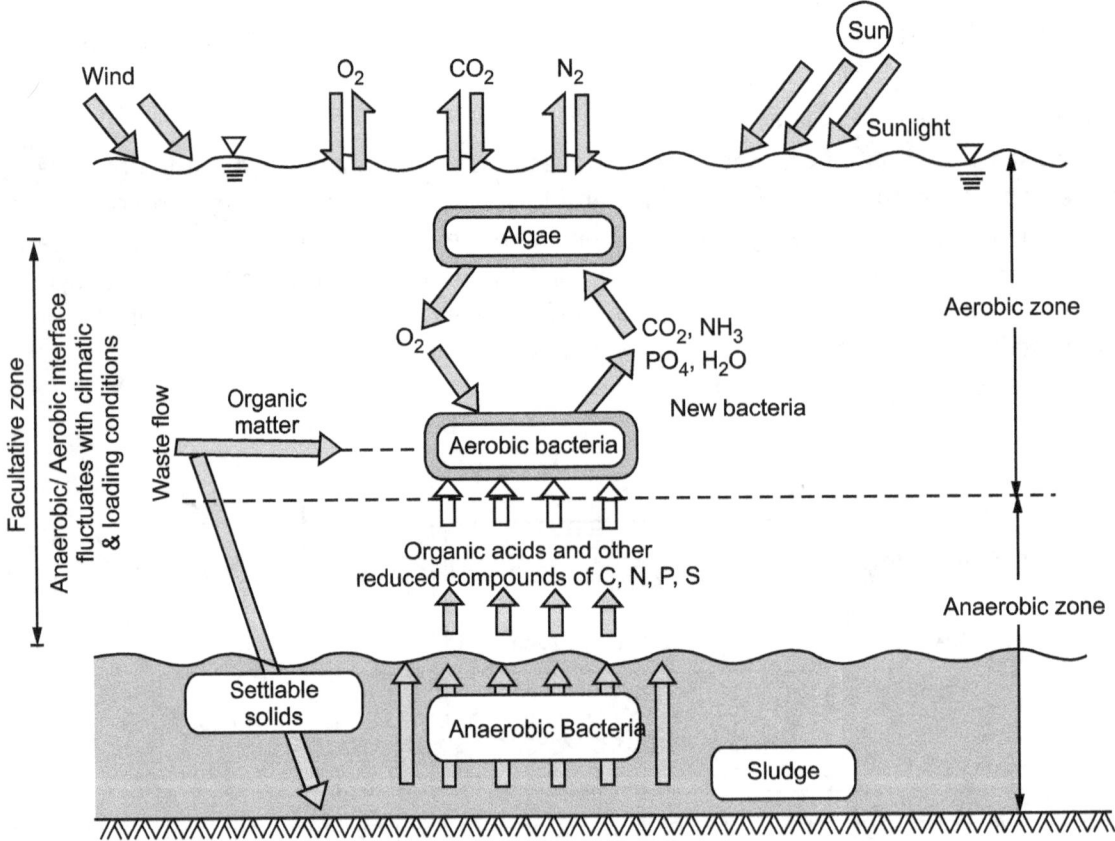

Fig. 9.3 : Diagram of facultative pond reaction

The boundary as shown in Fig. 9.3 between the aerobic and anaerobic zones is not stationary. Aerobic area may extend downward due to mixing (by wind action) and penetration (by sunlight). Conversely, calm waters and weak lighting result in the anaerobic layer rising towards the surface. Diurnal changes in light conditions may lead in diurnal fluctuations in the aerobic – anaerobic interface.

9.2.2.3 Anaerobic Stabilisation Ponds

In this type of ponds, the entire depth is in anaerobic condition except an extremely shallow top layer. Generally, these ponds are used in series after facultative pond for complete treatment of a waste.

Process Description : In this system, free dissolved oxygen is not available to the sewage, so anaerobic decomposition, called putrefaction occur. An anaerobic bacteria is survived by extracting and consuming the bounded molecular oxygen present in compounds like sulphates (SO_4) and nitrates (NO_3).

Process Microbiology : Firstly, acid producing bacteria produce organic acids like acetic, butyric and propionic by decomposition of dissolved organic waste. Further the organic acids converted into methane gas ($CH_4 \uparrow$), carbon dioxide gas ($CO_2 \uparrow$) etc. by the methane-producing bacteria, which is represented by the following equation and also shown in Fig. 9.4.

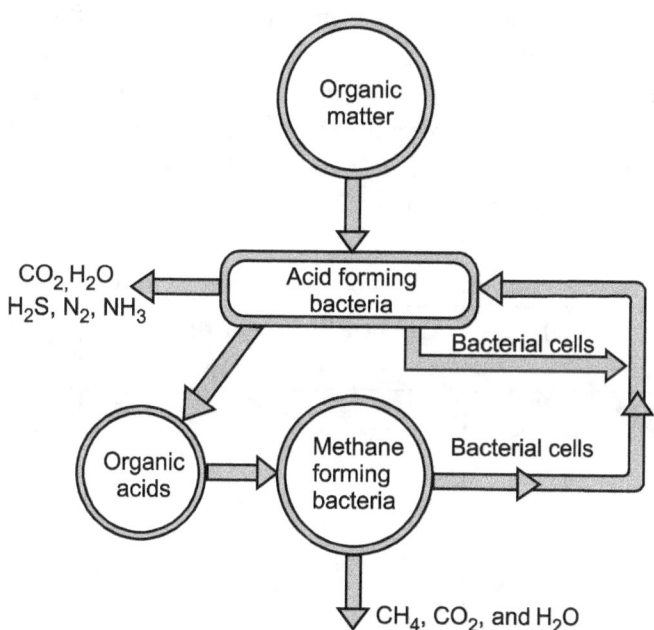

Fig. 9.4 : Anaerobic decomposition

$$\text{Organic acids} \xrightarrow[\text{anaerobic bacteria}]{\text{Methane forming}} CH_4 \uparrow + CO_2 \uparrow + \text{Heat}$$

Sludge or solids build up is much less in this anaerobic system because some quantity of waste is used by the anaerobic biosystem as source of energy and in the synthesis of new bacterial cells. If the contents of anaerobic pond are in the black colour, it indicates proper functioning of anaerobic pond.

9.2.3 Design Criteria   (Dec. 2010, May 10, May 09, May 2011)

The stabilisation ponds design parameters are not well defined. Due to the simultaneous involvement of the operations like sedimentation, oxidation, digestion, photosynthesis, evaporation, seepage etc., the mathematical modelling of the process of stabilisation in the pond is difficult.

Here, two separate methods are described, the first method applicable for aerobic pond only and the second applicable for aerobic and facultative ponds.

9.2.3.1 First Method (Applicable for Aerobic Pond)

In this method, the oxygen resources of the pond are equated to the applied organic loading. The principle source of the oxygen is photosynthesis and is also dependent on solar energy. The solar energy is related to geographical, astronomical and meteorological phenomena, and varies with time in the year and the latitude of the place. Based on studies conducted by the National Environmental Engineering Research Institute (NEERI), Nagbur, Table 9.2 shows the values of yield of photosynthetic oxygen in different latitudes IS : 5611 recommends the BOD loading equal to the yield of photosynthetic oxygen, as shown in column 4 of Table 9.2. The values shown in Table 9.2 may be modified for elevation above mean sea level (MSL) by dividing by a factor (1 + 0.003 H), where H is the elevation of the pond site above MSL in hundred meters. Other correction is the pond volume which has to be made when the sky is clear for less than 75% of the days at the rate of 3% for a fall of every 10%.

Table 9.2 : Yield of Photosynthetic Oxygen and Recommended BOD Loading

Sr. No.	Latitude (°N)	Yield of Photosynthetic O_2 (kg/ha/day)	BOD_5 Loading (kg/ha/day)
(1)	(2)	(3)	(4)
1.	8	325	325
2.	12	300	300
3.	16	275	275
4.	20	250	250
5.	24	225	225
6.	28	200	200
7.	32	175	175
8.	36	150	150

(**Ref. :** Manual on sewerage and sewage treatment, 2nd Edition)

If the amount of solar energy is cal/m^2/day and the efficiency of the conversion of light energy to fixed energy in the form of algal cells are known, yield of photosynthetic oxygen can be calculated directly.

As we know,

$$\text{Flow} \times \text{Detention time} = \text{Depth} \times \text{Surface area}$$

Detention time can be calculated by using the following equation.

$$t = \frac{1}{K_1} \log_{10} \left(\frac{L_a}{L_a - Y} \right) \qquad \qquad \text{... (9.0)}$$

where,

L_a = BOD of the effluent entering the pond

Y = BOD removed (say 90% of L_a or 95% of L_a)

The organic surface loading in kg of BOD per hectare per day can be estimated using the following equation :

$$L_o = 10 \left(\frac{d}{t} \right) BOD_L \qquad \qquad \text{... (9.1)}$$

where,

L_o = Organic loading in kg/ha/day

d = Depth of pond in m

t = Detention time in days

BOD_L = Ultimate soluble BOD in mg/lit

The equation (9.1) is also useful to calculate oxygen requirement for the aerobic decomposition of the waste in kg/ha/day in aerobic ponds.

Design Steps (First Method) :

The following are the steps of design of aerobic ponds (with slight modification and ponds can be designed as facultative ponds by first method, see the following note) :

1. Calculate ultimate BOD (BOD_L).
2. Then calculate yield of photosynthetic oxygen related to latitude from Table 9.2.
3. From equation (9.1), calculate (d/t) ratio.
4. Assume suitable depth of pond (d).
5. By knowing value of d, calculate t.
6. Detention time can be calculated by using equation (9.0) (see example 9.5).
7. Calculate the required surface area, by using the following equation :

$$\text{The required surface area} = \frac{\text{Flow} \times \text{Detention time}}{\text{Depth of pond}}$$

Note : The above method may be applied with slight modification in the **design of facultative ponds**, taking into consideration the BOD stabilization of solids in the bottom zone by anaerobic reaction. In this case, the oxygen requirement is corrected to take into account the non-settleable portion of BOD which undergoes the aerobic decomposition in the aerobic zone. Normally, a correction factor of 0.5 is taken. In other words, in step 3 modify equation (9.1) as follows :

$$L_0 = 10 \left(\frac{d}{t}\right) BOD_L \times 0.5 \qquad \text{... (9.2)}$$

Refer example (9.1) for design of facultative pond by first method.

9.2.3.2 Second Method

In this method, the principle of biological treatment kinetics are applied. For the removal of BOD in the pond, assuming a retarded first order reaction kinetics, the following equation (9.3) gives the relationship between the efficiency of the treatment in BOD removal, first order BOD removal rate constant, and the detention time in a **complete mix system**.

$$\frac{S_1}{S_0} = \frac{1}{1 + K (V/Q)} \qquad \text{... (9.3)}$$

where,　　　　S_0 = Influent BOD (substrate) concentration

　　　　　　　　S_1 = Effluent BOD concentration

　　　　　　　　Q = Waste flow rate

　　　　　　　　V = Volume of the reactor

　　　　　　　　K = First order BOD removal rate constant

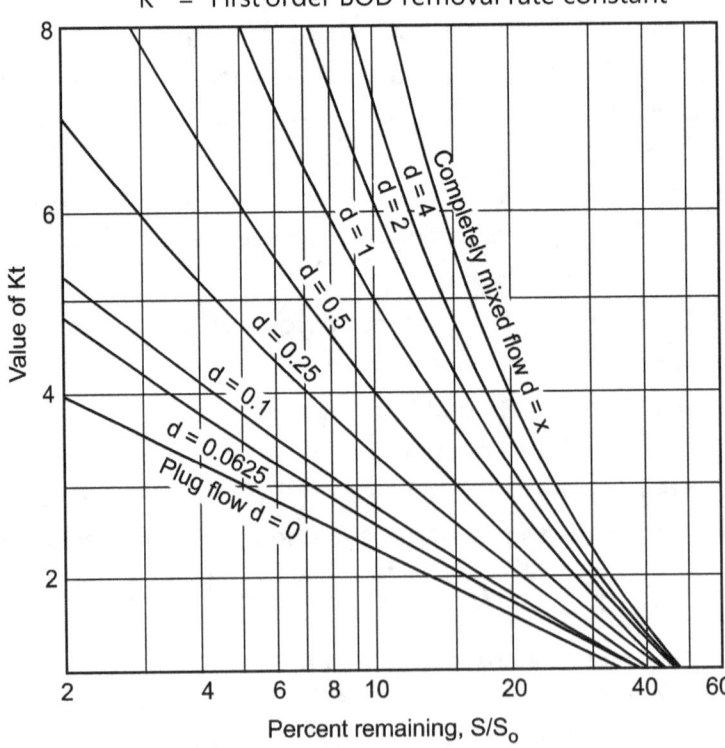

Fig. 9.5

But in actual practice the stabilisation ponds are never the complete mix type. The hydraulic regime within the tank assumes an intermediate condition in between plug flow and complete mix system i.e. partially mix system therefore, these may be considered as plug flow system with certain amount of axial dispersion of the materials.

Wehner and Wilhelm have developed an equation for partially system correlating the efficiency, axial dispersion, detention time, first order BOD removal rate constant etc.

Thirumurthi developed design curves related to that equation as shown in Fig. 9.5, which gives the product of first order BOD removal rate constant (K) and detention time (t) corresponding to percent BOD remaining (S_1/S_0) for different values of dispersion factors.

The values of dispersion factors and BOD removal rate constant are given in the following Table 9.3 and Table 9.4 respectively.

Table 9.3 : Values of Dispersion Factors

Sr. No.	Description	Value of Dispersion Factor
1.	For idealized complete mix system	∞
2.	For idealized plug flow	zero
3.	For most stabilization ponds	0.1 to 1.0
4.	For aerobic ponds	1.0
5.	For facultative ponds	0.3 to 1.0 (typical value 0.5)

Table 9.4 : Values of BOD Removal Rate Constant

Sr. No.	Description	Value of BOD Removal Rate Constant
1.	In stabilisation ponds (temperature 20 to 35°C)	0.05 to 1.0 per day
2.	For primary ponds (temperature 20°C)	0.22 per day
3.	For secondary ponds (temperature 20°C)	0.1 per day
4.	For tertiary ponds (temperature 20°C)	0.06 per day

Note : *Generally, most ponds are bound to receive some amount of settleable organics and at the bottom layer anaerobic action will develop due to thick layer of accumulated sludge.*

Design Steps (Second Method) :

The following are steps of design for facultative ponds :

- Calculate % BOD_5 remaining (if not given) by assuming desired effluent BOD_5 and considering 50% of the BOD is stabilised by anaerobic decomposition alone. (See example 9.1).

- Calculate Kt from Fig. 9.5, by knowing value of dispersion factor and BOD_5 removal efficiency.

- Calculate the value of K for different temperatures (for winter and summer or maximum and minimum as per requirement) from the following equation :

$$(K)_{T°C} = (K)_{20} \cdot (\theta_K)^{T-20}$$
$$= K_{20} \cdot (1.06)^{T-20}$$

- Calculate value of t, by substituting value of K (which is calculated from step 3) in step 2.
- Calculate the surface area from the following relationship for different temperatures and select higher value of surface area. (Generally, minimum temperature gives higher value of surface area, so the pond can be designed for minimum or winter temperature).
- If surface aerators are provided, then the power and number of aerators are required to be calculated. (See example 9.2).

Design Parameters :

The following Table 9.5 shows typical design parameters for ponds.

Table 9.5 : Typical Design Parameters for Ponds

Sr. No.	Parameters	Aerobic pond	Anaerobic pond	Facultative pond
1.	BOD_5 loading, kg/ha/day	150 to 200 (for winter season)	500 to 1000 (winter) 1000 to 2000 (summer)	See table 9.1
2.	Depth, m	See Table 9.1	2.5 to 7	1 to 1.5
3.	Detention time, day	7	2 to 5	At least 6.5 days
4.	BOD removal efficiency	80 to 95% under normal conditions, decrease during winter months	45 to 65% during winter. 65 to 80% during summer	80 to 90%

9.2.4 Construction Details

The following Table 9.6 shows construction details of pond.

Table 9.6 : Construction Details of Pond

Sr. No.	Item	Description
1.	**Shape of Pond**	• Round, square or rectangular ponds with length not exceeding three times the width are acceptable. • Avoid narrow or elongated portions. • Adopt maximum basin length of 750 m. • To minimise accumulations of floating matter and to avoid dead pockets, keep rounded corners.

Contd...

2.	Embankment	• Prepared well compacted embankment of soil.
		• Top width – 1.5 to 3 m for large ponds
		• Freeboard – minimum 0.5 m
		                    – For larger ponds, 1.5 times the wave height.
		• Outer slopes – 2 : 1 to 2.5 : 1
		• Inner slopes – 1 : 1 to 1.5 : 1, if fully pitched
		                    – 2 : 1 to 3 : 1, if face is unprotected.

3.	Inlets When sewage is discharged by pump When sewage is discharged under gravity	• Pipeline should extend into the pond atleast 15 to 20 m from the water edge. • When the sewage is to be pumped, the pipeline should be laid at bottom of the pond to discharge through an upward inclined 90° bend. • In case of gravity flows, the outfall sewer terminate at a manhole. • The invert of the manhole should be atleast 0.2 m above the MWL of the pond.
4.	Outlets	• To avoid short circuiting, outlet should be so located with reference to inlets. • Provide one outlet for every 0.5 ha pond area.
5.	Multiple Units of Ponds	• Multiple units should be provided when the required area of pond exceeds 0.5 ha. • These units can be either in series/in parallel/ in series-parallel system. • **Parallel System :** – Provide better distribution of settleable solids. – Also, from operation point of view, one unit at a time can be taken out of operation temporarily for desludging.
		• **Series System :** – Reduced algal concentration in the effluent. – Coliform removal efficiency is less. – Implies a high BOD loading in the primary cell, they should have 65 to 75% of the total surface area requirements to avoid anaerobic conditions in these cells.

Contd...

		• **Parallel - Series System :**
		– In this system, getting advantages of both parallel and series operations.
		(See Fig. 9.6 for arrangement of pond for these three different systems).
6.	**Pond Interconnections**	• Pond interconnections are needful in case ponds are designed in multiple cells in series.
		(See Fig. 9.7 for arrangement of pond interconnections).

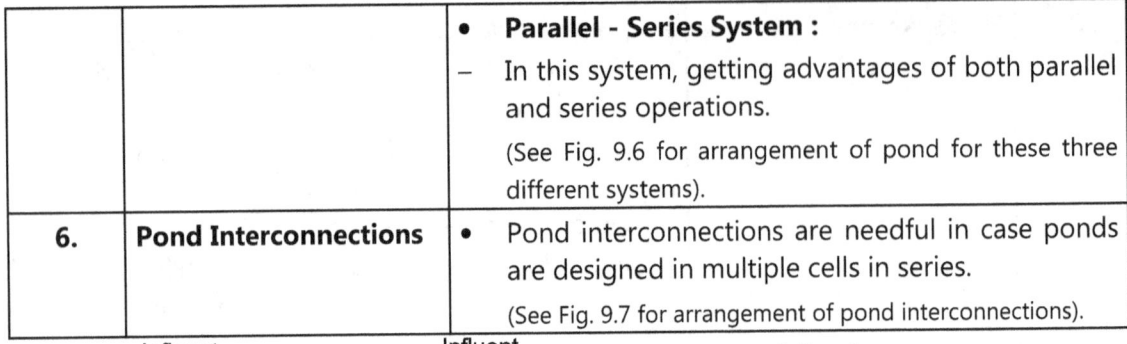

(a) Parallel system   **(b) Series system**   **(c) Parallel-series system**

Fig. 9.6 : Arrangement of ponds for different systems

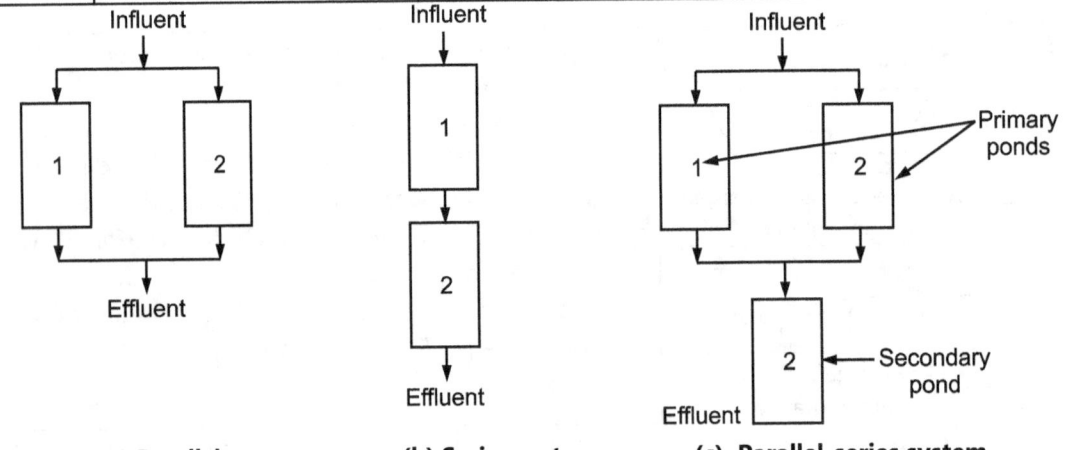

Section A-A

Plan

In section A-A it is seen that, the effluent from first cell withdrawn from the aerobic layer and introduced at the bottom of next cell.

Fig. 9.7 : Arrangement of pond interconnections for series system

Following Fig. 9.8 shows a neat diagram of stabilisation pond.

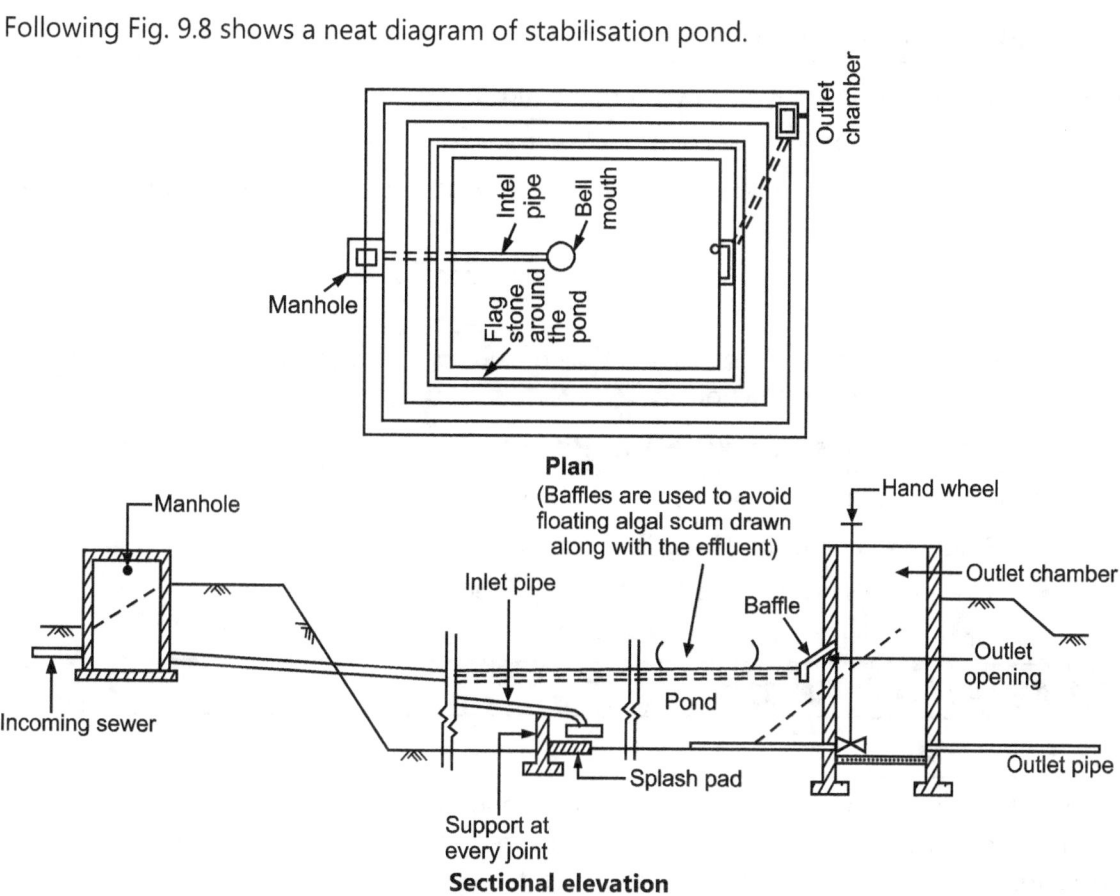

Plan
(Baffles are used to avoid
floating algal scum drawn
along with the effluent)

Sectional elevation
Fig. 9.8 : Stabilisation pond

9.2.5 General Considerations

•	BOD loading to maintain aerobic layer in the top at all times (In India)	– 330 to 560 kg/ha/day
•	Accumulation of sludge and grit in the pond	– 2 to 5 cm depth per year/minimum 0.3 m adopted for all the time. OR 0.06 to 0.09 m³/capita/year (Typical value for design 0.07 m³/capita/year)
•	Cleaning of ponds	– Once in 6 years for 1.2 m deep pond and once in 12 years for 1.5 m deep pond.
•	If the surface area of tank is too large	– Provide two or more number of ponds.
•	If the soil is too pervious	– The bottom and dikes should be sealed to prohibit seepage, a commonly used sealing agent is bentonite.

9.2.6 Advantages of Oxidation Ponds

The following are the advantages of oxidation ponds :

- They are suitable in hot countries like India.
- In small cities or towns, they are more advantageous one where large land areas are cheaply available.
- Capital cost is less as compared to conventional system (activated sludge process or trickling filters).
- Operating cost is less as no skilled supervision is required at any stage of operation or construction.

9.2.7 Disadvantages of Oxidation Ponds

The following are the disadvantages of oxidation ponds :

- Effluent standards of 30 mg/lit for suspended solids are not met.
- The main disadvantage is the mosquito breeding and bad odour.
- Only useful in rural areas where land costs are less.

9.3 AERATED LAGOONS

9.3.1 General

Aerated lagoons are one sort of deep oxidation ponds in which the oxygen is introduced by means of surface aerators. For aerated lagoons, required less area and detention time as compared to oxidation pond. In this system, wastewater is treated either on a flow through basis or with solids recycle.

9.3.2 Process Description

Aerated lagoons are a simple holding earthen basins with a continuous supply of oxygen by surface aerators. This will keep the contents of the basin in suspension and they are initially seeded by the same type of micro-organisms which are used in biodegradation of activated sludge process.

9.3.3 Process Microbiology

Aerated lagoon's process is same as the activated sludge process, the microbiology is also similar. Some differences occur due to the large surface area of the aerated lagoons can cause more significant temperature effects than are normally happening in the conventional activated sludge process.

9.3.4 Design Criteria

Aerated lagoon may be designed as a complete mix biological reactor without cell recycle using micro-organism growth kinetics.

BOD Removal :

Generally, in the aerated lagoons, it is assumed that BOD removal can be described by the first order removal function. From a steady state mass balance of the organic materials across the complete mix single lagoon. Based on that analysis, the equation for a single aerated lagoon is

$$\frac{S_1}{S_0} = \frac{1}{1 + K X_1 \ (V/Q)} \qquad \qquad ... (9.4)$$

where, S_1 = Effluent soluble BOD_5, mg/lit

S_0 = Influent soluble BOD_5, mg/lit

X_1 = Micro-organism mass concentration in the reactor, mg/lit

K = Specific soluble BOD_5 removal rate coefficient, l /mg/day

V = Volume of the reactor, litre

Q = Rate of flow of waste, l/day

The following Fig. 9.9 shows general flow diagram of aerated lagoon.

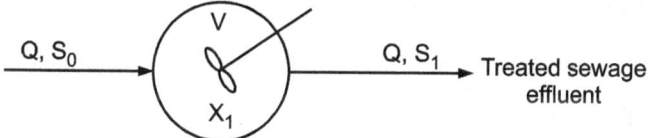

Fig. 9.9 : Flow diagram for aerated lagoon

The value of X_1 in equation (9.4) can be calculated by the following relationship which is developed from the mass balance for the mass of micro-organisms across the system in a steady state :

$$X_1 = \frac{Y \ (S_0 - S_1)}{1 + K_d \ (V/Q)} \qquad \qquad ... (9.5)$$

where, Y = Yield coefficient

K_d = Specific decay coefficient, day^{-1}

For design purpose, the following values of K, Y and K_d can be used, where temperature rarely falls below 15°C.

K = 0.05 l/mg/day at 20°C, Y = 0.5 and K_d = 0.05 per day.

The values of K at other temperatures can be calculated as :

$$K_T = K_{20} \ \theta^{T-20} \qquad \qquad ... (9.6)$$

where, θ = Temperature coefficient

= 1.060

$$= 1.097 \text{ (for cold climates)}$$

But at first approximation, X_1 can be calculated as follows :

$$X_1 = Y (S_0 - S_1) \qquad \text{... (9.7)}$$

Temperature : The temperature of the aerated lagoon can be calculated by the following relationship (for complete mix system) :

$$T_w = \frac{Q\,T_i + A f\,T_a}{Q + Af} \qquad \text{... (9.8)}$$

where,

T_w = Lagoon water temperature, °C

T_i = Temperature of influent, °C

T_a = Ambient air temperature, °C

f = Proportionality factor, 0.5

A = Surface area of lagoon, m²

Q = Flow rate through the lagoon, m³/day

Oxygen Requirement :

Oxygen requirement may be calculated by using the following equation :

Weight of oxygen required/day

$$= Q (S_0 - S_1) (1.47 - 1.42\,Y) + 1.42\,K_d\,X_1\,V \qquad \text{... (9.9)}$$

Field transfer rate N can be calculated by the following relationship :

$$N = N_0 \left[\frac{C_s - C_o}{C_w} (1.024)^{T-20} \cdot \alpha \right] \qquad \text{... (9.10)}$$

where,

N = kg of O_2/W/hr transfer under field conditions

N_0 = kg of O_2/W/hr transferred in water at 20°C and zero DO

C_s = Saturation oxygen concentration for waste at operating temperature and altitude (see Fig. 9.10).

C_o = Operating oxygen concentration

C_w = Saturation oxygen concentration for water at 20°C

$= 9.17$ mg/lit

T = Temperature of lagoon in °C

and α = Salinity - surface tension correction factor, generally 0.8 to 0.85.

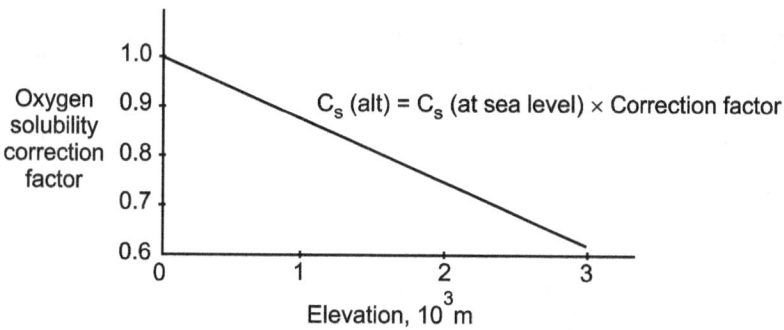

Fig. 9.10 : Oxygen-solubility correction factor versus elevation

9.3.5 Design Steps for Design of Aerated Lagoons   [May 2009, 2011]

- Calculate approximate X_1 by using equation (9.7).

- Calculate the approximate hydraulic retention time $\left(\dfrac{V}{Q}\right)$, from equation (9.4).

$$\frac{V}{Q} = \frac{S_0 - S_1}{S_1 \, K \, X_1} \qquad\qquad \dots (9.11)$$

- Calculate required volume.
- Calculate surface area.
- Calculate lagoon water temperature from equation (9.8).
- Calculate X_1 from equation (9.5).

- Again use equation (9.11) and calculate $\left(\dfrac{V}{Q}\right)$.

- Calculate required volume related to step 7.
- Now keeping the surface area same as calculated in step 4; calculate depth of aerated lagoon.
- Calculate oxygen requirement.
- Calculate surface aerators power requirement.
- Calculate the field transfer rate, N.

9.3.6 Design Parameters of Aerated Lagoons

The following Table 9.7 shows design parameters of aerated lagoons.

Table 9.7 : Design Parameters of Aerated Lagoons

Sr. No.	Parameters	Values
1.	Flow regime	Completely mixed.
2.	Detention time, days	2 – 3
3.	Depth, m	2.5 – 4
4.	BOD removal	50 – 60%

(Ref. Manual on sewerage and sewage treatment 2nd edition).

9.3.7 Advantages of Aerated Lagoons   [May 09, 10, 11]

The following are the advantages of lagoons :

- Sludge production is low.
- Low sensitivity to toxicity, pH disturbance and load variations.
- Odour problem is less.

9.3.8 Disadvantages of Aerated Lagoons   [May 09, 10, 11]

The following are the disadvantages of aerated lagoons :

- Energy is required to run aerators.
- It requires large area.
- It is sensitive to cold climate.

SOLVED EXAMPLES ON STABILISATION POND (OXIDATION POND)

Example 9.1 : Design a facultative stabilisation pond to treat a domestic sewage flow of 3 mld, at a place, the latitude of which is 24°N. The 5 day 20°C BOD of the sewage is 250 mg/lit. Assume necessary data.

Solution :

Given :

Domestic sewage flow	=	3 mld
	=	3×10^6 litres/day
	=	3×10^3 m^3/day
Latitude	=	24°N
∴ Yield of photosynthetic oxygen	=	225 kg/ha/day
BOD$_5$ of the sewage	=	250 mg/lit

Assume,   1st stage BOD removal constant, K = 0.23 per day

The facultative pond can be designed by both methods (first and second).

(A) First Method :

1.   Determine the ultimate BOD (L$_a$) :

As we know,

$$BOD_5 = L_a [1 - e^{-K \cdot t}]$$

∴   Ultimate BOD, $L_a = \dfrac{250}{[1 - e^{-0.23 \times 5}]}$

$$= 365 \text{ mg/lit}$$

2. Determine the detention period :

Now, from equation (9.1),

$$L_o = 10 \left(\frac{d}{t}\right) BOD_L$$

$$= 10 \times \frac{d}{t} \times 365 \ \text{kg/ha/day}$$

Assuming that (i) 50% of this load is non-settleable and, (ii) it undergoes aerobic decomposition in the top layer,

$$\text{Oxygen requirement} = 10 \left(\frac{d}{t}\right) \times 365 \times 0.5 \ \text{kg/ha/day}$$

$$\therefore \qquad 225 = 10 \times \left(\frac{d}{t}\right) \times 365 \times 0.5$$

$$\therefore \qquad \frac{d}{t} = 0.123$$

Now providing the depth of pond, d = 1.5 m

$$\therefore \qquad \frac{1.5}{t} = 0.123$$

$$\therefore \qquad t = \frac{1.5}{0.123}$$

$$t = 12.20 \ \text{days}$$

3. Determine the surface area :

Now, $$\text{Surface area} = \frac{\text{Flow} \times \text{Detention time (t)}}{\text{Depth}}$$

$$= \frac{3 \times 10^3 \times 12.20}{1.5}$$

$$= 24.40 \times 10^3 \ \text{m}^2$$

Providing two ponds in parallel, area of each = $12.20 \times 10^3 \ \text{m}^2$.

Assuming length (L)/width (B) ratio = 2,

$$\therefore \qquad 2B^2 = 12.20 \times 10^3$$

$$\therefore \qquad B = 78 \ \text{m}$$

$$\therefore \qquad \text{The size of each pond} = 78 \ \text{m} \times 156 \ \text{m}$$

and $$\text{overall depth} = (1.5 + 1) = 2.5 \ \text{m}$$

$$\therefore \qquad \text{Size of pond} = 7.8 \ \text{m} \times 156 \ \text{m} \times 2.5$$

(B)   Second Method :

1.   Determine the detention time :

Assuming desired BOD_5 effluent = 30 mg/lit and 50% of the BOD is stabilized by anaerobic decomposition alone,

$$\% \ BOD_5 \ remaining \ = \frac{S}{S_o} = \frac{30}{250/2} = 24\%$$

Assuming a dispersion factor in the facultative pond = 0.5

∴   From Fig. 9.5,

$$Kt = 2.1$$

Now, assuming winter temperature in the pond = 15°C, and the value of K in the pond = 0.22 per day at 20°C,

∴

$$K_{15°C} = 0.22 \ (1.06)^{15 \ – \ 20}$$

$$= 0.1645 \ per \ day$$

∴

$$t = \frac{2.1}{0.1645}$$

$$= 12.77 \ days$$

2.   Determine the surface area :

Now,

$$Surface \ area = \frac{Flow \times Detention \ time}{Depth}$$

$$= \frac{3 \times 10^3 \times 12.77}{1.5}$$

$$= 25.53 \times 10^3 \ m^2$$

Providing two ponds, area of each = $12.76 \times 10^3 \ m^2$.

∴   Size of each pond = 80 m × 160 m

and the overall depth = (1.5 + 1) = 2.5 m.

∴   Size of pond = 80 m × 160 m × 2.5 m

Example 9.2 : Design a facultative pond to treat a wastewater flow of 4000 m³/day. As the ponds are to be installed near a residential area, surface aerators will be used to maintain oxygen in the upper layers of the pond. Use the following data :

1.	Influent suspended solids	=	220 mg/lit
2.	Influent BOD_5	=	200 mg/lit
3.	Summer liquid temperature	=	37°C

4.	Winter liquid temperature	=	15°C
5.	Overall first order BOD_5 removal rate constant	=	0.25 d^{-1} at 20°C
6.	Temperature coefficient, θ_K	=	1.06
7.	Depth of pond, d	=	1.8 m
8.	Pond dispersion factor	=	0.5
9.	Overall BOD_5 removal efficiency	=	80%

Solution :

1.   **From Fig. 9.5, determine the value of Kt** for a dispersion factor of 0.5 and a BOD_5 removal efficiency of 80 percent i.e. % BOD_5 remaining is 20%.

∴   Kt = 2.4

2.   **Determine the temperature coefficient for summer and winter conditions :**

(a) Winter : K_{15} = (0.25) [(1.06)$^{15-20}$] = 0.187 d^{-1}

(b) Summer : K_{37} = (0.25) [(1.06)$^{37-20}$] = 0.673 d^{-1}

3.   **Determine the detention time for winter and summer conditions :**

(a) Winter :

As,   Kt = 2.4

∴   0.187 × t = 2.4

∴   t = 12.8 days

(b) Summer :

0.673 × t = 2.4

t = 3.57 days

4.   **Determine the surface area requirement :**

(a) Winter :

As,   Surface area $= \dfrac{\text{Flow} \times \text{Detention time}}{\text{Depth}}$

∴   Surface area $= \dfrac{4000 \times 12.8}{1.8}$

$= 28.444 \times 10^3 \, m^2$ ... (i)

(b) Summer :

Surface area $= \dfrac{4000 \times 3.57}{1.8}$

$= 7.93 \times 10^3 \, m^2$ ... (ii)

Selecting the larger of (i) and (ii),

∴   The surface area $= 28.444 \times 10^3\,m^2$ (2.8 ha).

(It means winter conditions control the design).

Providing two ponds.

Area of each pond $= 14.22 \times 10^3\,m^2$

∴   Size of each pond $= 84\,m \times 168\,m$ and overall depth $= (1.8 + 1) = 2.8\,m$.

∴   Size of pond $= 84\,m \times 164\,m \times 2.8\,m$

5.   Determine the surface loading :

$$kg\ BOD_5/ha{\cdot}d\ =\ \frac{Flow \times Influent\ BOD_5}{Surface\ area}$$

$$=\ \frac{4000 \times 200}{2.8} \times \frac{1}{10^3}$$

$$=\ 285.7\ kg/ha/day$$

6.   Determine the power requirements and number of surface aerators :

Assume that the capacity of the aerators in terms of oxygen transferred is equal to double the value of the BOD_5 applied per day and that a typical aerator will transfer about 24 kg O_2/kW · day.

∴   kg O_2/d required $= 2 \times Flow \times Influent\ BOD_5$

$$=\ \frac{2 \times 4000 \times 200}{10^3}$$

$$=\ 1600\ kg/d$$

$$kW\ =\ \frac{1600\ kg/d}{24\ kg/kW{\cdot}d}$$

$$=\ 66.67\ kW\ \cong\ 70\ kW$$

Use seven 10 kW units.

7.   Check the power input (if mixing will occur) :

$$kW/10^3\,m^3\ =\ \frac{70\ kW}{28.44 \times 10^3\,m^3}$$

$$=\ 2.46\ kW/10^3\,m^3$$

This is insufficient power for surface aerator to mix the pond contents, as minimum requirement is 3 kW/10^3 m³.

Example 9.3 : Design an oxidation pond for treating sewage from a hot climatic residential colony with 6000 persons. The sewage generation is about 130 litres per capita per day. The BOD_5 of sewage is 350 mg/lit.

Solution :

Given :

Total number of persons	= 6000
The sewage generation rate	= 130 l/capita/d
BOD_5 of sewage	= 350 mg/lit
BOD loading or organic loading or yield of photosynthetic oxygen in hot climates (assume)	= 300 kg/ha/d

1. **Determine the quantity of sewage :**

   The quantity of sewage to be treated $= 6000 \times 130$

   $$= 0.78 \times 10^6 \ \text{litres/day}$$

   $$= 780 \ \text{m}^3\text{/day}$$

2. **Determine the ultimate BOD (L_a) :**

   Assuming 1st stage BOD removal rate constant, K = 0.23 per day.

   As we know,

   $$BOD_5 = L_a [1 - e^{-Kt}]$$

   $\therefore$ $\qquad$ Ultimate BOD, $L_a = \dfrac{350}{[1 - e^{-0.23 \times 5}]}$

   $$= 512.17 \ \text{mg/lit}$$

3. **Determine the detention period :**

   Now, from equation (9.1),

   $$L_o = 10 \left(\frac{d}{t}\right) \times BOD_L$$

   $$= 10 \times \frac{d}{t} \times 512.17 \ \text{kg/ha/day}$$

   Assuming that (i) 50% of this load is non-settleable and, (ii) it undergoes aerobic decomposition in the top layer.

   $$\text{Oxygen requirement} = 10 \left(\frac{d}{t}\right) \times 512.17 \times 0.5$$

   $\therefore$ $\qquad$ $300 = 10 \times \dfrac{d}{t} \times 512.17 \times 0.5$

$$\therefore \qquad \frac{d}{t} = 0.117$$

Now, providing the depth of pond, d = 1.5 m

$$\therefore \qquad \frac{1.5}{t} = 0.117$$

$$\therefore \qquad t = 12.82 \text{ days}$$

4.   Determine the surface area :

Now,   Surface area $= \dfrac{\text{Flow} \times \text{Detention time (t)}}{\text{Depth}}$

$$= \frac{780 \times 12.82}{1.5}$$

$$= 6.6 \times 10^3 \text{ m}^2$$

Assuming length (B)/width (L) ratio = 2

$$\therefore \qquad 2B^2 = 6.6 \times 10^3$$

$$\therefore \qquad B = 57.73 \text{ m} \text{ say 58 m}$$

$$\therefore \qquad L = 116 \text{ m}$$

$\therefore$ The size of pond is 58 m $\times$ 116 m and overall depth = (1.5 + 1) = 2.5 m.

$$\therefore \qquad \text{Size of pond} = 58 \text{ m} \times 116 \text{ m} \times 2.5 \text{ m}$$

5.   Design of inlet pipe :

Assuming an average velocity of sewage as 0.9 m/sec. and daily flow for 8 hours only,

$$\text{Discharge (cumecs)} = \frac{\text{Sewage flow (m}^3\text{/day)}}{8 \times 60 \times 60} = \frac{780}{8 \times 60 \times 60}$$

$$= 0.027 \text{ cumecs}$$

$\therefore$ Area of inlet pipe required (m²)

$$= \frac{\text{Discharge (cumecs)}}{\text{Velocity (m/sec)}}$$

$$= \frac{0.027}{0.9}$$

$$= 0.03 \text{ m}^2$$

$$\therefore \qquad \text{Diameter of inlet pipe} = \sqrt{\frac{4 \times 0.03}{\pi}}$$

$$= 0.195 \text{ m}$$

$$= 195 \text{ mm} \text{ say 200 mm}$$

6.   **Design of outlet pipe :**

Assume the diameter of outlet pipe is 1.5 times the diameter of inlet pipe,

∴   Diameter of outlet pipe = 1.5×200

= 300 mm

Example 9.4 : Design an oxidation pond to treat 10 m³/d of sewage discharge.

Assume :   BOD of raw sewage = 210 mg/lit

Design temperature = 10°C

BOD loading = 140 kg/ha/d

Sketch the details.   **[Pune University Exam.]**

Solution :

1.   **Determine ultimate BOD (L_a) :**

Assume, 1st stage BOD removal constant,

$$K = 0.23 \text{ per day}$$

As we know,

$$BOD_5 = L_a [1 - e^{-K \cdot t}]$$

∴ $$L_a = \frac{210}{[1 - e^{-0.23 \times 5}]}$$

= 307.3 mg/lit

2.   **Determine the detention period :**

Now, from equation (9.1),

$$L_o = 10 \left(\frac{d}{t}\right) \times BOD_L$$

$$= 10 \times \frac{d}{t} \times (307.3)$$

Assuming that (i) 50% of this load is non-settleable and, (ii) it undergoes aerobic decomposition in the top layer.

$$\text{Oxygen requirement} = 10 \left(\frac{d}{t}\right) \times 307.3 \times 0.5 \text{ kg/ha/d}$$

∴ $$140 = 10 \left(\frac{d}{t}\right) \times 307.3 \times 0.5$$

$$\frac{d}{t} = 0.09$$

Now, providing the depth of pond, d = 1.5 m

$$\therefore \qquad \frac{1.5}{t} = 0.09$$

$$\therefore \qquad t = 16.67 \text{ days}$$

3. **Determine the surface area :**

Now, $\qquad$ Surface area $= \dfrac{\text{Flow} \times \text{Detention time (t)}}{\text{Depth}}$

$$= \frac{10 \times 16.67}{1.5}$$

$$= 111.11 \text{ m}^2$$

Assuming length/width ratio = 2

$$\therefore \qquad 2B^2 = 111.11$$

$$\therefore \qquad B = 7.45 \text{ m} \quad \text{say } 7.5 \text{ m}$$

$$\therefore \qquad L = 15 \text{ m}$$

∴ The size of the pond is 7.5 m × 15 m and the overall depth = (1.5 + 1) = 2.5 m.

$$\therefore \qquad \text{Size of pond} = 7.5 \text{ m} \times 15 \text{ m} \times 2.5 \text{ m}$$

4. **Sketch of pond :**

Refer Fig. 9.8 and show dimensions on the same.

Example 9.5 : Design an oxidation pond for the following data :

1. Sewage flow $\qquad\qquad$ = 10 m³/d
2. BOD of raw sewage $\qquad$ = 300 mg/lit
3. Mean monthly temperature = 30°C maximum and 10°C minimum
4. Desired effluent BOD $\qquad$ = 30 mg/lit
5. Location $\qquad\qquad\quad$ = 20°C latitude
6. Yield of photosynthetic O_2 = 250 kg/ha/d. $\qquad$ **(Pune University Exam.)**

Solution :

1. **Determine the detention time :**

Design the pond for minimum temperature i.e. 10°C.

By using equation (9.0),

$$t = \frac{1}{K_1} \log_{10} \left(\frac{L_a}{L_a - Y} \right)$$

$$(K_1)_{10°C} = 0.1 (1.047)^{10-20}$$

$$= 0.06317 \text{ per day}$$

$$\therefore \quad t = \frac{1}{0.06317} \log_{10} \left(\frac{300}{30}\right)$$

$$(L_a - Y = 30 \text{ mg/lit i.e. BO.D. remaining})$$

$$\therefore \quad t = 15.83 \text{ days} \approx 16 \text{ days}$$

2. **Determine the surface area :**

(Consider depth of pond is 1.5 m)

Now, $\qquad$ Surface area $= \dfrac{\text{Flow} \times \text{Detention time (t)}}{\text{Depth}}$

$$= \frac{10 \times 16}{1.5 \text{ m}} = 106.67 \text{ m}^2$$

Assuming length/width ratio = 2

$$\therefore \quad 2B^2 = 106.67$$

$$\therefore \quad B = 7.3 \text{ m say } 7.5 \text{ m}$$

$$\therefore \quad L = 15 \text{ m}$$

∴ The size of pond is 7.5 m × 15 m and overall depth $= (1.5 + 1) = 2.5$ m.

$$\therefore \qquad \text{Size of pond} = 7.5 \text{ m} \times 15 \text{ m} \times 2.5 \text{ m}$$

Note : *Depth of pond can be determined by proper calculations (see example 9.6).*

Example 9.6 : Design an oxidation pond for 8000 population and a sewage flow of 150 lit/head/day with a BOD of 300 mg/lit. The BOD of effluent should not be more than 30 mg/lit. Assume temperature as 24°C. Assume sludge accumulation rate as 0.05 m³/capita/year and desludging interval as 5 years. Assume $K_{20} = 0.20$/day, given $K_T = K_{20}$ $(1.047)^{T-20}$. **(10 Marks, Pune University Exam.)**

Solution :

Given : Population $\qquad = 8000$

Sewage flow $\qquad = 150$ lit/head/day

$\qquad = 150 \times 8000$ lit/day

$\qquad = 1.2 \times 10^3$ m³/day

BOD of sewage $\qquad = 300$ mg/lit

Temperature $\qquad = 24°C$

BOD of effluent $\qquad \not> 30$ mg/lit

Sludge accumulation rate	=	0.05 m³/capita/year
Desludging interval	=	5 years
Assume BOD loading	=	300 kg/ha/day

1.   Determine total BOD load :

$$\text{BOD per capita/day} = (150 \times 300) \times 10^{-6}$$
$$= 0.045 \text{ kg/day}$$

∴ $$\text{Total BOD load} = 8000 \times 0.045$$
$$= 360 \text{ kg/day}$$

2.   Determine pond area :

$$\text{Pond area} = \frac{\text{Total applied BOD}_5}{\text{BOD loading}}$$

$$= \frac{360 \text{ kg/d}}{300 \text{ kg/ha/d}}$$

$$= 1.2 \text{ ha}$$

$$= 1.2 \times 10^4 \text{ m}^2$$

3.   Determine detention period :

By using equation (9.0),

$$t = \frac{1}{K_1} \log_{10}\left(\frac{L_a}{L_a - Y}\right)$$

Now, $$(K_1)_{24°C} = K_{20} (1.047)^{T-20}$$
$$= 0.2 (1.047)^{24-20}$$
$$= 0.24 \text{ per day}$$

∴ $$t = \frac{1}{0.24} \log_{10}\left(\frac{300}{30}\right)$$

$$(L_a - Y = 30 \text{ mg/lit i.e. BOD remaining})$$

$$t = 4.2 \text{ days}$$

4.   Determine pond liquid volume and pond liquid depth :

$$\text{Pond liquid volume} = \text{Flow} \times \text{Detention time}$$
$$= 1.2 \times 10^3 \times 4.2 = 5040 \text{ m}^3$$

$$\text{Liquid depth} = \frac{5040 \text{ m}^3}{1.2 \times 10^4 \text{ m}^2}$$

$$= 0.42 \text{ m}$$

Also, provide free board of 0.6 m.

Total pond area is 1.2 ha. Adopt a **parallel-series** system of 6 ponds with 4 primary ponds and 2 secondary ponds of equal area, with 2 primary ponds feeding a secondary pond in each set as shown in the following Fig. 9.11. This would give the primary pond area as 66.67% which is within the required range of **65 to 75%** of the total pond area.

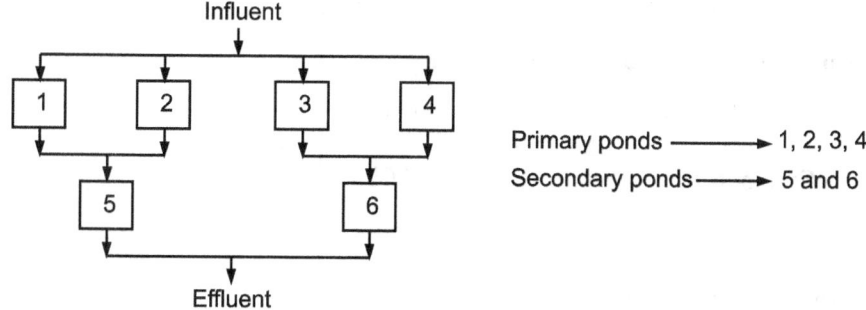

Primary ponds ⟶ 1, 2, 3, 4
Secondary ponds ⟶ 5 and 6

Fig. 9.11

$$\text{Area of each pond} = \frac{1.2 \times 10^4}{6} = 2000 \text{ m}^2$$

Provide rectangular ponds with length to breadth ratio as 2.0.

$$\therefore \qquad 2B^2 = 2000$$
$$\therefore \qquad B = 31.62 \text{ m} \approx 32 \text{ m}$$
$$\therefore \qquad L = 32 \times 2 = 64 \text{ m}$$
$$\therefore \qquad \text{Actual area of each pond} = 32 \times 64$$
$$= 2048 \text{ m}^2$$

5. **Determine volume of sludge and depth of sludge**

$$\text{Volume of sludge} = 0.05 \text{ m}^3/\text{capita/year}$$
$$\text{Desludging interval} = 5 \text{ years}$$

$\therefore$ Adopt minimum 0.3 m depth for sludge accumulation (Refer article 9.1.5).

Example 9.7 : Design an oxidation pond for the following data :

1.	Location	= 20°N
2.	Elevation	= 1000 m above MSL
3.	Mean monthly temperature	= 35°C maximum & 10°C minimum
4.	Population to be served	= 9000
5.	Sewage flow	= 160 l pcd
6.	Desired effluent BOD_5	= 30 mg/lit
7.	Pond removal constant at 20°C	= 0.1/d
8.	Sky is clear for 15% of the days.	
9.	BOD of sewage	= 300 mg/lit.

Solution :

1. **Determine total BOD load :**

$$\text{BOD per capita/day} = (160 \times 300) \times 10^6 = 0.048 \text{ kg/d}$$

$\therefore$ Total BOD load $= 9000 \times 0.048 = 432$ kg/d

2. **Determine permissible area/BOD loading :**

Area/BOD loading at 20°N $= 250$ kg/ha/day.   (Refer Table 9.2)

$$\text{Correction factor for elevation} = 1 + 0.003 \times \frac{1000}{100}$$

$$= 1.03$$

Correction factor for sky clearance

$$= \frac{100}{100 + 3 \times \frac{15}{10}} = \frac{100}{104.5} = 0.96$$

$\therefore$ Corrected area/BOD loading $= \dfrac{250}{1.03} \times 0.96$

$$= 232.27 \text{ kg/ha/d}$$

$$\approx 232 \text{ kg/ha/d}$$

3. **Determine pond area :**

$$\text{Area of pond} = \frac{\text{Total applied BOD}_5}{\text{Area/BOD loading}}$$

$$= \frac{432 \text{ kg/day}}{232 \text{ kg/ha/d}}$$

$$= 1.86 \text{ ha}$$

$$= 1.86 \times 10^4 \text{ m}^2$$

4. **Determine the detention period :**

Design for minimum temperature 10°C.

By using equation (9.0),

$$t = \frac{1}{K_1} \log_{10} \left(\frac{L_a}{L_a - Y} \right)$$

$$(K_1)_{10°C} = 0.1 \, (1.047)^{10-20}$$

$$= 0.06317 \text{ per day}$$

$\therefore$

$$t = \frac{1}{0.06317} \log_{10}\left(\frac{300}{30}\right)$$

$$(L_a - Y = 30 \text{ mg/lit i.e. BOD remaining})$$

$$t = 15.83 \text{ days} \approx 16 \text{ days}$$

5.   **Determine the volume and depth of pond :**

Pond volume   = Flow × Detention time

= (160 × 9000) × 16

= 23040 × 10³ litres/day

= 23040 m³/day

Depth of pond $= \dfrac{23040}{1.86 \times 10^4}$

= 1.23 m   ≈ 1.25 m

Provide a depth of 1.25 m, also provide a F.B. of 0.6 m.

Provide a parallel-series system of 6 ponds, as same is provided in example 9.6.

Area of each pond $= \dfrac{1.86 \times 10^4}{6}$ = 3100 m²

Assume rectangular ponds with length to breadth ratio as 2.

$\therefore$ 2B² = 3100

$\therefore$ B = 39.34 m   say 39.5 m

Length = 2 × 39.5

= 79 m

Actual area of each pond = 39.5 × 79

= **3120.5 m² say 3120 m².**   ... **Ans.**

SOLVED EXAMPLES ON AREATED LAGOONS

Example 9.8 : Design a complete mix aerated lagoon system to treat a domestic sewage flow of 2.5 MLD. Use the following data :

1.   Influent suspended solids   =   250 mg/lit
2.   Effluent suspended solids after settling   ≯   20 mg/lit
3.   Influent BOD$_5$ =   220 mg/lit
4.   Effluent BOD   ≯   20 mg/lit
5.   Volatile suspended solids = 80% of total solids produced.

6. Summer temperature   =   38°C

7. Winter temperature   =   15°C

8. Wastewater temperature   =   22°C

9. Oxygen concentration to be maintained in the lagoon   =   1.5 mg/lit

10. Lagoon depth   =   3.0 m

11. Specific substrate removal coefficient, K = 0.05 l/mg/day at 20°C; Growth yield coefficient, Y = 0.5; Decay coefficient, K_d = 0.05 per day,; f = 0.5.

12. Oxygen transfer coefficient of the aerator, α = 0.8.

13. Temperature coefficient, θ = 1.065

14. Elevation = 1000 m.

Solution :

Given :   Flow = 2.5 mld = 2.5 × 10³ m³/day , S_0 = 220 mg/lit

Now the total effluent BOD$_5$ = 20 mg/lit and effluent SS after settling = 20 mg/lit .

X = 0.80 × 20 = 16 mg/lit.   (As VSS = 80% of total SS)

1.   Determine X_1 :

∴ S_1 = Soluble BOD$_5$ in the effluent

                                           = (20 − 0.54 × 16)   (Assuming ESS BOD$_5$ @ 0.54 kg/kg)

                                           = 11.36 mg/lit

As first approximation X_1 can be calculated from equation (9.7),

∴ X_1 = Y ($S_0 - S_1$) = 0.5 (220 − 11.36)

                                           = 104.32 mg/lit

2.   Determine retention time :

Now,
$$\boxed{\frac{V}{Q} = \frac{S_0 - S_1}{S_1 \, K \, X_1}}$$

$$= \frac{220 - 11.36}{11.36 \times 0.05 \ \times 104.32} = 3.5 \text{ days}$$

3.   Determine surface area :

                     Volume = Flow × Retention time

                                = 2.5 × 10³ × 3.5

                                = 8.75 × 10³ m³

$$\text{Surface area} \quad = \quad \frac{8.75 \times 10^3}{2.5} \qquad \text{... (Assuming a depth = 2.5 m)}$$

$$= \quad 3.5 \times 10^3 \ m^2$$

4.   **Determine waste water temperature of the water in the aerated lagoon :**

Summer and winter temperature of the water in the aerated lagoon can be calculated by equation (9.8).

   (a)   Summer temperature,

$$T_W \quad = \quad \frac{Q\,T_i + AF\,T_a}{Af + Q} \quad = \quad \frac{2.5 \times 10^3 \times 22 + 3.5 \times 10^3 \times 0.5 \times 38^oC}{3.5 \times 10^3 \ \times 0.5 + 2.5 \times 10^3}$$

$$\therefore \qquad\qquad\qquad T_W \quad = \quad 28.58^oC$$

   (b)   Winter temperature,

$$T_W \quad = \quad \frac{Q\,T_i + Af\,T_a}{Af + Q}$$

$$= \quad \frac{2.5 \times 10^3 \times \ 22 + 3.5 \times 10^3 \times 0.5 \times \ 15^oC}{3.5 \times 10^3 \times 0.5 + 2.5 \times 10^3}$$

$$= \quad 19.11^oC$$

Note : As related to winter temperature, the value of surface area becomes larger than related to summer temperature, therefore, always design the lagoon for winter temperature.

Value of K at temperature 19.11°C

$$= \quad 0.05 \times (1.065)^{19.11 - 20}$$

$$= \quad 0.047 \ l/mg/day$$

5.   **Determine value of X_1 :**

$$X_1 \quad = \quad \frac{Y\,(S_0 - S)}{1 + K_d\,(V/Q)}$$

$$= \quad \frac{0.5\,(220 - 11.36)}{1 + 0.05 \times 3.5}$$

$$= \quad 88.78 \ mg/lit$$

6.   **Determine (V/Q) :**

$$\frac{V}{Q} \quad = \quad \frac{S_0 - S_1}{S_1\,K\,X_1}$$

$$= \quad \frac{220 \ - 11.36}{11.36 \times 0.047 \times 88.78} \quad = \quad \frac{208.64}{474}$$

$$= \quad 4.4 \ days \ \approx \ 4.5 \ days$$

Now, modifying our design, after using

$$\frac{V}{Q} = 4.5 \text{ days}$$

$$\text{Volume required} = 4.5 \times 2.5 \times 10^3$$

$$= 11.25 \times 10^3 \text{ m}^3$$

7.   Determine the depth of lagoon :

Now keeping the surface area same as in the 1st trial i.e. 3.5×10^3 m²

$\therefore$ The depth required $= \dfrac{11.25 \times 10^3}{3.5 \times 10^3}$

$$= 3.2 \text{ m}$$

$\therefore$ Provide the depth of aerated lagoon $= 3.2$ m.

8.   Determine the oxygen requirement :

By using equation (9.9),

$$O_2 \text{ kg/day} = Q (S_0 - S_1) (1.47 - 1.42 \text{ Y}) + 1.42 K_d X_1 V$$

$$= [2.5 \times 10^3 (220 - 11.36) (1.42 - 1.42 \times 0.5)$$

$$+ 1.42 \times 0.05 \times \quad 88.78 \times 11.25 \times 10^3] \times 10^{-3}$$

$$= 441.25 \text{ kg/day}$$

9.   Determine the ratio of oxygen required to BOD$_5$ removed :

$$\frac{O_2 \text{ required}}{BOD_5 \text{ removed}} = \frac{441.25 \text{ kg/day}}{[(220 - 11.36)] \times 2.5 \times 10^3 \times 10^{-3}}$$

$$= 0.85$$

10.   Determine the surface aerator power requirements :

Assume that the aerators to be used are conservatively rated at 2.0 kg O_2/kW·h.

Determine the field transfer rate for surface aerators for summer condition by using equation (9.10). Oxygen saturation concentration at 28.58°C

$$= 7.84 \text{ mg/lit} \qquad\qquad \textbf{(Refer Appendix A)}$$

Oxygen saturation concentration at 28.58°C corrected for altitude

$$= 7.84 \times 0.9 = 7.056 \text{ mg/lit}$$

Now, $N = N_o \left[\dfrac{C_s - C_o}{C_w} (1.024)^{T - 20} \cdot \alpha \right]$

$$= 2.0 \text{ kg } O_2/\text{kW} \cdot \text{h} \left[\frac{7.056 - 1.5}{9.17} \times (1.024)^{28.58 - 20} \times 0.8 \right]$$

$$= 1.19 \text{ kg } O_2 /\text{kW·h}$$

The amount of O_2 transferred per day per unit is equal to 28.56 kg O_2/kW·d.

The total power required,

$$kW = \frac{441.25 \text{ kg } O_2/d}{28.56 \text{ kg } O_2/kW·d}$$

$$= 15.45 \text{ kW}$$

11. **Check the energy requirements for mixing :**

Assume the power requirement for a completely mixed flow regime is 15 kW/10^3 m³

$$\text{Volume of lagoon} = 11250 \text{ m}^3$$

$$\text{Power required} = (15 \text{ kW}/10^3 \text{ m}^3) \times (11250 \text{ m}^3)$$

$$= 168.75 \text{ kW}$$

$$\cong 169 \text{ kW}$$

Use six 30 kW surface aerators.

Example 9.9 : Design an aerated lagoon to treat a wastewater (W/W) discharge of 1200 m³/d, with the following data :   **(10 Marks : Pune University Exam.)**

1. BOD of influent W/W = 200 mg/lit.
2. BOD of treated W/W effluent to be limited to 20 mg/lit.
3. Growth constants, Y = 0.6 and K_d = 0.06/day.
4. BOD removal rate constant = K_{20} = 2.5/day.
5. Mean temperature of W/W = 25°C.
6. Temperature coefficient = 1.06.
7. Aeration constants, α = 0.85 and β = 1.0.
8. Minimum D.O. to be maintained = 2 mg/lit .
9. SRT = 4 days.

Solution :

Please refer example 9.8 for the procedure.

Note : Here SRT = 4 days is given.

So 1st trial is not required, the example can be solved from step 3 onwards.

9.4 PHYTOREMEDIATION TECHNOLOGY FOR WASTEWATER TREATMENT

Due to industrial and agricultural activities, there is an increasing trend in areas of land, surface waters and groundwater affected by contamination. The build-up of toxic pollutants not only affects natural resources but also causes a major strain on ecosystems. Remediation of contaminated sites using conventional practices, such as 'pump-and-treat' and 'dig-and-dump' techniques, is often expensive, has limited potential, and is usually only applicable to small areas. Additionally, these conventional approaches to remediation often make the soil infertile and unsuitable for agriculture and other uses by destroying the microenvironment. Hence, there is the need to develop and apply alternative, environmentally sound technologies, taking into account the probable end use of the site once it has been remediated.

Phytoremediation is the name given to a set of technologies that use different plants as a containment, destruction, or an extraction technique. Phytoremediation as a remediation technology that has been receiving attention lately as the results from field trials indicate a cost savings compared to conventional treatments.

Phytoremediation ('phyto' means plant and 'remediation' means correct evil) is a generic term for the group of technologies that use plants for remediating soils, sludges, sediments and water contaminated with organic and inorganic contaminants. Phytoremediation can be defined as the efficient use of plants to remove, detoxify contaminants in a soil, water or sediments through the natural biological, chemical or physical activities and processes of the plants.

9.4.1 Applications of Phytoremediation

The following are the applications of Phytoremediation :

- Degradation

- Extraction

- Containment and Immobilization

9.4.1.1 Degradation

Plants may enhance degradation in the rhizosphere (root zone of influence). Microbial counts in rhizosphere soils can be 1 or 2 orders of magnitude greater than in non-rhizosphere. Plants may enhance degradation in the rhizosphere. Microbial counts in rhizosphere soils can be 1 or 2 orders of magnitude greater than in non-rhizosphere soils. It is not known whether this is due to microbial or fungal symbiosis with the plant, plant exudates including enzymes or other physical/chemical effects in the root zone. There are, however, measurable effects on certain contaminants in the root zone of planted areas. Several projects examine the interaction between plants and such contaminants as trinitrotoluene between plants and such contaminants as trinitrotoluene (TNT), Total Petroleum Hydrocarbons (TPH), pentachlorophenol (PCP), and Polynuclear Aromatic Hydrocarbons (PAH). Another possible mechanism for contaminant degradation is metabolism within the plant. Some plants may be able to take in toxic compounds and in the process of metabolizing the available nutrients, detoxify them. Trichloroethylene (TCE) is possibly degraded in poplar trees and the carbon used for tissue growth while the chloride is expelled through the roots.

9.4.1.2 Extraction

Phytoextraction or phytomining is the process of planting a crop of a species that is known to accumulate contaminants in the shoots and leaves of the plants, and then harvesting the crop and removing the contaminant from the site. Unlike the destructive degradation mechanisms, this technique yields a mass of plant and contaminant (typically metals) that must be transported for disposal or recycling. This is a concentration technology that leaves a much smaller mass to be disposed of when compared to excavation and landfilling. This technology is being evaluated in a Superfund Innovative Technology Evaluation (SITE) demonstration, and may also be a technology amenable to contaminant recovery and recycling. Rhizofiltration is similar to phytoextraction in that it is also a concentration technology. It differs from phytoextraction using hydroponic (soil-less) growing techniques. This is useful for separating metal contaminants from water. Volatilization or transpiration through plants into the atmosphere is another possible mechanism for removing a contaminant from the soil or water of a site. It is often raised as a concern in response to a proposed phytoremediation project, but has not been shown to be an actual pathway for many contaminants. Mercury (Hg) has been shown to move through a plant and into the air in a plant that was genetically altered to allow it to do so. The thought behind this media switching is that elemental Hg in the air poses less risk than other Hg forms in the soil. However, the technology or the associated risk has not been evaluated.

9.4.1.3 Containment and Immobilization

Containment using plants either binds the contaminants to the soil, renders them non-bioavailable, or immobilizes them by removing the means of transport. Physical containment of contaminants by plants can take the form of binding the contaminants within a humic molecule (humification), physical sequestration of metals as occurs in some wetlands, or by root accumulation in nonharvestable plants. Certain trees sequester large concentrations of metals in their roots, and although harvesting and removal is difficult or impractical, the contaminants present a reduced human or environmental risk while they are bound in the roots. Risk reduction may also be achieved by transforming the contaminant into a form that is not hazardous, or by rendering the contaminant non-bioavailable. Hydraulic control is another form of containment. Groundwater contaminant plume control may be achieved by water consumption, using plants to increase the evaporation and transpiration from a site. Some species of plants use tremendous quantities of water, and can extend roots to draw from the saturated zone.

9.4.2 Advantages of Phytoremediation

The following are the advantages of Phytoremediation :

- It is a most useful at sites with shallow, low levels of contamination.
- It is useful for treating a wide variety of environmental contaminants.
- It is a good alternative method in place of mechanical cleanup methods.

9.5 ROOT ZONE CLEANING SYSTEM

The economical development and industrialization followed by urbanization in India are creating problems for waste disposal arising from domestic and industrial activities. Treatment of industrial wastewater is mandatory by law. However untreated sewage is discharged into receiving water bodies. Urban areas are growing at the rate that is far more than capacity of local authority like Municipal Committee and Municipal Corporation for collection, treatment and disposal of sewage. This problem is very serious in the newly expanded urban areas.

Sewerage system provided at residential complexes and individual houses collect the wastewater and partially treat it in the septic tanks under anaerobic condition. The overflow from these septic tanks either goes to the soak pit or joins the nearby nullah. Drawbacks of this system are Partial Treatment, Causes of smell; Sludge gets accumulated and requires removal once in 2 to 3 years and Causes ponding in soak pit if percolation rate of soil is poor. Where sewerage system is laid down, sewage is collected and directly disposed off into receiving water bodies or treated by conventional treatment with physical and biological treatment units. The principle of conventional sewage treatment is based on removal or destruction of pollutants by physical, chemical and biological methods to bring down pollutants within permissible limits. Conventional treatment system requires Capital cost, Energy to operate system, Skilled manpower and Maintenance cost for mechanical equipments.

Conventional sewage treatment includes simple technology like stabilization pond to the complex module of activated sludge process. Stabilization ponds use natural purification system driven by solar energy coupled with photosynthesis by algae. Aerated lagoon, activated sludge and trickling filter require electrically driven equipments to transfer oxygen to water. Another natural treatment system existing in nature and well known to this subcontinent is use of wetland species for sewage treatment.

Root zone systems are artificially prepared wetlands comprising of clay or plastic lined excavation and emergent vegetation growing on gravel/sand mixtures and is also known as constructed wetland. This method combines mechanical filtration, chemical precipitation and biological degradation in one step for the treatment of wastewater. A number of factors like low operating cost, less energy requirement and ease of maintenance attribute to making root zone system an attractive alternative for wastewater management.

9.5.1 Process Desctription

The process in a root zone system to treat the sewage begins with passing the raw effluent (after removing grit or floating material) horizontally or vertically through a bed of soil having impervious bottom. The effluent percolates through the bed that has all the roots of the wetland plants spread very thickly, nearly 2,500 types of bacteria and 10,000 types of fungi, which harbor around roots get oxygen form the weak membranes of the roots and aerobically oxidize the organic matter of the effluent. The characteristics of plants of absorbing oxygen through their leaves and passing it down to roots through their stems which are hollow, is utilized as a bio-pump. Away from the roots, anaerobic digestion also takes place. The filtering action of the soil bed, the action with fungi etc. and chemical action with certain existing or added inorganic chemicals help in finally obtaining very clear and clean water. The system of plants regenerates itself as the old plants die and form useful humus. Hence, the system becomes maintenance free and can run up to 50 to 60 years without any loss of efficiency.

9.5.2 Advantages

The following are the advantages of root zone cleaning system :

- As no use of machinery and associated maintenance, the root zone system provides for low maintenance cost.
- Low operating and monitoring cost.
- It enhances the landscape and gives the site a green appeal.
- It provides natural habitat for birds and after a few years gives an appearance of a Bird's sanctuary.
- It does not have mosquitoes problem.
- Reed beds can be survive as there is no salinity problem.
- In the horizontal flow system, the sewage percolates through bed and that has all roots of the wetland plants spread very thickly nearly with 2500 types of bacteria and 10,000 types of fungi and aerobically oxidized organic matter of the effluent.
- This system gives a very good performance of removing 90% BOD and 63% nitrogen.

EXERCISE

1. What are the factors that affect the design of oxidation pond ?
2. Discuss the biological principle on which the oxidation ponds work.
3. State the importance of latitude of a place in the design of oxidation ponds.
4. Enumerate the different low cost waste treatment methods for sewage and write in detail about the 'stabilisation pond'.
5. Write short notes on :
   (a) Aerated lagoon.
   (b) Oxidation pond.
   (c) Low cost wastewater treatment - Necessity.
   (d) Symbiosis and oxidation pond design.
   (e) Algal-bacterial symbiosis.
   (f) Discuss with sketch – oxidation ditch.
6. What do you understand by 'stabilisation ponds' ? Give classification of 'stabilisation ponds'.
7. Explain the mechanism of purification in facultative ponds.

8. Explain how do you determine the size and detention period for a facultative type stabilisation pond.

9. Design an oxidation pond based on the following given data :
   (i)   Location   ...   26°C Latitude
   (ii)   Elevation   ...   150 m above sea level
   (iii) Mean monthly temperature   ...   35°C max. and 10°C min.
   (iv)   Population served   ...   8000
   (v)   Sewage flow   ...   150 $lpcd$
   (vi) BOD_5 for raw sewage   ...   300 mg/lit
   (vii) Desired effluent BOD   ...   30 mg/lit
   (viii) Sky is clear for 15% of the days
   (ix)   Per capita BOD contribution per day   ...   0.045 kg/day
   (x)   Pond removal constant at 20°C   ...   0.1/day

10. Describe phytoremdiation Technology for wastewater treatment.

11. Explain in detail Root zone cleaning system.

12. State the advantages of root zone cleaning system.

UNIVERSITY QUESTIONS

1. Explain 'Bacteria-Algae symbiosis in oxidation ponds'.
   (6 M) (May 2011, Dec. 2010, May 2010)

2. Write the design steps required for oxidation pond.
   (6 M) (Dec. 2010, May 2010, May 2009)

3. Write about constructional details and design criteria of oxidation pond.
   (6 M) (Dec. 2010, May 2011)

4. How the detention period of oxidation pond is estimated ?
   (4 M) (Dec. 2010, May 2010)

5. Classify the different types of oxidation ponds.   **(4 M) (May 2010, May 2011)**

6. What are the advantages and disadvantages of aerated lagoons ?
   (6 M) (May 2010, 2011, 2009)

7. What are the different methods of aeration in the treatment of aerated lagoon ?
   (6 M) (May 2011, 2009)

8. Explain diagrammatically the algae-bacteria symbiotic relations. **(4 M) (May 2009)**

9. What is the difference between oxidation pond and aerated lagoon ?
   (4 M) (Dec. 2010)

10. Draw a neat figure of unlined soak pit filled with broken brickbats. Explain its working. **(6 M) (Dec. 2010)**

✠ ✠ ✠

Chapter 10

SEPTIC TANKS AND ANAEROBIC TREATMENT OF SLUDGE AND PACKAGE SEWAGE TREATMENT PLANT

10.1 SEPTIC TANKS

Septic tanks are horizontal continuous flow, small sedimentation tanks. The sewage is allowed to flow slowly so that the suspended sewage solids settle to the bottom of the tank. The settled solids are digested anaerobically and settled effluent is disposed off safely. The thick layer of scum is formed at the surface which helps to maintain anaerobic conditions into the tank. The anaerobic bacteria convert the organic sewage solids into gaseous, liquid and sludge. The digested sludge is removed from the tank at regular intervals usually once every 1–5 years. To maintain anaerobic conditions, the tank must be air-tight and water-tight. The septic tank is constructed into masonry or RCC. The shape of the tank is usually rectangular. The bottom of the tank should be 1.2 m above the ground water table. The septic tank should be provided in such a area where site condition is favourable for effluent disposal preferably at the lowermost contour. The effluent from septic tank is highly offensive with bad odour and dark in colour.

In rural areas and the fringe areas of suburban towns and also in cases of isolated buildings and institutions such as hotels, hospitals, schools, small residential colonies, septic tanks are provided. Septic tanks are recommended for individual homes and small communities and institutions whose contributory population does not exceed 300.

10.2 DESIGN AND CONSTRUCTION FEATURES

[Dec. 2010, May 2009, 2010, 2011]

Since a septic tank is a settling cum digestion tank, its rational design is based on the following three functions :

- Sedimentation to remove maximum possible amounts of suspended solids from sewage.
- Digestion of settled sludge resulting in a much reduced volume of dense and digested sludges.
- Storage of sludge and scum accumulating in between successive cleanings, thereby preventing their escape.

Hence, the dimensions of tank should be such that the above mentioned requirements are fulfilled.

10.2.1 Sewage Flow

The maximum sewage flow does not depend on number of users but it depends on the number of plumbing fixtures discharging simultaneously.

Tables 10.1, 10.2, 10.3, 10.4 give the idea about the determination of sewage flow.

Table 10.1 : Equivalent Fixture Units

Sr. No.	Facility	Equivalent Fixture Unit	Sr. No.	Facility	Equivalent Fixture Unit
1.	Water closet	1	8.	Combination fixture	1
2.	Bath kitchen	1/2	9.	Shower bath	1
3.	Wash basin/kitchen sink	1/2	10.	Bath tub	2
4.	Urinal (autoflush)	1	11.	Drinking fountain	½
5.	Urinal (ordinary)	1/2	12.	Ablution tap	½
6.	Slop tank	1	13.	Dish washer	½
7.	Lab sink	2			

Table 10.2 : Estimated Peak Discharges for Small Tanks upto 50 Users

No. of Users	No. of Fixtures	Probable No. of Fixture Units Discharging Simultaneously	Probable peak Discharge (lpm)
5	1	1	10
10	2	2	20
15	3	2	20
20	4	3	30
25	5	4	40
30	6	4	40
35	7	5	50
40	8	6	60
45	9	6	60
50	10	7	70

Table 10.3 : Estimated Peak Discharge for Residential Housing Colonies

No. of Users	No. of Households	No. of Fixture Units	Probable Peak Discharge (Based on 60% Fixture Units Discharging Simultaneously) (lpm)
100	20	40	240
150	30	60	360
200	40	80	480
300	60	120	720

Table 10.4 : Estimated Peak Discharge for Eating Establishments, Boarding Schools etc.

No. of Users	W.C.	Baths	Wash Basin / kitchen Sinks	No. of Fixture Units	Probable Peak Discharge (Based on 70% Fixture Units Discharging Simultaneously) (lpm)
50	6	6	6	12	84
100	12	12	12	24	168
150	19	19	19	38	266
200	25	25	25	50	350
300	37	37	37	74	518

10.2.2 Dimensions of Tank

The capacity of tank depends on the functions to be performed i.e. sedimentation, sludge digestion and sludge storage.

1. Sedimentation :

Design criteria to determine surface area is 0.92 m^2 for every 10 lpm peak flow rate. A minimum depth of 25–30 cm is necessary. The length is maintained 2–4 times the breadth.

2. Sludge Digestion :

The volume of fresh sludge can be considered as 0.00083 m^3/head/day.

The volume of digested sludge = 0.0002 m^3/head/day.

In septic tank, the digestion zone contains both fresh sludge and space for digestion. Hence, the total volume required will be equal to 0.000515 m^3/head/day. Assuming the digestion period of 63 days for average sludge, the capacity of sludge digestion is 63 × 0.000515 = 0.032 m^3/head.

3. Space for Sludge and Scum :

Volume of digested sludge = 0.0002 m^3/head/day. The capacity for 100 persons with the cleaning period of one year works out to be

$$0.0002 \text{ m}^3/\text{head/day} \times 365 \text{ days} \times 100 \text{ persons} = 7.3 \text{ m}^3.$$

The total capacity will be sum of the above three requirements.

10.2.3 Detention Period   [Dec. 2010, May 2010]

A detention period of 24 to 48 hrs is provided based on the design criteria discussed above.

10.2.4 Sludge Withdrawal

The period of sludge withdrawal may vary from 6 months to 3 years.

10.3 CONSTRUCTION DETAILS   [MAY 2009]

Fig. 10.1 shows the details of a septic tank. The material of construction may be brick, stone or concrete. The watertight and airtight cover is provided to maintain anaerobic conditions. Ventilating pipe, extending at least 2 m above the top of the highest building with a radius of 20 mm is provided. Only one compartment for smaller capacities and two compartments for larger capacities are provided. The partition wall at a distance of about 2/3 the length from the inlet is provided.

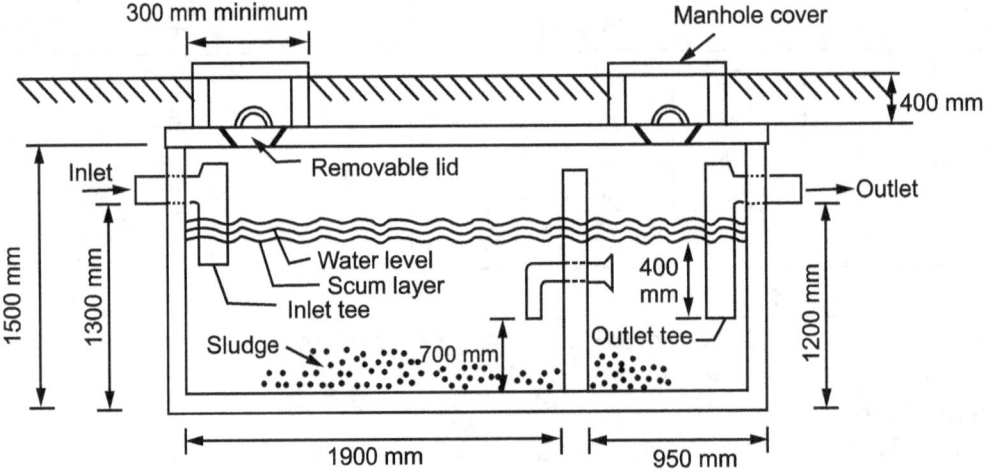

Fig. 10.1 : Septic tank

The inlet and outlet are located at the two opposite ends. The baffles are generally provided at both inlet and outlet and should dip 25 to 30 cm into and project 15 cm above the liquid level. The invert of outlet pipe should be placed at a level of 5 to 7 cm below the invert level of inlet pipe. The bottom of the tank will have slope towards the sludge outlet.

10.4 TREATMENT AND DISPOSAL OF SEPTIC TANK EFFLUENT

The effluent from septic tank generally is septic and malodorous. It is necessary to dispose off this effluent safely because of presence of pathogens. The effluent can be disposed off by one of the following methods :

- By subsurface irrigation.
- By surface irrigation.

- By discharging into nearby water courses.
- By soil absorption system.

Soil Absorption System :

It has two types :

- Seepage pit or soak pit.
- Dispersion trenches.

10.4.1 Seepage Pit

These are circular pits more than 1 meter in diameter and 1 meter depth below the invert of the inlet pipe. These pits are lined with dry bricks or stone and are filled with brick bats or coarse aggregate more than 7.5 cm in size. In the case of large pits, the top portion is reduced in size for the reduction in the size of R.C.C. cover. The lining above the inlet level should be finished with mortar. The details are shown in Fig. 10.2.

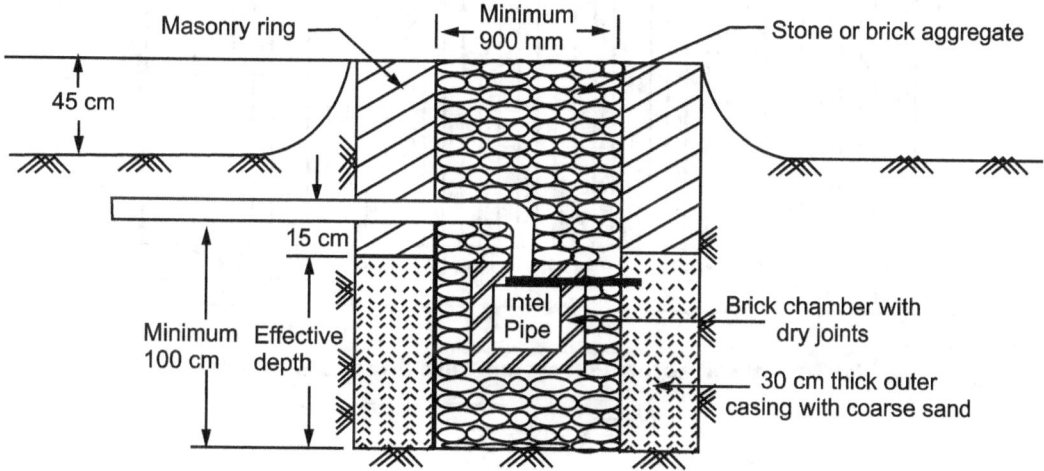

Fig. 10.2

Soak pit or seepage pit can be used in all porous soils where percolation rate is below 25 min/cm and depth of water table is 180 cm or more from ground level.

The total surface soil area required for the soak pits or dispersion trenches is given by the following empirical relation :

$$Q = \frac{130}{\sqrt{t}}$$

where, Q = Maximum rate of effluent application in lpd/m² of leaching surface

t = Standard percolation rate for the soil, in minutes per cm.

While calculating the effective leaching area required, only area of trench bottom in case of dispersion trenches, and effective side wall area below the inlet level for soak pits should be taken into account.

10.4.2 Dispersion Trenches

In this system, the septic tank effluent is uniformly distributed into a large area of subsoil through open jointed or perforated tile drains, each housed in a dispersion trench as shown in Fig. 10.3. Dispersion trenches consist of relatively narrow and shallow trenches about 0.5 to 1 m deep and 0.3 to 1 m wide excavated to a slight gradient of about 0.25%.

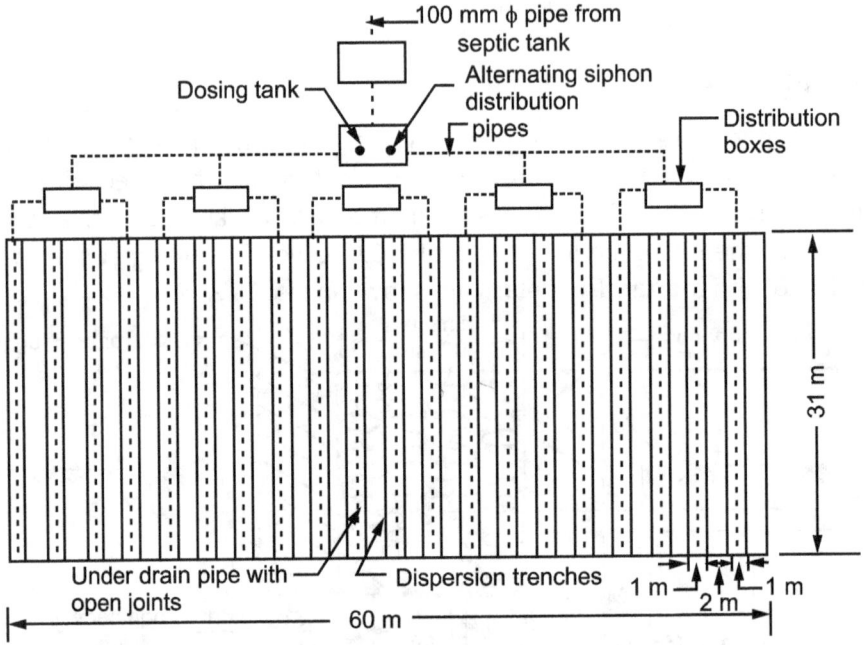

(a) Typical soil absorption system with dispersion trenches

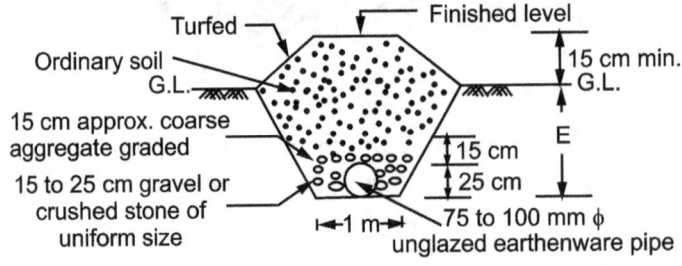

(b) Enlarged section through filled dispersion system

Fig. 10.3 : Dispersion trench system

Open jointed earthen ware or concrete pipes of 70 mm to 100 mm dia. Are laid in the trenches over a bed of 15 to 25 cm of washed gravel or crushed stone. The maximum length of each trench is kept as 30 m and these are spaced not closer than 2 m apart. One distribution box is provided for a group of about 3 to 4 trenches.

10.5 ADVANTAGES AND DISADVANTAGES OF SEPTIC TANKS

Advantages :

- Easy to construct.
- No skilled supervision is necessary.
- The quantity of sludge produced is relatively low and with no odour.
- The cost of construction, operation and maintenance is affordable to private house holders.
- No moving parts are required for operation.
- The effluent can be disposed off easily.
- When once installed, it gives long carefree service.

Disadvantages :

- The size required is large and uneconomical.
- The functioning of tank is eratic.
- The effluent is dark and foul smelling with high BOD.
- Leakage of gases from top cause bad smell.
- Periodic cleaning, removal and disposal of sludge is often tedious.

SOLVED EXAMPLES ON DESIGN OF SEPTIC TANK

Example 10.1 : Design a septic tank for a hostel housing 150 persons. Also design the soil absorption system for the disposal of the septic tank effluent, assuming the percolation rate as 15 minutes per cm.

Solution :

[A] From table the estimated peak discharge for 150 persons is equal to 360 lpm.

Let us assume sludge withdrawal once in a year.

Ταβλε 9.   Surface area of tank @ 0.92 m² for every 10 lpm

$$= \frac{0.92 \text{ m}^2}{10 \text{ lpm}} \times 360 \text{ lpm} = 33.12 \text{ m}^2$$

Let us assume depth for sedimentation = 0.3 m.

Also provide a free board of 0.3 m. The total volume of tank will be as follows :

1. For sedimentation 33.12×0.3 = 9.936 m³
2. For digestion 0.032×150 = 4.8 m³
3. For sludge storage $\frac{7.3}{100} \times 150$ = 10.95 m³

4. Free board 33.12×0.3 $= 9.936 \ m^3$

$$\text{Total} = 35.622 \ m^3$$

$\therefore$ Total depth of tank $= \dfrac{35.622}{33.12} = 1.075 \ m$

          Provide depth $= 1.1 \ m$

Let us keep L/B ratio as 2.5.

$\therefore$ $[2.5 \ B] \ [B] = 33.12$

$\therefore$ $B = 3.64 \ m$

          and $L = 9.1 \ m$

Hence, tank dimensions are 9.1 m $\times$ 3.64 m $\times$ 1.1 m

[B] For absorption system, $Q = \dfrac{130}{\sqrt{t}}$

Here, $t = 15 \ min/cm$

$\therefore$ $Q = \dfrac{130}{\sqrt{15}} = 33.56 \ lpd/m^2$

Let us assume sewage flow @ 135 lpcd.

$\therefore$ Total flow per day $= 150 \times 135$

          $= 20250 \ lpd$

$\therefore$ Total trench area required $= \dfrac{20250}{33.56} = 603.39 \ m^2$

    Let us assume trench width as 1 m and separation between trenches as 2.0 m, total land area required $= 3.9 \ m \times 603.39 = 1810.17 \ m^2$.

    Let us provide length of each trench $= 30 \ m$.

          Hence width of land $= \dfrac{1810.17}{30} = 60.34 \ m$

          Hence provide $\dfrac{60.34}{3.0} = 20 \ trenches$

$\therefore$ Actual percolation area provided $= 20 \times 30 \times 1$

          $= 600 \ m^2$

SLUDGE TREATMENT AND DISPOSAL

A by-product in the treatment of wastewater is the huge volume of sludge that must be disposed off. The problem of disposing sludge is complex because –

- It is largely composed of the substances that make the wastewater objectionable.
- It is composed of organic matter that can decompose making it objectionable.
- The sludge solid itself is only a small portion of the total sludge, resulting in large sludge volume with only little solids to dispose off.

Sludge contains only from 0.25 to 16% solids. To dispose sludge economically, its volume must therefore be reduced.

10.6 SOURCES OF SLUDGE

The sources of solids in the treatment plant vary according to the type of plant and its method of operation. The principle sources of solids and sludge and the types generated are given in Table 10.5.

Table 10.5 : Sources of Solids and Sludge from a Conventional Wastewater-Treatment Facility

Unit Operation or Process	Type of Solids or Sludge	Remarks
Screening	Coarse solids	Coarse solids are often comminuted and returned to the wastewater for removal in subsequent treatment facilities.
Grit removal	Grit and scum	Scum removal facilities are often omitted on grit removal facilities.
Preaeration	Scum	In some plants, scum removal facilities are not provided in preaeration tanks.
Primary sedimentation	Primary sludge and scum	The quantities of both sludge and scum depend on the nature of the collection system and whether industrial wastes are discharged to the system.
Aeration tank	Suspended solids	Suspended solids are produced from the conversion of BOD. If wasting is from the aeration tank, flotation thickening is normally used to thicken the waste activated sludge.
Secondary sedimentation	Secondary sludge and scum	Provision for scum removal on secondary settling tanks is now a requirement of the U.S. Environmental Protection Agency.
Sludge-processing facilities	Sludge and ashes	The characteristics and moisture content of the sludge and ashes depend on the operations and processes that are used.

10.7 CHARACTERISTICS OF SLUDGE

To treat and dispose off the sludge produced from wastewater treatment plants in the most effective manner, it is important to know the characteristics of the solids and sludge that will be processed. The characteristics vary depending on the origin of the solids and sludge; the amount of aging that has taken place, and the type of processing to which they have been subjected. The physical and chemical characteristics of untreated sludge are given in Tables 10.6 and 10.7 respectively.

Table 10.6 : Characteristics of Sludge Produced during Wastewater Treatment

Solids or Sludge	Description
Screenings	Screenings include all types of organic and inorganic materials large enough to be removed on bar racks. The organic content varies, depending on the nature of the system and the season of the year.
Grit	Grit is usually made up of the heavier inorganic solids that settle with relatively high velocities. Depending on the operating velocities, grit may also contain significant amounts of organic matter, specifically fats and grease.
Scum	Scum consists of the floatable materials skimmed from the surface of primary and secondary settling tanks. It may include grease, vegetable and mineral oils, animal fats, waxes, soaps, food wastes, vegetable skins, hair, paper and cotton, cigarette tips, plastic suppositories, rubber prophylactics, grit particles, and similar materials. The specific gravity of scum is less than 1.0 and usually around 0.95.
Primary sludge	Sludge from primary sedimentation tanks is usually gray and slimy and, in most cases, has an extremely offensive odour. It can be readily digested under suitable conditions of operation.
Chemical-precipitation sludge	Sludge from chemical precipitation tanks is usually dark in colour, though its surface may be red if it contains much iron. Its odour may be objectionable, but not as bad as odour from primary sedimentation sludge. While it is somewhat slimy, the hydrate of iron or aluminium in it makes it gelatinous. If it is left in the tank, it undergoes decomposition like the sludge from primary sedimentation but at a slower rate. It gives off gas in substantial quantities and its density is increased by standing.
Activated sludge	Activated sludge generally has a brown flocculant appearance. If the colour is quite dark, it may be approaching a septic condition. If the colour is lighter than usual, there may have been underaeration with a tendency for the solids to settle slowly. Sludge in good condition has an inoffensive characteristic odour. It tends to become septic rather rapidly and then has a disagreeable odour of putrefaction. It will digest readily alone or mixed with fresh wastewater solids.

Contd...

Trickling-filter sludge	Trickling-filter humus is brownish, flocculant, and relatively inoffensive when fresh. It generally undergoes decomposition more slowly than other undigested sludges, but when it contains many worms it may become offensive quickly. It is readily digested.
Digested sludge (aerobic)	Aerobically digested sludge is brown to dark brown and has a flocculant appearance. The odour of aerobically digested sludge is not offensive; it is often characterized as musty. Well digested aerobic sludge dewaters easily, and the resulting dry solids are inoffensive.
Digested sludge (anaerobic)	Anaerobically digested sludge is dark brown to black and contains an exceptionally large quantity of gas. When thoroughly digested, it is not offensive, its odour being relatively faint and like that of hot tar, burnt rubber, or sealing wax. When drawn off on porous beds in thin layers, the solids first are carried to the surface by the entrained gases, leaving a sheet of comparatively clear water below them which drains off rapidly and allows the solids to sink down slowly on to the bed. As the sludge dries, the gases escape, leaving a well-cracked surface with an odour resembling that of garden loam.
Septage	Sludge from septic tanks is black. Unless well digested by long storage, it is offensive because of the hydrogen sulphide and other gases it gives off. The sludge can be dried on porous beds if spread out in thin layers, but objectionable odours are to be expected while it is draining unless it has been well digested.

Table 10.7 : Typical Chemical Composition of Untreated Sludge

Item	Untreated Primary Sludge	
	Range	Typical
Total dry solids (TS), %	2.0–8.0	5.0
Volatile solids (% of TS)	60–80	65
Grease and fats (ether-soluble, % of TS)	6.0–30.0	...
Protein (% of TS)	20–30	25
Nitrogen (N, % of TS)	1.5–6.0	4.0
Phosphorus (P_2O_5, % of TS)	0.8–3.0	2.0
Potash (K_2O, % of TS)	0–1.0	0.4
Cellulose (% of TS)	8.0–15.0	10.0
Iron (not as sulphide)	2.0–4.0	2.5

Silica (SiO_2, % of TS)	15.0–20.0	...
pH	5.0–8.0	6.0
Alkalinity (mg/lit as $CaCO_3$)	500–1500	600
Organic acids (mg/lit as HAc)	200–2000	500
Thermal content (MJ/kg)	14–23	16.5

10.8 QUANTITY OF SLUDGE

The quantity of daily sludge varies depending upon the degree of removal of suspended solids in primary and secondary settling tanks, moisture content and specific gravity of sludge. In case of primary sludge, continuously desludged solids do not generally exceed 4 to 5%, while in secondary settling tanks, they range between 0.5 to 1%. When the secondary sludge is combined with the primary sludge, the solids content in the mixed sludge range between 2.5 to 5%. The solids content in the digested sludge is usually in the range between 6 to 13% when reduction in bulk takes place due to separation of supernatant.

Guidelines to calculate quantity of sludge –

- Quantity of suspended solids in raw sewage : 90 gm/day per head.
- Concentration of suspended solids in raw sewage : 200 to 250 mg/lit.
- Solids removed in PST : 60%.
- Solids generated in biological process :
  (a) Fixed/Attached growth process : 0.4 to 0.5 kg of BOD_5 applied.
  (b) Suspended growth process : 0.2 – 1.0 kg of applied BOD_5.

Typical values of solids are given in Table 10.8.

Table 10.8 : Solids in Sludges (Per Capita Per Day)

Treatment Process		Total (gm)	Volatile (g)	Fixed (g)	Sp. Gr. Of Dry Solids	% Solids in Wet Sludge
(1)		(2)	(3)	(4)	(5)	(6)
Sr. No.	Raw sewage					
1.	Total solids	90	63	27	1.22	
2.	Settleable solids (60%)	54	38	16	1.22	
3.	Non-settleable solids (40%)	36	25	11	1.22	
I.	Primary (Pr.) sedimentation and digestion					
1.	Solids removed as fresh sludge	54	38	16	1.22	4–5
2.	Solids digested*	–	–25	+6		
3.	Solids remaining in primary digested sludge	35	13	22	1.6	10–13

Contd...

II.	Activated sludge Process (AS)					
1.	Non-settleable solids affected	36	25	11	1.22	
2.	Solids digested during activation (10%)	–	−2.5	+0.5		
3.	Solids to be removed	34	22.5	11.5		
4.	Solids removed as fresh activated sludge (90%)	31	20	11	1.25	
5.	Combined primary (I) and secondary excess AS (II)	54 + 31 = 85	38 + 20 = 58	16 + 11 = 27	1.22	2.5 – 4
6.	Solids digested	–	−38	+10		
7.	Solids remaining in digested combined Pr. & Excess AS	57	20	37	1.65	6 – 7
III.	Trickling filter (T.F.) Process					
1.	Non-settleable solids	36	25	11	1.22	
2.	Solids digested during filtration (10%)	–	−2.5	+0.5		
3.	Solids to be removed in sedimentation tank	34	22.5	11.5		
4.	Solids to be removed in SS Tank (40%)	14	9	5		
5.	Combined Pr. (I) and TF humus (III)	68	47	21	1.22	4 – 5
6.	Solids digested in digester	–	−32	+8		
7.	Solids remaining in digested Pr. and T.F. humus	44	15	29	1.66	8 – 10

The quantity of solids removed in PST can be calculated by the following formula :

$$M_p = \eta \times SS \times Q$$

where,

M_p = Mass of primary solids, kg/d

η = Efficiency of PST for solids removal

SS = Total SS in effluent, kg/m³

Q = Flow rate, m³/d

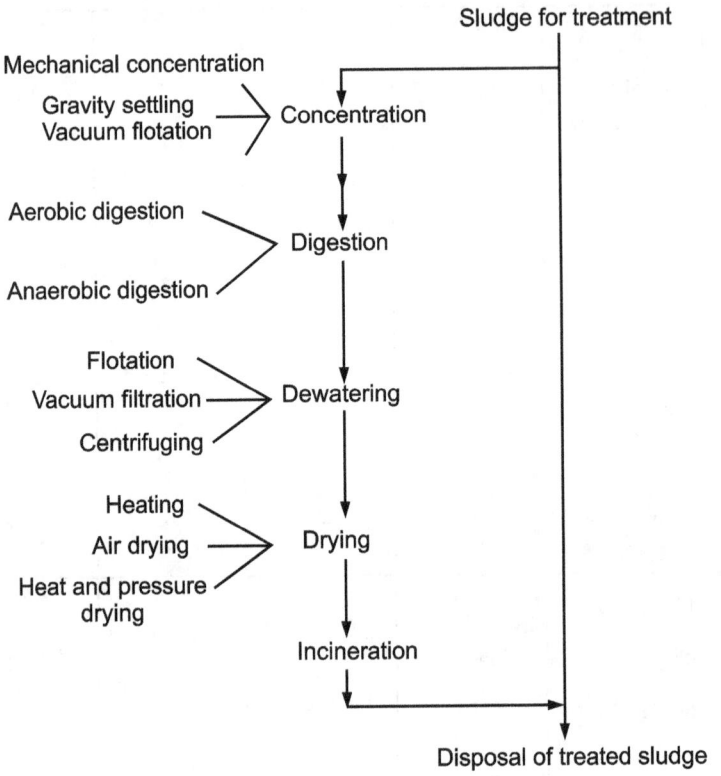

Fig. 10.4 : Flow chart for possible treatment of sludge

Secondary sludge composed primarily of biological solids, the quantity of which can be estimated by the equation :

$$M_S = Y' \times BOD_5 \times Q$$

where, M_S = Mass of secondary solids, kg/d

Y' = Biomass conversion factor

Q = Flow rate, m³/day

To calculate volume of sludge, the following equation can be used :

1. If sludge contains organic (volatile), inorganic (fixed) solids :

$$\frac{W_S}{S_S} = \frac{W_f}{S_f} + \frac{W_v}{S_v}$$

or

$$\frac{100}{S_S} = \frac{\% \text{ of mineral matter}}{\text{Sp. gr. of mineral matter}} + \frac{\% \text{ of volatile matter}}{\text{Sp. gr. of oganic matter}}$$

where, W_S = Wt. of solids

S_S = Sp. gr. of solids

W_f = Wt. of fixed solids

S_f = Sp. gr. of fixed solids (2.4 to 2.65)

W_v = Wt. of volatile matter

S_v = Sp. gr. of volatile matter (1.0 to 1.2)

2. Specific gravity of Wet Sludge (S_{sl}) :

$$\frac{100}{S_{sl}} = \frac{\% \text{ moisture}}{\text{Sp. gr. of water}} + \frac{\% \text{ of solids}}{S_s}$$

3. Once the sp. gr. of wet sludge and % solids in wet sludge are known, volume of wet sludge can be determined, using the relationship :

$$V_{sl} = \frac{W_s}{\rho_w \, S_{sl} \, P_s}$$

where,

V_{sl} = Volume of sludge

W_s = Wt. of dry solids

S_{sl} = Sp. gr. of sludge

P_s = Percent solids expressed as decimal

ρ_w = Density of water

10.9 SLUDGE TREATMENT PROCESSES

Techniques for processing waste sludges depend on the type, size and location of the wastewater treatment plant, unit operations employed in treatment, and the method of ultimate disposal. The system selected must be able to receive the sludge produced and economically to convert it to a product that is environmentally acceptable for disposal.

Popular methods for handling, processing and disposing of waste sludge are given below :

1. **Storage Prior to Processing :**
    - In the primary clarifiers.
    - Separate holding tanks.

2. **Thickening Prior to Dewatering or Digestion :**
    - Gravity settling.
    - Dissolved air flotation.

3. **Conditioning Prior to Dewatering :**
    - Chemical treatment.
    - Stabilisation by aeration.
    - Stabilisation by anaerobic digestion.

4. **Dewatering :**
    - Pressure filtration.
    - Drying beds or lagoons.
    - Centrifugation.
    - Composting.
    - Vacuum filtration.

5. Solids Disposal :

- Burial in landfill.
- Incineration.
- Spreading on farmland.
- Production of soil conditioner.

Typical unit operations selected for processing sludge from filtration plant and activated sludge process are shown in Fig. 10.5 and Fig. 10.6.

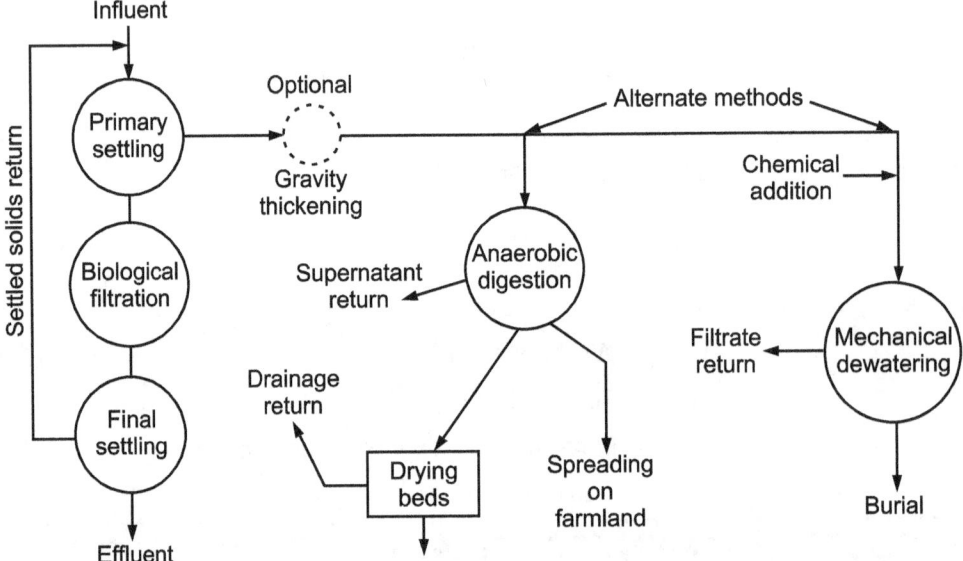

Fig. 10.5 : Typical unit operations for processing waste sludge from filtration plants

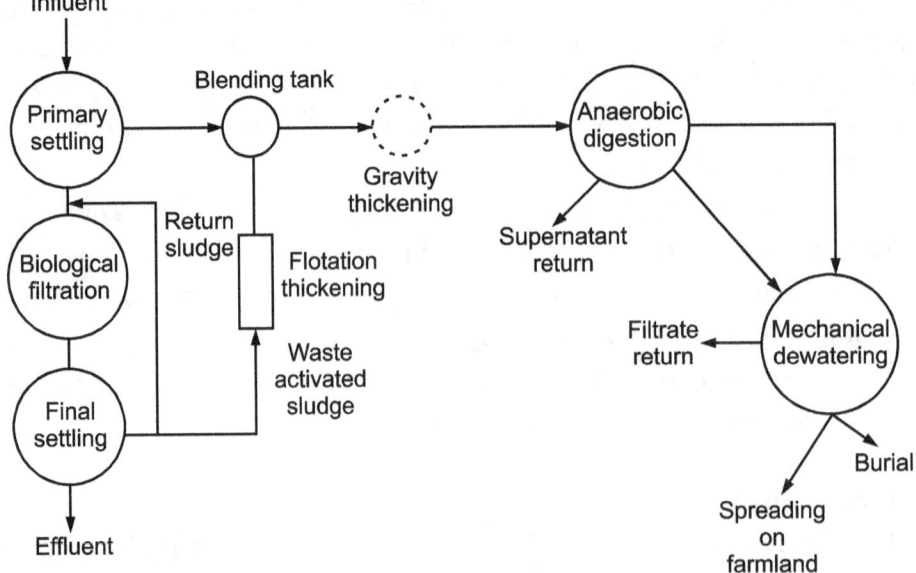

Fig. 10.6 : Possible alternatives to handling waste sludges from activated-sludge treatment

10.9.1 Sludge Thickening

Sludge contains large volumes of water. Thickening of sludge is used to concentrate solids and reduce the volume. Thickened sludge requires less tank capacity and chemical dosage for stabilization and smaller piping and pumping equipment for transport.

Common methods of sludge thickening :

1. Gravity thickening
2. Dissolved air floatation.

1. Gravity Thickening :

This is accomplished in circular sedimentation tank similar to those used for primary and secondary clarification of liquid waste. Solids coming to thickener separate into three distinct zones. The top layer is relatively clear liquid. The next layer is the settling zone, which usually contains a stream of denser sludge moving from influent end toward the thickening zone.

Water is squeezed out of interstitial spaces and flows upwards to the channels. Arrangement is done to provide gentle stirring of sludge blanket and move the gases and liquid towards the surface. The supernatant from the sludge thickener passes over an effluent weir and is returned at the inlet of plant.

The thickened sludge is withdrawn from the bottom.

Gravity thickening is used to concentrate solids in sludges from the primary clarifier, trickling filter and activated sludge.

The degree of thickening may vary from 2 to 5 times the concentration of solids in the incoming sludge.

Maximum solids concentration achieved in gravity thickening is normally less than 10 per cent.

The equipment includes :

- Rotating bottom scraper arm.
- Vertical pickets.
- Rotating scum collecting mechanism with scum baffle plates.

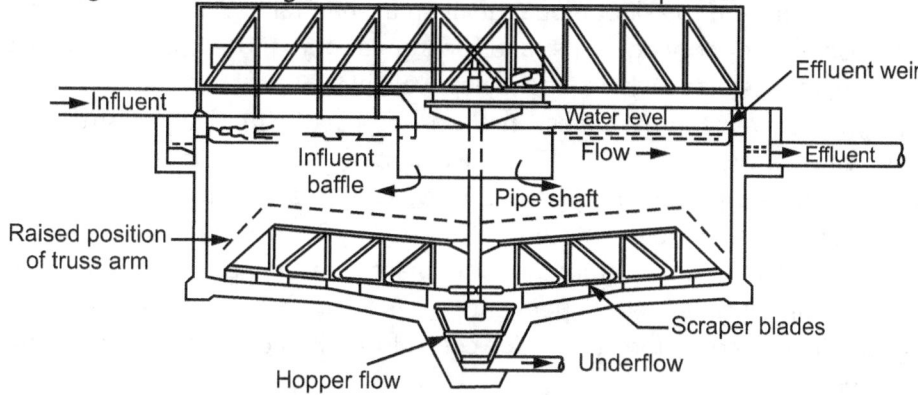

Fig. 10.7 : Gravity sludge thickener

2. Dissolved Air Floatation :

Air floatation is primarily used to thicken the solids in chemical and waste activated sludge. Separation of solids is achieved by introducing fine air bubbles into the liquid. The bubbles attach to the particulate matter which then rise to the surface. In this system, the air is dissolved in the incoming sludge under pressure. The pressurised flow is discharged into a floatation tank that operates at normal pressure.

Fine air bubbles rise that cause floatation of solids.

The principle advantages of floatation over gravity thickening is the ability to remove more rapidly and completely those particles that settle slowly under gravity. The amount of thickening achieved is 2-8 times the incoming solids. Maximum concentration of solids in the float may reach 4-5 per cent.

The common equipments includes :

1. Sludge feed pump with air compressors.
2. Floatation tank with skimmer.
3. Chemical storage and feed system.
4. Thickened sludge pump.

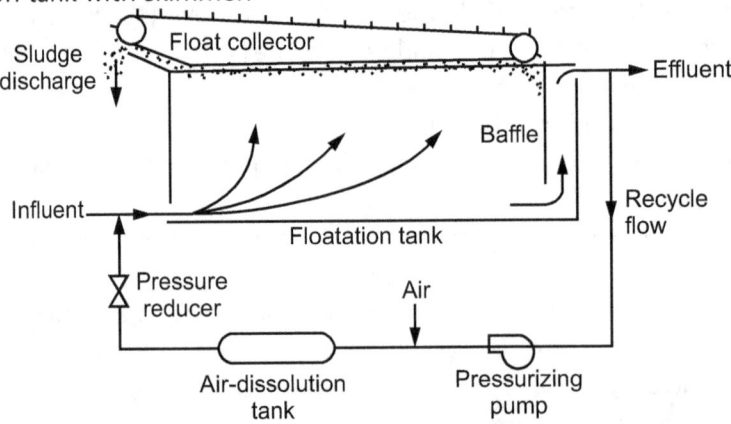

Fig. 10.8 : Schematic diagram of a dissolved air floatation system

10.9.2 Sludge Drying Beds

When land is available and the sludge quantity is small, natural dewatering systems are more attractive. These include drying beds and drying lagoons. The mechanical dewatering systems are generally selected where land is not available.

Sludge drying beds even though oldest method, still used extensively in small to medium size plants to dewater digested sludge. Typical sand bed consists of layer of coarse sand 15-25 cm in depth and supported on a graded gravel bed that incorporates selected tiles or perforated under drains. Sludge is placed on the bed in 20 to 30 cm layers and allowed to dry. The under drained liquid is returned to the plant. The drying period is 10-15 days and moisture content of the cake is 60-70 per cent.

Depending on climatic conditions and odor control requirements, the drying beds may be open or covered.

Design criteria :

Sludge drying bed area :
  0.14 – 0.28 m² per capita for uncovered beds.
  0.1 – 0.2 m² per capita for covered beds.

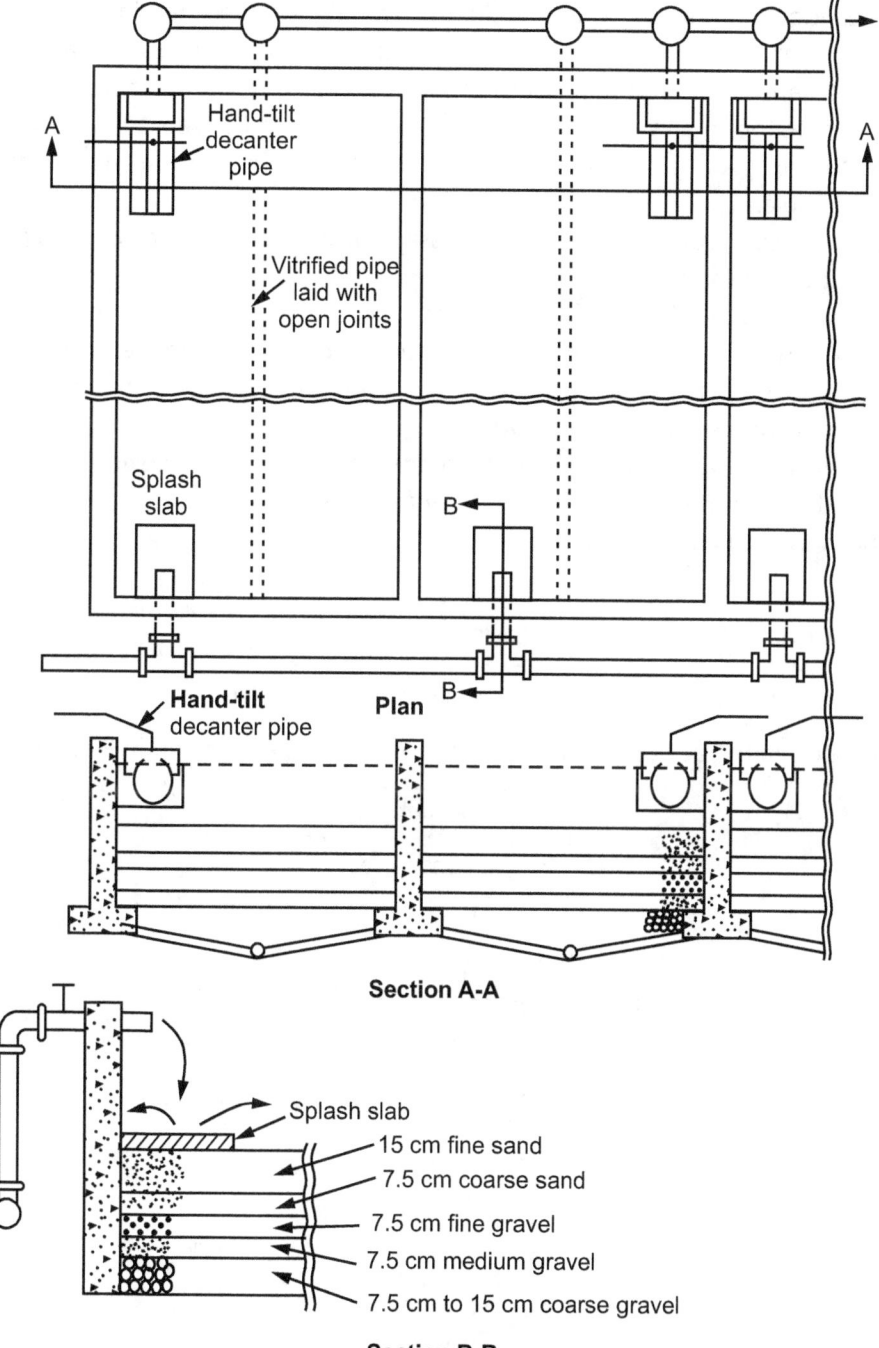

Section B-B
Fig. 10.9 : Details of sludge drying beds

10.10 ANAEROBIC DIGESTION   [MAY 2010, 2009; DEC. 2010]

Anaerobic digestion is by far the most common method of sludge processing with the wastewater sludges containing primary sludge. Primary sludge contains large amounts of readily available organics that would induce a rapid growth of biomass if treated aerobically. Anaerobic decomposition produces considerably less biomass than aerobic processes.

The principle function of anaerobic digestion, therefore, is to convert as much of the sludge as possible to end products such as liquids and gases, while producing as little residual biomass as possible.

The bacterial process consists of two successive processes that occur simultaneously in digesting sludge as given below :

- Breaking down large organic compounds and converting them to organic acids along with gaseous by-products of carbon dioxide, methane and trace amounts of hydrogen sulphide. This is done by variety of facultative bacteria operating in an environment devoid of oxygen.
- Converting the organic acids to methane and carbon dioxide. This is done by methane formers which are strictly anaerobes.

The reaction is as shown below :

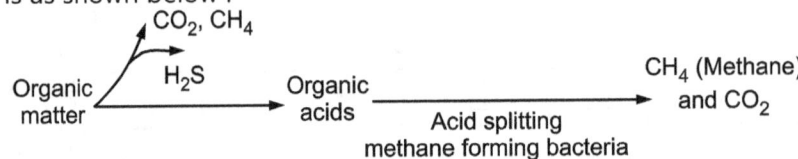

Specific products in the above anaerobic digestion process are shown in Fig. 10.10.

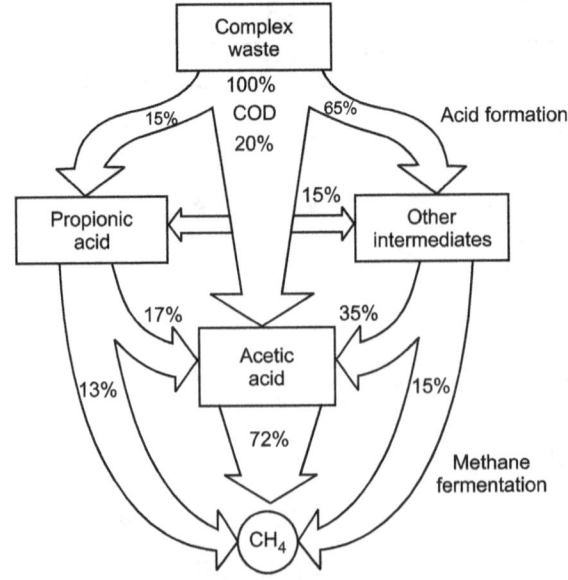

Fig. 10.10 : Pathways and products of anaerobic digestion of wastewater sludge

Typically, about 50 to 60% organics are metabolized, with less than 10% being converted to biomass.

10.11 TYPES OF DIGESTERS

Reactors for anaerobic digesters consist of closed tanks with airtight covers. Sludge digestors are of two types :

1. Conventional or low rate digester or standard rate digester.

2. High rate digesters.

10.11.1 Conventional or Low Rate Digesters

A typical standard rate anaerobic digester consisting of a single stage operation is as shown in Fig. 10.11.

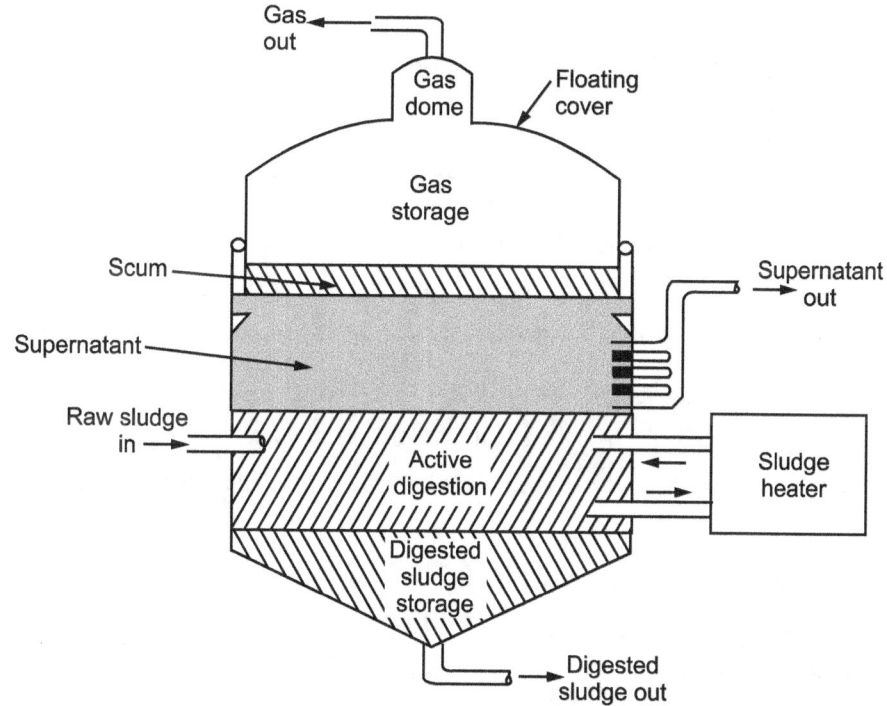

Fig. 10.11 : Diagram of a standard rate anaerobic digester

*   The conical bottom facilitates sludge withdrawal while the floating cover accommodates volume changes due to sludge addition and withdrawals.

*   The sludge separates in the reactor as shown, although some mixing occurs in the zone of active digestion and in the supernatant because of withdrawal.

*   In two stage process, two tanks are provided – first tank meant for digestion and second stage is used for storage, thickening and supernatant formation.

- The high rate digestion process differs from conventional single stage process, in that the solids loading rate is much greater.

- Sludge is fed into the digester on the intermittent basis and the supernatant is withdrawn and returned to the secondary treatment unit.

- The digested sludge accumulates in the bottom, its removal often being determined by subsequent sludge disposal facilities rather than by operational needs of the digester.

Digester Capacity :

The capacity of the low rate/standard rate digester is determined by loading rates, digestion period, solids reduction and sludge storage. The capacity can be determined by the following rational formula :

$$V = \frac{V_f + V_d}{2} T_1 + V_d T_2$$

However, since the process of digestion is parabolic, the capacity of the digester is given by the following expression :

$$V = \left[V_f - \frac{2}{3} (V_f - V_d) \right] T_1 + V_d T_2$$

where,

V = Volume of digester

V_f = Volume of fresh sludge added per day

V_d = Volume of digested sludge withdrawn per day

T_1 = Digestion time in days

T_2 = Monsoon storage in days

The checks for digester capacities can be made based on the following parameters :

- Per capita capacity :
  - (a) Primary sludge .... $0.05 - 0.075$ m^3
  - (b) Combined sludge .... $0.1 - 0.15$ m^3
- Loading factor :

  Primary or combined sludge ...... $0.3 - 0.75$ kg/m^3/day

10.11.2 High Rate Digesters

These digesters are more efficient and often require less volume than low rate single stage digesters. The sludge is more or less continuously added and vigorously mixed either mechanically or by recirculating a portion of digestion gases through a compressor. Mechanical mixing ensures better contact between the organics and the micro-organisms. The unit is heated to increase the metabolic rate of micro-organisms (thus speeding up the digestion process). Optimum temperature is around 35°C.

Because of good mixing, there is no stratification and hence loss of capacity does not arise due to supernatant or scum or dead pockets.

High rate digestion systems normally consist of two tanks operated in series. (Fig. 10.12). The first stage is a complete mixing, heated, floating or fixed cover digester fed as continuously as possible, whose function is anaerobic digestion of volatile solids.

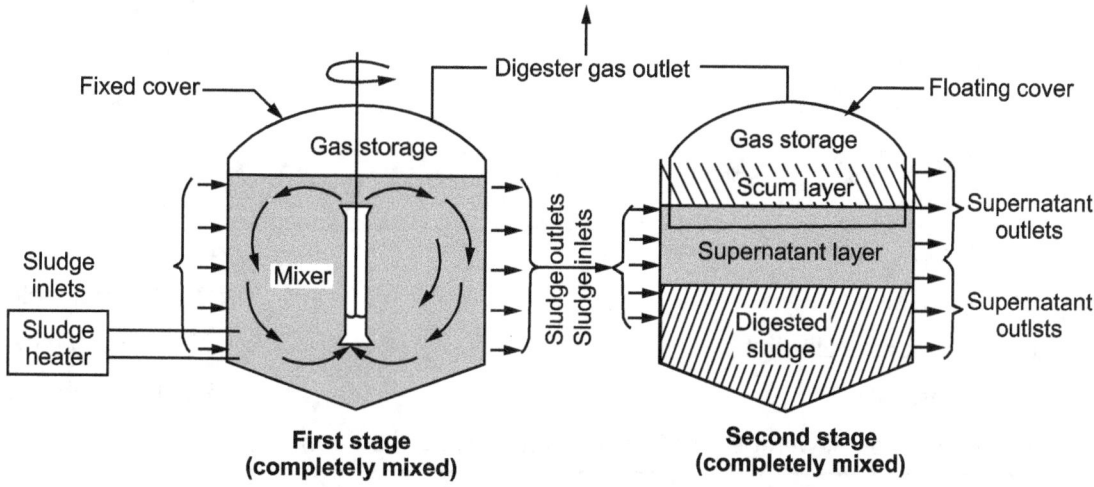

Fig. 10.12 : Diagram of high-rate, two-stage anaerobic sludge digester

In the second stage digester, separation of supernatant accompanied with a reduction in volume of sludge due to gravity thickening takes place. Little gas is generated in the second stage, but the influent is supersaturated with gases that are released in the second stage reactor. Consequently second stage reactor is usually covered and equipped with gas recovery. The second stage reactor is not heated.

Table 10.9 : Design Parameters for Anaerobic Digesters

Parameter	Standard Rate	High Rate
Digestion period, days	30 – 40	10 – 20
Volatile solids loading, kg/m³/day	0.6 – 1.6	1.6 – 6.4
Digested solids concentration, %	4 – 6	4 – 6
Volatile solids reduction, %	35 – 50	45 – 55
Gas production (m³/kg VSS destroyed)	0.5 – 0.9	0.6 – 0.65
Methane content, %	60 – 70	60 – 70

10.12 PERFORMANCE OF DIGESTERS

The following parameters give the idea about the performance of digesters :

1. Gas production on per capita basis   :   0.025 m³/day

2.	Gas production per kg of volatile matter added	:	0.4 m^3
3.	Gas production per kg of volatile matter destroyed	:	0.9 m^3
4.	pH of digesting sludge	:	7 to 8
5.	Methane content of gas produced	:	60 to 70%
6.	Dry solids in digested sludge	:	6 to 10%
	(a) Primary	:	10 to 15%
	(b) Secondary	:	6 to 10%
7.	Volatile acids	:	200 to 400 mg/lit
8.	Colour	:	Black
9.	Odour	:	Inoffensive
10.	Drainability	:	Quickly drainable
11.	Bicarbonate alkalinity	:	2000 – 5000 mg/l
12.	Grease	:	Practically absent

(Ref. Manual on Sewerage and Sewage Treatment, 2nd Edition)

10.13 DISPOSAL OF SLUDGE

Final disposal for the sludge and solids from treatment facilities can be done by the following methods :

(a) Spreading on Land : Dewatered sludge may be disposed off by spreading over farm-lands and ploughing under after it has dried. Wet dewatered sludge can be incorporated into the soil directly by injection. The humus in the sludge, conditioned the soil and involves its moisture retentiveness.

(b) Sludge Lagooning : A lagoon is an earth basin into which untreated and digested sludge is deposited. Untreated sludge lagoons stabilizes the organic solids by anaerobic and aerobic decomposition which may give rise to objectionable odours. Hence, the lagoons should be located away from the town. The stabilised solids settle to the bottom of lagoon and accumulate. Excess liquid from the lagoon is returned to the treatment plant. The lagoons are shallow 1 to 1.5 m, if they are cleaned by scraping.

(c) Dumping : Dumping, such as in an abondoned mine quarry, is a suitable disposal method. The stabilised sludges without any nuisance condition only can be disposed off by this method.

(d) Land Filling : If a suitable site is convenient, a sanitary landfill can be used for disposal of sludge, grease, grit, and other solids, whether stabilised or not. However, dewatering is recommended before such disposal. The sanitary land fill is most suitable if it is also used for disposal of other solid wastes. In a true sanitary land fill, the wastes are deposited in a designated area, compacted in place with a roller and covered with a 30 cm layer of clean soil. With daily coverage of the newly deposited wastes, nuisance conditions, such as odours and flies are minimised.

(e) Disposal in Water or Sea : This is not common method of disposal because it is contingent on the availability of a large body of water adequate to permit dilutions. At some sea-coast cities, the sludge either raw or digested may be barged to sea far enough to make available the required dilution and dispersion. The method requires careful consideration of all factors for proper design and siting of outfall to prevent any coastal pollution or interference with navigation.

10.14 UP-FLOW ANAEROBIC SLUDGE BLANKET (UASB) REACTOR

10.14.1 Introduction

The idea of UASB treatment came as a modified version of the contact process in which the wastewater is applied in the upward direction through a dense blanket of anaerobic sludge. This UASB system was developed by Lettinga and his co-workers in 1970. After that it has received a widespread acceptance and has been successfully used to treat variety of industrial wastewater.

A schematic diagram of the UASB reactor is as shown in Fig. 10.13.

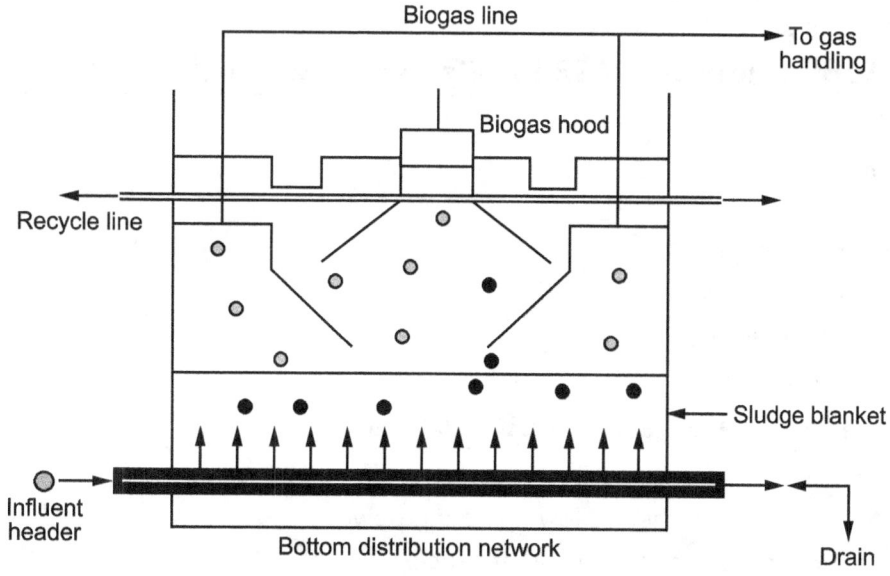

Fig. 10.13: UASB reactor

UASB is a technology which offers the best cost-benefit ratio by reducing pollutant levels, meeting regulated standards and generating biogas – an environment-friendly fuel.

10.14.2 Process

- The UASB system consists of an up-flow anaerobic sludge blanket (UASB) reactor with a three phase settler.
- The settler is at the top of the reactor and is designed for specific organic loading and hydraulic loading throughout.
- It separates the sludge, liquid and biogas. Raw effluent is pumped through a distribution network that ensures effluent flow over the base of the reactor.
- The network eliminates short-circuiting and facilitates easy online cleaning thereby eliminating potential plugging problems.
- Bacterial cells formed in the reactor aggregate into flocs with good settling characteristics. The biogas produced by the bacteria in the form of small bubbles rise upward through the sludge-bed and provides a natural mixing action.
- Treated effluent rises to the top of the reactor along with fine sludge particles.
- The three phase settler separates out the gas, liquid and sludge particles.
- Biogas is allowed to leave through a collection and distribution system.
- The liquid overflows through weirs into gutters.
- Suspended solids are allowed to settle down in the sludge blanket.
- Biogas is carried through frame arresters and foam-trap to the gas-burning system or for other appropriate end use.

10.14.3 Applications of UASB in Different Industries

- Distillery.
- Sugar.
- Brewery.
- Pulp and paper.
- Maize and tapioca starch.
- Food processing.
- Municipal sewage.

10.14.4 Salient Features of UASB Process

- Low life-cycle cost.
- No moving parts, hence, low operating power.
- Easy operation, minimum maintenance.
- Reactor in concrete M20. Hence, no corrosion and longer life.

- Unique bottom distribution system improves mixing.
- Formation of sludge blanket. No media, no clogging.
- In-built three-phase settler.
- High methane content in biogas, high calorific value.
- Consistent performance. Absorption of shock loads.
- Quick start-up after shut down.

10.15 ONSITE SANITATION AND INTRODUCTION TO PACKAGE SEWAGE TREATMENT PLANT

10.15.1 Introduction

Onsite sanitation means the storage of waste within the premises and it is treated and disposed of on site.

The term "package plant" originated from the fact that these types of treatment plants were constructed and assembled at a factory and then shipped and installed "pre-packaged" as a complete unit. They became popular during the 1960's and are still being installed today. Typically they were constructed of 1/4" plate steel and divided into several components. The components always included an aeration tank where most of the treatment occurs and a clarifier for settling. Some systems included a sludge waste compartment and chlorine contact tank. Package plant tanks would be shipped on a flat bed truck and off-loaded with a crane and set on a poured-in-place concrete slab. The piping and equipment is generally installed at the installation site after the tanks have been set.

10.15.2 Types of Package Sewage Treatment Plants

The following are the types of package sewage treatment plants:

1. Activated Sludge Plants

A raw sewage is collected into a septic tank and then passes into an aeration tank where is it aerated. The sludge is settled from the mixed liquor in the clarifier and returned to the septic tank or the aeration tank or, to drying beds. The effluent is then passed through the clarifier, settled, then disinfected and discharged.

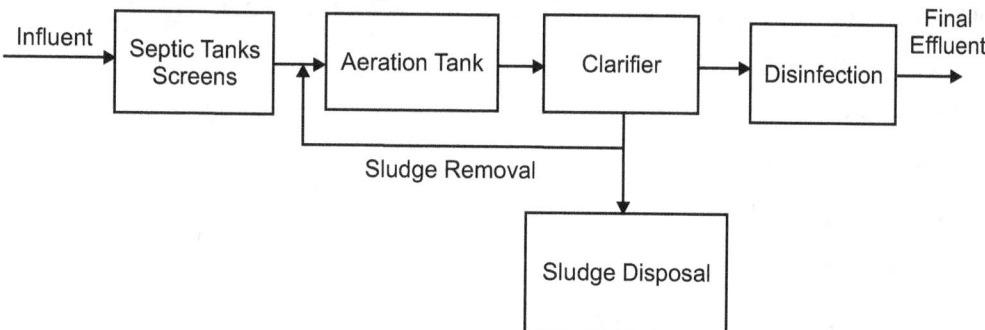

Fig. 10.14 : A flow diagram of a typical package treatment plant with extended aeration activated sludge process

2. Trickling Filter Plants

A raw sewage is collected into a septic tank and then the supernatant is distributed evenly over a bed of media by rotating arms of trickling filter. The biomass which contains a large number of purifying organisms is established on the media and aerobically treats the effluent as it passes through. The effluent is then passed through a humus tank, settled, then disinfected and discharged.

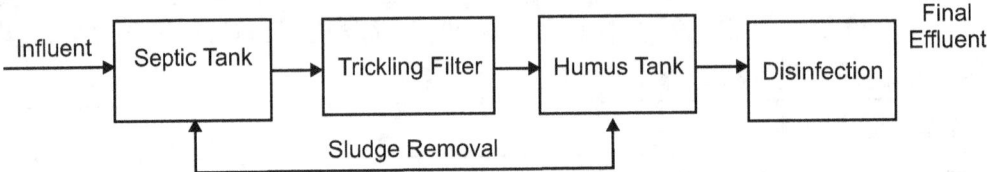

Fig. 10.15 : A flow diagram of a typical package treatment plant with a trickling filter

3. Rotating Bio-Contactors Plants

A raw sewage is collected into a septic tank and then the supernatant passes through troughs containing rotating discs that are partially submerged in the sewage. A film of biomass develops on the discs and sloughs off as soon as the layers grow too thick. As the discs rotate the biomass is exposed to the air, resulting in aeration of the biofilm. After sedimentation in the humus tank, the final effluent is then disinfected and discharged.

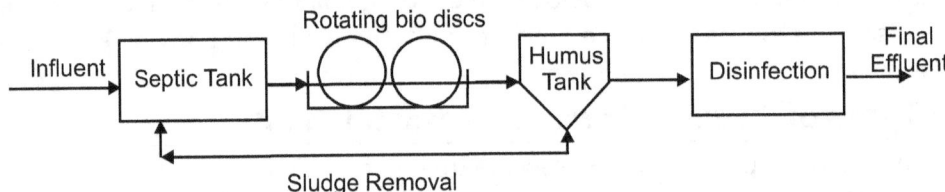

Fig. 10.16 : A flow diagram of a typical package treatment plant with a rotating bio-contactor system

10.15.3 Applications

The package sewage treatment plant can be used at the following places:

- Townships.
- Hotels (5 stars, 3 stars).
- Small and medium sized cities.
- Mobile Home Parks.
- Remote construction sites.
- Recreational areas such as parks, etc.
- Educational hubs.

10.15.4 Advantages

- It is having lower cost because of pre-fabricated structures.
- It is easy for transportation to the site.
- The time require for installation is less.
- Wastewater Treatment System is simple to operate.
- The operation cost is less as requires low manpower.
- The maintenance cost is less.

EXERCISE

1. Assuming a four person occupancy, design an on-site septic tank system for a wealthy residential home in an unsewered area. The sewage production is 390 lit-capita/day. Assume an equilibrium percolation rate of 0.02 mm/day.

2. Design a septic tank for the following data :

   Number of users : 150

   Sewage/capita/day : 125 litres

   Desludging period : 1 year

   Percolation rate : 15 min/cm.

3. Discuss the advantages and disadvantages of septic tank.

4. Write a note on – Disposal of septic tank effluent.

5. What are the sources of sludge from an ETP ?

6. Explain the characteristics of sludge.

7. Explain how the quantity of sludge is to be determined.

8. Explain with the help of flow chart, various processes involved in sludge treatment and disposal.

9. What is the necessity of stabilisation of sludge ?

10. What do you understand by digestion of sludge ? Explain the principle of anaerobic digestion of sludge.

11. Write a note on – Different types of digesters.

12. Compare low rate digester and high rate digester.

13. Explain the different methods of disposal of sludge.

UNIVERSITY QUESTIONS

1. Describe with the help of neat sketch the components of septic tank, along with the functions of each.   **(6 M) (Dec. 2010; May 2011, 2010)**

2. Explain the design criteria of a septic tank.   **(6 M) (May 2009)**

3. Write the various design parameters of anaerobic digesters.

    (6 M) (May 2010, 2009)

4. What are the advantages and disadvantages of anaerobic treatments ?

    (6 M) (May 2010, 2011; Dec. 2010)

5. What are the different stages of digestion in case of anaerobic digesters ?

    (4 M) (May 2009, 2010, 2011; Dec. 2010)

6. Discuss the design criteria of a septic tank.   **(8 M) (May 2009)**

7. What are the various gases generated in anaerobic digesters and their percentage.   **(6 M) (May 2009)**

8. Design a septic tank for a hostel housing 200 persons. Also design the soil absorption system for the disposal of the septic tank effluent, assume the percolation rate as 1500 minutes per m, L/B ratio = 4 and Desludging period = 1 year.   **(10 M) (May 2010, 2011; Dec. 2010)**

9. Design a septic tank for small colony of 300 persons with average daily sewage flow 100 lit per head per day.   **(8 M) (May 2009, 2011)**

✠ ✠ ✠

INDUSTRIAL WASTEWATER TREATMENT

11.1 INTRODUCTION

All industrial wastes affect, in some way, the normal life of a natural stream or river or lake. Industrial wastewaters are generally much more polluted than the domestic or commercial wastewaters. If they are discharged directly in the receiving waters, it may result in discolouring, foul smell and killing of aquatic life, apart from making the water unfit for various other purposes. The industries are, therefore, generally prevented by legal laws, from discharging their untreated effluents. It, therefore, becomes necessary for the industries to treat their wastewaters in their individual effluent treatment plants (PET) or common effluent treatment plants (CETP) i.e. collect the wastewaters from different industries and give the treatment, before discharging their effluents on land or natural streams or rivers or lakes as per availability of disposal point.

11.2 SAMPLING

The sampling techniques used in a wastewater survey must assume that representative samples are obtained.

11.2.1 Grab Sample

Samples are taken at a point beneath the surface where the turbulence is thoroughly mixing up the sewage particles.

11.2.2 Composite Sample

Grab samples are collected at regular intervals during a day. These different samples are now mixed together and amount utilised from each specimen is proportional to the rate of flow at the time the specimen was collected.

11.2.3 Sample Preservation

Sample preservation is must to maintain the physical, chemical and biological integrity of the samples during the interim periods between sample collection and sample analysis. Table 11.1 shows preservation of wastewater samples.

Table 11.1 : Preservation of Wastewater Samples

Sr. No.	Parameter	Preservative	Maximum Holding Period
1.	pH	None available	–
2.	BOD	Refrigeration at 4°C	6 hrs
3.	COD	2 ml/l H_2SO_4	7 days

Contd...

4.	Colour	Refrigeration at 4°C	24 hours
5.	Dissolved oxygen (DO)	Determined on site	No holding
6.	Oil and grease	2 ml/l H_2SO_4, 4°C	24 hours
7.	Solids	None available	–
8.	Turbidity	None available	–
9.	Acidity – Alkalinity	Refrigeration at 4°C	24 hours
10.	Hardness	None required	–
11.	Metals, total	5 ml/l HNO_3	6 months
12.	Metals, dissolved	Filtrate : 3 ml/l 1 : 1 HNO_3	6 months
13.	Nitrogen, ammonia	40 mg/l $HgCl_2$, 4°C	7 days
14.	Nitrogen, Kjedahl	40 mg/l $HgCl_2$, 4°C	Unstable
15.	Calcium	None required	–
16.	Chloride	None required	–
17.	Cyanide	NaOH to pH 10	24 hours
18.	Fluoride	None required	–
19.	Phosphorus	40 mg/l $HgCl_2$, 4°C	7 days
20.	Phenolics	1.0 g $CuSO_4$ + H_3PO_4 to pH 4, 4°C	24 hours
21.	Sulphate	Refrigeration at 4°C	7 days
22.	Sulphide	2 ml/l Zn acetate	7 days

11.3 CHARACTERISTICS OF WASTEWATER

The characterization of the raw waste is essential in the planning for effective and economical methods of water pollution control. As the varying nature of the industrial wastes, many of the recent installations have designed their treatment units with due consideration to the raw waste characteristics and the effluent characteristics as established by the Indian Standards Institution (ISI), State Pollution Control Boards or Central Pollution Control Boards (CPCB) or by the local administrative authorities.

Table 11.2 shows pollution characteristics of certain typical Indian Industries.

Table 11.2 : Pollution Characteristics of Certain Typical Indian Industries

Industry	Pollution Characteristics	Suggested Treatment Methods
Paper and pulp	High BOD, strong colour, high COD/BOD ratio, highly alkaline, high sodium content.	Lime treatment for colour, chemicals recovery, biological treatment.
Sugar	High volatile solids, high BOD, low pH.	Biological treatment
Textile (cotton)	High BOD, highly alkaline, high suspended solids.	Chemical and biological treatment
Dairy	High suspended solids, high dissolved solids, high BOD, presence of oil and grease.	Biological treatment.
Distillery and Brewery	High chloride, strong colour, very high BOD, high sulphate.	Biological treatment.

11.4 EFFLUENT STANDARDS

Table 11.3 shows ISI tolerance limits for the sewage and industrial effluents and that of inland surface water.

Table 11.3 : ISI Tolerance Limits for the Sewage and Industrial Effluents and that of Inland Surface Water

Characteristics	Tolerance Limits for Sewage Effluents Discharged into Inland Surface Water. IS : 4764–1973	Tolerance Limits for Industrial Effluents Discharged into		Tolerance Limits for Inland Surface Water, When Used as Raw Water for Public Water Supplies and Bathing Ghats IS : 2296-1974
		Inland Surface Water IS : 2490-1974	Public Sewers IS : 3306-1974	
1	2	3	4	5
BOD (5 day, 20°C), mg/lit	20	30	500	3
COD, mg/lit	–	250	–	–
pH	–	5.5 – 9.0	5.5 – 9.0	6.0 – 9.0
Total suspended solids, mg/lit	30	100	600	–
Temperature, °C	–	40	45	–

Contd...

Oil and Grease, mg/lit	–	10	100	0.1
Phenolic compounds, mg/lit	–	1.0	5	0.005
Cyanides (as CN), mg/lit	–	0.2	2.0	0.01
Sulphides (as S), mg/lit	–	2.0	–	–
Fluorides (as F), mg/lit	–	2.0	–	1.5
Total residual chlorine, mg/lit	–	1.0	–	–
Insecticides, mg/lit	–	zero	–	zero
Arsenic (as As), mg/lit	–	0.2	-	0.2
Cadmium (as Cd), mg/lit	–	2.0	–	–
Chromium, hexavalent (as Cr), mg/lit	–	0.1	2.0	0.05 (Total chromium)
Copper, mg/lit	–	3.0	3.0	–
Lead, mg/lit	–	0.1	1.0	0.1
Mercury, mg/lit	–	0.01	–	–
Nickel, mg/lit	–	3.0	2	–
Selenium, mg/lit	–	0.05	–	0.05
Zinc, mg/lit	–	5.0	15.0	–
Chloride (as Cl), mg/lit	–	–	600	600
Sulphates, mg/lit	–	–	–	1000
% Sodium	–	–	60	–
Ammoniacal Nitrogen, mg/lit	–	50	50	–
Nitrates (as NO_3), mg/lit	–	–	–	50
Radioactive materials :				
α-emitters, µc/ml	–	10^{-7}	–	10^{-9}
β-emitters, µc/ml	–	10^{-6}	–	10^{-8}
Dissolved Oxygen, mg/lit	–	–	–	40% of the saturation value, or 3 mg/lit, whichever is higher.
Coliform organism (monthly average) – MPN per 100 ml	–	–	–	Should not exceed 5000. (should not exceed 20000 with less than 5% samples, and 5000 with less than 20% samples).

11.5 POLLUTANTS IN INDUSTRIAL WASTEWATER

The following materials can cause pollution :

1. **Inorganic Salts :** These are present in most industrial wastes as well as in nature itself, cause water to be hard and make a stream undesirable for municipal, industrial and agricultural usage. These include carbonates, chlorides, nitrogen, phosphorus, etc.

2. **Acids and/or Alkalies :** Due to acids and/or alkalies, a stream unsuitable not only for recreational uses such as swimming and boating, but also for propagating of fish and other aquatic life.

3. **Organic Matter :** Due to the presence of organic matter this exhausts the oxygen resources of rivers and creates unpleasant tastes, odours and general septic conditions.

4. **Suspended Solids :** These are settled to the bottom and decomposed causing odours and depleting oxygen in the river water.

5. **Floating Solids :** These include oil, greases and other materials which float on the surface.

   Some of the specific objections to oil in streams are that, it (1) is toxic to aquatic life, (2) interferes with natural reaeration, (3) creates a fire hazard when present in the water surface, (4) renders boiler feed and cooling water unusable.

6. **Colour :** It is contributed by tanneries, textile, paper mills etc. Colour producing substances impart objectionable colour in the receiving water bodies. Colour interferes with the transmission of sunlight into the stream and therefore lessens photosynthetic action.

7. **Toxic Chemicals :** These include sulphides, cyanides, acetylene, alcohol, phenols, heavy metals (i.e. zinc, cadmium, copper, hexavalent chromium, arsenic etc.) due to which flora and fauna of receiving waters is greatly affected.

11.6 METHODS OF TREATMENT

Treatment of industrial wastewater generally consists of one or more of the following processes :

(a) Equalization and proportioning.

(b) Neutralization.

(c) Physical treatment.

(d) Chemical treatment.

(e) Biological treatment.

(a)   Equalization and Proportioning :

Equalization is a method of retaining wastes in a mixed basin until the effluent discharged is fairly uniform in its sanitary characteristics (colour, pH, turbidity, BOD etc.). Air is sometimes injected into these basins to provide : (i) chemical oxidation of reduced compounds, (ii) better mixing, (iii) agitation, to keep suspended solids from settling out.

Only holding of waste is not sufficient to equalize waste. Adequate mixing must take place, so that each unit volume of waste discharged will be mixed with other unit volume of waste discharged many hours ago. The mixing may be brought about in the following ways :

- Proper distribution and baffling.
- Mechanical agitation.
- Aeration.
- Combinations of all three.

Proportioning means discharge of industrial wastes in proportion to the flow of municipal sewage. The objective of proportioning is to keep the percentage of industrial wastes entering the municipal sewage plant constant. This procedure has several purposes : (1) To minimise fluctuations in sanitary standards in the treated effluent, (2) to protect biological treatment devices from receiving shock loads of industrial wastes; which may inactive the bacteria.

(b)   Neutralization :

Neutralization means neutralizing the excessive acidity or alkalinity of the particular wastewater, by adding alkali or acid respectively to the wastewater. This may be done either in the equalization tank, if the conditions so permit, or else in a separate neutralization tank.

There are many acceptable methods for neutralizing overacidity or alkalinity of wastewaters. Some of these methods include : (1) passing acid wastewaters through beds of limestone, (2) mixing wastes so that the net effect is a near-neutral pH, (3) adding the proportions of concentrated solutions of soda ash (Na_2CO_3) or caustic soda (NaOH), (4) mixing acid wastes with lime slurries, (5) adding compressed CO_2 to alkaline wastes, (6) adding sulphuric acid to alkaline wastes.

(c)   Physical Treatment :

It is similar to primary treatment of domestic wastewater. It consists of domestic wastewater. It consists of separating the suspended inorganic matter by physical processes, like screening, sedimentation, floatation and filtration.

Sedimentation is necessary to remove high percentage of heavy organic solids. Floatation is provided to remove the finer particles. In floatation, create fine air bubbles, by injecting air into the tank from the bottom. The rising air bubbles lift the finer particles to the surface from where these are removed by skimming.

(d)   Chemical Treatment :

Physico-chemical treatment is applied to the industrial wastewaters in absence of biological treatment or in conjunction with biological treatment.

The chemical treatment is used to recover the dissolved organic matter from the wastewater. One or more of the following chemical processes, that are used for industrial wastewater treatment, are :

- Chemical oxidation;
- Chemical coagulation or chemical precipitation;
- Hyper filtration or reverse osmosis;
- Electrodialysis;
- Adsorption;
- Deionisation;
- Thermal reduction; and
- Air-stripping.

(e)   Biological Treatment :

When industrial wastewaters contain large quantities of biodegradable substances, then biological treatment is essential.

Type of treatment depends on the following BOD/COD ratio.

$\dfrac{BOD}{COD}$ Ratio	Type of Treatment
$\dfrac{BOD}{COD} > 0.6$	Biologically treatable, without acclimatisation.*
$\dfrac{BOD}{COD} > 0.3 \text{ and } < 0.6$	Acclimatisation is essential for biological treatment.
$\dfrac{BOD}{COD} < 0.3$	Biological treatment is not necessary.

*Acclimatisation is a process of seeding or raising initial microbial population under a controlled condition, by gradual exposure of the wastewater in increasing concentration.

The following various biological treatment methods that can be used are :

- Trickling filter;
- Activated sludge process;
- Oxidation pond;
- Aerated lagoon;

- Oxidation ditch; and

- Oxidation lagoon, followed by aerated lagoon.

11.7 INDUSTRIES

11.7.1 Sugar Industry   [Dec. 2010, May 2010]

11.7.1.1 Manufacturing Process and Sources of the Waste

Fig. 11.1 (A) shows a flow diagram of the manufacturing process of a typical sugar industry.

Mill House : In the mill house, the sugarcanes are cut into pieces and crushed in a series of rollers to extract the juice.

Lime Treatment : The milk of lime is then added to the cane juice and heated. During this treatment much of the colour is removed, when all the colloidal and suspended impurities are coagulated.

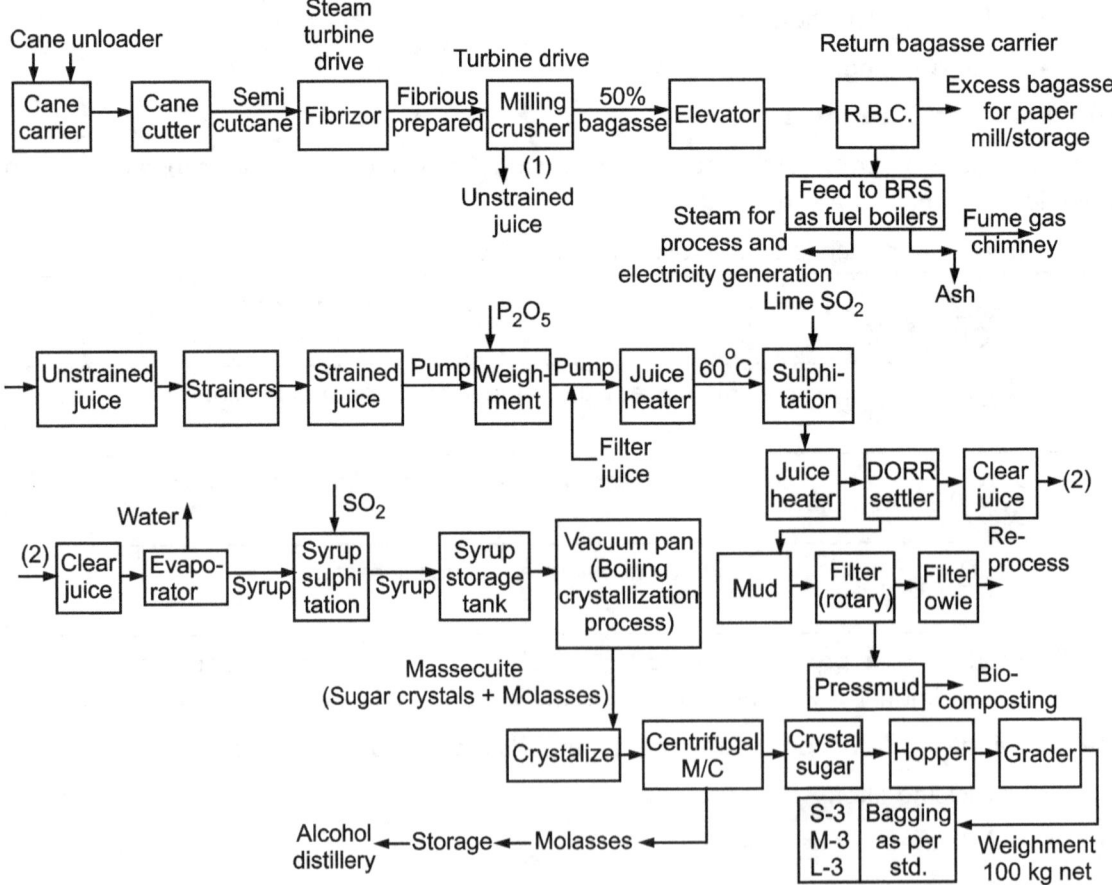

Fig. 11.1 (A) : Flow diagram of the manufacturing process of a typical sugar industry

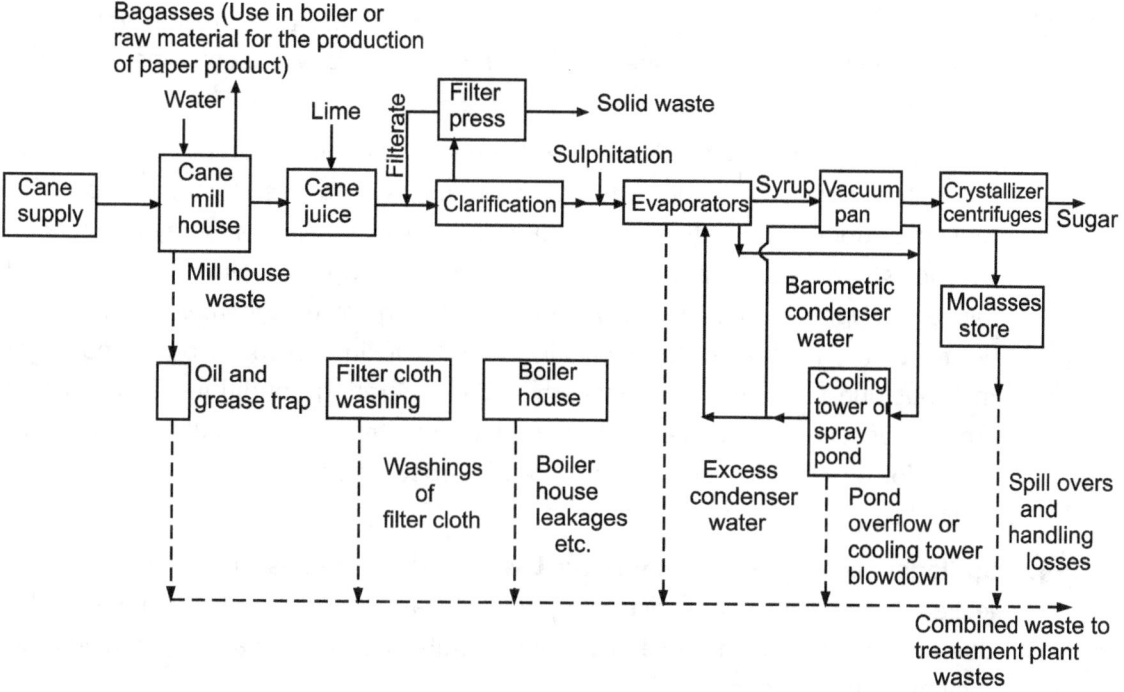

Fig. 11.1 (B) : Source of wastes

Clarification : To remove the sludge, coagulated juice is then clarified. This clarified sludge is filtered through filter presses and then disposed off as solid waste. The filterate is recycled to the process.

Sulphitation Process : The clarified juice is treated by passing sulphur dioxide gas through it. The process is called as "Sulphitation Process". Due to this process, colour of the juice is completely bleached out.

Evaporators and Vacuum Pans : The clarified juice is then preheated and concentrated in evaporators and vacuum pans.

Massecuite : The partially crystallized syrup from the vacuum pan known as 'massecuite" is then sent to crystallizers.

Crystallizers : Here complete crystallization of sugar occurs. After this massecuite is centrifuged, to separate the sugar crystals from the mother liquor.

The spent liquor is discarded as "black strap mollases", which can be used in distilleries. The sugar is then dried and bagged for transport.

Bagasses : Bagasses means the fibrous residue of the mill house which may be burnt in the boilers, or may be used as a raw-materials for the production of paper products.

Sources of Wastewater :

   1. **Mill House Waste :** It includes the water used as splashes to extract maximum amount of juice. Due to the presence of sugar and oil from the machineries, this waste contains high BOD.

2. **Filter Cloth Washing Waste :** The wash water produced is small in volume as occasional cleaning of the filter cloths is required. This waste contains high BOD and suspended solids.

3. **Pond Overflow or Excess Condenser Water :** The cooling water of a spray pond or cooling tower, as it picks up some organic substances from the vapour of boiling syrup in evaporators and vacuum para. The water from spray pond when overflows, becomes a part of the wastewater or when cooling tower is used instead of spray pond, the blow down of cooling tower becomes a part of the wastewater. This wastewater is usually of low BOD in a properly operating sugar mill. But due to poor maintenance and bad operating conditions, a substantial amount of sugar may entrain in the condenser water, so this polluted water is not useful for recirculation and is therefore discarded as excess condenser water. The BOD of such waste is moderate.

4. **Spillages, Leakages and Handling Losses :** These wastes originate due to the leakages, and spillages of juice, syrup and mollasses in different sections and also due to the handling of mollasses. Even though these wastes are small in volume, they have got a very high BOD.

Boilers Blow Down :

The periodical blow down of boilers generate waste. This waste is high in suspended solids, low in BOD and alkaline.

11.7.1.2 Characteristics of the Sugar Industry Waste

Table 11.4 shows the characteristics of the combined waste of the sugar industry.

Table 11.4 : Characteristics of the Combined Waste of the Sugar Industry

Sr. No.	Parameter	Unit	Value
1.	pH	–	4.6 – 7.1
2.	COD	mg/lit	600 – 4380
3.	BOD (5 days, 20°C)	mg/lit	300 – 2000
4.	Total solids	mg/lit	870 – 3500
5.	Total volatile solids	mg/lit	400 – 2200
6.	Total suspended solids	mg/lit	220 – 800
7.	Total nitrogen	mg/lit	10 – 40
8.	COD/BOD ratio		1.3 – 2.0

11.7.1.3 Treatment of the Sugar Industry Waste

Fig. 11.2 and Fig. 11.3 shows flow diagrams for treatment of sugar mill wastes.

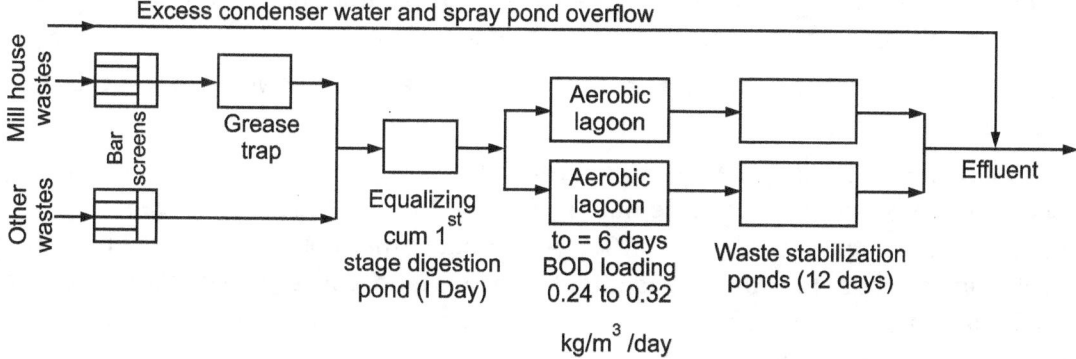

Fig. 11.2 : Flow diagram for treatment of sugar mill waste

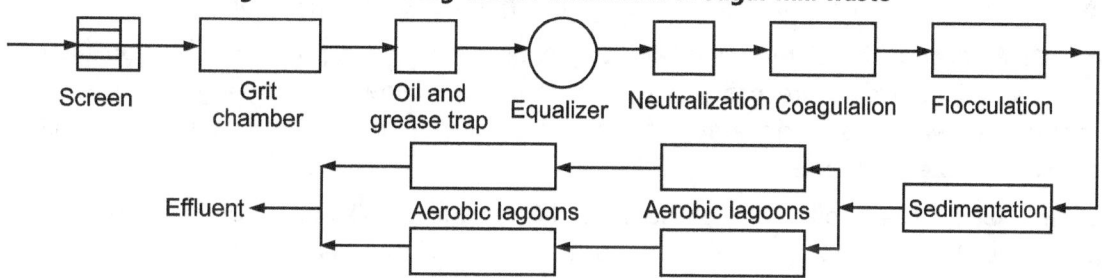

Fig. 11.3 : Flow diagram for treatment of sugar mill waste

11.7.2 Dairy Industry   [Dec. 2010]

11.7.2.1 Manufacturing Process and Sources of Waste of Dairy Industry

Large quantities of wastewater originate due to the following different operations of dairy industry : (i) Receiving station; (ii) bottling plant; (iii) cheese plant; (iv) butter plant; (v) casein plant; (vi) condensed milk plant; (vii) dried milk plant; (viii) ice cream plant; (ix) water softening plant and (x) bottle and can washing plant.

Receiving Station : Here, the milk is received from the farmers, inspects the same and emptied into large containers for transport to bottling or other processing plants. Then, the empty cans are rinsed, washed, sterilized and are returned to the farmers.

Bottling Plant : Here, the raw milk which is collected from receiving station is stored. The processing includes cooling, clarification, filtration, pasteurization and bottling.

Receiving Station and Bottling Plant Waste : From these two sections, the liquid wastes originate out of rinse and washing of bottles, cans and equipments and due to this, liquid wastes contain milk drippings and chemicals used for cleaning containers and equipments.

Cheese Plant : Here, whole milk or skimmed milk is pasteurized and cooled and placed in a vat, where a lactic acid producing bacterial culture as a starter and rennet are added. This separates the casein of the milk in the form of curd. The whey is then withdrawn by compressing curd. Now, other ingredients are added and the cheese blocks are cut and packaged for sale. The wastewater generated from this plant includes the washwater used for cleaning vats, equipments, floors etc. and discarded whey.

Creamery Process : Here, to separate the cream from the milk, the whole milk is preheated to about 30°C.

Butter Plant : In this plant, the cream is pasteurized and may be ripened with a bacterial culture and selected acid. To produce butter granules, the pasteurized and ripened cream is churned at a temperature of about 7 – 10°C. At a proper time, a butter milk is drained out of the churn and the butter is washed and after standardisation, packaged for sale. To clean the churn, butter milk and wash waters are used. From the butter plant, small quantity of butter comes out of a liquid waste.

Bottling : Now, skimmed milk may be sent for bottling or to dry milk plant.

Dry Milk Plant : The skimmed milk may be used for other products like non-fat milk powders. Milk powders are produced by evaporation followed by drying by either roller process. The waste water generated from this plant due to wash waters is used to clean containers and equipments.

Casein Plant : The spoiled and sometimes the skimmed milks are processed to produce caseins used for preparation of some plastics. The waste generated from this section includes washings, whey and the chemicals used for precipitation. Very big dairies also produce ice creams and condensed milks.

Cooling Tower Wastes : In addition to the wastes from all the above milk processing units, some amount of uncontaminated cooling water comes from cooling tower blowdown as wastes.

11.7.2.2 Characteristics of the Dairy Industry Waste

Table 11.5 shows characteristics of the dairy industry waste.

Table 11.5 : Characteristics of the dairy industry waste

Sr. No.	Parameter	Unit	Value
1.	pH		7.2
2.	Alkalinity	mg/lit as $CaCO_3$	600
3.	Total dissolved solids	mg/lit	1060
4.	Suspended solids	mg/lit	760
5.	BOD	mg/lit	1240
6.	COD	mg/lit	84
7.	Total Nitrgen	mg/lit	84
8.	Phosphorous	mg/lit	11.7
9.	Oil and grease	mg/lit	290
10.	Chloride	mg/lit	105

11.7.2.3 Treatment of the Dairy Waste

Fig. 11.4 shows a flow diagram for treatment of the dairy industry waste.

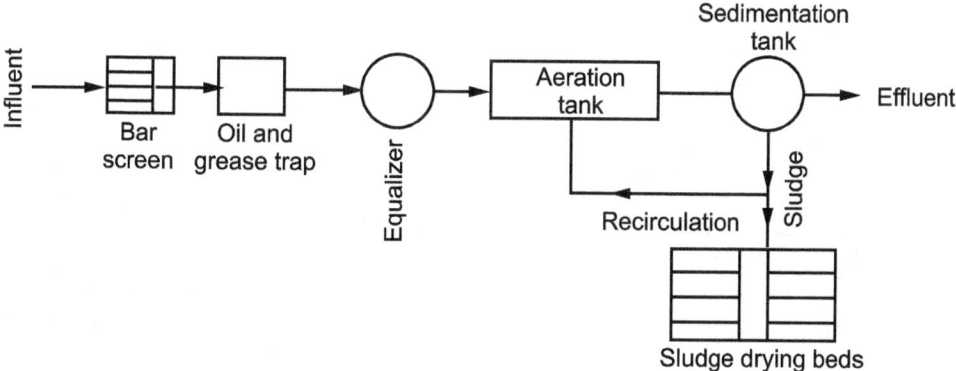

Fig. 11.4 : Typical flow chart for treating dairy wastewater

11.7.3 Brewery, Winery and Distillery

Breweries produce 'Beer' and Wineries produce 'Wine', a large number of products of varying origin are obtained in distilleries. Various products that are manufactured in distilleries include industrial alcohol, silent spirit, rectified spirit, absolute alcohol, beverage alcohol etc.

11.7.3.1 Breweries Waste

Following are two stages of making beer : (i) preparation of malt from grains like barley and, (ii) brewing the barley.

The wastewater is generated from both these stages.

Malt House Waste : The spent water from the steeping process comes from this section. This wastewater contains the water soluble substances of the grain that are diffused into it. This section contributes a high BOD in the range of 400 – 800 mg/lit, low suspended solids and alkaline in nature.

Brewing Plant Waste : In this plant, the major potential pollutant is the fermentation residue or the spent grains. Waste is also generated in the preparation of yeast suspension, from washing of containers, equipments and floors and in the process of by-product recovery from spent grains. This section contributes a high BOD and a high suspended solids and acidic in nature.

Large volume of unpolluted water also comes from the blowdown of cooling tower.

11.7.3.2 Characteristics of Breweries Waste

Table 11.6 shows characteristics of combined breweries waste.

Table 11.6 : Characteristics of combined breweries waste

Sr. No.	Parameter	Unit	Values
1.	pH	–	4.0 – 7.0
2.	COD	mg/lit	30 – 1225
3.	BOD	mg/lit	70 – 3000
4.	Total solids	mg/lit	272 – 2724
5.	Suspended solids	mg/lit	16 – 516
6.	Total nitrogen (N)	mg/lit	7 – 42

11.7.3.3 Treatment of the Brewery Waste

Fig. 11.5 shows a flow diagram for the treatment of Brewery waste.

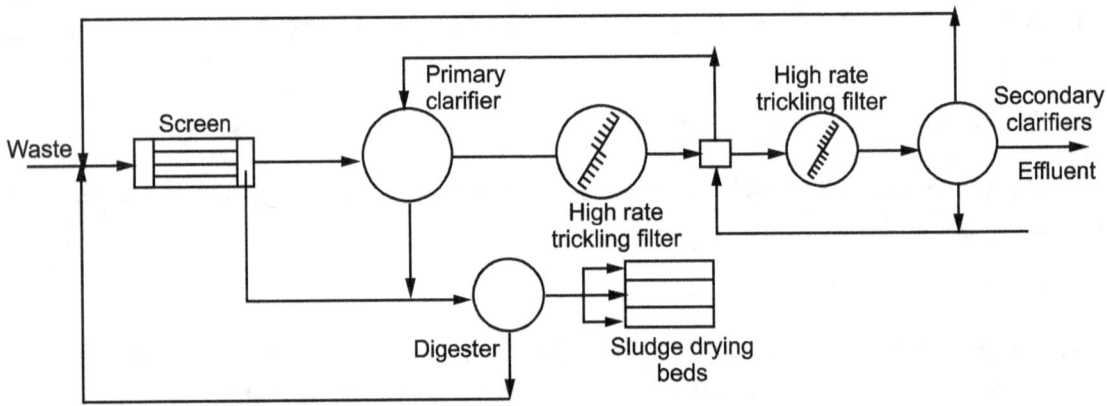

Fig. 11.5 : Flow diagram for the treatment of brewery waste

11.7.3.4 Distilleries Waste

The 'spent wash' is the major polluting component of the distilleries. The other pollutants include yeast sludge and generally the same is mixed with spent wash and discharged.

In addition to these wastes, floor washes, waste cooling water and wastes from the operations of yeast recovery or by-product recoveries processes also contribute to the volume of these wastes.

11.7.3.5 Characteristics of Combined Distilleries Waste   (May 2010)

Table 11.10 : Characteristics of Combined Distilleries Waste

Sr. No.	Parameter	Unit	Value
1.	pH	–	3.9 – 4.3
2.	COD	mg/lit	27900 – 73000
3.	BOD	mg/lit	12230 – 40000
4.	Total solids	mg/lit	16640 – 26000
5.	Suspended solids	mg/lit	4500 – 12000

11.7.3.6 Treatment of the Distilleries Waste

Fig. 11.6 shows a flow diagram for the treatment of distilleries waste.

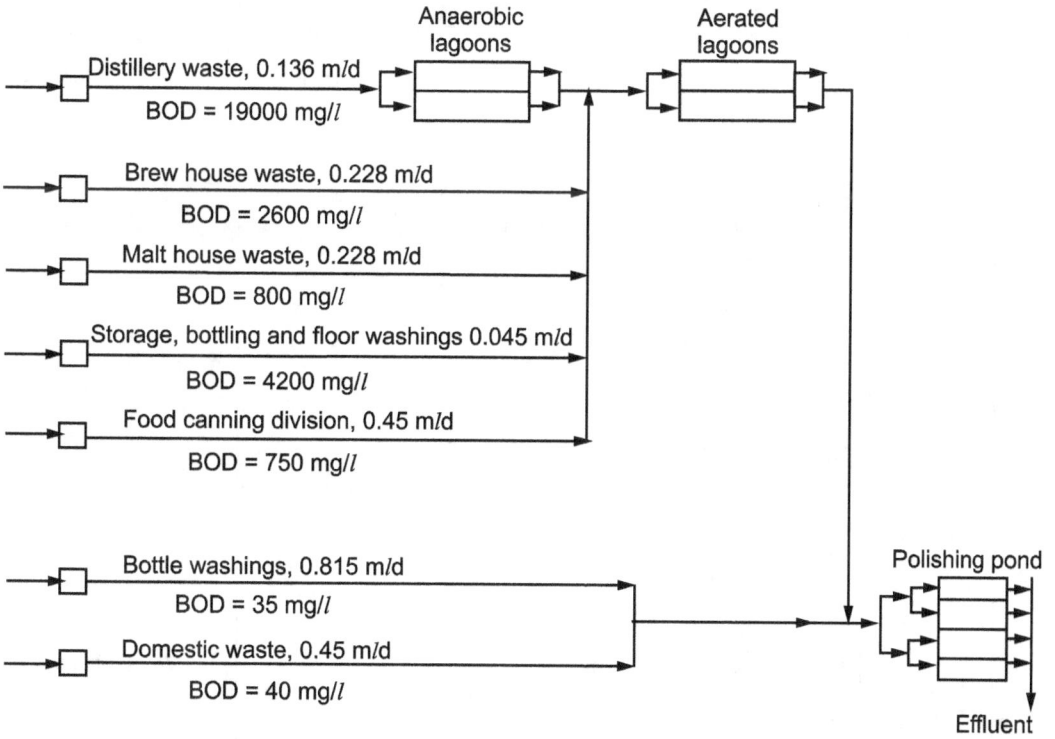

Fig. 11.6 : Flow diagram for treatment of distilleries waste

11.8 DISCHARGE STANDARDS AS PER CPCB NORMS

Sr. No.	Industry	Parameter	Standards	
1	2	3	4	5
1.	Sugar	Effluents	Concentration not exceed, milligramme per litre	
		Bio-chemical oxygen demand, [3 days at 27° C]	100 for disposal on land 30 for disposal in surface water	
		Suspended Solids	100 for disposal on land. 30 for disposal in surface waters	
2.	Dairy	Effluents	Concentration in mg/l except pH	Quantum per product processed
		pH	6.5-8.5	--
		Bio-chemical oxygen demand, [3 days at 27° C]*	100	--
		Suspended Solids**	150	--
		Oil and Grease	10	--
		Waste water generation	--	$3m^3$/Kl of milk

Contd...

Note

:*BOD may be made stringent upto 30 mg/l if the recipient fresh water body is a source for drinking water supply. BOD shall be upto 350 mg/l for the chilling plant effluent for applying on land provided the land is designed and operated as a secondary treatment system with suitable monitoring facilities. The drainage water from the land after secondary treatment has to satisfy a limit of 30 mg/l of BOD and 10 mg/l of nitrate expressed as N'. The net addition to the groundwater quality should not be more than 3 mg/l of BOD and 3 mg/l of nitrate expressed as N'. This limit for applying on land is allowed subject to the availability of adequate land for discharge under the control of industry, BOD value is relaxable upto 350 mg/l, provided the wastewater is discharged

into a town sewer leading to secondary treatment of the sewage.

** Suspended solids limit is relaxable upto 450 mg/l, provided the wastewater is discharged into town sewer leading to secondary treatment of the sewage

Ref.: www.cpcb.nic.in (The Environment (Protection) Rules, 1986)

EXERCISE

1. Identify the points of origin of wastewater streams, characterise the streams and discuss in detail one method of treatment in the case of any two of the following industries :

    (a) Paper and pulp industry.

    (b) Textile industry.

    (c) Dairy industry.

2. What is the necessity of treatment of industrial effluent ?

3. Discuss in brief various treatment processes adopted for treating industrial wastewater.

5. Write a note on 'characteristics' of industrial wastewater.

UNIVERSITY QUESTIONS

1. Discuss the characteristics and treatment of any of the following industrial waste :
    (i) Dairy industry

    (ii) Sugar factory waste

(iii) Pulp and paper mill.

(8 M) (May 2011, Dec. 2010)

2.   Explain any one of the following :

(a)   Sugar,

(b) Pulp and paper,

(c) Dairy with respect to the following :

    (i)   Sources of W/W,

    (ii)   Manufacturing process,

    (iii) Characteristics of W/W,

    (iv) Method of W/W treatment.   **(9 M) (May 2011)**

3.   Draw a flow chart for treating sugar mill and dairy wastewater.

(12 M) (May 2010)

4.   What are the characteristics of distillery spend wash ?   **(6 M) (May 2010)**

✠ ✠ ✠

APPENDIX A

Table A-1 : Saturation Values of Dissolved Oxygen (DO) in Fresh Water at Different Temperatures and 1 Atmospheric Pressure

Temperature (°C)	Dissolved oxygen (mg/lit)	Temperature (°C)	Dissolved oxygen (mg/lit)
0	14.62	20	9.17
1	14.23	21	8.99
2	13.84	22	8.83
3	13.48	23	8.68
4	13.13	24	8.53
5	12.80	25	8.38
6	12.48	26	8.22
7	12.17	27	8.07
8	11.87	28	7.92
9	11.59	29	7.77
10	11.33	30	7.63
11	11.08	31	7.51
12	10.83	32	7.42
13	10.60	33	7.28
14	10.37	34	7.17
15	10.15	35	7.07
16	9.95	36	6.96
17	9.74	37	6.86
18	9.54	38	6.75
19	9.35		

APPENDIX B

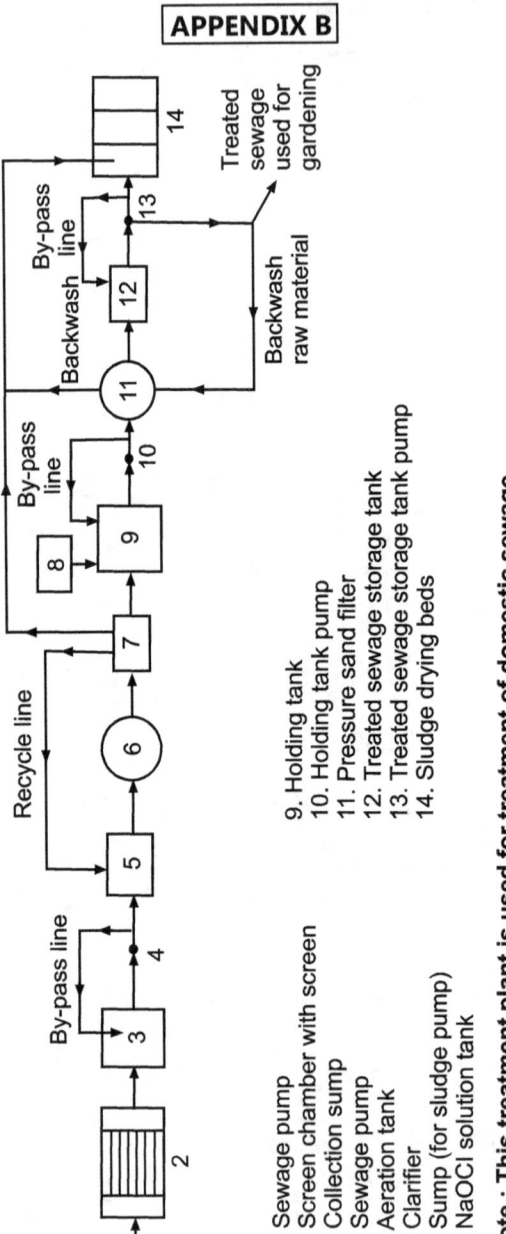

1. Sewage pump
2. Screen chamber with screen
3. Collection sump
4. Sewage pump
5. Aeration tank
6. Clarifier
7. Sump (for sludge pump)
8. NaOCl solution tank
9. Holding tank
10. Holding tank pump
11. Pressure sand filter
12. Treated sewage storage tank
13. Treated sewage storage tank pump
14. Sludge drying beds

Note : This treatment plant is used for treatment of domestic sewage

Fig. : General layout of sewage treatment plant (STP)

APPENDIX C

Common Effluent Treatment Plant (CETP)

Treatment Units :

1. Screen chamber
2. Grit chamber
3. Equalisation tank
4. Flash mixer
5. Clariflocculator
6. Chemical sludge drying beds
7. Biological sludge drying beds
8. Extended aeration tank
9. Secondary settling tank
10. Pressure sand filter
11. Activated carbon column
12. High rate transpiration system (HRTS)
13. Reverse osmosis

Dosing Tanks :

1. Ferrous sulphate dosing tank
2. Lime dosing tank
3. Polyelectrolyte dosing tank

APPENDIX D

India : Environmental Legislation

1.   The Water (Prevention and Control of Pollution) Act 1974, as amended upto 1988.

2.   The Water (Prevention and Control of Pollution) Rules, 1975.

3.   The Water (Prevention and Control of Pollution) Cess Act 1977, as amended upto 1991.

4.   The Water (Prevention and Control of Pollution) Cess Rules 1978, as amended upto 1992.

5.   The Air (Prevention and Control of Pollution) Rules 1982 and 1983.

6.   The Environment (Protection) Act, 1986.

7.   The Environment (Protection) Rules, 1986.

8.   The Hazardous Wastes (Management and Handling) Rules, 1989.

9.   Manufacture, Storage and Import of Hazardous Chemical Rules, 1989.

10. Manufacture, Use, Import, Export and Storage of Hazardous Micro-organisms, Genetically Engineered Micro-organisms or Cells Rules, 1989.

11. The Public Liability Insurance Act, 1991.

12. The Public Liability Insurance Rules, 1991.

13. Environmental (Protection) Rules, 1992 and 1993 – "Environmental Statement".

14. Environmental (Protection) Rules, 1993 – "Environmental Standards".

15. Environmental (Protection) Rules, 1994 – "Environmental Clearance".

APPENDIX E

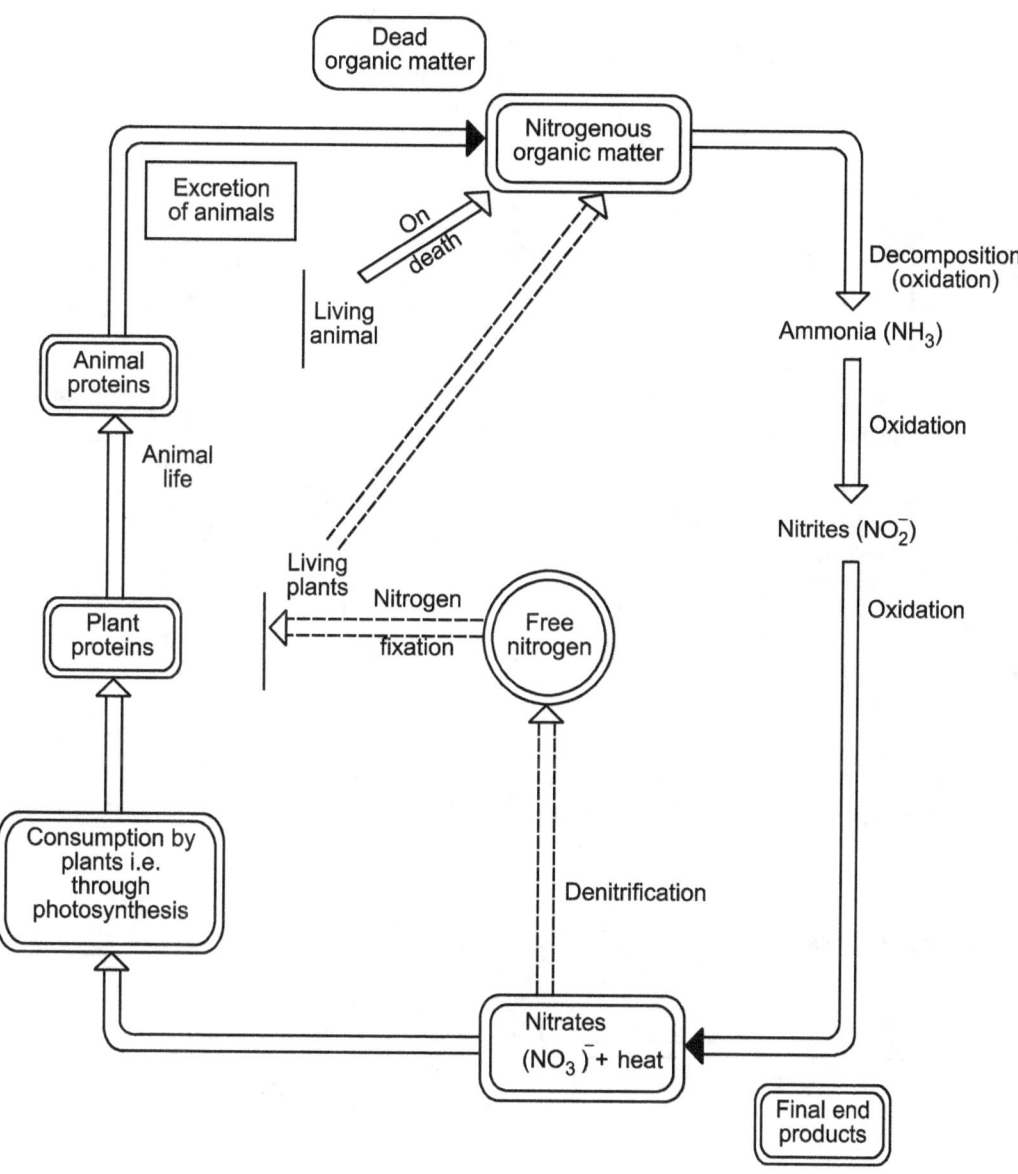

Fig : Nitrogen cycle (Aerobic oxidation)

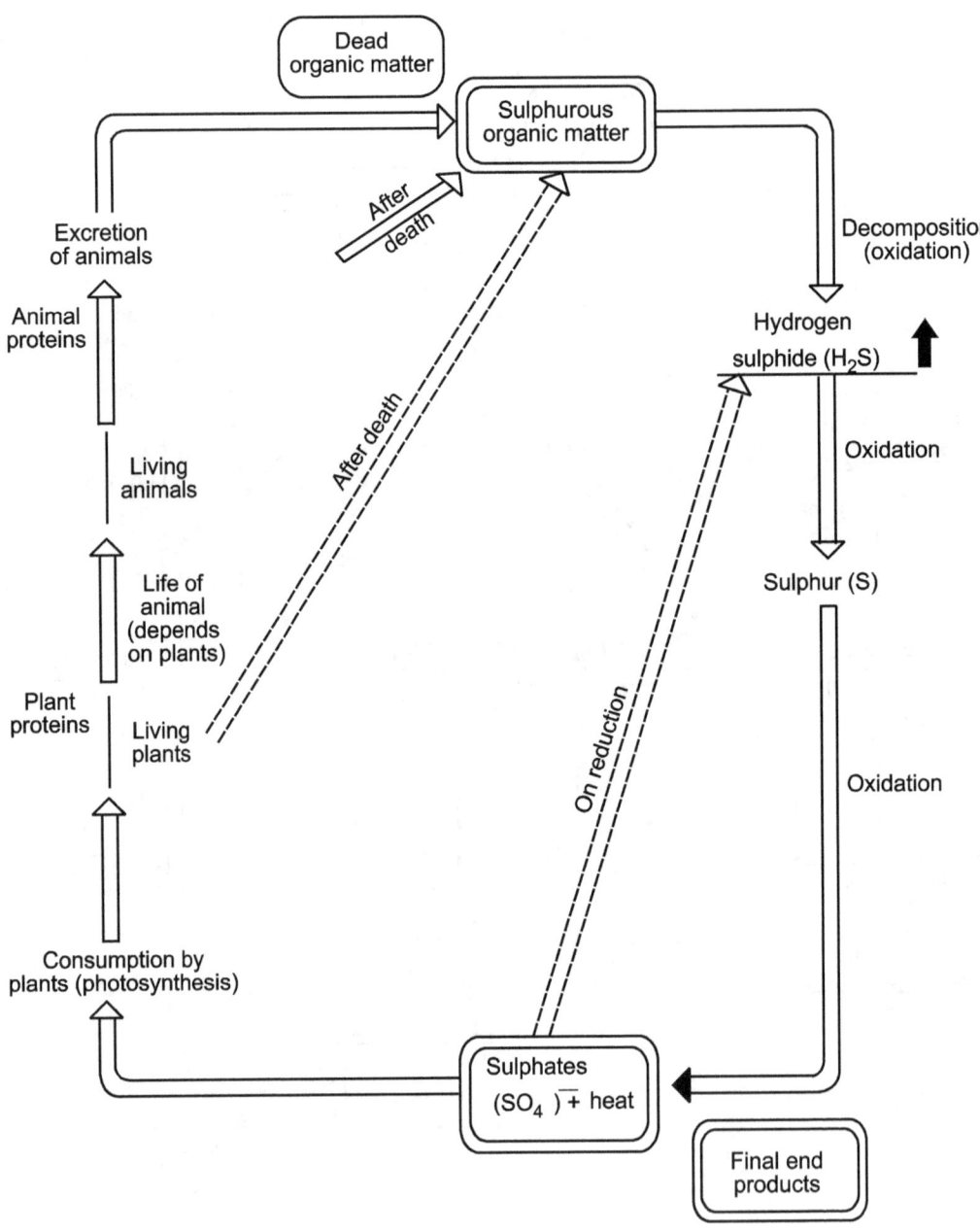

Fig. : Sulphur cycle (Aerobic oxidation)

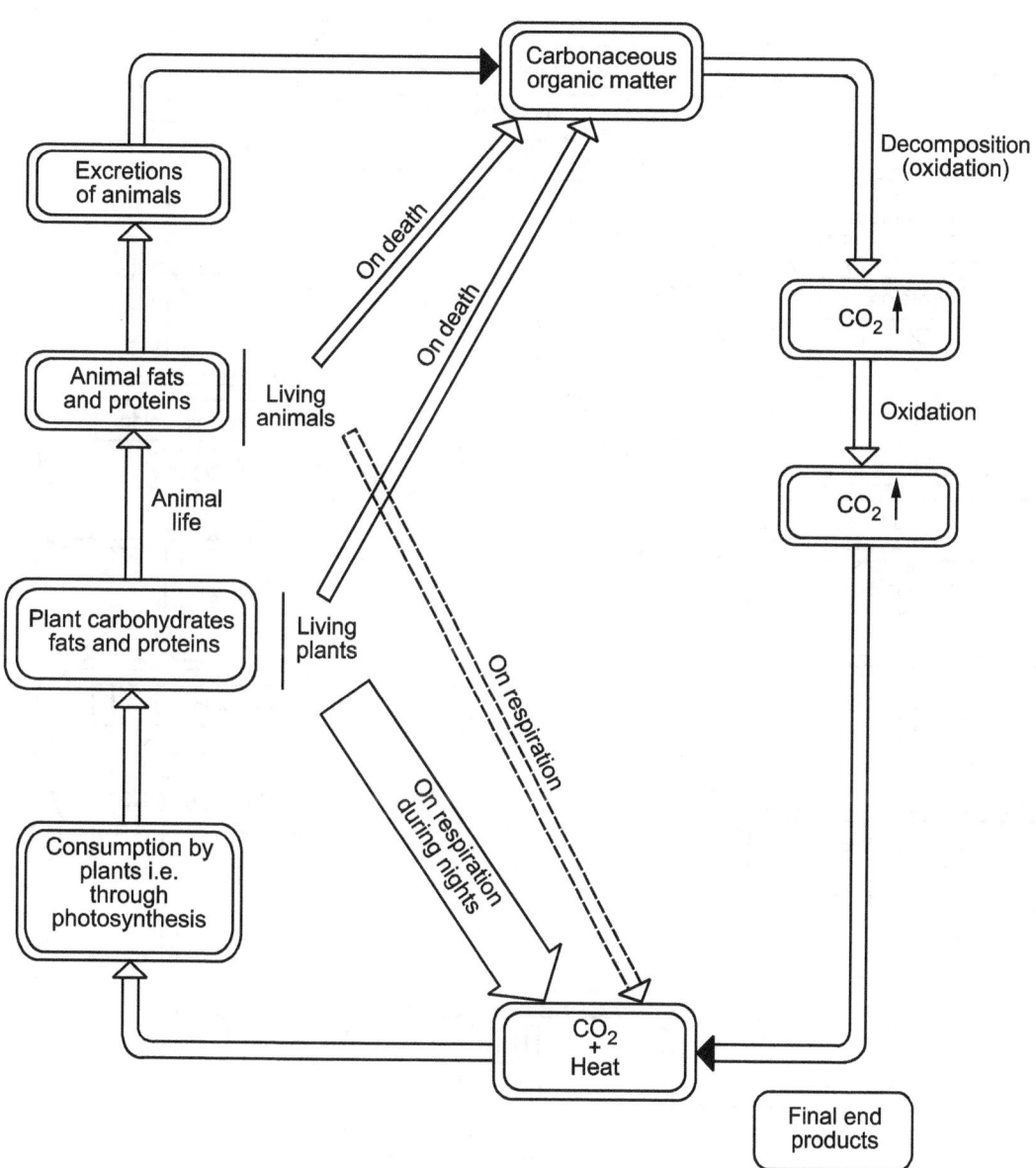

Fig. : Carbon cycle (Aerobic oxidation)

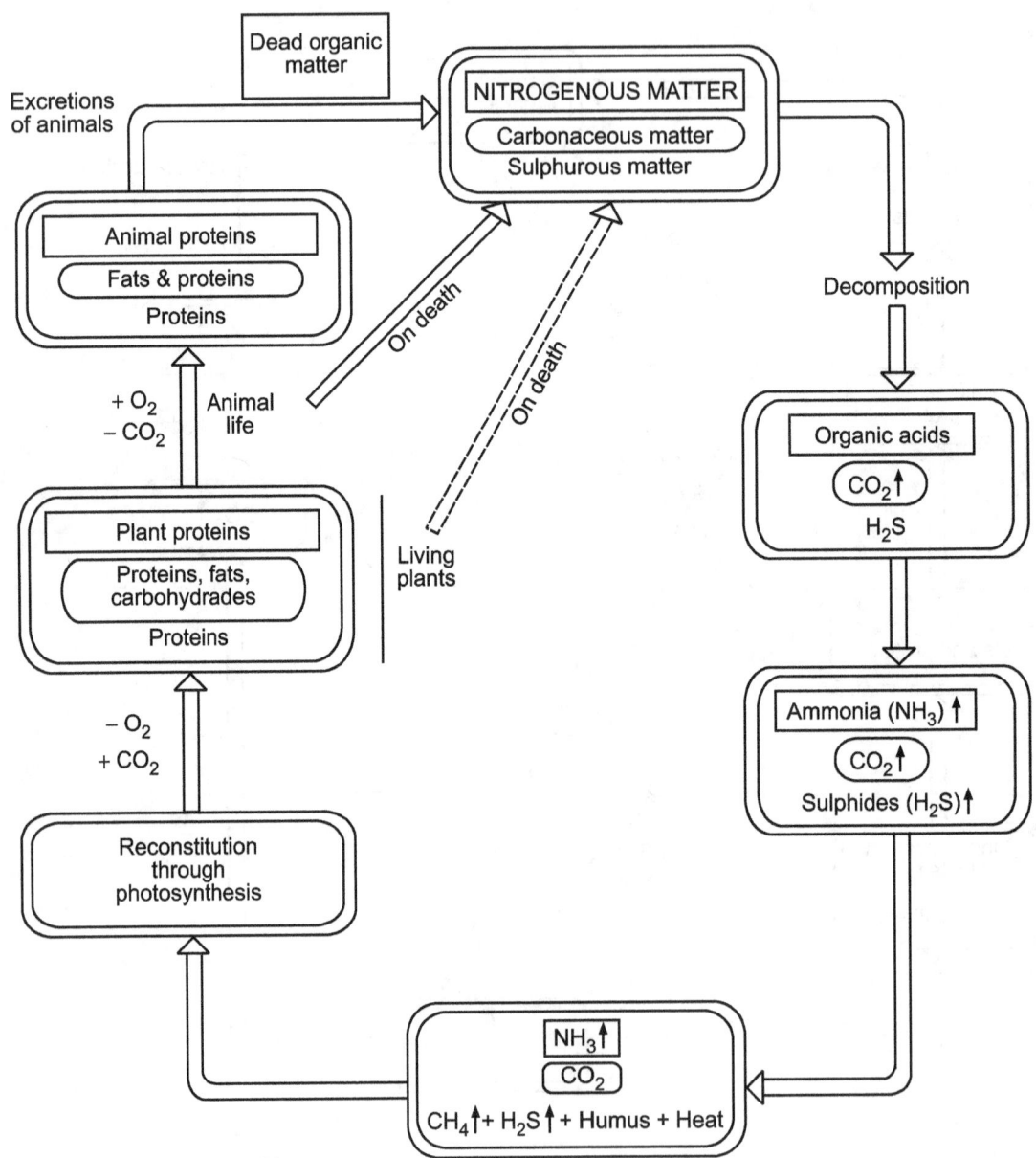

Fig. : Nitrogen, carbon and sulphur cycles (Anaerobic oxdation)

✠ ✠ ✠

1. (a) Differentiate between BOD and COD. What is the significance of treatability index ?
                                                                        [6 M]
   (b) Differentiate between separate and combined sewerage system.   **[4 M]**

OR

2. (a) The BOD_5 of a waste has been measured at 500 mg/l. The rate constant is 0.12. Determine ultimate BOD and 3 day BOD at 27°C.   **[6 M]**
   (b) What are the sources of sewage ? Explain the variations in sewage flow.   **[4 M]**

3. (a) A screen consisting of 10 mm diameter bars, at a clear spacing of 40 mm, treats a maximum hourly flow of 1200 m^3. Velocity of flow through the screen chamber is 0.75 m/sec.
   (i) Length and number of bars.
   (ii) Head loss in the chamber.   **[6 M]**
   (b) Write a short note on proportional flow weir.   **[4 M]**

OR

4. (a) Design a grit chamber for the following data :
   (i) Maximum flow : 30 mld.
   (ii) Diameter of particle to be removed : 0.2 mm and more.
   (iii) Specific gravity of particle : 2.65.
   (iv) Average temperature : 20°C.   **[6 M]**
   (b) Explain different treatment units in preliminary treatment of wastewater.   **[4 M]**

5. (a) Given the following data of operating Activated Sludge Process.
   (i) Waste water flow = 30,00 m m^3/day.
   (ii) Influent total solids = 600 mg/lit.
   (iii) Influent suspended solids = 120 mg/lit.
   (iv) Influent BOD = 170 mg/lit.
   (v) Effluent total solids = 480 mg/lit.
   (vi) Effluent suspended solids = 20 mg/lit.
   (vii) Effluent BOD = 20 mg/lit.
   (viii) MLVSSS concentration = 3000 mg/lit.
   (ix) Return sludge solid concentration = 9800 mg/lit.

Calculate :

(1) Volume of reactor

(2) F/m ratio

(3) Oxygen required per day   **[6 M]**

(b) Describe with sketch the treatment of sewage by Activated Sludge Process.   **[4 M]**

OR

6. (a) A single stage filter is to treat a flow of 3.79 mld of raw sewage with BOD of 240 mg/l. It is to be designed for a loading of 11086 kg of BOD in raw sewage per hectare metre and the recirculation ratio is to be 1. What will be the strength of the effluent, according to the recombination of NRC ?   **[6 M]**

(b) Explain with sketch the biological process in trickling filter.   **[4 M]**

Sample Question Paper for
In-Semester Examination

Marks: 30   **Time: 1 Hour**

---

1. (a) What are the units of measurements for the following :   **[6 M]**
   (i) Solids, (ii) Colour, (iii) Test and odour, (iv) Turbidity.
   (b) Explain giving reasons, when to adopt separate and combined systems.   **[4 M]**

                                OR

2. (a) Design a sanitary sewer for the following data :   **[6 M]**
   (i) Rate of water supply = 200 lpcd.
   (ii) Value of N = 0.013.
   (iii) Peak factor = 3.
   (iv) Slope = 1 in 700.
   (b) Explain the necessity of DO fixation while determining DO in water and state
       procedure for the same.   **[4 M]**

3. (a) Design a grit chamber for the following data :   **[6 M]**
   (i) Flow = 15000 m^3 per day,
   (ii) Settling velocity of particle 0.016 to 0.022 m/sec
   (iii) Flow through velocity 0.3 m/sec.
   (b) Draw a flow diagram for sewage treatment plant   **[4 M]**

                                OR

4. (a) Design bar screen for a peak flow of 60 million litres per day.   **[6 M]**
   (b) Write design criteria for grit chamber.   **[4 M]**

5. Data given :   **[10 M]**

1.	Municipal waste water flow rate,	Q	=	10,000 m^3/day
2.	BOD of settled effluent,	S_o	=	150 mg/lit
3.	BOD of treated effluent,	S_e	=	5 mg/lit
4.	Yield coefficient,	Y	=	0.5 kg/kg
5.	Endogenous decay coefficient,	K_d	=	0.05 d^{-1}
6.	MLSS concentration,	X	=	3000 mg/lit
7.	Return sludge solids concentration,	X_r	=	10,000 mg/lit
8.	Mean cell residence time,	θ_c	=	10 days.

Determine :

(a) The volume of the reactor.

(b) F/M ratio.

(c) Volumetric loading rate.

(d) Oxygen requirement.

(e) Recycle ratio.

(f) BOD removal efficiency.

OR

6. Design a high rate trickling filter using N.R.C. equation for the following data :   **[10 M]**

(i) Sewage flow = 8 mld.

(ii) Recirculation ratio = 1.5.

(iii) BOD of raw sewage = 300 mg/lit.

(iv) BOD removal in primary clarifier = 30%.

(v) Final effluent BOD desired = 30 mg/l.

Marks: 70   **Time: 2.5 Hour**

1. (a) Define :
   (a) Sewage, (b) Sullage. **[5 M]**

   (b) The BOD_5 of a waste has been measured as 450 mg/lit. If rate constant is 0.12, find out ultimate BOD and 3 day BOD at 27°C. **[5 M]**

OR

2. (a) Explain :
   (a) Conservancy system.
   (b) Water carriage system. **[5 M]**

   (b) Derive the BOD equation with usual symbols **[5 M]**
   $y_t = L_0 (1 - 10^{-Kt})$.

3. (a) What are the advantages of high rate T.F. over conventional or low rate T.F. ? **[6 M]**
   (b) Design a grit chamber for the following data :
   (i)   Maximum flow : 30 mld.
   (ii) Diameter of particle to be removed : 0.2 mm and more.
   (iii) Specific gravity of particle : 2.65.
   (iv) Average temperature : 20°C. **[4 M]**

OR

4. (a) Determine the size of a circular sewer for a discharge of 600 lps running half full. Assume s = 0.0001 and n = 0.015. **[6 M]**

   (b) What is the significance of treatability index ? **[4 M]**

5. (a) Explain 'Bacteria-Algae symbiosis in oxidation ponds'. **[5 M]**

   (b) Write about constructional details and design criteria of oxidation pond. **[5 M]**

   (c) Design a complete mix aerated lagoon system to treat a domestic sewage flow of 2.5 MLD. Use the following data : **[8 M]**
   1. Influent suspended solids=250 mg/lit
   2. Effluent suspended solids after settling 20 mg/lit
   3. Influent BOD_5=220 mg/lit
   4. Effluent BOD=20 mg/lit
   5. Volatile suspended solids = 80% of total solids produced.
   6. Summer temperature =38°C
   7. Winter temperature =15°C

8. Wastewater temperature=22°C

9. Oxygen concentration to be maintained in the lagoon=1.5 mg/lit

10. Lagoon depth=3.0 m

11. Specific substrate removal coefficient, K = 0.05 l/mg/day at 20°C; Growth yield coefficient, Y = 0.5; Decay coefficient, K_d = 0.05 per day,; f = 0.5.

12. Oxygen transfer coefficient of the aerator, α = 0.8.

13. Temperature coefficient, θ = 1.065

14. Elevation = 1000 m.

OR

6. (a) What are the advantages and disadvantages of aerated lagoons ?   **[5 M]**

(b) Describe phytoremdiation Technology for wastewater treatment.   **[5 M]**

(c) Design a facultative stabilisation pond to treat a domestic sewage flow of 3 mld, at a place, the latitude of which is 24°N. The 5 day 20°C BOD of the sewage is 250 mg/lit. Assume necessary data.   **[8 M]**

7. (a) Explain the different methods of disposal of sludge.   **[5 M]**

(b) Write a short note on package sewage treatment plant.   **[5 M]**

(c) Design a septic tank for the following data :
    Number of users : 150
    Sewage/capita/day : 125 litres
    Desludging period : 1 year
    Percolation rate : 15 min/cm   **[6 M]**

OR

8. (a) Write a note on – Disposal of septic tank effluent.   **[5 M]**

(b) What is the necessity of stabilisation of sludge ?   **[5 M]**

(c) What do you understand by digestion of sludge ? Explain the principle of anaerobic digestion of sludge.   **[6 M]**

9. (a) What is the necessity of treatment of industrial effluent?   **[6 M]**

(b) Draw a flow chart for treating sugar and dairy wastewater.   **[10 M]**

OR

10. (a) Discuss in brief various treatment processes adopted for treating industrial wastewater.

                    [6 M]

(b) Discuss the characteristics and treatment of the distillery waste.   **[10 M]**

Sample Question Paper for
End-Semester Examination

Marks: 70   **Time: 2.5 Hour**

---

1. (a) What are the advantages and disadvantages of conservancy and water carriage system ?   **[5 M]**

   (b) The BOD_5 of a waste has been measured at 500 mg/l. The rate constant is 0.12. Determine ultimate BOD and 3 day BOD at 27°C.   **[5 M]**

OR

2. (a) Discuss the advantages of the separate and combined system of sewage and give the conditions favourable for the adoption of each of them.   **[5 M]**

   (b) What are the sources of sewage ? Explain the variations in sewage flow.   **[5 M]**

3. (a) What is meant by activated sludge ? Describe with sketch the treatment of sewage by ASP.   **[6 M]**

   (b) Design the screen chamber of an ETP to treat peak flow of 80 mld of sewage.

   Assume inclination of bars 45° with horizontal, size of bars : 10 mm × 70 mm; 10 mm dimension facing the flow, clear spacing between bars as 50 mm and the velocity through the screen as 0.8 m/sec at peak flows.   **[4 M]**

OR

4. (a) Design a sanitary sewer for the following data :   **[6 M]**

   (i) Population = 120000 persons.

   (ii) Rate of water supply = 200 lpcd.

   (iii) Value of N = 0.013.

   (iv) Peak factor = 3.

   (v) Slope = 1 in 700.

   (b) Differentiate between BOD and COD.   **[4 M]**

5. (a) Write the design steps required for oxidation pond.   **[5 M]**

   (b) Classify the different types of oxidation ponds.   **[5 M]**

   (c) Design an oxidation pond based on the following given data :   **[8 M]**

   (i)   Location   ...   26°C Latitude

   (ii) Elevation   ...   150 m above sea level

   (iii) Mean monthly temperature   ...   35°C max. and 10°C min.

   (iv) Population served   ...   8000

(v)   Sewage flow   ...   150 *l*pcd

(vi) BOD$_5$ for raw sewage   ...   300 mg/lit

(vii) Desired effluent BOD   ...   30 mg/lit

(viii)Sky is clear for 15% of the days

(ix) Per capita BOD contribution per day   ...   0.045 kg/day

(x)   Pond removal constant at 20°C   ...   0.1/day

OR

6. (a) What are the different methods of aeration in the treatment of aerated lagoon? **[5 M]**

(b) Explain in detail Root zone cleaning system.   **[5 M]**

(c) Design an oxidation pond for treating sewage from a hot climatic residential colony with 6000 persons. The sewage generation is about 130 litres per capita per day. The BOD$_5$ of sewage is 350 mg/lit.   **[8 M]**

7. (a) What are the sources of sludge from an ETP?   **[5 M]**

(b) Compare low rate digester and high rate digester.   **[5 M]**

(c) Assuming a four person occupancy, design an on-site septic tank system for a wealthy residential home in an unsewered area. The sewage production is 390 lit-capita/day. Assume an equilibrium percolation rate of 0.02 mm/day.   **[6 M]**

OR

8. (a) Discuss the advantages and disadvantages of septic tank.   **[5 M]**

(b) What do you understand by digestion of sludge ? Explain the principle of anaerobic digestion of sludge.   **[5 M]**

(c) Write a applications and advantages of package sewage treatment plant.   **[6 M]**

9. (a) Write a note on 'characteristics' of industrial wastewater.   **[6 M]**

(b) Draw a flow chart for treating distillery and dairy wastewater.   **[10 M]**

OR

10. (a) Write a note on 'characteristics' of industrial wastewater.   **[6 M]**

(b) Discuss the characteristics and treatment of the sugar industry waste.   **[10 M]**

✠ ✠ ✠